equations*of*life

H   gasped, and blinked his eyes to clear them of splinters of
light.

vo men, two women, and him lying on bare wooden boards
in   etween. Two guns on one side, one on the other, no clear
lea of what was going on or where he was. He could see stone
lars, broken coloured light, dark-stained wood. He could smell
h and prayers.

A church, then; he was in a church.

He tried to sit up, feeling every flicker of pain from his
ribcage as a white-hot flame. He made it to his elbows before
the effort grew too great. The only comfort he had was that the
would-be kidnappers were aiming their Glocks at someone else
for a change.

He flopped his head over to see who they were trying to
threaten now.

She was a nun, fully robed, white veil framing her broad,
serious face. A silver crucifix dangled around her neck, and a
rosary and a holster hung at her waist. She had the biggest
automatic pistol Petrovitch had ever seen clasped in her righteous
right hand.

equations*of*life

*simon*morden

orbit

www.orbitbooks.net

ORBIT

First published in Great Britain in 2011 by Orbit
Reprinted 2011, 2012, 2013

Copyright © 2011 by Simon Morden

Excerpt from *Theories of Flight* by Simon Morden
Copyright © 2011 by Simon Morden

A CIP catalogue record for this book
is available from the British Library.

ISBN 978-1-84149-948-2

Typeset in Garamond by Palimpsest Book Production Limited,
Falkirk, Stirlingshire
Printed and bound by CPI Group (UK) Ltd, Croydon, CR0 4YY

Papers used by Orbit are from well-managed forests
and other responsible sources.

MIX
Paper from
responsible sources
FSC
www.fsc.org
FSC® C104740

Orbit
An imprint of
Little, Brown Book Group
100 Victoria Embankment
London EC4Y 0DY

An Hachette UK Company
www.hachette.co.uk

www.orbitbooks.net

ACKNOWLEDGEMENTS

A story: once upon a time, way back when, I was just finding my feet in the publishing world. I didn't really know what was going on, or how to do it – write, for sure, but how to write better, how to edit, how to find markets for finished stories, how to write a covering letter – but I was fortunate to find a number of people who held my hand gently and guided me through the maze with encouragement, good advice and honest opinions.

One of these was an American writer and editor called Brian Hopkins. Brian had his own e-publishing outfit long before the Kindle was a twinkle in Amazon's eye, and he was putting together an anthology of fantasy and horror short stories "from the ends of the Earth". I could do that, I thought in my naivety: he was in the USA, I was in Britain, and I could set something just down the road and make it look exotic. So I wrote something, sent it off, had it rejected with kind words. Rinse and repeat. But finally, I wore him down. He accepted one of my stories.

The first anthology eventually stretched to a series of five. I ended up in all of them. Then I pitched something different — a collection of linked stories, twenty in all, about the lives of people caught up in a wave of religiously inspired nuclear terrorism that would sweep across Europe and leave chaos in its wake. That collection has become, eight years later on, the world of *Equations of Life* and the books that follow. They are stories that probably wouldn't have happened otherwise.

So this one's for Brian. Thank you.

I

Petrovitch woke up. The room was in the filtered yellow half-light of rain-washed window and thin curtain. He lay perfectly still, listening to the sounds of the city.

For a moment, all he could hear was the all-pervading hum of machines: those that made power, those that used it, pushing, pulling, winding, spinning, sucking, blowing, filtering, pumping, heating and cooling.

In the next moment, he did the city-dweller's trick of blanking that whole frequency out. In the gap it left, he could discern individual sources of noise: traffic on the street fluxing in phase with the cycle of red-amber-green, the rhythmic metallic grinding of a worn windmill bearing on the roof, helicopter blades cutting the grey dawn air. A door slamming, voices rising – a man's low bellow and a woman's shriek, going at it hard. Leaking in through the steel walls, the babel chatter of a hundred different channels all turned up too high.

Another morning in the London Metrozone, and Petrovitch had survived to see it: *God, I love this place.*

Closer, in the same room as him, was another sound, one that carried meaning and promise. He blinked his pale eyes, flicking his unfocused gaze to search his world, searching . . .

There. His hand snaked out, his fingers closed around thin wire, and he turned his head slightly to allow the approaching glasses to fit over his ears. There was a thumbprint dead centre on his right lens. He looked around it as he sat up.

It was two steps from his bed to the chair where he'd thrown his clothes the night before. It was May, and it wasn't cold, so he sat down naked, moving his belt buckle from under one arse cheek. He looked at the screen glued to the wall.

His reflection stared back, high-cheeked, white-skinned, pale-haired. Like an angel, or maybe a ghost: he could count the faint shadows cast by his ribs.

Back on the screen, an icon was flashing. Two telephone numbers had appeared in a self-opening box: one was his, albeit temporarily, to be discarded after a single use. In front of him on the desk were two fine black gloves and a small red switch. He slipped the gloves on, and pressed the switch.

"Yeah?" he said into the air.

A woman's voice, breathless from effort. "I'm looking for Petrovitch."

His index finger was poised to cut the connection. "You are who?"

"Triple A couriers. I've got a package for an S. Petrovitch." She was panting less now, and her cut-glass accent started to reassert itself. "I'm at the drop-off: the café on the corner of South Side and Rookery Road. The proprietor says he doesn't know you."

2::

"Yeah, and Wong's a *pizdobol*," he said. His finger drifted from the cut-off switch and dragged through the air, pulling a window open to display all his current transactions. "Give me the order number."

"Fine," sighed the courier woman. He could hear traffic noise over her headset, and the sound of clattering plates in the background. He would never have described Wong's as a café, and resolved to tell him later. They'd both laugh. She read off a number, and it matched one of his purchases. It was here at last.

"I'll be with you in five," he said, and cut off her protests about another job to go to with a slap of the red switch.

He peeled off the gloves. He pulled on yesterday's clothes and scraped his fingers through his hair, scratching his scalp vigorously. He stepped into his boots and grabbed his own battered courier bag.

Urban camouflage. Just another immigrant, not worth shaking down. He pushed his glasses back up his nose and palmed the door open. When it closed behind him, it locked repeatedly, automatically.

The corridor echoed with noise, with voices, music, footsteps. Above all, the soft moan of poverty. People were everywhere, their shoulders against his, their feet under his, their faces — wet-mouthed, hollow-eyed, filthy skinned — close to his.

The floor, the walls, the ceiling were made from bare sheet metal that boomed. Doors punctured the way to the stairs, which had been dropped into deliberately-left voids and welded into place. There was a lift, which sometimes even worked, but he wasn't stupid. The stairs were safer because he was fitter than the addicts who'd try to roll him.

Fitness was relative, of course, but it was enough.

He clanked his way down to the ground floor, five storeys away, ten landings, squeezing past the stair dwellers and avoiding spatters of noxious waste. At no point did he look up in case he caught someone's eye.

It wasn't safe, calling a post-Armageddon container home, but neither was living in a smart, surveillance-rich neighbourhood with no visible means of support — something that was going to attract police attention, which wasn't what he wanted at all. As it stood, he was just another immigrant with a clean record renting an identikit two-by-four domik module in the middle of Clapham Common. He'd never given anyone an excuse to notice him, had no intention of ever doing so.

Street level. Cracked pavements dark with drying rain, humidity high, the heat already uncomfortable. An endless stream of traffic that ran like a ribbon throughout the city, always moving with a stop-start, never seeming to arrive. There was elbow-room here, and he could stride out to the pedestrian crossing. The lights changed as he approached, and the cars parted as if for Moses. The crowd of bowed-head, hunch-shouldered people shuffled drably across the tarmac to the other side and, in the middle, a shock of white-blond hair.

Wong's was on the corner. Wong himself was kicking some plastic furniture out onto the pavement to add an air of unwarranted sophistication to his shop. The windows were streaming condensation inside, and stale, steamy air blew out the door.

"Hey, Petrovitch. She your girlfriend? You keep her waiting like that, she leave you."

"She's a courier, you *perdoon stary*. Where is she?"

Wong looked at the opaque glass front, and pointed through it. "There," the shopkeeper said, "right there. Eyes of love never blind."

4::

"I'll have a coffee, thanks." Petrovitch pushed a chair out of his path.

"I should charge you double. You use my shop as office!"

Petrovitch put his hands on Wong's shoulders and leaned down. "If I didn't come here, your life would be less interesting. And you wouldn't want that."

Wong wagged his finger but stood aside, and Petrovitch went in.

The woman was easy to spot. Woman: girl almost, all adolescent gawkiness and nerves, playing with her ponytail, twisting and untwisting it in red spirals around her index finger.

She saw him moving towards her, and stopped fiddling, sat up, tried to look professional. All she managed was younger.

"Petrovitch?"

"Yeah," he said, dropping into the seat opposite her. "Do you have ID?"

"Do you?"

They opened their bags simultaneously. She brought out a thumb scanner, he produced a cash card. They went through the ritual of confirming their identities, checking the price of the item, debiting the money from the card. Then she laid a padded package on the table, and waited for the security tag to unlock.

Somewhere during this, a cup of coffee appeared at Petrovitch's side. He took a sharp, scalding sip.

"So what is it?" the courier asked, nodding at the package.

"It's kind of your job to deliver it, my job to pay for it." He dragged the packet towards him. "I don't have to tell you what's in it."

"You're an arrogant little fuck, aren't you?" Her cheeks flushed.

Petrovitch took another sip of coffee, then centred his cup

on his saucer. "It has been mentioned once or twice before." He looked up again, and pushed his glasses up to see her better. "I have trust issues, so I don't tend to do the people-stuff very well."

"It wouldn't hurt you to try." The security tag popped open, and she pushed her chair back with a scrape.

"Yeah, but it's not like I'm going to ever see you again, is it?" said Petrovitch.

"If you'd played your cards right, you might well have done. Sure, you're good-looking, but right now I wouldn't piss on you if you were on fire." She picked up her courier bag with studied determination and strode to the door.

Petrovitch watched her go: she bent over, lean and lithe in her one-piece skating gear, to extrude the wheels from her shoes. The other people in the shop fell silent as the door slammed shut, just to increase his discomfort.

Wong leaned over the counter. "You bad man, Petrovitch. One day you need friend, and where you be? Up shit creek with no paddle."

"I've always got you, Wong." He put his hand to his face and scrubbed at his chin. He could try and catch her up, apologise for being . . . what? Himself? He was half out of his seat, then let himself fall back with a bang. He stopped being the centre of attention, and he drank more coffee.

The package in its mesh pocket called to him. He reached over and tore it open. As the disabled security tag clattered to the tabletop, Wong took the courier's place opposite him.

"I don't need relationship advice, yeah?"

Wong rubbed at a sticky patch with a damp cloth. "This not about girl, that girl, any girl. You not like people, fine. But you smart, Petrovitch. You smartest guy I know. Maybe you smart enough to fake liking, yes? Else."

"Else what?" Petrovitch's gaze slipped from Wong to the device in his hand, a slim, brushed steel case, heavy with promise.

"Else one day, pow." Wong mimed a gun against his temple, and his finger jerked with imaginary recoil. "Fortune cookie says you do great things. If you live."

"Yeah, that's me. Destined for greatness." Petrovitch snorted and caressed the surface of the case, leaving misty fingerprints behind. "How long have you lived here, Wong?"

"Metrozone born and bred," said Wong. "I remember when Clapham Common was green, like park."

"Then why the *chyort* can't you speak better English?"

Wong leaned forward over the table, and beckoned Petrovitch to do the same. Their noses were almost touching.

"Because, old chap," whispered Wong faultlessly, "we hide behind our masks, all of us, every day. All the world's a stage, and all the men and women merely players. I play my part of eccentric Chinese shopkeeper; everyone knows what to expect from me, and they don't ask for any more. What about you, Petrovitch? What part are you playing?" He leaned back, and Petrovitch shut his goldfish-gaping mouth.

A man and a woman came in and, on seeing every table full, started to back out again.

Wong sprung to his feet. "Hey, wait. Table here." He kicked Petrovitch's chair-leg hard enough to cause them both to wince. "Coffee? Coffee hot and strong today." He bustled behind the counter, leaving Petrovitch to wearily slide his device back into its delivery pouch and then into his shoulder bag.

His watch told him it was time to go. He stood, finished the last of his drink in three hot gulps, and made for the door.

"Hey," called Wong. "You no pay."

Petrovitch pulled out his cash card and held it up.

"You pay next time, Petrovitch." He shrugged and almost smiled. The lines around his eyes crinkled.

"Yeah, whatever." He put the card back in his bag. It had only a few euros on it now, anyway. "Thanks, Wong."

Back out onto the street and the roar of noise. The leaden sky squeezed out a drizzle and speckled the lenses in Petrovitch's glasses so that he started to see the world like a fly would.

He'd take the tube. It'd be hot, dirty, smelly, crowded: at least it would be dry. He turned his collar up and started down the road towards Clapham South.

The shock of the new had barely reached the Underground. The tiled walls were twentieth-century curdled cream and bottle green, the tunnels they lined unchanged since they'd been hollowed out two centuries earlier, the fans that ineffectually stirred the air on the platforms were ancient with age.

There was the security screen, though: the long arched passage of shiny white plastic, manned by armed paycops and monitored by grey-covered watchers.

Petrovitch's travelcard talked to the turnstile as he waited in line to pass. It flashed a green light, clicked and he pushed through. Then came the screen which saw everything, saw through everything, measured it and resolved it into three dimensions, running the images it gained against a database of offensive weapons and banned technology.

After the enforced single file, it was abruptly back to being shoulder to shoulder. Down the escalator, groaning and creaking, getting hotter and more airless as it descended. Closer to the centre of the Earth.

He popped like a cork onto the northbound platform, and glanced up to the display barely visible over the heads of the other passengers. A full quarter of the elements were faulty, making the scrolling writing appear either coded or mystical. But he'd had practice. There was a train in three minutes.

Whether or not there was room for anyone to get on was a different matter, but that possibility was one of the few advantages in living out along the far reaches of the line. He knew of people he worked with who walked away from the centre of the city in order to travel back.

It became impossible even to move. He waited more or less patiently, and kept a tight hold of his bag.

To his left, a tall man, air bottle strapped to his Savile Row suit and soft mask misting with each breath. To his right, a Japanese woman, patriotically displaying Hello Kitty and the Rising Sun, hollow-eyed with loss.

The train, rattling and howling, preceded by a blast of foulness almost tangible, hurtled out from the tunnel mouth. If there hadn't been barriers along the edge of the platform, the track would have been choked with mangled corpses. As it was, there was a collective strain, an audible tightening of muscle and sinew.

The carriages squealed to a stop, accompanied by the inevitable multi-language announcements: the train was heading for the central zones and out again to the distant, unassailable riches of High Barnet, and please – mind the gap.

The doors hissed open, and no one got out. Those on the platform eyed the empty seats and the hang-straps greedily. Then the electromagnetic locks on the gates loosened their grip. They banged back under the pressure of so many bodies, and people ran on, claiming their prizes as they could.

And when the carriages were full, the last few squeezed on, pulled aboard by sympathetic arms until they were crammed in like pressed meat.

The chimes sounded, the speakers rustled with static before running through a litany of "doors closing" phrases: English, French, Russian, Urdu, Japanese, Kikuyu, Mandarin, Spanish. The engine span, the wheels turned, the train jerked and swayed.

Inside, Petrovitch, face pressed uncomfortably against a glass partition, ribs tight against someone's back, took shallow sips of breath and wondered again why he'd chosen the Metrozone above other, less crowded and more distant cities. He wondered why it still had to be like this, seven thirty-five in the morning, two decades after Armageddon.

2

He was disgorged at Leicester Square, where he spent a minute hauling air that was neither clean nor cold into his lungs. It tasted of electricity and sweat: its saving grace was that it was abundant.

He had to walk now, through the city streets, moving in time with the lights and the crowds, stealing the occasional glance up at the spires and slabs of mutely reflective glass that rose above and blotted out the sky, a sky that was itself crowded with private helicopters flitting from rooftop to rooftop without ever touching the ground.

He knew the route well, no need for HatNav or gawking like a tourist at the holographic signposts. The route that still – and he marvelled at the inefficiency of it – still followed the medieval roads and possessed names that no longer had any meaning save to denote an address.

So Leicester Square was square, but there was no Leicester: Shakespeare brooded on his grimy plinth, and the trees were all dead. Coventry Street remembered a city destroyed and rebuilt, then abandoned. Then through Piccadilly, with its love-lorn statue sealed in a dust-spattered plexiglas dome.

Onwards. Thousands of people, all of them having to be some-where, moving in dense streams, sometimes spilling out onto the roads and into the gutters. Couriers running and gliding down the lines that separated the traffic, millimetres from disaster.

Green Park. No longer green, no longer a park, the domik sprawl thrown up on it in the first spasm of Armageddon long gone. Towers grew there now, brilliant high buildings that reflected the grey sky all the way to their zeniths. At their feet, marble and granite blocks wet with fountains. Workers filing in to the lobbies, suited, smart, plugged in to the day's to-do list and already voicing memos, compiling reports, buying, selling.

A woman was coming the other way, out of one of the towers and against the flow of bodies. Her boldness caught his eye. She crossed the plaza, repelling people with an invisible field composed of fear and deference. In the time it took Petrovitch to shuffle another twenty metres, she'd strode fifty, her silks and perfume trailing in her wake.

He thought that, surely, there had to be someone with her. From the backward stares of those she passed, he wasn't alone in that thought. The woman – the girl – no, he couldn't decide which – should have had a retinue with her, glasses, earpieces, bulges under their jackets, the works. There was no one like her, but there was no one with her.

They were on a collision course. She was walking like she meant it, expecting a path to open up before her, until they were no more than a metre apart. She looked up from under her asymmetric black fringe, and saw the seething mass of humanity passing before her.

She hesitated, breaking step, as if she'd never seen such a

sight before. Petrovitch tried to slow down, found that it wasn't possible. He was carried on, and she looked through him as he passed in front of her. He had the memory of her slanting eyes glazed with indecision.

Then, abruptly, stupidly, he was moving backwards. For a moment, he couldn't understand why, because crowds like the one he was in had their own momentum: they went, and you went with them.

A slab of chest pushed him aside as if he were no more than a swinging door. An arm reached out, and a hand tightened around the woman's shoulder, engulfing it in thick, pink fingers.

The man who owned the chest and the hand lifted her off her feet and started for the kerb, wading through the crowd like it was thigh-deep water. And somehow, Petrovitch was caught up in the bow wave. He struggled this way and that and always found himself inexorably propelled towards a waiting car, its rear door open and its interior dark.

He knew what this was. He knew intimately. He knew because he'd seen this from the other side.

She was being kidnapped. She wore the mask of mute incomprehension, the one that would transform into blind rage at any moment.

He waited, and waited, and her reaction still didn't come.

They were at the car, and there were figures inside: two in the front, another in the rear, and they were staring at him, wondering who the hell this kid was, either too inept or too stupid to get out of the way.

The steroid-pumped man wanted him gone: Petrovitch was blocking his path. He raised his free hand to swat at him, a blow that would send him flying and leave him insensible and bleeding.

Petrovitch ducked instinctively, and the hand brushed the top of his head. As he looked up, he caught sight of the one vulnerable point amidst all the muscle. Still, he should have run, stepped back, crouched down. It wasn't his fight.

But he couldn't help but ball a fist, point a knuckle, and drive it as hard as he could at the man's exposed Adam's apple.

The woman landed next to him, her hands steadying herself against the filth-covered pavement.

He had one more chance. He could turn his back, make good his escape, disappear into the crowd. She could work her own salvation out from here.

Petrovitch reached out a hand, and hers slapped into it, palm against gritty palm.

They were off, not back towards the glittering towers of Green Park. That way was blocked by too many people and the rising man gagging and clutching at his throat. He dragged her out into the road, round the back of the car, back down the street against the flow of traffic – because that car would never be able to turn around. He pulled her behind him like a streamer, his own legs skipping like hers to turn their bodies sideways to avoid the wing-mirrors that rushed at their midriffs. Horns blared, collision warnings squealed, drivers beat on their windows and mouthed obscenities.

Behind them, the lights changed. The traffic stiffened to a halt, and Petrovitch vaulted over a bonnet to the faded white lines that marked the centre of the road. The vehicles coming the other way were like a wall of glass, reflecting their fear off every smooth surface.

He stopped for the first time since . . . since he'd got involved in someone else's madness, and wondered what the *chyort* he thought he was doing. He looked down his arm at the woman still attached to the other end, trying – like he was – to make herself as thin as possible.

Two men from the car were moving purposefully down the line of stopped traffic. Not running, but striding in that way that meant nothing but trouble. The lights changed and the one lane that was still free to proceed jerked into life. The men in dark suits stumbled and shouted, and Petrovitch saw his chance: the cars in front were slowing. He ran to match their speed, then weaved between bumpers until he made the other pavement.

She was still there. She wasn't going to let go.

Neither were the men. One, fed up with barking his shins and negotiating his vast muscles through the narrowest of gaps, pulled a flat-black automatic out and sighted down his arm. A red dot flickered across Petrovitch's chest like a fly trying to land, and a shot banged out, amplified by the facades of the buildings.

A man, a black man with a phone clipped to his ear and in the middle of a conversation, span violently round and vanished backwards into the crowd.

Petrovitch blinked once, tightened his grip and fled. He was aware of the sounds around him: there were shouts, cries, and screams, varying in pitch and intensity, and there was the methodical crack of a pistol. Every time he heard it, he expected to feel bright pain, and every time it was someone close by who spasmed and sank to the ground. Not him, not yet.

It was impossible to judge how far ahead he was. The closeness of the structures, the intensity of the crowded pavement, the noise that was washing back and forth: all he knew was that he was ahead, a metre or ten or fifty, enough that whoever was trying to kill him couldn't target him long enough to make sure.

And he was sure they were trying to kill him. They wouldn't risk this, risk everything, shooting random strangers in a central Metrozone street, if whoever's hand he held wasn't worth keeping alive. They could have killed her half a dozen times on the way from the Green Park building to the kerb. They hadn't, and yet they kept on firing in an attempt to make him let go.

He was tempted. Even as he saw a side-street, less dense with traffic, actual visible corroded tarmac on the road, he thought about jinking left, loosening his grip, vanishing into the nearest alley and lying low until it was all over.

They'd grab her around the waist, lift her up to deny her the ground, maybe inject something through her pale-cast skin to knock the fight or flight from her, bundle her away, and it wouldn't be his problem any more.

He turned left anyway, aiming for the centre markings on the road, but he kept hold of her. He didn't leave her behind.

Now there was space for them to run freely, side by side. He had the chance to steal a glance at her, to check she hadn't been hurt by a stray bullet, and he caught her doing the same for him. Neither of them had a hole torn in their clothing, nor a spreading dark stain.

Petrovitch flashed her a grin of pure nervous energy. She looked at him as if he was mad.

There hadn't been the sound of a gunshot for ten whole seconds. Two in quick succession shattered a windscreen and burned past his ear so close he could feel its passage. They were still coming. Obviously. Crowd density was dropping fast – the word of an incident was out, and those plugged into news feeds and navigation 'ware were steering a course around them. Good in that Petrovitch could run. Bad in that he couldn't hide.

Still no police. Not even the wail of a siren. Then again,

Petrovitch had grown up on the lawless prospects of St Petersburg. He knew to rely only on himself.

A right turn this time, and then another left. A wider street, busier, or should have been: automatic steel shutters were beginning to close over always-open foyers, and even the nose-to-tail of the rush hour was down to three sets of tail-lights scurrying for cover.

They were becoming exposed, isolated. People were pressed in doorways, cowering, covering their heads, or peering over the rims of basement wells. There were faces at windows and toughened glass portals, safe and watching the spectacle of two young idiots try and outrun a couple of pumped-up killers who wouldn't take no for an answer.

Petrovitch looked up. Regent Street was ahead, the lines of cars stalled, unable, like him, to escape. He didn't even break step. Over the bonnet of one, the roof of another, one, two, three, and jump down on the other side. A single shot crazed a first-floor pane of smoked glass. Then left again, up the road towards the covered arcade of Oxford Street.

The mall barriers were closing. Paycops in fluorescent vests were willing them to close faster, and Oxford Circus tube was being denied them in the same way: thick metal armour rolling down over the entrances to the underground.

He had to swerve left again, turning parallel to the main street, use the back roads to get to the far end. As he got to the corner, he looked down the empty pavement. He glimpsed the two men – the same two men who had started the chase – running purposefully. They moved like athletes, for all their size. They looked like they could keep going all day.

From the first twinges in his chest and flickering darkness behind his eyes, Petrovitch knew that he couldn't. The woman didn't seem to be in much better shape: mouth-breathing, sweat-drenched, letting out little grunts of pain at each footfall. This was going to finish badly even if it didn't finish earlier.

He put his head down and kept on going because he had to. She was going to be the death of him, and he didn't even know her name. An empty space opened up in front of them: Hyde Park, all mute shadows and shades of grey. The stink rose from the site like a solid wall. A shrouded Marble Arch, always being cleaned but never quite finished, lay hidden behind wind-torn sheets of polythene and a skeleton of scaffolding. The traffic on all the roads was gridlock-solid, with barely room to squeeze between. The tube was sealed.

His vision started to grow jagged and discordant. It wasn't the stinging perspiration that was trickling down his forehead and into his eyes; it *was* his eyes; the first signs of a faint. He was running out of time. He could hear a klaxon blare over the sound of his heartbeat in his ears, but couldn't decipher what it meant.

He was going down, and his pace faltered.

She took over. She was surprisingly strong. She looked small and light and weak, but Petrovitch felt the tendons in his arm stretch as she pulled him along. Their positions reversed, he trailed uselessly, almost blind.

He could tell enough to know that they were going the wrong way. They should have headed into the park, lost themselves in the labyrinthine shanties, and perhaps even the gunmen would have balked at going in after them: crossing Hyde Park was something that no one chose to do of their own free will.

Instead, they ran through lane after lane of stalled, cringing cars and down a broad, deserted pavement.

And the two men still pursued them. They were gaining on

them, arms pumping, knees lifting and slamming down like pistons, driving them closer. Petrovitch was past caring. Any second now.

When it didn't happen, when the pain grew so intense that his whole being felt touched by fire, that was the moment he stumbled and fell, sprawling half in the gutter. She stopped, and started to drag him by his shoulders.

Then there was someone else who scooped him up like a bundle of damp washing and carried him to a place that was cool and high.

The device in his chest finally, finally decided it was going to work. He jerked like a fish, shuddered and twitched. Once wasn't enough, not this time. It tripped again, sending enough current down implanted wires to shock his heart into remembering how to pump blood properly.

He gasped, and blinked his eyes to clear them of splinters of light.

Two men, two women, and him lying on bare wooden boards in between. Two guns on one side, one on the other, no clear idea of what was going on or where he was. He could see stone pillars, broken coloured light, dark-stained wood. He could smell polish and prayers.

A church, then; he was in a church.

He tried to sit up, feeling every flicker of pain from his ribcage as a white-hot flame. He made it to his elbows before the effort grew too great. The only comfort he had was that the would-be kidnappers were aiming their Glocks at someone else for a change.

He flopped his head over to see who they were trying to threaten now.

She was a nun, fully robed, white veil framing her broad,

serious face. A silver crucifix dangled around her neck, and a rosary and a holster hung at her waist. She had the biggest automatic pistol Petrovitch had ever seen clasped in her righteous right hand.

3

More frightening than the gun she was holding was her attitude of utter invulnerability. She stood like a soldier, right arm braced around the wrist by the left hand, sighting with her dominant eye, stance open and finger tickling the trigger.

She knew with absolute certainty they would never dare shoot a nun.

"Turn around, walk away," she said. "You've lost this time."

Of course, she could only aim at one of them at a time, and she did so without mercy. The target of her intentions started to crumble.

"We just want the girl," said the man. "Just the girl."

"No," said the nun. The girl in question took a step back behind the nun's skirts and played with her necklace.

"She can't get both of us," said the other man, and took an exploratory step forward.

"I wouldn't bet my life on it," said the nun. "More to the

point, you shouldn't bet your life on it. I don't carry this cannon around for show."

"If I can interrupt," said Petrovitch from the floor. He swallowed around the knot of acid pain in his throat. "You don't have time for this. You see that pendant in your target's hand? It's a panic button. I'm guessing she's had her thumb jammed on it for the last few minutes, and the signal it's giving off is stationary. Which means the cavalry are going to be no more than, what, thirty seconds away?"

He would have said more, but his vision flashed white again, and he momentarily lost muscle control. The back of his head banged against the floorboards.

He heard, "What the hell's the matter with him?" and "What are we going to do?"

They weren't smart. They weren't even up to the standards of Petrovitch's old boss. He struggled to his elbows again, blinking at their stupidity. "Really. You'd better go now. Go."

The surge of electricity through his heart took him down again. For the fourth time. It had never done that before. The sparks in his sight looked like angels against the vaulted roof space.

"*Chyort*," he whispered, then he noticed that no one had moved. He gathered what was left of his strength and hissed "Run!"

They started to edge away, and their first tentative movements rapidly translated into full flight. They burst out into the daylight, and it was there, framed against the shadow, that they were scythed down.

At the first shot, the nun flattened the girl with a sweep of her legs and threw herself on top of Petrovitch. Her veil covered his face, forming a seal over his mouth. He couldn't breathe, but as she lay across his ribs with her full weight, there wasn't much point in trying. She had even managed to pin his arms;

he couldn't so much as bat his hands against her. He struggled weakly and uselessly. He was powerless to save himself; of all the stupid ways to go, crushed by a nun.

The roar of gunfire went on for longer than was ever necessary. Someone determinedly made a point while Petrovitch meekly suffocated.

It became abruptly silent, and after a pause that was almost his undoing, the nun looked up. Her veil swung to one side, and he managed to drag in a wheezing gasp of air.

He coughed, and filled his lungs again. The air tasted of dust, cordite and blood.

"Stay down," she said, not realising that Petrovitch had no option but to obey. Figures made their way through the haze and picked their way over the ruined bodies of the two dead men.

These men also had guns; long-barrelled assault rifles with smoke still curling from their muzzles. They carried them easily, like workmen who knew they'd completed the day's task.

"Miss Sonja?" said one, a pocket-sized man with a shaved head. He stepped out of the clearing air and looked sadly around him.

"I'm here," said the woman. She picked herself off the floor and shook out the hem of her skirt.

"We should go," said the man, "Your father is worried about you." He brushed a chip of plaster off his suited shoulder while he too waited. The rest of his team materialised behind him. To a man – and they were all men – they were Japanese.

"I'm ready." She walked towards the doors, the security men surrounding her. She stopped at the entrance to the porch, and looked round at the only other people who had helped her that morning. She screwed up her face, and came back. She leaned over them, and Petrovitch thought it an extraordinary thing that her hair had managed to fall into place with no effort at all.

"Miss Sonja? The police will be here soon. It would be best to avoid them at the moment."

She held up her hand in a way that indicated that she was in charge now.

"Is he going to be OK?" she asked the nun.

"I think," she said, with a surprising amount of viciousness for someone in holy orders, "he needs an ambulance."

"I'll have one called. Hijo?"

"Yes, Miss Sonja. At once."

"I do have to go." But then she knelt next to Petrovitch, her presence forcing the nun back on her haunches. "Who are you?"

Petrovitch panted to give himself a voice. "If you're *yakuza*, I don't want you to know."

"*Yakuza*? What a ridiculous idea."

His gaze moved from her outrage to the nun's scepticism, to the gun-toting suits glancing out of the door and eager to be away.

"I'm not getting involved with you," he said.

"Involved? You saved my life."

"Stupid me. Now do me a favour and save mine: go."

She looked hurt; more upset at his slight than at nearly getting kidnapped. Sirens penetrated the thick stone walls, and she picked herself up from the floor. The man she called Hijo was trying to bury his agitation beneath the sheen of civility; he even had the temerity to take her gently at one elbow and guide her outside.

The last rifle-toting gunman left the church, leaving Petrovitch, the nun, and two ruined corpses.

"Do I get to find out who you are?" she asked. She released

the slide on her automatic, discharging the shiny unspent bullet into her palm.

"Petrovitch," said Petrovitch.

"Just Petrovitch?" She clicked on the safety and slid out the magazine to click the bullet back into the clip.

"It'll do."

"Sister Madeleine," she said. "I'm a Joan."

"Yeah. Figured. What with the Papal seal on your *pushka* and your complete lack of fear." He gave up trying to sit, and attempted to roll over instead. The effort was too much for him, and he concluded that he might actually be dying.

"Is there anything I can do?"

He looked up into her big brown eyes properly, now that no one was trying to kill him. His heart stopped again, only for a moment, but he put it down to his arrhythmia. "If you haven't got a scalpel, some bolt cutters and a set of rib spreaders, no. The defibrillator that's part of my pacemaker seems to have crashed."

"Crashed?"

"Normally I go to a hospital and they reprogramme it. Five-minute job. Only I need it to work right now and I don't think I have five minutes.

She slung her automatic into her holster and scooped him up in her arms. It was only then that he realised that she was huge. Tall, proportionately built; a giantess. She carried him out to the streetside and stood on the last wide step of a series that led up to the main doors.

The traffic had flooded back onto the road, as had the pedestrians to the pavement. Sister Madeleine spotted over everyone's heads that, miracle of miracles, an ambulance was fighting its way through to the kerb in a blizzard of red and blue.

"At least your little friend did that right." She adjusted the weight in her arms, aimed his feet towards the mass of people that stood in her way, and barged through. From the way he kept feeling impacts on the soles of his boots, he realised that the sight of a two-metre-tall fully-robed novice nun cradling a semi-conscious man wasn't strange enough for hardened Metrozone residents to take much notice. The sister was determined, however, and they met the ambulance as it shuddered to a halt.

The paramedics took him from her, and laid him efficiently on a stretcher inside the van. He watched as they attacked his shirt with scissors and pasted cold electrodes to his skinny chest. It was only when they tried to put a mask over his face that he rebelled and turned his face away.

"The nun. Where is she?"

She climbed up and crouched down. "What is it?"

If she'd been expecting a message for someone or a death-bed confession, she was going to be disappointed. "My bag."

"Your what?"

"My bag. Courier bag."

"It's back in the church." She pulled back the side of her veil so she could press her ear close to his mouth. "Is there something important in it?"

"Hardware. Cost me a small fortune and I've not even turned it on yet."

She sat back. "A computer? Your heart's about to fail and you're worried about a shiny new computer?"

"Look after it for me."

"Petrovitch," she said, "you, you geek."

"Sister," said the paramedic who was wincing at the vital signs on his handheld screen. "In or out, but we're moving."

She made to leave, but ended up reaching out of the cabin

and pulling the doors shut, trapping herself inside. "Just drive," she muttered, and sat awkwardly in a fold-down seat that wasn't anywhere near her size. She pulled her veil straight and reached for her rosary to compose herself.

Sister Madeleine watched Petrovitch flat-line three times in the ten minutes it took to get him to the hospital, and each time he came back to life again he searched the interior of the ambulance for her.

Some of the time, he was thinking about his beautiful piece of bespoke kit, lying untended on a pew in a city-centre church where anyone could just walk in and take it.

But part of him wondered what she was thinking, and he couldn't work that out at all.

It involved less surgery and more coding. No one cut him wide open, which he was grateful for. The chip that was supposed to control his errant heart was pulled bloodily out through a hole, and a new one slotted into place. He was kept conscious throughout.

The morphine and exhaustion made him drowsy though, and at some point when they were sewing up the access wound with short, blunt tugs of black thread, he allowed himself the luxury of falling asleep.

He dreamed: cold snow, cold wind, crystal-black nights and needle-bright stars. He dreamt of ribbons of auroral colour above the blank skyline, of the Soviet murals that decorated the foyers of the underground. He dreamt of good vodka and good friends.

When he woke up, he found that he'd left all that behind and exchanged it for a pale cream room with hospital bed, polarising filters on the window and an amazonian nun in the corner. Perhaps the nun was optional; then again, for one to come as standard made as much sense as anything in his life ever did.

"How long?" he asked.

"Hour, maybe," she said. She stood by his bed and looked around. "This must cost a fortune."

"More than my modest insurance could afford." Petrovitch pushed himself up with his hands and accepted the automatic movement of his pillows. Sister Madeleine looked down to see what her hands were doing – shaping and plumping – and she consciously stopped herself.

"So?"

Petrovitch leaned back. He could feel the tightness in his chest, but no pain. That was good. "Miss Sonja wanted to know who I was. The only way she could do that was to pick up the tab on my hospital bill. It'll be no more than small change for someone like her, and she'll consider herself clever because she's found out who I am."

Sister Madeleine shrugged. "You got something out of it too."

"Yeah. Why do you think I didn't tell her my name?"

She saw his sly smile. "You were dying, and you saw the opportunity to get a room upgrade?".

"And a private ambulance. I didn't need her gratitude, I needed her influence. And look: I'm still alive."

Her eyes grew large. "That's, that's . . ."

"What?" Petrovitch was nonplussed by her reaction. "Just because you didn't work it out."

"Why? Why would someone like you want to help someone like her?" She put her hands on her hips and waited for Petrovitch to answer. When he didn't, she said: "You know what? I don't care. I haven't got the energy to waste on it. You know where to find me if you want your little box of tricks back."

She strode to the door, the second time that day a pretty woman had turned her back on him and walked away.

"I don't," he said. "I don't know where to find you. I wasn't aware of where I was for the last five minutes or so of the chase."

She faced the closed door. "So you want me to tell you? What if I don't? What then?"

"I'll work it out. It can't be that difficult. Five minutes, maybe. Ten, then — tops. All I want is my bag back. Really." He had no idea why he was having this conversation. "Sister?"

"Saint Joseph of Arimathea, Edgware Road." She twisted the doorknob, and the door swung aside.

"Sister?"

"What?"

He thought about mentioning that she had nearly suffocated him with that stupid head-dress of hers, and for once found that sarcasm died on his tongue. "Thank you. I'm grateful."

She shrugged again. "Doing good things is in the job description, Petrovitch." She looked down at the patient, crumpled man sitting across the corridor from her. "Police are here."

She left, robes billowing out behind her. Neither man, the one in the bed, the one in the chair, had the authority to stop her.

4

Eventually, having watched the sister stamp angrily down to the first corner and disappear, the policeman got wearily from his chair and wandered in. He ignored Petrovitch at first, and walked around, touching the furnishings, playing with the window controls, pouring himself a glass of water from the jug on the bedside table.

Petrovitch looked over the top of his glasses at the man as he drank, one gulp, two gulps, three.

"Do you mind if I sit down?" the man asked, wiping his mouth on his jacket sleeve, then sat down anyway without waiting for an answer. "There's always too much standing up in this job."

He patted his pockets for his warrant card, and passed it over to Petrovitch with an air of distraction: he was already looking for something else in a different place.

Petrovitch inspected the card: Chain, Henry – Detective Inspector, Metropolitan Police. The hologram looked twenty years out of date, because the Chain in front of him had far more wrinkles and much less hair. His head was flaring under the lights, the thin strands dotted haphazardly over his scalp illuminated from below as well as above.

Petrovitch passed the card back, and Chain opened the cover of his police handheld. The detective chewed the stylus for a moment, then pecked at an icon.

"Right then," said Chain, and interrupted himself with a volley of wet coughing. "Sorry. It's the air. I'll start again: Petrovitch, Samuil. Twenty-two, citizen of the Russian Federation, here on a university scholarship. Address, three-four-one-five, Clapham Transit A. You will stop me if I mess up here? I know these things are supposed to be accurate, but you know what it's like." He paused. "You do know what it's like, don't you?"

Petrovitch cleared his throat. "I know."

"Your English good? Don't need a translator or a dictionary?"

"I'm fluent."

"This is just an interview, you know. You haven't done anything wrong. I'm just asking a few questions. If you think you might need a lawyer, do say." Chain coughed again, an episode that left him breathless. He twisted round in his chair and poured himself some more water. "Nice room."

Petrovitch nodded slowly. Either the man was brilliant or a buffoon. Only time would tell which.

"You are OK to answer a few questions, aren't you? Doctors told me you'd died several times on the way here. I can come back later." Chain touched the video icon on his handheld and hunted for the right clip.

"*Yobany stos!* Get on with it."

Chain glanced up. "I know that one. Just so you know, *yeban'ko maloletnee.*"

Petrovitch chuckled, then grimaced at the discomfort. "Ask your questions, Detective."

"This," said Chain, "this is you, early this morning." He passed Petrovitch the handheld.

Petrovitch watched himself, identified with a floating yellow tag, crawl along the pavement at Green Park. A red tag moved into view, and the two crossed briefly. The screen went blank.

"Where's the rest?" he asked.

"The cameras over the whole block went down." Chain took the handheld back. "Very professional. But we know what happened. We know where you went, and we know how it ended."

He opened up another file, and showed Petrovitch a picture of two bullet-ridden gangsters lying in a mutual pool of thick red blood.

Petrovitch looked, then looked away. "If you know what happened, why do you need me?"

"We – I – was hoping you could tell me why. Why would Samuil Petrovitch risk his scrawny neck intervening in a kidnapping that has nothing to do with him? Or at least, seems to have nothing to do with him. You weren't some sort of Plan B, were you?"

"Why don't you ask them?" Petrovitch nodded at the screen. "They look like the sort of guys who could come up with a really good Plan B."

"Point taken." Chain reamed an eye with his finger until it squelched. "Do you know who it was you saved?"

"No. Never seen her before in my life."

Chain pressed his lips together and ruminated. "If I had a euro for every time someone said that to me. "Oh, Detective, I have no idea whose body this is in the boot of my car. Never seen her before in my life." You genuinely don't know?"

"No."

"Don't keep up with the celebrity news?"

"Do I look like someone who uses celeb porn?" Petrovitch grunted. "I study high-energy physics."

The detective sighed. "She's Sonja Oshicora. Ring any bells now?"

"No."

"Oshicora Corporation?"

"No."

"You heard what happened to Japan, right? The whole falling-into-the-sea thing?"

"I heard. It wasn't my fault, though."

"Very droll, Petrovitch. So, let's just recap." He dropped the handheld in his lap and held out his sausage-like fingers. "One, you were minding your own business, proceeding in a westerly direction on Green Park. Two, you witnessed the attempted kidnapping of some woman you don't know or recognise. Three, you drop one of the kidnappers – good work, by the way – and run for it, keeping this woman with you despite the fact you're now being shot at."

"How many?"

"Six dead. Twelve wounded, five of them critically. They're in a different hospital somewhere, in wards a lot less posh than this one." Chain waggled his little finger. "Four, after a tour of central London, you pitch up in a Catholic church. The kidnappers enter, then leave without their intended target. They die on the steps – how, I can guess, but the CCTV goes mysteriously blank again. Five, I get there. Oshicora's gone, you've gone, the Joan's gone. Have I got it about right?"

"More or less," admitted Petrovitch.

"So I'll ask you again: why?" The detective leaned back in

his chair, and closed his eyes. A little while later, he murmured, "I'm still here."

Petrovitch stroked the end of his nose, and eventually pushed his glasses back up his face. "I don't know why," he said.

"You don't sound so certain of that."

"I genuinely don't." His tone of voice earned him a glance from one heavy-lidded eye.

"Altruism? Chivalry? Civic duty? Random act of kindness? Perhaps you're a secret crime fighter, and you didn't have time to put your underpants on the outside of your trousers."

"*Idi v'zhopu.*"

"We get them, you know. Costumed vigilantes, and for good or ill, without the superpowers." Chain shuffled himself more erect, and played with the computer in his lap. "They're just about one step up from the death squads we used to have during Armageddon. Were you here for that?"

"Before my time, Inspector. Look, I don't know what I can do for you. I'm the victim of a crime, but the two criminals who shot at me and murdered all those people are dead. This Sonja woman . . ."

"Girl. Seventeen."

"I don't know her. It was an accident." Petrovitch scratched at his chest. "Would you rather I'd not done anything?"

Chain said nothing, just looked into the distance with narrowed eyes.

"Oh, you're joking." Throwing off the bed covers, Petrovitch swung his legs out over the side of the bed. "I've walked into someone's private crusade. So what did they do to you? Kill your rookie partner, blow up your car, boil your pet rabbit?"

"No," said Chain. "They just really piss me off."

"I'm not playing your game, Inspector. You can take your

questions and you can shove them up your *zhopu*." He found his clothes in the bedside locker. Except his shirt, of course. "Despite the tendency my heart has to stop working at critical moments, I quite like the life I have."

He sat on the edge of the mattress and pulled off the hospital's green gown, dressing as quickly as he could. Chain made no effort to stop him, just watched him as he efficiently laced his boots.

"I know where to find you," said Chain as Petrovitch stood warily, testing which way was up. "So, of course, do they."

"I don't care."

"Perhaps you ought. Perhaps you'll find it harder than you think to pretend all this never happened." Chain tucked his handheld away, and gripped the arms of the chair. He pushed himself up.

"I don't owe them. Quite the reverse." Petrovitch decided he could make it outside without falling over, and tried his luck.

"My point precisely," said Chain. He beat Petrovitch to the door handle, and held the door open. "They owe you. This – this lovely room, the ambulance, the private doctors, the best of care. That's just the start."

Petrovitch hesitated, one hand on the wall. "What do you mean?"

"Honour, Petrovitch. You saved Hamano Oshicora's only child from a fate worse than death. You saved both her and the family name. They owe you big time. Why," he said, "you're almost one of the family yourself now."

"If I don't have to play along with you, I don't have to play along with them."

Chain motioned Petrovitch through the door first. "You'll find them a lot more persuasive than me."

"I'm pretty good at saying no." Petrovitch limped out into the corridor. "Now, if you'll excuse me. I'm late for work."

"You're a student, you don't get to use that excuse. But I'll give you a lift if you want." Chain smiled; it wasn't pleasant. "You get to ride in a police car."

"I'm not a little kid, Inspector."

"No. You're a poor immigrant who's just had a run-in with two of the biggest crime syndicates in the Metrozone and ended up in hospital because your heart is on its last legs. If hearts have legs, of course."

Petrovitch walked away, dismissing the policeman with a wave of his hand. "Yeah. I'll be fine."

"It's not what your doctor said."

He came back. "What did he say?"

Chain shrugged his shoulders. "If you're going to discharge yourself without telling anyone, you'll never find out. Until it's too late."

Petrovitch stared him down.

Chain reached out and tapped Petrovitch's sternum. "He said you've damaged that one beyond repair. You need a replacement."

"Maybe."

"You can always ask for a second opinion. But I wouldn't take too long about it."

Petrovitch considered matters. "Your bedside manner sucks. See you, Inspector." He turned on his heel and buried his hands in his pockets.

"New hearts cost," called Chain. "You could always ask the Oshicoras to cough up for a replacement, seeing how you wrecked the old one in their service."

"Yeah. *Perestan' mne jabat' mozgi svojimi voprosami.*" Petrovitch walked to the end of the corridor, past the verdant pot-plants balanced on every window sill, through the doors that cut him off from the despondent figure of Detective Inspector Chain.

He reached for his wrist and ripped off the hospital tag: somewhere on a computer, the action would have been registered, and someone would already be looking for him. Not because he was important, but because the people picking up the bill were.

Petrovitch didn't want to be an asset. He wanted to be invisible again.

He threw the tag into the leaf crown of a fern and caught the first lift down to the ground. He watched the counter topple towards zero, and rested his forehead against the cool metal of the wall. By the time he reached the foyer, he'd made his decision.

It didn't look like a hospital. It looked like a hotel, which he supposed it was, really: a hotel with operating theatres. It was busy, controlled, efficient. Customers and staff moved through their booking-in procedures with whispered courtesies.

Paycops guarded a screen at the ever-revolving door. Even they looked happy and relaxed.

Petrovitch spotted a vacant chair in front of a huge circular desk. He sat down and waited for the clerk behind it to focus on him through her holographic screen.

"Good afternoon, sir," she said accurately: the clock had just tipped past noon. "Welcome to Angel Hope Hospital."

"I need a new heart," he said baldly. "How much?"

He had her attention. "It very much depends on what is clinically necessary. If you can submit a cardiologist's report, I might be able to book an appointment for you." While she talked, he could tell she was judging both him and the size of his bank balance. "Our transplant teams pride themselves on using only the very latest technology."

"OK, save me the sales pitch. I knew this day would come

sooner or later, so I've had a lifetime of weighing up the pros and cons. How much for a vat-grown organic heart?"

She smiled sweetly, revealing two rows of perfect white teeth. "I'm afraid that currently comes in at two hundred and fifty thousand euros. Surgery, post-operative care and rehabilitation are extra. I can download a list of charities that might be able to help in funding all or part of a less expensive clinical package. We offer several budget solutions that solve most chronic cardiac conditions."

Petrovitch was watching carefully for her reaction. He pushed his glasses back up his nose, and asked: "Do you take cash?"

5

Petrovitch put the hospital's datacard in his top pocket and followed the sweep of the revolving doors out into the daylight.

Private cars were queuing to drop people off under the covered entrance before pulling back out to join the mayhem of the midday roads. As one drove off, another replaced it, wheelchairs or a walker unit being brought to the passenger door as required.

Two cars weren't moving, though. They were parked opposite, one behind the other, fat wheels up on the concrete kerb. One was new – clean, black paintwork, black tinted glass, a beast of a car, tall and proud and sturdy. The other was a dented wreck with mismatched wings and a plastic bag taped over the rear-offside window.

Sitting nonchalantly around the first car were three Japanese men, wrap-round info shades on their expressionless faces. Their suits were identical down to the creases in their trousers and the bulges in their jackets. He even recognised one of them: shaven-headed Hijo.

Lolling on the bonnet of the other car was Chain, who was glaring at the world in general and the men in front of him in particular.

Hijo spotted Petrovitch first. He stood erect, adjusted his black leather gloves, and nodded to his men. Chain saw the change in attitude of his quarry and glanced over to the doors. He slid off his car and shuffled his feet.

Petrovitch looked from one car to the other like he was sizing up two different but equally unappealing destinies. One of Hijo's men even gave a little bow.

"Thank you, gentlemen," said Petrovitch under his breath, "but I'm not stupid."

He turned away, feeling four sets of eyes burning into his back until he disappeared into the crowd. He let himself be carried for a while, crossing two intersections, taking the opportunity before the lights cycled green to look around him and see if he was being followed.

That idea was ludicrous – or had been when he'd woken up that morning. Now, it had to be part of his mental map, along with needing a new heart and accidentally abandoning a perfectly decent piece of hardware in a church.

He crossed one more road, and the buildings changed. The tall two-centuries-old town houses stopped and the massive domik sprawl of Regent's Park started: a vast heap of rusting shipping containers, stepped like blood-smeared Aztec pyramids until the peaks were high in the heavens. It made his own Clapham A look tiny, and legends had grown around the most inaccessible habs, deep inside the pile: Container Zero, the last Armageddonist, the Zoo.

He hadn't realised he was so close, didn't want to be so close. No one should think he had a connection with it. He took a step back so that he was in the lee of an anonymous grey box, a piece of left-over street furniture from an earlier age. He looked up to the topmost container, adorned with a fluttering green banner and a small windmill that span to a blur in the wind.

Petrovitch pushed his glasses up his nose, and walked off, heading west down Marylebone.

It was only a kilometre or so. He should have been able to manage it without effort. He had to stop twice, once at a road-side kiosk to swap all of the low value coins he could find in the depths of his pockets for a bar of chocolate, and once because he needed to sit down, just for five minutes.

By the time he was walking in the shadow of the flyover, he was spent. He should have gone home, slept, had something to eat. Work could have waited, collecting his rat could have waited. He'd made the wrong decision, temporarily thrown by the recep-tion party outside the hospital. He needed to be thinking more clearly.

At least he was at the church. Seven broad brick semi-circular steps led up to the open doors. There was a railing; he made use of it. When he got to the top, he saw brushed sand and smelled bleach. Perhaps it had been Sister Madeleine's job to scrub the blood out of the stonework.

He stepped around the sea of sand, taking time to run his finger around one of the pale bullet holes splintered into the dark wood door. Inside, a priest with crow-black hair was standing at the front, obscuring the altar with his outstretched arms, and maybe a dozen people scattered throughout the echoing space.

The crucifix hanging from a roof beam had extra stigmata, and the Holy Mother was missing her outstretched hand even while she was cradling the Infant in the other. White marks on the floorboards indicated hurriedly swept plaster dust.

Petrovitch sat himself in the very back pew and waited for this particular piece of religious theatre to end. The host was elevated while a white-robed acolyte rang a bell. As the priest turned to face the congregation, his gaze fixed on the latecomer.

A breath of air tickled the hairs on the back of Petrovitch's neck. The nun was standing behind him, clicking through her rosary with one hand, the other resting on the butt of her Vatican special. She looked down sternly and dared him to speak, move, or do anything that might interrupt mass.

He didn't have the energy to defy her, no matter how much fun it might have been. And he wanted his bag back without it being stamped on. He sat through the rest of the liturgy, hearing the words in plain English, but not understanding the symbols. People stood, sat and knelt at intervals, then trooped to the altar rail to receive a piece of translucent wafer.

Then the service was over, and it was him, the priest and Sister Madeleine.

"So soon, Petrovitch?" said the nun. She turned and heaved the doors shut. "Strange the things you find important."

"Yeah," he said. The priest had disrobed, and was walking slowly down the centre aisle in his black cassock and Roman collar. "It's not like I came to see you."

"That would never happen," she said, banging the bolts into place. The sound reverberated around the nave. "This is Father John, priest in charge."

"Father," said Petrovitch, and raised his hand briefly. The man who came over and shook it with wary firmness couldn't have been much older than he was.

"What do I call you?" said the father, scraping his fingers through his heavy fringe.

"Petrovitch will do. Is it me, or is the world being run by a bunch of kids?"

"Father O'Donnell was murdered two months ago. The parish needed someone." Father John sat in the pew in front and twisted round to face Petrovitch. "I go where I'm sent."

"Very noble, I'm sure."

"But bringing extra trouble to our doorstep when we've more than enough of our own, that's not. The sanctuary's violated yet again, mass is delayed, and the police are here, throwing their weight around."

"When Father O'Donnell died, they didn't want to know," said Sister Madeleine. "No investigation, no forensics, no arrests, no one to face justice. We know who did it, but no one's interested."

"I'm sorry about that," said Petrovitch.

"I'm here to make sure they don't need to let us down again," she said. Her face hardened and she stared into the distance.

The priest picked underneath his nails. "A good man dies, and nothing. You and that girl turn up, and we have everything we didn't have before. And who for? Two dead criminals."

"If it was a detective inspector called Chain, don't take it personally: he's got a grudge against the Oshicoras."

Father John scratched at his ear, where there was a notch missing from the cartilage. "Sister Madeleine shouldn't have left the church, either. I've told her novice master. Penance will have to be done."

Petrovitch glanced at the men and raised his eyebrows. "She's in trouble? Because of me?" He started to smile.

Father John tried to wipe the smirk off Petrovitch's face with sheer force of will, but Petrovitch was having none of it. "Yes.

She's here to protect her church and her priest. Not passing strangers. A member of the Order of Saint Joan has legal exemptions whilst she's doing her duty, none when she goes off and does her own thing."

"She didn't shoot anyone."

"She could have done a life sentence if she had." Father John's voice rose in volume until he was yelling, bare centimetres from Petrovitch. "She's not the police. She's not even a paycop. I don't thank you for putting her vocation in jeopardy before it's barely begun."

"Yeah. OK. I get the message, Father. Just get me my bag; sooner I get what I want, the sooner you can get me out of here." Petrovitch made sure his smile grew wider and he snorted. "You take yourself far too seriously."

The father got up and cast him a baleful look. "Don't bring bad people here."

"Since I've been called a bad man once already this morning, I'll have to count myself among their number."

Father John stalked off to the vestry to collect Petrovitch's bag. Sister Madeleine leaned down and waited until the father was out of sight. "Come with me," she whispered.

"I'm just going to get you into more trouble, and none of it the interesting kind."

"I can look after myself. Just come." She walked to a side door, turned the heavy key and pulled the bolts aside. Stale air blew in as she worked the latch. Petrovitch dragged himself out of the pew and followed.

There were stairs, going up in a tight spiral, which she had difficulty negotiating because of the width of each step and the height of the ceiling, and he had problems with because he grew rapidly breathless as he ascended.

She opened another door, a trap door which she unbolted and threw back. Light poured in, making them both blink. She led the way onto the roof of the tower, and turned a full circle, taking in the view.

It wasn't much. Immediately to the north was a raised section of dual carriageway, crammed with traffic. South and east were the cramped streets of old London, the skyline filled with the skeletons of cranes and new buildings, each trying to outdo the last for height. To the west was the rising ground of Notting Hill, where the wealthier post-Armageddon refugees had squatted.

Petrovitch leaned heavily on the parapet and wiped his damp forehead with the back of his hand. "I can't believe you've got me all the way up here just for this."

"Look," she said, pointing beyond the flyover. "See those buildings? That's the Paradise housing complex. It used to be St John's Wood, before they bulldozed half of it."

"Yeah," said Petrovitch. There were seven tower blocks, ugly, utilitarian shapes, their bases hidden in a yellow haze. The concrete looked scarred and cracked. "Doesn't look like they deserve the new name."

"They call themselves the Paradise militia," she said, and leaned on an adjacent piece of brickwork, staring out over the city with faraway eyes. "They run the blocks, and everybody in them. It's like a city-within-a-city, with an economy based on crime. That's who Father O'Donnell took on."

"So they killed him. Shame, but I don't know why you're telling me this."

"I want you to understand." She tilted her head to face him, brushing the side of her veil away where it obscured her view of him. "Father John . . ."

"I understand too well. He's just a boy. Like me." Petrovitch laughed, and it hurt in a way that reminded him that he was still alive and how much he had to lose. "Father John thinks he can take the place of the martyred O'Donnell and win the souls of Paradise. He's deluded by dreams of glory and can't see that he's going to go the same way."

"They hate us. They act like we're another gang, moving in on their territory. You're right: they'd kill Father John, 'too, if they could. But he has me," she said.

"So what's your life expectancy measured in? Weeks or days?" He looked her in the eye, briefly, before feeling the need to count the lace holes in his boots.

She gathered her blowing veil and held it over her shoulder. "Someone has to do something."

"I bet that's what the Armageddonists said, right before they . . ."

He didn't finish his sentence. His feet left the ground and, for a moment, he thought he was going over the parapet.

"Don't," she screamed in his face. Her fists were balled up in his collar. "Don't ever. This is their fault. Everything. I could have been little Madeleine instead of this. I could have been normal."

Then the calm after the storm. She lowered him rather than just letting go. His toes gratefully found the concrete roof.

"I'm not like them," she said. She straightened his jacket out, sweeping her long fingers over the folds in the cloth. His skin burned under her touch. "I could never be like them."

Petrovitch dared to move, retreating until his back was against the brickwork. When it eventually came, his voice was high and panicked. "I'm going now. For both our sakes."

She waited until he was ducking down out of sight before calling after him. "Do you believe me?" she asked.

"What? That you feel the need to die in a futile gesture?

Yeah. Russians have been throwing their lives away for nothing for centuries: it's in the blood." He started down the steep steps. "I don't intend to join them."

"So why did you try and save that girl?"

"I didn't try," he whispered defiantly. "I succeeded."

Father John was waiting for him at the bottom of the staircase, holding up Petrovitch's bag in one hand. His expression said that he'd won at least one small victory.

Petrovitch took the bag from him, unzipped the pouch and slid his hand inside. The rat had gone. All he found was his nearly-spent cash card and a flimsy piece of paper.

"Oh, this has gone completely *pizdets*." He pulled out the paper, knowing what was on it already. But he still had to look.

It was a Metropolitan Police Evidence Seizure form. A serial number, a few ticked boxes, and a place for the officer's printed name and signature. Petrovitch screwed it up in his fist and threw it at the floor.

"It turns out you didn't need to come back here after all," said the young priest. "I appreciate the irony, even if you don't."

"Why the hell didn't the bastard *ment* tell me this in hospital?" Petrovitch bent down to scoop up the crumpled form, and laboriously started to flatten out the creases over his knee.

"I'm sure he had his reasons. By the way, this is a church. I'd appreciate you not swearing in it."

Petrovitch considered his options. If the priest didn't hold to turning the other cheek, hitting him might end badly. But just skulking off didn't strike him as being appropriate either. *"Past' zakroi, podonok."*

Though the words were incomprehensible, his sentiment was resonant in his delivery. Father John's face grew hard, and he took a step forward. "Get out."

"Gladly." Still pressing the piece of paper flat between his hands, he walked towards the doors. He caught sight of Sister Madeleine standing quite still beside the tower staircase.

He wondered if she would have intervened between him and the father. He knew it was her duty, but she looked so disappointed with him that he rather thought she would have just stood by and watched him get the beating he most likely deserved.

6

Petrovitch had had enough; enough for one day, most likely the week. And still he didn't go home.

He rode the nearby Circle Line tube to South Kensington, then the underground travelator the length of Exhibition Road. All the way, he felt a dull, distant fear, a sense of having done something that might mean nothing or everything. He'd succeeded in saving a stranger – this Sonja Oshicora – and failed himself: burned out his heart, become exposed to the unwanted attentions of both criminals and police.

He'd been noticed, and that wasn't what he wanted at all. Time would tell whether he'd been snagged enough by events for his life to unravel like an old knitted jumper.

He still had one place of safety though, somewhere he could slip into a comfortable, familiar role without anyone asking stupid questions like "why?"

Pif was there already, standing at the whiteboard, marker pen in hand, perfectly still but for the flick of her eyes. She was so absorbed in her work that she didn't initially notice Petrovitch wander in and slump into a wheely chair behind her. The chair rolled back across the floor and clattered into a redundant filing cabinet, empty but for empties.

He leaned back and prised two strips of an ancient set of Venetian blinds apart to see the world outside. "The limits on that integral should be minus infinity to plus infinity, not one to infinity," he said. "It's a waveform."

"It wasn't meant to be," she said, "when I wrote this stupid equation out. Where have you been?"

"Getting shot at." He let the blinds ping back. "Being thrown into the back of an ambulance, I think, or how else would I have got to hospital? Having my internal defib machine poked. Nearly thrown off the top of a church by a two-metre-tall nun."

"Orly?" She stepped forward, made her black hand blacker by rubbing out the offending symbols and replacing them with the correct ones, using her impossibly neat copperplate.

"Yeah. Really." He unzipped his jacket and peered at his chest. The ends of black thread sprouted from his skin like a half-buried spider. He had a thought and scooted across the room to his desk. Buried in the bottom of a drawer was a T-shirt, the relic of a death metal concert some six months earlier.

Pif turned around just as Petrovitch had shucked his jacket onto the back of the chair.

"Eww," she said. "Sam, some warning, OK?"

He ignored her protests and dragged the black T-shirt on over his head. It was slightly too small; it accentuated his thinness and rode up above his waistband when he raised his arms.

"Have you got anything to eat?" he asked, looking through the rest of his desk, then under the piles of printout and monographs. "I'm not feeling so good."

"In a minute," she replied, glancing back over her shoulder at the whiteboard.

"I'll never do your coding for you again."

"All right, all right." She threw up her hands and raided her bag for an energy bar.

When she'd launched it across the room at him, and he'd missed it, she pulled her own chair towards his and sat backwards on it, resting her chin on the back-rest.

Petrovitch scrabbled on the floor for the foil-wrapped bar, and crawled awkwardly to sitting again. They looked at each other, then she reached forward and took his chin in her fine fingers, turning it left and right. Her fingernails were painted with randomly generated Mandelbrot sets.

"How bad is it?" Her beaded hair jiggled softly as she talked.

"Bad enough," he said, and finally tore through the wrapping. He continued around mouthfuls of sweet, sticky crumbs. "The defib machine took too long to kick in, and then it wouldn't stop firing. A lot of heart muscle had gone anoxic, and I won't get that function back."

"What are you going to do?"

"I have two options. Get a new heart or die soon."

She blinked slowly. "You mean cake or death?"

"Pretty much, except the cake I want costs two hundred and fifty kiloeuros, plus expenses."

Pif whistled air out of her mouth. "So what are you going to do? Will the university spring for it?"

"I'm a private student. The foundation that supplies my scholarship will cover it." He screwed up the wrapper and dropped it in the bin. "Have you anything else?"

"Yes, but . . . that's very generous of them. You've talked to them already?" She rolled away and dug out another energy bar.

"I didn't want to hang around. I haven't exactly got time on my side. It'll happen next Monday, when the funds are in place."

Pif was distracted again by her equation. She swung around to face it. "Why did you say it was a wave?"

Petrovitch held out his hand for the energy bar, and she placed it deftly without looking around. "I don't know. You've written it like a zeta function, but it looks more like the bastard child of a Fourier transform."

"I should be able to solve this." She glanced at him as he crammed his mouth with food. "Do you want second place on the paper?"

"It can't hurt: Ekanobi and Petrovitch, twenty twenty-five. What is it?"

"Quantum gravity. Part of it, anyway."

He stopped chewing and got up slowly, energy bar lying forgotten on the edge of his desk. He walked to the board. "Which part?"

"The last part. I'm going to do all the calculations again, from scratch, and see if I can get to this point again. I've got it all written down . . ." She was breathless, more than that, hyperventilating. "Sam, I just caught a glimpse of creation."

Her body started to sway, and Petrovitch caught her, and managed to get her head down between her knees.

He crouched next to her, feeling a cold sweat spring up on his own forehead. "You've probably made a mistake, somewhere," he said.

"Probably," she agreed. "At least one. Promise me you won't die until I've gone through the proof."

"I'll try not to." He pointed at the board. "*Yobany stos*, if you pull this off . . ."

She looked out from under her fringe. "It means I'll never have to put up with you taking my lunch again."

"Yeah. But in Russia, lunch takes you." He sat back on his haunches and squinted at the symbols on the board through half-closed eyes. He almost saw it too, the flicker of recognition of something wholly and completely true. "How certain are you of this?"

"Certain? No. But look at it! It's beautiful."

"Take a picture of it. For posterity."

Pif gave him her phone, and he rested his elbows on her desk to reduce the camera shake. It clicked, and she was frozen in time for ever, arms folded, grinning like a loon.

"Perfect," he said.

He left her bent over her notebooks. His exit elicited no more than a soft murmur and a slight inflection of her hand. He knew from past experience that she'd be like that, not moving except when absolutely necessary, blocking everything else out and using her ferocious concentration to map out all the little steps she'd made that preceded the giant leap drawn out in black marker.

Petrovitch left the university the same way he'd entered. Home for sure this time, beating the more spread out but nevertheless impressive migration to the outer parts of the Metrozone. He passed a copy of the iconic Underground map as he glided along the travelator, squashed to one side by a phalanx of marketeers who did nothing but talk into their headset microphones and eye up their prey.

He noticed that to get to Embankment, he'd have to go through St James's Gate. He shrugged his shoulders enough to be able to get into his bag, and look at the address on the evidence form he'd been left with.

The police station was just around the corner, and getting his hardware back was starting to become urgent. How long could it take to make a fuss at the front desk, threaten Chain with non-existent lawyers and finally get his hands on it?

He went through the screen, the turnstile, through the unconscious motions of travelling. There were three stops to go, then two, then one.

The lights flickered in a rippling pattern, from the front of the carriage to back, came on again. Then they snapped off, all the lights, plunging the passengers into utter, tunnel-enclosed darkness.

The train faltered, losing power to the motors, and someone banged hard into Petrovitch's side, driving the air from his lungs and causing him to collide with half a dozen soft, yielding shapes who cushioned the impact.

He thought he was going to fall, to slide under their feet and become trampled. At the last moment, he found vertical again.

He was almost catapulted the other way when the lights blinked on and the train surged forward. He snaked out an arm and held tightly on to a pole, looking back down the chasm his wild movement had carved in the crowded carriage.

At the far end, even as the sea of people closed the gap, was a woman, a teenager with puff-ball white hair, a black jacket that was all zips and buckles, an object in her hand that was made from transparent plastic but had a single serrated edge.

He used his free hand to press against his T-shirt; no wetness, no spreading stain. But his courier bag had a hole in it, just about kidney height. They made the damnedest things out of kevlar these days.

She disappeared from sight as the train roared out into the

next station and began to squeal to a stop. He knew she was there, her mind racing like his, trying to out-think his next move even as he was trying to anticipate hers.

Shouting "She's got a knife" would only serve to make everyone rush away. He needed it tightly packed. She could work her way through the crowd and have another go, but he knew she knew if she got anywhere near him, he'd have nothing to lose by exposing her; if she made the hit, she'd be gunned down by the first paycop she encountered.

He decided she'd missed her only opportunity. She should have waited, followed him out onto the platform. That's how he would have done it. Get close, in with the blade and step away. Shriek herself hoarse and panic. No one would suspect her until very much later and she'd changed her appearance completely.

"St James's Gate. Doors opening."

If he left the train, she'd stay on. She'd let her controller know she'd failed. There might be another attempt, another day.

As passengers poured out onto the platform and away, he could see her watching him. He waited until he could slip along the glass partition to the door. She stayed where she was, her plastic knife hidden behind one of her zips. He was at the threshold, foot hovering over the gap between train and platform. She gave an almost imperceptible jerk of her head, an indication that she'd been thwarted, but that there were no hard feelings.

Petrovitch walked along beside the carriage, feeling her gaze burn between his shoulder blades. The barriers opened, and people poured on. She was gone, lost from sight. The buzzer sounded, the doors closed, and the train whipped away, chased by a whirlwind of litter and stink.

He stopped to watch the red lights slide away around the

next bend, and started to shake. He gripped his bag tight and made his knuckles go white while his stomach flooded with acid that burned all the way up to his throat. He swallowed and screwed his eyes shut.

Another train was coming, buffeting the air ahead of it. He couldn't stand there for the rest of the day. He left the platform, the passengers from a westbound train pushing through the connecting tunnels ahead of him all the way to the surface.

The crush around the towers of St James's Park was intense, but he managed to spot what he wanted within a few seconds of leaving the Underground; a basement datashop that would sell him access by the minute. He had to fight his way through to the steps down, then wrestle with the door that was swollen with heat and humidity.

Other users were glazed and expressionless as they passively absorbed their porn of choice. While Petrovitch was being led by the manager to a free cubicle, he saw one elderly man stare with fascination at a line of windswept rock peaks, the sun rising red over the col between two of them and flooding the scene with light.

"Real?"

"VR. Somewhere Outzone, up north," said the blue-turbaned proprietor. "How long do you want?"

"Five minutes on the net. You OK with proxy servers?"

"I will be if I charge you for ten."

Petrovitch hid his location and identity behind his usual proxy, a Tuvalu-based computer whose existence seemed to have been forgotten by its true owners. From there he went after Chain's number, and simultaneously bought a single-use virtual phone from a provider.

"Chain," said Chain.

"Detective Inspector Chain? It's Petrovitch."

"Petrovitch? That Petrovitch. How's the heart?"

"Just about intact. Yeah, Chain, look . . ."

"I take it this isn't a social call. Where are you now?"

"Datashop. Raj Singh's. Chain . . ."

There was a brief pause while he was away from the microphone. "I can see it from the window. I take it there's a reason you're not at the front desk."

"Chain, listen. Someone just tried to kill me."

Chain coughed liquidly. "They did? That was quick off the mark."

"You knew?"

"It was only a matter of time. There's probably one or two things you need to know about the mess you've got yourself into. Come up and we can have a chat."

"If I'm being watched, I don't want to step foot inside a police station. So the only way I want my kit back, you thieving *ment*, is for you to bring it here."

"There's paperwork to fill in," he said mildly. "Why don't I meet you, and take you over to the station?"

"You're not listening, Chain. I'm not going to appear to be helping you. I don't even want to be anywhere near you." Petrovitch checked the timer. "If this conversation is going to go nowhere, tell me now so I can set some lawyers on you."

"You can have your whatever-it-is back. It's clean. But there genuinely is paperwork, and you're not worth my while cheating the system. Come on, Petrovitch, a little trust goes a long way."

"You stole my property just so I'd have to call you, and you talk about trust?"

"OK, point taken. I did want to check it, make sure you weren't a low-level Oshicora foot soldier, but I could have

done so on the quiet and brought it back to you in hospital."
He coughed again. "I sort of believe you now, and maybe I
can let the other side know you're just some stupid kid who
doesn't know any better than to meddle in the affairs of gods.
What do you reckon?"

Petrovitch reined in his anger. "Will you do that? Will it
work?"

"Tell you what: I think I owe you, so yes. I'll do what needs
to be done, though talking to Marchenkho's *organitskaya* leaves
me with heartburn. Wait there, and I'll come and collect you
when it's done."

"*Organitskaya?*" said Petrovitch. "*Yobany stos.*"

"I imagine you probably are," said Chain, and cut the
connection.

7

Petrovitch was drinking coffee, brewed in a chipped mug in the Raj Singh back office, when Chain knocked politely on the door and let himself in.

"Ready to go, Petrovitch?" He nodded at the Sikh. "Sran? Keeping it legal?"

"As ever, Inspector Chain." Sran winked.

"One day, Sran."

"And until that day, Inspector, we'll keep trading."

"Of course you will. Leave the coffee, Petrovitch. I've better in my office." Chain looked around at all the notes pinned to the office walls, testing names, numbers, addresses for a tickle of memory.

Sran wanted Chain out quickly: he leaned forward and took the mug from Petrovitch's hands. "Pleasure doing business with you."

Petrovitch threw his bag over his shoulder, and Sran ushered them out: he shooed them all the way to the bottom of the basement steps that led up to street level to make sure the policeman didn't have time to see clearly what some of the shop's customers were doing.

The door was shut firmly behind them.

"You know him, then?" said Petrovitch, his ears adjusting to the blare of noise falling on him from above.

"I know everyone," said Chain, checking inside his jacket. He patted his shoulder holster, and unfastened a tab. "Let's make this unremarkable, shall we?"

"I thought you'd talked to whoever it was you needed to talk to."

"I did. You're not the only one with a price on your head." Chain led him up the steps, then elbowed his way into the pedestrian stream. Petrovitch was almost standing on the man's heels so as not to lose him.

They made it to the crossing and, on the next green light, shuffled across the road to a building that sat squat and lonely, surrounded on all sides by streets. Armed police – not paycops, but the real thing – guarded the entrance. They were tall and wide in their armour and utterly anonymous behind their targeting visors. One of them watched Petrovitch as he trailed after Chain, and Petrovitch saw his reflection in the curved faceplate.

He wasn't looking anywhere near as angelic as he had first thing that morning.

He also had to sign in at the desk. The man behind the bullet-proof glass was brisk and businesslike, but Petrovitch still felt a frisson of fear as the optical scanner was pressed against his eye socket.

His identity passed muster, and he was issued with a tag similar to the one he'd worn in hospital.

"It's an offence not to keep this on while you're in the

building," said the man as he watched Petrovitch clip it around his wrist. "Offence as in five years and a ten-thousand-euro fine."

"Is that all?" said Petrovitch.

"We can choose to shoot you." His gaze left Petrovitch and slid onto Chain. "He's all yours."

"You're a humourless bastard, George. Give the kid a break." Chain took Petrovitch by the arm and pulled him away towards the lifts. "Nothing else in that bag I need to know about, is there?"

"Apart from the hole where someone tried to cut me a new *zhopu*, no."

While they waited, Chain inspected the damage. "What did they use?"

"A clear plastic knife. Behind the screen, too."

"Perspex. Covert weapon of choice at the moment." The lift doors shuddered apart. "Get in, and we can have our little chat."

Petrovitch and Chain rode the lift to the seventh floor and walked along the corridor until they reached a door marked "DI H. Chain SCD6". Petrovitch hadn't seen another soul the entire time. The place was a ghost ship, adrift in the heart of the Metrozone.

Despite his disquiet, he dropped gratefully into a leather chair opposite Chain's desk, and watched without comment as the detective busied himself with the domestic chore of making proper coffee.

"I like you," said Chain, once the water had started gargling noisily through the machine. "So I'll tell you how the conversation with Marchenkho went."

"Marchenkho? The *organitskaya* boss?"

"I've got him on speed dial. Now Marchenkho might be a vodka-soused old villain who models himself on Stalin, but we

go back a long way, so he takes my calls. I tell him that two
of his lieutenants are in the mortuary, having been scraped off
the steps of a church, and guess what?"

"He already knows?"

"He already knows." Chain went to the window and peered
past the vertical blinds at the face of the glass monolith being
erected opposite. "But he's not apologising. Marchenkho apol-
ogises a lot, especially when he doesn't mean it, so I guess he's
livid that his carefully planned, once-in-a-lifetime chance at
taking Oshicora's daughter hasn't worked out."

"This isn't sounding good," said Petrovitch, slumping further
down.

"I mention that I'd talked to some of the witnesses. That I
can link all the innocent bystanders gunned down by those two
idiot slabs of Ukrainian pork directly to him." Chain ambled
back to the coffee pot, which hadn't finished, and opened up a
packet of nicotine patches lying on the table. "He doesn't like
that."

"Does that mean the hired help screwed up?"

"It does indeed." He peeled a patch off its backing strip, and
pulled up his sleeve. He pressed it into place above his wrist,
revealing that there was another just further up under his shirt
cuff. "You catch on quick, Petrovitch. Tell me what happens
next."

Petrovitch frowned. "You traded me," he said after a moment.

"Pretty much. I wouldn't be able to stick anything on
Marchenkho, but I might take out one or two of his upper
management and they'd be watching their backs for months. So
he's called off the attack dogs on you in exchange for some peace
and quiet." Chain got fed up of waiting, and grabbed the coffee
pot. As he poured the black liquid into two mugs, spatters of

steam hissed on the hot plate. "Want to know how much you were worth?"

"Not particularly."

"Two fifty."

"Thousand?" Petrovitch sat bolt upright. "*Huy na ny!*"

"Enough for a new heart, even. Marchenkho was really very cross with you." Chain pushed the coffee along the desk at Petrovitch, and sat awkwardly on one corner. "I hope you don't take milk, because I haven't got any. Or sugar. Anyway, putting out a contract takes no time at all. Information like that moves fast, and it reaches all the right people – or wrong people – very quickly. Rescinding that same contract takes longer. News that no one wants to hear crawls along. Sometimes it doesn't get to everyone who needs to know until it's too late."

"Too late. As in me."

"You've got an uncomfortable week ahead, Petrovitch." Chain slurped at his coffee. "Bugger. Hot."

While Chain dabbed at his scalded lip, Petrovitch pushed his glasses up his nose and made little ticking noise with his tongue. "How did they get on to me so fast? I mean, I went from the church, to hospital, to the church, to the university, and suddenly I'm a target."

"Two unpalatable options, each equally likely. First, that your face has been lifted from a CCTV file, run through facial recognition software, and your government file rifled for information on where you live, where you work, everything official about you."

"A *krisha.*"

"As you say, a bent copper. More likely, you've been bugged. At the hospital, I would guess."

Petrovitch looked down. Now even his own clothes were

betraying him. "So for all I know, they're lining up outside to have a go at me."

"They'd have to know roughly where you are first." Chain went behind his desk and pulled out a magic wand from his top drawer. "Abracadabra."

He waved the wand mystically over Petrovitch, top to toe, and gradually zeroed in on his right boot.

"I'm not taking it off for you," said Chain, looking up from the floor.

Petrovitch unlaced the boot and pulled it off his foot. Chain wrinkled his nose.

"Sorry," said Petrovitch.

"I'm guessing girls don't feature much in your life." Chain ran the wand around the boot, then inside. He plunged his hand in after it, and after a few moments of pulling faces, retrieved a sticky label. "There."

Petrovitch took the wand from the detective and inspected it. A line of lights ran up one side, the bottom four already lit. When he brought it close to the label stuck to the end of Chain's fingers, all the lights flickered on.

He peeled the label off Chain, and as he held it up to the window, he could see shadows of circuitry inside. "What do I do with it?"

"Tear it in half. But if they have access to the CCTV network, they can still track you with cameras, and they know where you live. Anywhere you can hole up safe for a few days?" Chain dragged his coffee closer, and warily tried to drink it.

"I'm a physicist, not a spy."

"A holiday in Russia?"

"Yeah. That really isn't a good idea."

Chain raised his eyebrows. "How so?"

"It just isn't. OK?" Petrovitch stared up at the detective, who eventually shrugged and muttered something under his breath.

"Look," said Chain, "let me explain something to you. I can't stop you from being killed. I don't have the resources. I can make it difficult for them, but not impossible. I might even be able to catch your murderer, but I'm sure that's not going to be of much comfort to you. You're going to have to help yourself. Any good at that?"

Petrovitch nodded slowly. "Yeah. Not bad."

"Good. So what are you going to do?"

"I don't know yet. Chain, what is it with you and the Oshicoras?"

The detective slid off his desk and paced the floor. When he spoke, it was with messianic zeal. "I was here. Here for everything. Armageddon: the shock of the first explosions – Dublin, Belfast, Sellafield, the emptying of the countryside, the radioactive rain, the streets choked with refugees, kids – so many kids without their parents – everywhere. We could have lost control in so many different ways, torn apart from the inside, swamped from the outside, or just one of those fucking heretics with their holy nuclear bombs getting across the M25: but we didn't. We kept it together. We took everybody in. Housed them. Fed them. Found something for them to do."

Petrovitch sighed, and Chain made a rumbling cough.

"Am I boring you?" he asked.

"Just get on with it, Inspector."

"What we did was a miracle. Then Oshicora turned up, eight years ago, unseen amongst all the other refugees that were washing around the world. Marchenkho's *organitskaya* and every other criminal gang in the Metrozone has been losing ground to Oshicora's *yakuza* ever since."

"He's not *yakuza*," said Petrovitch. "His men have got too many fingers."

"Neo-yakuza, then. Corporate *samurai*, whatever you want to call them. They prey on us, suck us dry – virus and host. And if the infection was in just one place, it wouldn't matter, but Oshicora runs his organisation like a franchise, each outlet selling his specific brand of criminality to the masses. They're turning up everywhere, and what we've worked for, what I've worked for, will have been for nothing. This city brought to its knees by a . . ." Words finally failed him. He threw up his hands and dropped heavily into his seat.

Petrovitch scratched his chin and pushed his glasses up his nose. "All that must make him very rich."

"Most people don't get it. They don't understand why the police just can't do something about it. I'm guessing that you get it perfectly."

"Better than you could possibly imagine." His coffee at a drinkable temperature, Petrovitch gulped at it until it had gone. "Thanks for the lecture, but I think I should be going."

His abruptness startled Chain. "You said you had nowhere to go."

"That's because I hadn't. Now I do." He was halfway to the door, when he realised he'd forgotten what he'd originally come for. "You still have something of mine."

"Ah, yes: your Remote Access Terminal. Half-gigabyte band-width, two-fifty-six-bit encryption, satellite connectivity and a touch interface. Chinese kit, top of the range, does pretty much everything. Just how does a kid like you afford something like that? More to the point, what would you need one for?"

"You're the detective. You figure it out." Petrovitch's jaw jutted out. "Just get it for me, OK?"

Chain patted his pockets, and ended up using the hardwired desk phone. He said a few words, listened to the response, and a faint smile raised the corners of his mouth.

He put the phone down. "Hard luck."

"You're joking."

"I'm afraid not. Someone's swiped it from the evidence room. I'll be making enquiries, don't worry. You'll get it back, eventually." Chain looked almost happy. "So where are you going, Petrovitch?"

"Do you honestly think I'd tell you? You can't even keep evidence locked up. What good would you be with a secret?" Petrovitch wrestled with the unfamiliar door handle. "Just leave me alone."

"You know my number. Call me when you're ready."

"Ready for what?" He finally got the door open.

"Ready for when you tell me why you saved Sonja Oshicora."

"*Potselui mou zhopy*, Chain."

Petrovitch fumed all the way down to the ground floor. He still had the sticky bug on the end of his fingers. He made a face at it, then carefully pasted it on the inside of his police-issue wrist tag. When he passed the front desk, he ripped the tag off and slapped it face-up on the counter in a carefully calculated act of rage.

Outside, he looked at the buildings around him and headed north. Towards Green Park.

8

The Oshicora Tower was constructed in the phallocentric style: tall, narrow at the base before flaring out to a maximum girth halfway up. Silvered triangles of glass wrapped like a staircase around its circumference, making it impossible to see any of the internal structure.

He'd soon have an opportunity. He was going in. He wasn't sure it was the wisest course to take, but he gauged that the short-term benefits of staying alive outweighed any potential downside. He stood almost exactly where he'd been that morning, watching Sonja Oshicora striding towards him – then hesitating, as if she couldn't quite remember what it was she planned to do next.

Then he turned and walked down the wide, fountain-flanked concourse to the entrance lobby. The guards – he'd have called them paycops, but for the little cloth Rising Sun badge sewn on the front of their impact armour – must have thought him a courier, because they stood back and ignored him.

Inside was bright and airy and clean. Real plants scrubbed the air, real people busied themselves cleaning the marble floor or carrying boxes labelled with *katakana* or answering phone calls at a tiered bank of terminals.

Petrovitch was the only non-Japanese face on the entire ground floor. He'd crossed the threshold from the multi-ethnic Metrozone to something he'd never encountered before; a monocultural enclave. He stood there, in the middle of the lobby, marvelling at the strangeness of it all.

"Petrovitch-san?"

It took him a moment to realise there was someone behind him, and another to realise they were addressing him. He span on his heel to see a squad of three black-clad guards, two standing respectfully behind their leader, who Petrovitch knew.

"Hijo. Hijo-san." He knew to bow, and Hijo bowed lower, revealing the ceremonial sword strapped across his back.

"You are most welcome, Petrovitch-san. Please, come with me." Hijo walked away, just expecting Petrovitch to follow, which after a deep breath, he did.

Everything he saw was beautiful, clean, new. It was how he'd imagined his future to be, not the squalor of the domiks, not the hot, heavy air that filled his lungs, not the day-to-day grind of just getting from one place to another. He had to keep reminding himself who he was going to see and how they got their money.

The lifts ran up the core of the building, accessed from behind the receptionists with their terminals and headsets. Discreetly placed guards marked a line between the public space and the private – no physical barrier, but there was a steel strip set into the floor. Petrovitch had no doubt that he would have been challenged and turned back if he'd crossed it alone.

But he had his escort: Hijo in front of him and two more armoured men behind. Their presence didn't make him feel any more safe than he did on the streets, and he knew they had orders to protect him.

One set of lift doors were being held open for him. Hijo marched straight in, turned, and waited.

Petrovitch hovered, and pushed at the bridge of his glasses. "Can I just say something here?"

"Of course, Petrovitch-san."

"My turning up here is in no way to be taken as a sign of loyalty or joining sides or looking for favours. I'd very much like to keep everything informal, no contract implied or offered, that sort of thing. All I'd like is a quick word with your boss and ask his help in clearing up a little misunderstanding, then I'll be out of here never to bother you again."

Hijo smiled, and gave a little bow. "Oshicora-san is eager to meet you, too."

Petrovitch screwed his eyes up and joined Hijo in the lift. "That's not quite what I meant, but never mind."

The two guards stayed outside, and bowed as the lift doors closed. Hijo spoke up – "*toppu yuka*" – and the car started smoothly. Lights indicating the floor number turned over, *kanji* characters all.

Petrovitch scratched his chin. The thought that had occurred to him while he listened to Chain crystallised in perfect form: this tower wasn't just Japanese owned, Japanese staffed, but was actually Japan. It went beyond a yearning for what was lost; it was no pale recreation of a Tokyo office block, but the real deal, vibrant and alive with industry.

Chain saw Oshicora's neo-*yakuza* as a new model of crime syndication, but he'd missed the truth of the matter. Petrovitch had misspent his youth playing strategy games: he recognised the plan for what it was. Each franchise was a colony, and they were growing.

The lift chimed, and the doors opened on another world.

The light was blinding and, for the first time in his life, Petrovitch realised he'd lived in the dark. He could hear water, birdsong, feel a cool breeze on his face. As his eyes adjusted, he began to see how all this was created at the top of a building in the middle of a city.

The glass skin of the tower soared up over his head. Fans at the apex stirred the air, sucking in the heat and pushing out a frigid wind. Trees, planted in real soil, waved their leaves over streams of moving water that sometimes narrowed to run babbling over cobbles, sometimes widened to become slow pools dotted with lilies.

Gravel paths, carefully raked and rolled, wound across the rooftop until they arrived at graceful arched bridges. Birds — real birds — gave flashes of movement and colour.

Almost hidden amongst all of the garden was a single man dressed in loose grey trousers and a rough white shirt. He was standing at the edge of a square of white sand in which large black stones had been carefully placed.

Hijo guided Petrovitch onto the first path, and took a step back. Hijo would see nothing, hear nothing, until it was time for him to go. Petrovitch walked as if he was on holy ground, carefully, fearfully, until he was within coughing distance of Oshicora.

The man looked around. "Come," he said. "Closer."

Petrovitch joined him at the dark timber which separated gravel from fine sand. He could see the surface of the sand was patterned in circles and waves.

"I owe you a great debt of gratitude, Samuil Petrovitch. You rescued my daughter from her attackers, at a considerable personal cost. A relieved parent thanks you from the bottom of his heart." Oshicora bowed low and formally, showing his thinning hair. Then he straightened up. "You've heard stories about me? From Detective Inspector Chain?"

"One or two," admitted Petrovitch.

"He makes me out to be a monster. Most unfair." Oshicora spread his hands wide. "Could a monster have conceived all this?"

"It's . . . amazing. You must regret not spending more time up here."

"You mean, I am so busy running my empire of crime that I can snatch only brief moments of rest?" He laughed, loudly and freely, his head tipped back. "Really, there is not that much to do. The secret is to choose your key managers carefully. You only have to take the critical decisions, or at least those which your managers deem to be critical. I have plenty of time to devote to matters of culture and learning. Much like yourself."

"That's very kind," said Petrovitch.

"You are downplaying your achievements, Petrovitch-san. You obtained a first-class honours degree from a top-rank university. You have a scholarship supplied by wise benefactors in Russia. Soon you will be Doctor Petrovitch, and you will become eminent in your chosen field. Good. It becomes everyone, great or lowly, to achieve their potential." Oshicora rested his hand on his chin. "But you are wary of me, uncertain whether to accept a compliment in case it is snatched away and replaced with malice. Try not to fear me. Here we are: a young man on the cusp of his life, an older man imagining what his legacy will be."

"Yeah. About that life: it's why I came to see you." Petrovitch turned his toe in the gravel. "Did you hear about Marchenkho?"

"I hear lots of rumours about that man."

"The contract? The two-hundred-and-fifty-thousand-euro one on my head?"

Oshicora pretended to think for a moment. "I sent Hijo to the hospital to escort you to safety. He informed me you walked away."

"That'll be me not being in full command of the facts. I'll apologise to him later for his wasted journey. So I nearly ended up with a knife in my back today, and I'd rather not repeat the experience."

"You require my protection? It is yours."

"No," said Petrovitch slowly. "Not exactly."

"Perhaps we should take tea while you explain." Oshicora walked around the perimeter of the Zen garden and towards a small table set with a delicate white china tea service.

Petrovitch sat on the edge of his chair and gazed at Oshicora's deft movements setting out crockery and pouring fragrant green tea.

"It's like this," he said, cradling the tea bowl in both hands, "Chain has warned Marchenkho and his associates off by all but convincing him I'm not in your pay. The contract's been cancelled, but it seems that Marchenkho isn't too bothered about letting everyone know. The last thing I need is for him to see me with one of your men. Or women; I'm sure it's all equal opportunities here. Even if they're brilliant, I'll still be marked for death and I'll still have to explain to my tutor why I have an armed bodyguard following me around."

Oshicora leaned over his bowl and bathed in the rising steam. "Most interesting analysis. Carry on."

"So what I'd like you to do is trump the original contract. Anyone who kills me gets taken down for say, five hundred thousand. It'll spread like wildfire to everyone who needs to know, and I can go to the corner shop again without worrying about snipers."

"What if," asked Oshicora, "Marchenkho has a change of heart, and bids higher?"

"You can always top him. That's why I came to you." Petrovitch blew across the surface of his tea, watching the patterns the steam made. "This is going to be a nine-day wonder. Next week, no one will care who I am. But for those few days I need the extra insurance."

"Ingenious. I'm impressed by your grasp of the intricacies of such a dark subject. It is almost," he mused, "as if you have some experience with the way these things are done."

"I grew up in St Petersburg during Armageddon. Everybody there has some relevant experience."

"Ah yes. You're not a native to these shores, much like me. You arrived here when?"

Petrovitch narrowed his eyes, squinting into the past. "Twenty twenty-one. I started at Imperial in twenty twenty-two."

"When you were nineteen?" Oshicora demonstrated his recall of incidental facts. "That seems a little young to tackle so difficult a subject."

"I'd passed the exams. Didn't seem much point in waiting till my balls dropped."

Oshicora laughed again, sending waves across his tea. "Good, good. Tell me; what's the next big thing in the world of physics? Do we have fusion power yet, or is it still ten years away?"

"Not if I have anything to do with it," said Petrovitch. "But showing it can work on a computer and building a reactor are two different things."

"And," said Oshicora, looking across the table at him, "any closer to a Grand Unified Theory?"

Petrovitch almost dropped his bowl, which probably gave the game away there and then. Hot tea poured into the palm of his hand as he regained his grip, almost causing him to fumble his catch. He gritted his teeth and put the bowl on the table.

"Your colleague, Doctor Ekanobi, has an announcement to make?" Oshicora handed him a starched napkin.

"Not just yet." Petrovitch took the cloth and held it inside his fist. "It might be nothing."

"On the other hand, it might be everything. Do you know how close other research groups are?"

"No. I'm not even formally part of the Imperial GUT group." The pain was fading now, and he inspected the damage. His hand was wetly pink, but there were no blisters or peeling skin. "More of a hanger-on. I help where I can."

"Stanford believe they are, at most, two or three steps away." Oshicora drank tea, and topped up Petrovitch's cup before continuing. "I believe it vital to keep up with these matters. Others are too short-sighted. Their loss. So, has there been a breakthrough?"

"It's not for me to say." He looked away, across the garden. The lift shaft was invisible. He was on a floating island in a sea of concrete and steel. "To be honest, I feel a bit uncomfortable talking about it."

"Of course. You have your professional confidences as I have mine. I apologise. But," said Oshicora, "perhaps we can discuss the practical implications of such a discovery. Unlimited power from zero point energy. Transmutation of elements. Space travel that is not just affordable, but fast. Access to the solar system, to other stars. What else can you imagine for me?"

"The door to the universe is ajar," said Petrovitch, then shook his head as if he'd been in a dream. "Maybe in a hundred, a thousand years. Just because we know something is possible doesn't mean we can do it. Materials, equipment, gaps in our knowledge: anything might hold us up." He gave a wry smile. "Don't go to the bank just yet."

"Petrovitch-san. Finish your tea. There is something I would like to show you."

Nervously, Petrovitch finished the light green liquid in his refilled bowl and replaced it on the lacquered tray. Oshicora led him through the garden, over one of the bridges from where he could see the peaks of the central Metrozone skyscrapers around him and the slow, lazy motions of koi carp beneath his feet.

"Japanese companies have always looked ahead," said Oshicora. "Not a year, not five years. Not ten. They have business plans that stretch decades, a century or more. Now that we have no homeland, we must look even further."

A small shrine sat on a low mound in a dense grove of maple trees. The shrine was an ornate, curved roof resting on four carved pillars. Inside was a table, and at that table sat a man – a white man in a checked shirt and fraying shorts. He was looking at a screen and typing on the tabletop, oblivious to their approach.

They walked up steps to the platform. The boards creaked, and the seated man's eyes flickered to capture their image before turning their full attention back to the screen.

The screen was dense with code, which he was splicing together with reckless confidence.

"Petrovitch-san, may I introduce Martin Sorenson? He is helping me build the future."

9

Sorenson unfolded himself from his chair. He extended a shovel-like hand and grasped Petrovitch's in a knuckle-cracking hold.

"Pleased to meet you," he said in an inflected Midwest accent.

"You're . . ." Petrovitch bit his tongue and changed gear. Sorenson knew he was an American, and Petrovitch telling him so would only mark him out as socially inept. "Very busy."

"Mr Oshicora pays well for good work. You doing the project too?"

"Project?" He didn't know what the project was. "No."

Oshicora interrupted. "Petrovitch-san has been assisting me in another matter, where he has been most helpful. Sorenson is an expert in man–machine interfaces; his skills are most apposite."

Now Petrovitch wondered what Oshicora needed a cyberneticist for. "I thought you Americans were into gene splicing and wetware."

"I'm the exception to the rule, then, Mr Petrovitch." Sorenson scratched at his thinning sandy hair, looking more like a farmer worrying about his crop than a technologist. He reached into his back pocket and passed him a business card. "If you ever need a spare part, just call."

Petrovitch glanced across to Oshicora, whose face remained utterly unreadable. "Yeah, thanks," he said, sliding the card into his jacket. "If you ever need, I don't know, someone to design some building-sized electromagnets, I'm your man. Though I doubt there's much call for that sort of thing in your line of work."

Sorenson laughed and clapped Petrovitch on the shoulder. "You never know."

He forced his arm back into line. "What was it you wanted me to see, Oshicora-san?"

"If Mister Sorenson will close his work, I will show you."

Sorenson busied himself at the virtual keyboard, then moved out of Oshicora's way.

The older man tugged his sleeves away from his wrists and reset the terminal's language. The image of the keyboard changed and grew as it converted to use an extended Japanese character set. He typed in a single command line, and sat back.

The screen blinked, as if it were a giant eye. When it opened, it looked out on an aerial view of Japan.

"Here is *Nippon*, as it was on the evening of March twenty-eighth, twenty seventeen," said Oshicora. He touched the screen, and they descended through the clouds until they were over the island of Honshu. "Here is Tokyo."

The city sprawled around the bay, street after street. Piers jutted into the sea. Buildings rose up from the ground. Oshicora brought them down to pavement level, where the scene slowly rotated. Shops, brightly lit, filled with the goods of the world. Everything was as it had been, the day before the whole island chain started to turn into Atlantis. Everything, except the people.

equationsoflife

"I get it," said Petrovitch. "How detailed are you going to make this?"

"Perfectly so. Down to the feel of the silk on a kimono."

"That's ambitious. No wonder you need Sorenson. You want a totally immersive city."

"I beg to correct you, Petrovitch-san. A whole country. Every tree, every blade of grass, every grain of sand. Mapped and reproduced from the memories of one hundred and twenty million Japanese survivors. Not just houses, but everything in them. Not just parks, but the scent of chrysanthemums. Cherry blossom will fall like rain once more. It will be exact. Our homeland will rise from the sea as if it had never fallen. The *shinkansen* will run again."

Petrovitch wondered if his heart had skipped a beat. "*Nu ti dajosh!* What the hell are you running this on?"

"Below this building is a room. It is bombproof, fireproof, waterproof, electromagnetic and radiation hard. In it is a quantum computer. If every *nikkeijin* visited the simulation at the same time, it would still run flawlessly."

"Ooh." Petrovitch's fingers tingled. He started to think about all the things he could do with such massively parallel processing, and broke out in a cold sweat.

"Petrovitch-san? Are you unwell?"

"No, I'm fine." He rested his hands on the table. "Just taking a moment. That's really very impressive."

"I am happy. Now, I will leave you briefly in the care of Sorenson, while I attend to the other matter we discussed earlier. If you will excuse me?" Oshicora bowed and left the shrine, leaving the single chair unoccupied.

"Mind if I?" asked Petrovitch.

"Knock yourself out, kid," said Sorenson. "So what do you make of our employer?"

"He's not my employer," said Petrovitch firmly, searching for the toggle that would give him a standard Roman keyboard. "I sort of bumped into his daughter this morning."

"Sonja: I've seen her around, though I've been told not to talk to her. But I haven't seen a wife, and he doesn't wear a ring." Sorenson looked around to see if he could be overheard. "Not that you have to be married to have kids. Not over here, anyways."

"And how is the Reconstruction?" Petrovitch gave up, and used the touchscreen instead, navigating around the streets. The walls were solid. Doors were tabbed to open. When he ran a virtual hand over a clothes rail, the dresses moved in exquisite detail.

"You one of these people who expect every American to be a card-carrying Reconstructionist? That gets old real quick."

"No. I rather assumed you weren't one of them, since you're working for Oshicora."

"It's a few weeks' consultancy, nothing more." Sorenson dug his hands in his pockets. "What do you mean? What's wrong with working for Old Man Oshicora? Because he's a Jap?"

"Not at all." Petrovitch glanced over the top of his glasses. "Because he controls the fastest-growing criminal organisation in the Metrozone."

"He what?"

Petrovitch raised his eyebrows. "You didn't know? Oh dear."

"Hey now, wait just a . . ." Sorenson chuckled. "Funny, kid. You had me going for a minute."

"Sorenson," said Petrovitch, "it's not a joke. That 'other matter' that Oshicora's gone to see about is to save me from being shot by the Ukrainian *zhopu* who tried to kidnap his daughter this morning. I'm not here for any other reason but to try and keep my skin intact."

A look of doubt flickered across Sorenson's broad face. "Kid," he started.

"And stop calling me kid. 'Kid' would describe the girl who tried to drive a perspex pick into my guts on the tube."

"OK, Petrovitch. I don't know where you're getting your facts from, but this gig is legit." Sorenson was growing angry. Petrovitch could see the storm start to rise behind his eyes. "Just butt out of my business. What is this? Revenge for the Cold War?"

"Neither of us was alive for that." Petrovitch turned his attention back to the screen. "What you do with the information is up to you. Don't blame the messenger." He deliberately leaned forward and absorbed the sights of the eerily empty city.

"I don't have to take this." Sorenson stood behind the screen. "I don't even know you."

"Yeah, look." Despite his desire to keep on playing the man, Petrovitch was aware that Sorenson could not only beat the *govno* out of him, but seemed quite willing to do so. "I don't care. You're not interested in anything I have to say because it's me saying it. So I'm going to do the grown-up thing and let you get on with your coding."

He got up and walked away, letting the chair fall back with a bang onto the wooden boards. But he didn't know how far he was permitted to go in the park, so he sat down on the shrine's wide bottom step and waited.

The chair scraped as it was set upright. "Who's your source?"

Without turning around, Petrovitch said: "You seem bright enough. Work it out yourself."

"OK. I'm sorry. Tell me who I need to talk to." Sorenson sat down next to him, and had the grace to look troubled.

"DI Chain. Works out of Buckingham Gate." He looked up

and saw Oshicora making his stately way towards them. He finished in a hurried whisper: "Do not mention my name. I've no intention of renewing my acquaintance with the man."

Petrovitch scrabbled to his feet and went to meet Oshicora on the apex of the wooden bridge.

"Petrovitch-san," said Oshicora, bowing.

Petrovitch bowed in return.

"I have made the arrangements you requested. A counter-contract of five hundred thousand euros has been placed. I imagine you will be safe even from Marchenkho himself." He looked inordinately pleased with himself, getting one over on an old rival.

"Thank you, Oshicora-san. I kind of assume that our paths won't cross again." Petrovitch chanced a half-smile. "I'm rather hoping they won't. I like a quiet life."

"Stranger things have been known to happen. If you find that your life is not as quiet as you wish, I will instruct my staff to come to your assistance, as you did to my daughter's. If you call, they will come." Oshicora contemplated the carp moving in circles beneath his feet. He dipped his fingers in his pocket and came out with a few compressed pellets of fish food. He dropped them one at a time into the water, and the fish fought for the honour of eating.

"Thank you also for showing me this garden, and your quantum computer project. I hadn't known there were any in private hands. I wouldn't be so unwise as to spread that around, either."

"We understand each other perfectly, Petrovitch-san. Come; I will take you to Hijo, who will show you out."

As they walked, Petrovitch glanced behind him at Sorenson, stood by the shrine, fists clearly clenching and unclenching. "I think you should have told him."

"Told him? Ah, yes. Sorenson. You believe I have ruined his life?"

"I think you might have given him the choice first."

"Do not waste your sympathy on him," said Oshicora. "He appears to be what the Yankees call a hick, but he has a past which he manages to hide from his own Homeland Security, from himself even. I, however, believe I have discovered his secret. That aside, the mere fact of his relationship with me will ruin him when he has completed his work and tries to return home. It is good that he suspects nothing; it will be an unpleasant surprise for him."

Petrovitch nodded, and managed somehow not to swear out loud.

Oshicora appeared not to notice the abrupt whiteness of Petrovitch's skin, and he carried on. "One word from me, and he will lose his citizenship, his company, his assets. He will be stateless, a refugee like we once were. You, I will deal with honourably. After the way the Americans treated my countrymen and women, I have no compunction in exploiting any one of them mercilessly."

"Yeah, well." They were at the lift again. Hijo was as immobile as when Petrovitch had left him. "Thanks again, and goodbye."

"Goodbye, Petrovitch-san. I wish you good fortune and success in your studies. The secrets of the universe are elusive, but perhaps you are the man to catch them." Oshicora turned to Hijo, who bowed low. "Petrovitch-san is leaving us now. Please make certain he arrives home safely."

The last sight of Oshicora that Petrovitch had was his smiling face being narrowed to a line by the closing doors.

Hijo led him back through the sea of Japanese faces to the lobby, but didn't leave him there. Instead, they went through a side door and down a spiralling ramp to an underground loading bay. Sharp white light lit up a pillar-supported concrete chamber. A car sat silently, waiting for them.

It was big and black and crouched low on its suspension. Polarised glass rendered its windows opaque. Petrovitch wondered if there was anyone in it — whether or not it was completely automatic — when the rear door rolled aside electrically and the courtesy light came on.

"Please, Petrovitch-san." Hijo gestured to the open door, and Petrovitch climbed in. He'd been wrong. There was a driver, and someone riding shotgun. Then Hijo himself got in beside him and tapped the shoulder of the man behind the wheel.

"I didn't realise you were coming with me," said Petrovitch. He was eager to be away; he didn't trust Sorenson to keep his mouth shut.

Hijo pulled the seatbelt across his body and clicked it into place. "My employer would be most displeased with me if something happened to you while you were in our care," he said by way of explanation.

"So I get a ride in a bullet-proof car." Petrovitch took a deep breath, and followed Hijo's example with the seatbelt. "Does this thing go south of the river?"

Barely aware that the engine was running, Petrovitch felt the car ease forward towards a steel shutter that rolled upwards. They were outside in a recessed road that gradually rose to join another. He twisted in his seat: he could see the base of the Oshicora Tower behind him, but not its top. They turned, and he lost even that view.

He was driven down the Strand, and across Waterloo Bridge, which neatly skirted the parliamentary Green Zone, then back west along the river before heading south. He even caught sight of the old Palace of Westminster brooding, black and cold, behind concrete walls.

The driver's wrap-round sunglasses showed him which way to go, and Petrovitch became a mute passenger until he felt he was back on his own territory.

"If you drop me here, that'll be fine. I want to get a coffee." They knew where he lived, but he didn't have to take them to his door.

Hijo tapped the driver again, and the car pulled up next to the kerb nearest Wong's.

"*Chyort!*"

"Sorry, Petrovitch-san?"

Petrovitch pressed his fingers into his temples. "This morning, I had a brand new Random Access Terminal delivered. Detective Inspector Chain took it in for questioning, and it vanished from the evidence room. Your lot didn't have anything to do with that, did they?"

"I believe not, but I will ask. Should I return it to you if we have it?"

"Bring it here," he said, "Wong will look after it for me. No offence, but the less I get seen in your company, the better."

"As you wish, Petrovitch-san." Hijo slipped his seatbelt and opened the door. He got out first for a precautionary look around, before allowing Petrovitch to step out onto the litter-strewn pavement.

They were attracting more than a little attention, not least from Wong who was at his shop door with his arms folded disapprovingly.

"Right then," said Petrovitch. "*Dobre den.*"

"Please," said Hijo, "I would like to know: why did you help Miss Sonja?"

Petrovitch could already taste coffee in his mouth, bittersweet and strong. "Tell you what, Hijo," he said, pushing his glasses back up his nose, "I'll answer that if you tell me what the *yebat* she was doing out on her own."

Hijo looked like he'd just been slapped.

"Yeah. Thought so," said Petrovitch, and shouldered his way past Wong in search of an empty table, cries of what a bad man he was ringing in his ears.

10

He woke up, but this time not to the sounds of the streets and windmills and voices. Someone was hammering on his door with something hard and heavy.

The door was steel, reinforced with electrically operated bolts. No need to panic, he lied to himself even as ice water flooded his veins and his poor heart struggled to keep in time.

He grabbed his glasses from where he'd thrown them the night before and listened carefully. The banging wasn't the right rhythm for breaking in – he'd expect a slow, heavy concussion with sledgehammer or a ram. Neither was it someone with more technical expertise and a gas axe or plastique, he'd have woken with the room full of smoke and a masked man standing over him with a gun.

Petrovitch pulled on the death metal T-shirt from the day before and stood close to the door. Through the insulation he could just about hear his name being shouted out.

Bangbangbangbang. Petrovitch. Bangbangbangbang.

"*Ahueyet?* You *opezdol*, you *raspizdyai!* Go away," he called back, but the banging and shouting redoubled.

He pulled the first bolt, then the second, working his way around the door. Finally, he gripped the handle and pulled.

Sorenson stumbled in, shoe in hand. Petrovitch shoved him hard towards the far wall and glanced outside. Everyone there was staring at him. He let fly with *yob materi vashi* and slammed the door shut again.

"What the *chyort* are you doing here?"

Sorenson stared at him wild-eyed. He was in the same clothes – shirt and shorts – that he'd worn yesterday, and Petrovitch guessed that he'd not been back to his hotel at all.

"You were right," he muttered. "So now I need your help."

"You want what?" said Petrovitch. He reached for his trousers and dragged them on. "Why do you think I'd be either willing or able to help you? And how the *huy* did you get my address?"

Sorenson walked towards the chair and looked like he was about to sit down.

"No. You're not staying." Petrovitch jammed his feet into his boots and started to lace them with controlled savagery. "Who told you where I live?"

"Chain." Sorenson stuck his hands in his back pockets. "I went to see him."

"And you just happened to mention my name. Thanks, *pidaras!*"

"He wouldn't give me anything otherwise. Then he said he'd arrest me for money laundering if I took so much as one red cent off Oshicora. So I've come to you: we've got some planning to do."

"We?" Petrovitch threw on his jacket and his courier bag. "Let me say this in words even you might understand: I wouldn't plan so much as a piss-up in a brewery with you because you're a fucking idiot."

Sorenson winced.

"What? Your little Reconstructionist soul shrinking at the bad language the nasty Russian is using? Get used to it, because you'll be hearing plenty more." He stamped to the door. "Get your shoe on, you *raspizdyai kolhoznii*. Now tell me you have money."

"I've money." Sorenson dropped his shoe and shuffled his foot into it.

"Good. Now get going: you're buying breakfast." Petrovitch hauled his door open, shoved Sorenson out into the corridor and heaved the door shut. He waited for the bolts to clang back into place, before blazing a trail down towards the first stairwell.

Eventually, Sorenson caught up. "Petrovitch, what is this place?"

"Domiks, after the shipping containers used to build them. It's where refugees like me live."

"I thought you were a student."

"Doesn't mean I'm not a refugee. Now," said Petrovitch, shouldering a fire door, "straight to the bottom, and if you value what's left of your life, don't look at anyone."

"I made it up here all right." Sorenson blustered.

"All it means is that they're waiting for you on the way down. Go, and keep your mouth shut. Yankees aren't exactly flavour of the month."

They walked the long, lonely staircase all the way to the ground floor. Petrovitch considered them lucky to arrive unmolested; perhaps Sorenson's minimal dress and his aura of impotent rage made it appear that the American had already been mugged.

"Where are we going?" Sorenson blinked in the morning light and hugged himself.

"I told you. Breakfast."

They crossed at the lights and crashed through Wong's sticky door.

"Hey, Petrovitch. You still owe me for yesterday." Wong flicked a filthy tea towel at him.

"Yeah. Don't worry. The Yank's paying. Two full breakfasts, and coffee, strong as you like."

Wong folded his arms and regarded Sorenson. "Who this?"

"Just one of my *yakuza* friends. So, when you're ready with the coffee?"

"It not enough that you bad man: you now hang out with bad men. Big cars, guns, money. It ends in early grave." He dragged his finger across his throat.

They looked at each other across the counter, Wong swapping his attention between Petrovitch and Sorenson.

"Breakfast?" ventured Petrovitch. "Or should we go elsewhere?"

"Show me the money," said Wong.

"Show him the money, Sorenson."

"What? I guess." He dug in his pocket for his credit chip and handed it to Wong, who fed it into the reader.

His thunderous expression lightened a little. "OK, you sit down. No organising crime in my shop."

"Wouldn't dream of it." Petrovitch kicked Sorenson over to the corner table, and chose to sit with his back against the wall and a good view of the door. "Sit your arse down. We've got some serious eating to do."

Sorenson cast a suspicious glance over to the counter where his credit chip remained in the till. "I still don't understand what we're doing here."

"Look. You've been up all night, walking the streets – and God only knows how you survived that – and have been running on nervous energy since you realised just how catastrophic the mistake you made is. We're going to load up on caffeine and long-chain carbohydrates, then I'm going to beat you around the head until your brain restarts. Yeah?"

Sorenson stared at him.

"How old are you?" asked Petrovitch. He swept the tabletop with the palm of his hand and decrumbed it against his thigh. Wong banged down two mugs of coffee and rumbled deep in his throat. "Thanks, Wong. Really, you don't want to overhear any of this."

He walked away muttering about bad men.

"Thirty-six," said Sorenson.

"You've been through the draft, yeah?"

"Sure, I served my country. Corps of Engineers. Five years. I made sergeant and got me a chestful of medals, including two Purple Hearts."

Petrovitch leaned back. "Then grow a pair of *yajtza*, man."

"OK, so I screwed up taking work from Oshicora. Chain has given me one chance to put it right, and you're going to help me." Sorenson snagged his coffee and drank. Whatever he was expecting, it wasn't the scalding black slurry that sloshed around his mouth. His eyes bugged, his cheeks bulged, but he eventually swallowed. "That's . . ."

"That's what you'll be drinking at least two cups of, so get used to it." Petrovitch picked up his own mug and drank nonchalantly. "So you did a deal with Chain. You told him you'd get something on Oshicora in return for a clean getaway."

"I can take my lumps, kid. But it's not just me. It's my mother and my sister. They rely on my company for everything. If it goes under, they lose the roof over their heads."

"If the stakes were so high, why didn't you check who Oshicora was?"

"I don't know. I'm on a sales trip, visiting hospitals and pitching my implants. I get approached by that Hijo character. His employer would like to meet me, discuss a project he's working on. I say OK, because, hey, I'm on a sales trip. I'm here to drum up business."

"Don't tell me: you got so caught up in the idea of Virtual Japan that you let your guard down." The first hint of sympathy entered Petrovitch's voice. "He plucked you like a ripe apple."

"He's got his own quantum computer, damn it. I never thought for a moment." Sorenson ran his hand through his greasy hair. "That was my problem: I never thought."

"Did you not even find it slightly odd that a Japanese businessman was offering an American businessman a job?"

"I . . ."

"Do you not realise how much they hate you? All of you?"

"I, no. I guess I didn't. I didn't approve of the President's decision. I don't even vote Reconstruction." Sorenson sighed and started on his coffee in earnest, pulling a face every time.

"You should have made that clear to him. Oshicora's lumped you in with the perpetual President Mackensie and all the other Reconstructionists. As far as he's concerned, you're the public face of a policy that would have condemned him and one hundred and twenty million of his fellow citizens to a watery grave." Petrovitch looked up, and Wong was advancing on them with two plates piled high with heart-stopping amounts of fried food. "Incoming."

They sat back in their seats as Wong banged their breakfasts down. The proprietor glared at the two men, then turned his back on them.

Sorenson blinked like an owl. "What . . . is this?"

"It's better not to ask. Very little of it has ever seen the inside

of an animal, and most of the rest hasn't been grown in soil."
Petrovitch leaned over and snagged a bottle of ketchup from a
neighbouring table. "It's full of salt, fat, starch and protein, and
honestly, it's the best thing you can eat right now."

"But my heart!"

"You should worry," he said, brandishing his knife and fork.
"Sorenson, just stop your complaining and get it inside you."

The pair worked their way methodically through the bacon
shapes, sausage shapes, potato shapes, reconstituted egg, and
engineered beans. Petrovitch speared Sorenson's black pudding
after explaining precisely how it was made; the irony being it
was the only natural product on the plate.

They washed it down with more of Wong's oil-black brew.

"Ready to talk?" said Petrovitch.

"Guess so." Sorenson covered his mouth to stifle a burp.

"Right. So let's get the story so far: you're a regular straight-
up sort of guy, look after your sister and your mother, done
nothing illegal so far."

Sorenson's eyes twitched briefly. "That's right," he said.

"You wouldn't be holding out on me, would you?" Petrovitch
pushed his glasses up his nose. "Think very carefully before
answering."

"There's nothing."

"I can find out for myself." He sighed. "I could probably find
out right now if I had my rat. Forget it. Why do you think I
can do something about this?"

"I saw you with Oshicora. You've got leverage with him. You
can use that."

"I'm not crossing him. No way, never."

"You're the only one I've ever seen him with who he actually respects. He puts his guard down with you."

"Even if that was true . . ." Petrovitch chewed his lip. "No. Absolutely not. I already had one gang trying to kill me this week. Why would I want another?"

Sorenson picked his knife up and stared at the grease-stained end. "Is that your final answer?"

"Look, I already tried, OK? I talked to him. I told him that he was treating you badly."

"And what did he say?"

"That it was no more than you deserved because you're a stinking Yankee technocrat who did nothing while Japan drowned." Petrovitch glanced up at the American's flushed face and decided not to mention that Oshicora knew what it was he was hiding. "I chose not to push it. The only thing you can do is go back to work. Back to the Oshicora Tower and pray to whatever god you believe in that when you're done, you get shown some mercy."

"Chain will ruin me."

"Trust me, Oshicora will ruin you a whole lot faster. Buy yourself some time to come up with a better plan."

Sorenson leapt up and closed his hands on the tabletop, threatening to snap it in two. "I came to you for help."

"Chain told you to. He's using you as much as Oshicora is. All I am is a kid who knows a lot about maths and physics. How the *chyort* did anyone think I could help?" Petrovitch finished his coffee standing.

Sorenson kicked his own chair away in frustration.

"Hey," shouted Wong. "You stop that now."

Petrovitch bent down and picked the chair up. "He's leaving. So am I."

Wong threw Sorenson's credit chip towards them. Petrovitch snatched at it and missed. Sorenson's catch was more certain.

"Come on, before you get me barred." Petrovitch squeezed out onto the busy street, and Sorenson joined him, shivering slightly in the damp morning air. Despite the American's size, he looked small and pathetic at that moment. "Go back to your hotel. Get a shower, change your clothes. Then go to work. Go, Sorenson, just go."

A black car with darkened windows pulled up by the kerb; a door opened but no one emerged. Immediately Petrovitch was looking for a way out, but it was too late.

"Comrade Marchenkho would like a word." The man had stepped from behind him and pressed something hard into his back, pushing him towards the open door.

Sorenson looked ready for a fight. Petrovitch put a hand out and covered his fist, then gave a little sigh.

"Stop stroking your *yielda*," he told the gunman. "You're not going to use it on me. Unless you want a half-a-million-euro contract on you."

"That might be true." The object left his skin and Petrovitch saw Sorenson pale. "But your friend, on the other hand, has no such protection. Get in the car."

Petrovitch looked up at the grey sky and gave a small strangled cry.

The inside of the car smelled of stale vodka and sweat, and Petrovitch immediately thought of home. The Ukrainian gunman sat next to Sorenson, automatic jammed against his ribs.

"You know, it doesn't get much better than this," said Petrovitch.

"Shut up, Petrovitch," said Sorenson.

"Yeah, well. Hey, Yuri."

The Ukrainian leaned forward. "It's Grigori."

"To be fair, I'm not that bothered what you're called. Marchenkho's chancing his arm, and by extension, yours. Feel free to let us out any time."

"Your American friend has got the right idea; shut up."

"Why don't you bite me, *zhirniy pidaras*?"

The foot soldier stiffened, and Sorenson winced as the barrel of the gun drove deeper.

"Well, excuse my mouth." Petrovitch put his feet up against the back of the front seat. "It doesn't give me much confidence in your boss if his underlings lose it when I've called them a rude name."

"Petrovitch . . ."

He dismissed Marchenkho's whole gang with a gesture. "Yeah, I'm done talking to the monkeys. Get me the organ grinder."

The driver took them north and east, eventually crossing the Thames at Southwark. The old East End was a vast building site, with property demolished as fast as it was being erected – the curious consequence being that there was nothing finished and all that existed were streets of scaffolding and cranes.

The car pulled into one of the construction yards, busy with labourers and machines, and came to a halt outside a pile of domik containers. External steps bolted onto the outside serviced the doors cut into the steel sides. At the very top of the staircase stood a man in a heavy coat and a fur hat.

When he saw Petrovitch get out and look up, he stared for a moment before disappearing into the domik behind him.

Sorenson clambered out, and Petrovitch seized the brief opportunity: he bent forward on the pretext of helping the American, and whispered: "Say nothing."

"Noth . . . ow." Sorenson was left rubbing his shin.

The Ukrainian looked up from inside the car, no longer bothering to hide his gun – home turf for him. "What?"

"Nothing," said Petrovitch pointedly, and jerked his head in the direction of the domiks. "Up there?"

"No funny business." Grigori shepherded them to the foot of the stairs and indicated that Petrovitch should go first.

Petrovitch sarcastically mouthed "no funny business" to himself. "You've watched too many Hollywood films, *tovarisch*, unless Marchenkho's hiring straight from central casting. Let's get this over with."

He clanged his way up the steps and, despite himself, was tired and sweaty when he reached the top. He entered without knocking and found himself in a passable replica of a seventies-style Soviet apartment.

An ancient three-bar electric fire sat in the ersatz hearth, and a framed picture of the great bear, Josef Stalin, hung above the mantelpiece.

Marchenkho sat at the dark wood desk, stroking his luxurious moustache. He'd lost the hat and the coat, and revealed a commissar's uniform, an enamel red star pinned to his olive-green lapel.

"Sit," said Marchenkho.

There was one chair, and Petrovitch took it. They sat in silence as Sorenson and Grigori came in, and the door banged hollowly closed.

After an age, Marchenkho pulled a drawer open, and pulled out a bottle of vodka. He went back for three shot glasses, then unscrewed the bottle and dashed out a measure for him and his guests. Spilt spirit started to etch the varnish away and evaporate into the air.

"Nice set-up," said Petrovitch. "Not quite Oshicora's standard, but at least you've only fallen this far."

Marchenkho dipped his hand in the drawer a third time and laid a Glock on the rectangle of leather set into the desk top. He took one of the vodka glasses for himself, and pushed the other two on cushions of liquid towards Petrovitch and Sorenson.

Petrovitch passed Sorenson his, and looked Marchenkho square in the eye as they both flipped their wrists and swallowed hard. They slammed the empty glasses down on the desk within moments of each other.

"'S'OK."

Marchenkho sloshed more vodka into their glasses. "Your American friend seems less sure."

"Reconstruction has made him soft."

"We have to look elsewhere for worthy adversaries." Marchenkho ran his fingers across his moustache again. "And elsewhere for loyal partners."

"Yeah. About that." Petrovitch glanced round at Sorenson, who was still trying to brace himself to drink, the brimming glass hovering at his lips. He shook his head in disgust. "The Oshicora girl was an accident."

"A very fortunate accident for her. Less fortunate for me. And I am still very unhappy with you." Marchenkho pointedly looked at the Glock rather than Petrovitch. "You cost me, boy. Cost me dear."

"Maybe you should have had a better plan."

"You need to be careful how you speak to me."

"Bite me." Petrovitch leaned forward for his vodka, then crossed his ankles and propped his feet up on the edge of the desk. "Any plan that could be thwarted by a kid just wandering past was *govno*. If that was the height of your capabilities, you're screwed."

Marchenkho blushed red with fury and snatched his Glock off the table. He pointed it in Petrovitch's face. Sorenson took a step forward, but Grigori was already there, gun at the American's neck.

"You little . . ." said Marchenkho.

"*A huy li?*" Petrovitch slugged back the vodka and threw the glass onto the table. "You're the past. Oshicora's the future. How do I know this? Because even you won't kill me. Pull the trigger and Oshicora will destroy you," he said. "What little you have left will be taken from you."

"Why did you do it? Why? My one opportunity to beat him and you ruined it." Marchenkho was raving, spittle flying through the air from the foam at the corners of his mouth. "What's he paying you? I'll double it. I'll triple it. Just tell me why!"

"Fine." Petrovitch dragged his legs aside and slapped both his palms down on the tabletop. The vodka bottle jumped. "You want to know why I did it? Kindness. That's why I did it. Because I was being kind. Just once. Just to show the world that a complete bastard like me still has a shred of human decency left inside."

The gangster's jaw worked as if he was trying to gag down something so wholly unpalatable that it stuck in his throat.

"You don't like that, do you?" crowed Petrovitch. "You don't understand it. It doesn't compute. Maybe you'll understand this: *eede vhad e sgadie kak malinkey suka!*"

Marchenkho swept the tabletop clean with one movement. Everything crashed to the floor – desk set, photo frame, paperweight, bottle, shot glasses. The air thickened with alcohol fumes.

"I should kill you now, and to hell with the consequences."

"All half a million euros of consequences? You haven't got the *yajtza*." Petrovitch sat back and folded his arms.

Marchenkho started to smile, his moustache twitching. Eventually, he was helpless, roaring with laughter, tears streaming down his face. The gun slapped back down on the table, and Marchenkho fell wheezing and gasping into his chair.

"Are we done now?" asked Petrovitch.

Marchenkho wiped his eyes with his sleeve. "You: a few more like you and the Soviet Union would never have fallen." He looked past him to Sorenson. "Kill the American instead," he told Grigori.

A foot in Sorenson's back sent him sprawling. He made it to all fours, quickly for a big man, before he felt the gun at the back of his head. He froze, staring up at Petrovitch, who adjusted his glasses and leaned back even further.

"Yeah, you could do that. But what you should get through your radiation-addled skull is that if you hurt Sorenson in any way, he can't fit me with my new heart. I'd die, and you'd be back to worrying about those little laser dots bouncing all over your chest. What do you reckon, Yuri? Shall we see how keen you are to follow your boss's orders?"

They all waited on Marchenkho, who eventually said in a quiet voice. "Get out."

"Good call." Petrovitch reached down to help Sorenson back to his feet, then levered himself upright. "I'd like to say it was a pleasure meeting you – but I can't. I had loads of important stuff to do this morning and you've gone and ruined it all."

"Get out now."

Sorenson took hold of Petrovitch's arm and steered him irresistibly to the door. He almost wrenched the handle off in his haste to leave. When he'd finally got him outside, he turned on him.

"Say nothing, you said! You nearly got both of us killed, you lunatic."

"I nearly got you killed? I saved your life, farmboy, and don't you forget it." Petrovitch started down the staircase. "And we wouldn't have been in this position if you hadn't come banging on my door this morning."

"I could have bargained with him. We could have got Oshicora together."

"You want to work with Marchenkho? Be my guest. He ordered you dead on a whim not sixty seconds ago." He was a whole landing away. "Go on. Go back. See how long you last, you *zhopa*."

"Is it true about your heart?" called Sorenson.

"Yeah. Now, come on. I'm taking you back to Oshicora, then I'm going to wash my hands of this whole stupid *pizdets*." He waited for him to catch up, then negotiated his way around the pallets of building materials lying between him and the front gate.

Sorenson fell in beside him. "So it was just a coincidence: my business, your heart?"

"Yeah."

"Lucky. Lucky for me."

"Yeah."

"Do you really need a new heart?"

"What is this? Twenty questions?" Petrovitch scowled up at Sorenson. "Give me an ulcer as well, why don't you?"

Sorenson dug his hands in his back pockets. "I can get you a new heart."

"I don't need your help. I'm not owing you anything."

"New hearts are pricey. I can do it for cost." Petrovitch didn't respond. "Discount, then."

"I don't need your help," he repeated.

"Where are you going to get that sort of money?" Sorenson suddenly threw his head back and gave a cry of triumph. "That's why! Oshicora's daughter for a new, top-of-the-range heart. Tell you what – I'll do it for nothing. Donate the heart, pay for the surgery."

"*Perestan' bit dabayobom.*"

"I wish I knew what you were saying."

"No you don't. Really, you don't. Your ears would melt." Petrovitch stood on the kerb and tried to orientate himself. He turned north. "This way."

"I'm just saying it was smart thinking. I can trump that, though."

"You will not buy me, Sorenson, just in the same way that Oshicora won't buy me either. Now, please, just shut up and walk."

"But where are you going to find that sort of money?"

"You know, I should have let Marchenkho shoot you. It would have been quieter." Petrovitch walked away, and after a few moments of indignation, Sorenson followed.

As they walked away from the empty East End towards the heights of Stepney, the pavements slowly filled up until it was as dense with people as it was in the centre of the city. Petrovitch slipped between the bodies with practised ease, leaving Sorenson to crash into everyone and spend his entire journey apologising.

Whitechapel was the closest tube station: when Petrovitch turned around at the entrance, he found that Sorenson was still dogging his steps.

"Where are we going?" He was breathless, sore, and looked ridiculous in his shirt and shorts.

"Your hotel," said Petrovitch. "What's it called?"

"The Waldorf Hilton. You know it?"

"Yeah, I go to the tea dances every week. District Line to Temple. Go and get a ticket and meet me the other side of the screen."

Sorenson stepped closer as people streamed by, in and out of the station. They were in the lee of one of the pillars, a tiny island of stillness.

"I'm sorry," he started to say.

"Good. You should be. Thank whichever god you pray to that Marchenkho is a *skatina* who wouldn't know the truth if it gave him a *minyet*." Petrovitch sighed, and let his shoulders sag. "I didn't ask for any of this. I really did just want to help her. Do the right thing for once. And now look: I could die any moment, and it's either an assassin or my heart. I've got things to do, things that I can only do alive. The mysteries of creation don't discover themselves."

"I said I was sorry."

"And I said I won't help you. I won't help you, or Chain, or Marchenkho, or any combination of you, do anything to the Oshicoras. Got it?"

"I get it." Sorenson felt in his pocket for his credit chip. "But I don't buy your story about the Oshicora girl. Where else would someone like you get the money for an implant?"

"Yeah, well. I'm going organic." Petrovitch assumed his usual shrug.

Sorenson breathed in sharply. "How the hell . . .?"

"None of your business," said Petrovitch, and stepped out into the concourse where he let himself be swept away.

12

They were walking down the street in front of the Oshicora Tower. Sorenson had showered, changed, and set his face hard.

"I'll find some way to get me out of this."

"Whatever *pizdets* you're in is only going to get worse if you fight against Oshicora. He'll flay you alive if you cross him." Petrovitch looked up to the pinnacle of the glass dome; the park was lost behind the reflection of the sky. "If you serve loyally, he'll be more merciful than if you get antsy about it. You're nearly done, right?"

"Another day, or two. Debugging the beta version. I've never run it on a quantum platform before."

"What's it like?"

"The hardware? It's a box a yard square on each side." He looked across at Petrovitch. "That's not what you mean, is it?"

"No," said Petrovitch. They were at the start of the wide-open concourse, and he deliberately slowed down to stay in the crowd. "How does it feel?"

"Reality is imperfect compared to Virtual Japan. It flows, whatever the loading. I haven't found an upper limit to its bandwidth yet. I don't know if it even has a limit." Sorenson gazed at the tower, and was distracted for a moment. "Now, that's something I could do." He left without explanation, and Petrovitch watched him make the long walk to the revolving doors. He disappeared from view.

"Hello."

He span around. Sonja Oshicora stood in front of him, slightly away from the edge of the pavement. She was almost alone, but was protected by a loose circle of men that now surrounded him, too. The people who walked by on their way to the towers or along the side of the road moved around the circumference: inside was empty but for the two of them.

Most of the Oshicora guards were looking out, but two of them were watching Petrovitch, and they both had their hands inside their jackets. Petrovitch moved his own hands very slowly, so that they were always in view. He made certain that they went nowhere near his bag.

"Hello," he replied, uncertain of what else to say. Certainly nothing that would prolong the conversation.

She, however, had other ideas. "You do remember me, don't you?"

"I . . . I'm not likely to forget." He watched her tuck her exquisitely cut hair behind her ears and smile with impossibly white teeth.

"It's good to see you well again," she said, as if suffering multiple heart attacks was a minor inconvenience. "You are well, aren't you?"

"Yeah. Fine." He wanted to run again; away, as fast as he could.

"Good," she repeated. She talked like she was fey, otherworldly. Compared to Petrovitch, she was. "I understand my father has already thanked you for your actions."

Again, actions: fleeing through the Metrozone while Ukrainian gangsters tried to kill him. The word didn't do it justice at all.

"Everything's settled. No honour debt, no favours owing, nothing. It's all fine."

If she noticed his discomfort, she ignored it. "I wanted to thank you myself," she said. In one step, she was pressing her lips against his. Her breath was warm, tasting of spice, smelling of flowers.

In return, he was rigid with fear. What lasted only a moment seemed to go on for ever. He thought he might have another seizure there on the concourse.

She released him, and looked out from under her fringe. Her brown eyes seemed impossibly, animé large.

"Sam," she said. "I can call you Sam, can't I?"

"Yeah," he squeaked. Someone had stolen all his oxygen, and he had a good idea who the culprit was.

"Thank you, Sam." She smiled again, and that was it; his audience was over. She walked towards the Oshicora Tower, trailing her scent along with her bodyguards, leaving him pale and trembling in the humid, stinking air that blew across the city.

He stood motionless as the bubble of isolation that had surrounded him pricked. Again, he was shoulder to shoulder with the Metrozone. He wondered what Old Man Oshicora would make of it, and hoped that if he was watching, he'd make nothing of it at all.

It was a short walk to the lab. Time, finally, to do some work.

He opened the door slowly, so as not to disturb Pif. She was precisely where he'd left her, crouched over her desk, staring at sheets of minutely detailed equations. If she knew he was there, she made no sign of it.

He threw his bag on his chair, collected her empty mug and rinsed it out using bottled water and his fingers, pouring the brown-stained contents into a pot plant. Then he busied himself making coffee: spooning the granules, boiling the water, stirring and breathing the steam in.

She still hadn't moved. Even when he delivered the fresh mug to her desk, setting it down exactly on the sticky ring left by the previous brew.

"Pif? Are you catatonic again?"

One eye twitched.

She got like this sometimes, caught up in a recursive maths loop that rendered her higher functions incapable of voluntary action. Petrovitch waved his hand in front of her face; her eye twitched faster.

"Yeah, OK. A drop of the hard stuff should sort you out." He went behind her desk and opened the drawer that contained the bottle of lemon juice. He spilt some into the palm of his hand and brought it close to her nose.

She blinked, made a face, and recoiled.

"Sam," she said. "How long?"

"No idea. I just got in."

She stretched extravagantly, and Petrovitch disposed of the juice the same way he'd got rid of the coffee dregs. She gave a cry of pain.

"You OK?"

"Pins and needles. I'll be fine in a minute. Ow ow ow."

"How you don't get pressure sores is a miracle." He wiped his hand on a suitable leaf and used a wet wipe to clear the stickiness away.

"My neck hurts too."

"You're not safe to be left on your own." He pulled out two cellophane-wrapped pastries from his bag. "They're a bit squashed, but they're fresh. Ish. At least, I only just bought them."

"Give me a minute to boot up." She dug her knuckles into her left thigh and grimaced. "What's the time?"

"Half eleven." She clearly expected him to carry on. "On the Tuesday."

"Good. I thought I'd wasted a whole day." Pif tried to stand, using her desk for leverage. She wobbled like Bambi, then managed a semblance of upright. "I have good news and bad news."

Petrovitch passed her a pastry. "Good news, please. My life is so irredeemably *pizdets* that I can't cope with anything bad."

"We haven't got any competition. I may have been as subtle as a brick casing out the opposition, but we're in front."

"Stanford?"

"Out of sight." She took a few tentative steps and didn't find them too painful. "Are you sure you don't want the bad news? I mean, after yesterday, how could it get worse?"

"Well, I was woken up this morning by a desperate American trying to get me to gang up on some very serious Japanese criminals. After breakfast I got picked up by the *organitskaya* and threatened with not one, but two guns. Then I got kissed by the daughter of the Japanese crime boss right in front of all her bodyguards. To be fair, I haven't died today, but it's not even lunchtime yet."

"I can't get from the quantum to the classical," she said.

The gears in Petrovitch's mind span up to speed. "It didn't bother Maxwell."

"Maxwell was a genius standing on the shoulders of other

genii. He made *a priori* assumptions that happened to turn out to be right."

"He didn't predict wave-particle duality, or quantum effects."

"But we can't ignore them. Can we?" A note of doubt crept into Pif's voice.

"Yeah. We can. Look at the gravitomagnetic equations. They do just that. And frame dragging works."

"But . . . what about chromodynamics?"

Petrovitch reached forward and took one of the sheets of paper from her desk. "You're doing this arse-backwards. You're trying to mash the electrostrong into gravity and it just won't work. Well, it might, but remember: it's supposed to be beautiful, not ugly. This," he said, shaking the paper, "is ugly. I never liked it. It's inelegant. What you cooked up yesterday is poetry."

"If I can't prove it, it means nothing." She ripped at the pastry with her teeth, spitting out the cellophane and chewing on what was left.

"Start at the beginning. Ignore everything else. Gravity might not even be part of a theory of everything."

"It is," she said, spraying crumbs. "I feel it in my soul."

"So did Einstein and he took two decades at the end of his life to get precisely nowhere."

"You said it was poetry." Pif looked at him reproachfully.

"Arse-backwards poetry." Petrovitch stood in front of the whiteboard with his coffee.

Pif started to say something, and he held up his hand.

She waited and chewed and drank.

"Can you," he said, his voice no more than a whisper, "derive all the other forces from this equation? If we expand this to be multi-dimensional," and he swallowed, "we can find out just how many dimensions reality has."

She looked, and rubbed her eyes. "I . . . don't know. I'm too tired to think straight any more."

Petrovitch shook his head. "Look, this is your baby. And your maths is way better than mine. Go and get your head down: this will still be here when you get back."

She groaned. "I don't want to leave it. We're so close."

"It'll be fine. I don't want to come in here tomorrow and have to pry the finished proof out of your cold, dead hand. I'll try and do some of the easy stuff – if I can manage that. That still leaves the really hard sums and most of the credit for you."

"Don't break the symmetry," she warned.

"I thought I was supposed to."

"Try without."

"I'll try with, then try without. And I'm going to use some real data, whether you like it or not."

"Experimentalists. Have I told you how much I hate them?"

"Only about a thousand times." Petrovitch shrugged. "Science: it works."

Pif drank her coffee, and summoned enough strength to pick up her rucksack. "Are you sure about this?"

"Go," he said. "See you in the morning. You can go through my shabby maths while I cringe pathetically in a corner, then I can watch you reimagine the whole universe."

She slung the rucksack over her shoulder. "If you put it like that, I don't see how I can argue."

"I might even get some of my own work done. You never know."

"Boys and their toys," she said, edging towards the door. "Sam, are you . . .?"

"Go away. There won't be any sleep for a week if you crack this."

She bowed her head, her beaded hair falling forward like a curtain. "Sam?"

"What?"

"I'm glad I'm sharing a room with you. You get me."

"You mean you're as dysfunctional as I am, just in different ways? Yeah, that's about right. Now, in the name of whatever god you believe in, go."

She nodded. She was halfway out into the corridor when she stopped. "What?" she said with typical directness.

"Police," said a familiar voice.

"*Chyort voz'mi!*" He launched himself into his chair and folded his arms.

Pif put her head back around the door. "Sam? There's a policeman here."

"I know. Send him in, then go home. I'll be fine." He pushed his glasses up his face. "He's not staying for longer than he absolutely needs to. Which is about a minute, if he's lucky."

Chain wandered in, blinking. "Petrovitch."

"Detective Inspector Chain. Found my rat yet?"

"Ongoing inquiries," he said. He glanced down at Pif's desk and reached out to pick up one of her equations.

Petrovitch leapt up and slapped his hand down on top of the paper. "Touch nothing. Really."

Chain held his hands up. "It didn't look like it was going to break, but if you insist." He looked around. "I was expecting big machines that sparked and hummed."

"We keep those in the basement next to the reanimated bodies. What do you want?"

"Oh, I don't know. How about five hundred thousand euros?"

"Back of the queue, Inspector. I have to be dead before you collect."

"You think you're smart?"

"I think I now stand a better chance of staying alive than I would relying on you. And thanks ever so much for sending Sorenson around. Not only did it get us both picked up by Marchenkho, I then had to get farmboy back to Oshicora before he realised his pet coder had gone awol."

"You're welcome," said Chain. He opened a filing cabinet drawer and peered inside. "Interesting character, Sorenson. Did he give you his war hero spiel?"

"He might have mentioned something; it didn't get him very far. Why?"

"That sort of stuff goes down really well in America, gets the folks onside. He tried it on me, so I thought I'd try and find out what he actually did for Uncle Sam." He rolled the drawer shut. "It's not pleasant reading. His civilian file is pretty thick, too. Not like your records — what little there is seems to fit together very neatly."

"The truth has a habit of doing that."

"So does something manufactured. You see, I can't find any trace of a Samuil Petrovitch, aged twenty-two from St Petersburg at all. Which could mean one of two things."

Petrovitch pushed his glasses up his nose. "No, don't tell me. I like games. I'm an Armageddonist with a suitcase bomb and head full of righteous fury, biding my time for, what, six years now before I set my nuke and kill you all. Or alternatively, Russian record keeping isn't what its supposed to be. Your choice, I suppose."

"Something's not right, Petrovitch. I don't like that. It makes me nervous, and when I get nervous, I get curious. Like a dog with a bone."

"Your metaphors are all mixed, Inspector. You'd better watch out for that." Petrovitch flexed his fingers, making his thumbs crack. "If that's all, don't let the door hit your *zhopu* on the way out."

Chain harrumphed, then wandered to the door. He reamed at his eye, and coughed hard. When he'd done, he leaned on the handle and turned back to Petrovitch.

"Is she a good kisser?"

"*Ahueyet?* You've been following me!" Petrovitch stood up and went nose to nose with the detective. "No. You followed Sorenson. No, that's not all of it, either. You bugged Sorenson so you could follow him."

"Calm down, Petrovitch." Chain put his hands up between them.

"Do you know what Oshicora will do if they find a police tag on him?"

"Pretty much."

"They'll kill him." Petrovitch was breathing hard.

"Careful of your heart. But of course, you're getting a new one, so it won't matter soon." Chain stepped out of the way of the opening door. "I could deport Sorenson right now, but I'm increasingly interested in this VirtualJapan he's working on. I'd lose all that."

"And you wonder why people hate the police."

"No," said Chain, "I'm up to speed on that, too. Go carefully, Petrovitch."

13

Petrovitch only had half his mind on his tensors. The other half was gnawing furiously at an entirely different problem.

After ten minutes, he gave up, threw his pen down in disgust and dug around in his jacket pocket. Sorenson's card was white and shiny, with a little animated logo spinning around in one corner. It had the company phone number embossed across the front, along with the URL: the back was over-printed with Sorenson's name and mobile number.

He tapped the card on the desk, considered putting it back, considered throwing it in the bin, considered trying to tear at its hard plastic edges until it broke. He tossed it to one side and looked at the equation he'd started.

"*Raspizdyai kolhoznii*," he muttered. The card stared back at him.

But he couldn't concentrate.

He wrenched open a drawer and unrolled a keyboard. His screen was under a pile of books he hadn't quite got around to returning to the stacks: he dragged it out and propped it against the fading spines. Some of the pixels had failed due to the weight of paper, but he could see around them.

He tapped the rubbery keys to make sure he had a connection, then logged on to his own computer.

There was a touch-pad somewhere. He moved some monographs, and it was hiding underneath. He nudged it closer to the keyboard and got the two talking.

If he'd had his rat, the whole operation would have been simplicity itself, but he hadn't bought it to make his life easy. He'd bought it for his insurance policy, the one he'd have to cash in if his world came tumbling down around him.

He contemplated his need for his missing hardware while listening to the ringing of Sorenson's phone.

"Sorenson."

"Are you alone?"

"Who is this?"

"Shut the fuck up, Sorenson, and listen to me. Don't say my name. Are you alone?"

There was a pause. "Yes. He's just left."

"Right. There is a very good chance that you're still wearing a bug that Chain planted on you. I know you changed your clothes this morning, and I don't know if that makes a difference, but I wouldn't risk it."

The silence that followed was long enough that Petrovitch pinged Sorenson's phone to make sure it was still on.

"How do you know?"

"Because Chain's just been to see me and casually let slip that he's been listening to our conversation all morning."

"What should I do?"

"I'm not your agony aunt, Sorenson. I've done the right thing, and now I'm hanging up. Oh, and I might not care about whatever horrible things you've done in the past, but both Oshicora and Chain seem to know all about them. Goodbye."

He closed the connection and deleted the phone from his records, then cleared all the computer components away. He was reasonably confident that the phone call was untraceable and anonymous. Confident, but not certain.

He shook his head. There was nothing to worry about. Nothing at all. He picked up his pen again and adjusted his glasses, allowing his concentration to blot out all external distractions.

His pen hovered over the paper, and then started to write. Symbols and letters spilled out, each line getting progressively longer than the one before. Then, with a blink and a pair of raised eyebrows, he started whittling away at the expressions, reducing pairs of them to simpler equations or single values.

He'd almost finished, and he felt a rush of cold heat inside. Something was falling out of the mass of complex mathematics, something that he didn't recognise but which carried the elegance and beauty of true meaning.

He stared at the final line. Now that he was done, he felt growing doubt. Pif would look at it and laugh, then show him where he'd gone wrong. It wasn't that he was terrible at maths, just that he wasn't as good as she was. She only had to look at an equation to taste its use and quality.

Petrovitch started to work backwards, trying to justify each step to himself, testing each part for error, when he was interrupted by a polite knock at the door.

No one ever knocked. No one he knew was emotionally or socially equipped to knock and wait. Doors were to be shoulder-charged and burst through.

He set down his pen and cleared his throat. "Come in?"

It was Hijo who stepped in first. "Petrovitch-san? Is this a convenient time?"

Petrovitch felt the sudden drop in his blood pressure, and its equally sudden surge as his defibrillator compensated. His hands shook and he clamped them flat on his desk to stop their tell-tale movement.

"Petrovitch-san?" asked Hijo again.

"Convenient for what, precisely?"

"Mister Oshicora would like to talk to you about a matter of some delicacy."

Petrovitch had no idea what he meant. It didn't sound good but not only did he have nowhere to run to, he had no way of running. In his current state, he'd get halfway down the corridor before keeling over clutching at his chest.

"I suppose now's as good a time as any."

Hijo looked around the room, and took in the closed blinds, the pre-Armageddon paint, the unpleasantly sticky lino, the vague, haphazard attempts to humanise the workspace. He nodded and stepped back outside.

Petrovitch peeled his sweaty palms off the desk top and started to stand. Oshicora came in and closed the door. He smiled and gave his little bow.

"*Vsyo govno, krome mochee,*" said Petrovitch to himself, closing his eyes.

"Pardon, Petrovitch-san?"

"It's an old Russian saying, nothing to worry about." He decided to put a brave face on the situation. It might be his last few minutes on the planet, but he was determined to go out with his middle finger firmly extended in salute. "We're not exactly set up for visitors here, but you can have my chair."

"Your colleague, Doctor Ekanobi, is not here?"

"No. She went – I sent her – home. She was working all night and I thought it best."

"I will sit at her desk, if you have no objections." Oshicora moved the wheeled chair aside and sat on the very front of it. His attention was drawn, like Chain's before him, to the handwritten equations. He lifted the top sheet up and examined it carefully. "It seems strange, anachronistic even," he said, "that in this modern world there is still a place for pen, ink and paper."

"Computers can only do so much," said Petrovitch. "They can still only do what we tell them to do."

"So very true," mused Oshicora. He put the piece of paper down on the pile, exactly where he'd found it. "Your work progresses well?"

Petrovitch looked down at his own desk, at the lines of script that had fallen from his nib. "This isn't my work. I'm just helping out."

"You are a very talented man," said Oshicora. "Which is rare enough. You are also compassionate. The two qualities combine to make you an attractive prospect to a certain young woman of our mutual acquaintance."

It wasn't about tipping Sorenson off. It was about Sonja. Petrovitch's sense of relief was like being picked up by an ocean wave: cold, clear, irresistible. He even laughed.

"I have no feelings one way or another towards your daughter, Oshicora-san, romantic or otherwise."

"She kissed you," he said.

"She caught me off-guard. I didn't know she was going to do that until she did it."

"She is impulsive. Naïve and impulsive. I do my best to protect her without damaging her further." Oshicora looked pensive, before restoring his mask of equanimity. "May I explain?"

"Only if you don't have to kill me later. Otherwise, I'd rather not know."

"I do not wish you dead, Petrovitch-san. Many years ago, I met an English teacher in Tokyo. English, in both senses: she was English, back when there was an England to come from, and she taught English. She was charming, exotic, very different to the Japanese girls I knew. We became close. We married. We did all the things that married people do."

"I get the picture," said Petrovitch, looking away embarrassed.

"Quite. We had children, and it suddenly became difficult for us. I was Japanese, my wife was incurably English, but our children were neither. We loved them, but . . ." Oshicora's fingers curled into a fist. He forced them to relax. "It is difficult to say these things without sounding like a racialist. While Japan stood, these things did not matter. Our culture, our language, our existence was secure. With it gone, everything is in doubt. It would be very easy for us to lose our identity within a few generations."

Here was this man, this pitiless crime lord well on his way to owning half of the Metrozone by racketeering, theft and murder, talking honestly and openly about his family. From the joy of not being shot like the traitorous dog he was, Petrovitch was now grimacing as his gut contracted into a small, shrivelled knot.

"I said children," sighed Oshicora. "Sonja was all I had left after Japan fell. My wife, my two boys were lost. They disappeared, and although I have scoured the face of the planet for them, I cannot find them. All my hopes and dreams now rest in my daughter. For these reasons, she will marry a Japanese man of pure blood. And not, I regret to say, a radiation-damaged Slav."

equationsoflife

Petrovitch swallowed hard against his dry throat. "I don't want to marry your daughter, Oshicora-san."

"I am afraid our problem runs deeper than that. The attraction between me and my wife was partly because of our differences. It seems to be a case of like father, like daughter." He raised his eyebrows.

"*Chyort!*"

"Her infatuation will be short-lived, but I would appreciate your co-operation in not prolonging it. Do we have an understanding, Petrovitch-san?"

"Yeah. Absolutely. I'd cut off my little finger if I thought it would make you believe me more." The thought terrified him, but he'd do it.

Oshicora shook his head slightly. "That will not be necessary. Thank you for your discretion in this, and earlier matters. I have a policy of only employing *nikkeijin* within my organisation. Sorenson was an exception, and I had other reasons for that which you know about. You, Petrovitch-san, would have proved very useful, above your already great service to me. Sadly, it is not to be. Still, come the revolution, you will be spared."

Petrovitch blinked slowly, then caught the slight upturn on Oshicora's mouth. "Very funny. In Russia, the revolution has you."

"Have we concluded our talk, Petrovitch-san? Are we parting on good terms?"

"I believe so."

Oshicora stood up and bowed. "Again, I am in your debt."

"No, no you're not." Petrovitch got to his feet, and realised just how weak he was; physically and emotionally drained.

"You would have made a good son-in-law, I think."

"And a lousy husband."

On his way to the door, Oshicora said off-handedly: "I would have offered you money to stay away from my daughter. A great deal of money."

"And I would have turned it down," said Petrovitch. "It's more honourable this way."

"A good word for a virtue that is in short supply. *Sayonara*, Petrovitch-san."

When he'd gone, when Petrovitch had waited for five minutes and Hijo hadn't leapt into the room to behead him with a *katana*, he fell across his desk, limp and useless.

He'd got away with it. Again. He'd ridden his luck so hard, so far, that surely it had to be spent by now.

Coffee. He boiled up some more water, and shovelled granules into the dregs of the previous brew. Then he sat back down and couldn't quite believe he was still alive.

There was work to do, though: he had to have something to show Pif when she came back in, even though he knew from experience that when she chose to sleep, she could be out for the best part of a day. In the current circumstances, with everything that was at stake, he guessed she'd cat-nap. A couple of hours and she'd return, running on adrenaline, caffeine and sugar. Much like himself.

He looked at what he'd done that morning, and wondered if he'd made a mistake copying out the original equations of state. Pif would beat him with the stupid stick if he had, so he wheeled himself around to her desk, nudging the other chair aside.

He checked every symbol with exaggerated care, finally coming to the conclusion that his errors were entirely of his own devising.

Then he spotted it, stuck to the desktop under Pif's papers, in plain sight to anyone who looked. A bug, the same size and shape as the one he'd found in his shoe. Just like the one Marchenkho's hired killers had used to find him.

"*Sooksin,*" he breathed.

It wasn't Marchenkho. The one Sorenson had picked up had been Chain's. And this one, slipped under Pif's working-out when he'd fiddled with it, was Chain's. Which probably meant that the first one had been his, too. He'd been tricked.

Then the awful realisation struck him. Not that Harry Chain had let him believe that Marchenkho had bugged him, but that he was still bugged.

No, not that either. Why would Chain make an attempt to plant another device on Pif's desk? Because the first one had gone wrong. He took off his jacket and pulled it inside out, searching every seam, folding back the collar, examining every pocket. Then his T-shirt.

Then his trousers, again turned street-side in, and his socks, damn it. Even the waistband of his pants, though he was sure he'd have noticed Chain rummaging around in there while he was still wearing them.

His boots. He took each one off and felt around inside them, then by chance and out of desperation, turned them over. It was there, on the right boot, tucked in the angle between heel and arch. The glue hadn't adhered properly to the dirty underside, and half the tab was flapping around, folded back on itself. The plastic cover had worn through, and some of the circuitry had been severed.

Where had he gone? Walked the short distance up past the palace to Green Park. Straight from Chain's office to Oshicora's. It had to have malfunctioned before then, otherwise he'd have been overheard organising a half-million-euro counter-hit with Oshicora. That Chain had missed that was down to pure, unadulterated luck.

Petrovitch was at the end of the line. It was time to get off and change trains, right now.

14

On Monday morning, everything had been fine. By Tuesday lunchtime, he was teetering on the brink of disaster, and might even be over the edge of the abyss.

The thought he struggled with was that he'd walked right into Oshicora's private park and met with the man himself without getting the once-over for weapons or wires. Or maybe he had, and the security was so discreet that he hadn't noticed. Perhaps the inside of each and every lift was a screen.

Sorenson hadn't been pushed against a wall and shot – not yet. It was a good but confusing omen, adding another element of doubt to a critical choice: whether to ditch his current identity and sleeve up with a new one. He'd done it once before, to get out of St Petersburg in one piece. He'd prepared for this moment for years. He always told himself that he'd do it if it looked like someone was close to discovering who he really was. It should have been as automatic as a reflex.

Petrovitch was twelve months away from becoming

Dr Petrovitch. Petrovitch had just written down a way to combine two fundamental forces of nature. Petrovitch was about to get a free ride to glory on the coat-tails of a future Nobel Prize winner. None of that would matter one iota if Petrovitch got locked up for twenty years.

The drumming of his fingers on the desk were the only outward sign that he was in an agony of indecision. He'd always assumed that it'd be his past catching up with him. Instead, he'd collided catastrophically with the future. Every time he returned to the question whether any of this was worth imprisonment or worse, he looked down at his morning's calculations.

There was no point in prevaricating. He knew if he stayed, Chain would get him, and if not Chain, Oshicora, and if not Oshicora, someone else. It was time to say goodbye to Samuil Petrovitch.

He grabbed his bag and headed for the door. Then he reversed himself and grabbed the piece of paper from his desk. He dropped it on Pif's, and scrawled a big question mark at the bottom of the page. She'd know what he meant, even if she never saw him again.

Now he was ready.

He took the wheezing lift down to the ground floor and out onto Exhibition Road, from where he took the travelator to the Underground. He wouldn't normally go by tube at this time of day; if it was crowded in the early morning, by lunchtime it was unspeakable.

Since this was going to be one of the last times he'd have to endure it, he suffered the crush gladly. Where next? Somewhere cold, somewhere clean – Canada, Scandinavia, New Zealand's southern island.

If he'd had his rat, he'd be booking plane tickets under a different name, storing data before wiping it clean away, using the unparalleled power of his machine to hack the Metrozone Authority's database and activate a sleeper personality he'd stored on there years ago.

If he'd had his rat, he could have done it now, all in the space of a single journey to the airport: Petrovitch would vanish, and another man would arrive luggageless at the airport to fly away to a new life. Even his failing heart could be spirited away. He didn't need a Metrozone hospital for that. Any big city would do.

If, if, if.

It was why he'd bought the rat, to cover this very event. But he didn't have it any more. Plan B, then.

He'd have to disappear the old-fashioned way, and that gave him time to make one last appearance as Petrovitch.

He eventually emerged from the tube, breathless and bruised, at Edgware Road: not the Bell Street exit, because it was cordoned off and sealed, but the Harrow Road one, south of the Marylebone Road.

St Joseph's was opposite, the bullet-scarred doors open. He sat on the steps and waited. As he listened to the service going on inside, he could hear, over the growl of the traffic, distant but distinct pops of gunfire from Paradise. The natives were restless. A black speck against the grey sky, a police drone flew in lazy circles high above the towers, and it was likely that it was the flier that the militia were aiming for.

He watched their target practice until his name was shouted out behind him.

"What are you doing here?"

He looked over his shoulder. Father John was shaking the hand of an elderly parishioner; when he released his grip, the hand went on shaking. Parkinson's, vCJD, something like that.

"I'm saying sorry, Father." Petrovitch stood up and dusted his backside down.

"And what are you sorry for?" Half a dozen people, all of them bowed and grey-haired, trooped by, walked slowly down the steps and vanished into the crowd that streamed past.

"You mean, apart from your church getting shot up? I've met the bosses of both sides: neither of them seemed too bothered about carrying on a gun-battle on holy ground. I guess you could call them yourself if you want, see if you have any luck in screwing them for some compensation."

"Blood money, Petrovitch." Father John wiped one sweaty palm across the other. "You do understand the concept, don't you?"

"Yeah," said Petrovitch with a snort. "Yeah, I do."

"You said, apart from." A shadow fell across the priest from behind Petrovitch. "Why are you really here?"

He looked up at Sister Madeleine, and his heart did that thing that might have been a software glitch. "I lied to you," said Petrovitch. "Or rather, I didn't tell you the truth."

The sister frowned down at him, trying to remember. "Which bit?"

"All of it. But that's not important right now. Ask me again. Ask me again why I did what I did, and I'll tell you."

She glanced over at Father John, covered in confusion. "He's the priest. If you want to confess . . ."

"No," said Petrovitch. "I'm not confessing. I'm not ashamed of what I've done."

"Then what the hell are you talking about?"

Her choice of language startled him, he who used the most

obscene insults imaginable. He pushed his glasses back up his nose to buy him some time. "I just wanted you to know that sometimes the people you hate most can change for the better."

"I don't hate you," she said, equally startled. "Why would I hate you? I . . ."

"You will do. Go on: ask me," he dared her.

"Excuse me," said the father, but Petrovitch and Madeleine were staring so intensely at each other that his presence was forgotten.

"Why did you help her?"

"Because I used to be part of a gang that kidnapped people for ransom, and I didn't want to see it happen ever again."

Sister Madeleine's eyes were wide open. "You?"

"Thanks. I was hoping that it wouldn't be too hard to believe." He adjusted his bag. "Forget about me. You won't see me again."

He started off down the steps, quicker than he ought. She called after him.

"Petrovitch, where are you going?"

He almost stopped. His feet dragged on the pavement. Then he picked up speed again and vanished into the crowd.

Vast, anonymous and brooding, the Regent's Park domiks grew closer as he walked down the Marylebone Road. Petrovitch put a determined smile on his face. Even without the rat, the plan he had was pretty damn good.

Before he could put it into operation, though, he had to make sure he was free of any other little surprises that Harry Chain might have adhered to him. He needed a back-street electronics chop-shop that would take his money without asking questions. Fortunately, in the shadow of the huge domik pile, such establishments were two a cent.

He negotiated the purchase of a sweeper, and got the shopkeeper to throw in a battery and a demonstration of how the lipstick-sized device worked. He paid for it with the last of the money on his card, unwrapped the tiny black wand there and then, and swept himself in front of the counter.

He was clean, from the white-blond hairs on his head to the worn soles of his feet.

The sweeper went on a lanyard around his neck and under his shirt. He shouldered his bag, and crossed the road. There were cameras at the junction, looking down at the crowds that swarmed back and forth. He looked up and fixed one with a knowing stare. The next time he passed that way, the computers that could isolate and recognise a face would put a different name to his.

He kept on walking until the pyramid of domiks showed its entrance, shaped like an ancient megalith: a tunnel constructed of upright containers with others braced on top to create a space that was as high as a cathedral, the main street that pierced the core of Regent's Park. Sodium lights hung from above and burnt orange, illuminating the hawkers, the whores and the hustlers who bought and sold everything and anything.

It was like the Nevskiy Prospekt during the darkest days of Armageddon. Winter, freezing Arctic winds howling down from Siberia, the bass rumble of generators and babble of voices, flashes of light and colour, the whisper of rumours – they have bread, that stall sells poisoned vodka, those fish are radioactive – the stench of struggle. The good old days when he ran wild through the unlit streets, stealing books and candles.

He kept on through the market bustle until he got to the Inner Circle, a distribution road in the very heart of the pile. Some people, driven by madness or guilt, would walk the Circle until they dropped. There were others who would wait for them and then strip the corpses, and others still wouldn't wait even that long.

Regent's Park was like that.

Petrovitch found Staircase Eight and started climbing. He kept climbing until the stair-dwellers dwindled to nothing and the corridors were empty. There was one last bulkhead light, then nothing but blackness. He reached into his bag for a tiny key-ring torch.

The blue light was no more than a bubble, but it was enough to see by. He walked on until he was blocked by a door equipped with a mechanical combination lock. He held the torch in his teeth and slid the lock cover aside.

The keypad was numbered zero to nine in a circle, and the code was entirely crackable by someone who knew what they were doing. What else could hide Petrovitch's treasure but the Golden Ratio?

He pressed each button in turn, listening for the click of the mechanism: one six one eight zero three three nine eight eight seven four. There was the most subtle of noises, almost a sigh, and he leaned heavily on the handle beneath the lock. The bolts behind the door lifted clear of the frame and he swung inwards.

The air was warm and stale, but dry; a pharaoh's tomb.

Inside, he leaned on the door and felt it grate shut. The bolts dropped back into place with an echoing bang. Petrovitch held up his single spark of light: the container was empty, save for a trunk in the far corner. Everything was just as he'd left it.

He stepped up on the trunk's lid, and felt above him. High up, on the wall, was a bolt. He pulled at it, working it from side to side until it slid across. There was another one, stiffer, but eventually it gave up and moved.

He hit between them with the flat of his hand, and forgot

to turn his head or close his eyes. Light burst in, blinding him, flooding the domik, chasing out every shadow.

Petrovitch sat down on the trunk, took off his glasses and dabbed at his streaming face with his sleeves. He turned the torch off, then climbed back up to stand on tiptoe and look out.

He was in the highest level of containers, right at the very top, and he could see a swathe of the Metrozone, from south-west to north-west, hazy and indistinct at the ground, but the towers were clear and confusingly seemed closer. Oshicora's Tower was out of sight, to the south, but if he screwed his eyes up tight and wished, he could just about make out the subtle slope of the land that lay crushed beneath the weight of buildings; the Thames valley that stretched out beyond the M25 cordon, into the uninhabited wilds of the Outzone.

He realised that it wouldn't stay that way for ever. The centre could not hold.

Dreaming wouldn't solve any of his current problems. He turned his back on the view, and climbed down to the metal floor of the domik. He wondered if there was anyone beneath him, suddenly aware of new light footsteps over their heads. Maybe.

He opened the trunk. It wasn't locked, had no need to be locked, and the catches sprang aside easily. Inside were things of use, like a couple of blankets and bubble-wrapped electronics, and things of no use at all, just pieces of heavy paper bearing pictures of people who he'd never see again and thought him dead.

It was to those he went first, though. A pair of children playing in the low, red light of the midday sun, a girl called Irena and a boy called Alexander. A woman, the children's mother, face lined by hard work and exhaustion. A man, lying in a hospital bed, bald, emaciated, drips in his arms and tubes up his nose, grinning and waving to the camera.

Fifteen years of life that amounted to a thin stack of photographs, and they weren't even his own memories any more. They belonged to someone else, even if he could remember them in ice-sharp clarity.

He shook himself free of the reverie. He gathered up the items in bubble-wrap and laid them out on the floor: a laptop computer whose case was pre-Armageddon and components most definitely not; a solar panel, rolled up; a silvered umbrella, folded; a fat cube of nanotube battery; a bundle of wires to connect them all together. This whole collection of electronics was dusty, unused, untested. Ripe for replacement, in fact. He'd been thwarted in that: now all he could do was hope that everything would work as promised.

He took a methodical approach, getting power from the panel to the battery first, plugging in the computer, extending the antenna and aiming it through the window at one of the relay stations visible on a rooftop down below.

There was a signal. He could get online. He realised that he'd been holding his breath, and he let it all out with a moan.

He typed furiously, scripting and executing programme after programme. One to hide his access point, one to lock down his Clapham hab, one to copy and encrypt the contents of his hard drive, and another to send it in little packages to a hundred dormant mailboxes. One more to erase itself and then fall into dormancy.

He continued with his housekeeping, ripping up history. It took a little while. Some of the computers he was targeting were well defended.

He'd dealt with the past. Now for the future. He timed his death for just after midday tomorrow. He'd kill himself, swiftly, painlessly, and arrive dead at a hospital in Greenwich: cause of death, heart failure. The body would be shipped to the crematorium, his ashes claimed, and his sad demise would be registered with the Metrozone Authority.

He bought airline tickets to Wellington under another identity. In the morning, he'd tuck the little bundle of photographs in his bag, and Samuil Petrovitch would die. No one would mourn his passing.

15

It was still night when he woke up, but it could never be called dark. Swaddled in blankets, he climbed up onto the trunk to look out of the window, to see the brilliant lights of the city: from the fiery orange of sodium glare that burned at street level to the three-coloured laser banks that scrawled logos and messages on the underside of the clouds. In between was the white glow and moving pictures of the towers, pointing the way to salvation. Points of light slid across the umber sky and along the roads, red above and red below.

It was bright to the edge of pain, sharp enough to cast his shadow on the blank wall behind him.

His computer was blinking at him. Even with a new name, he was still an infovore. He had time to look at the news before he started for the airport. He climbed down from his perch and sat cross-legged in front of the keyboard. He flexed his fingers, cracking each joint in turn, and went to see what today had brought.

It had brought chaos. His Tuvalu-based server had been hit by a massive surge in traffic: an old-school Denial of Service attack so huge that he couldn't get through to change the settings, reset it, or even put it to sleep. He pulled the plug on his connection and worried at his thumb.

He used a commercially available proxy, hiding his identity in amongst a mass of other anonymous browsers, and sniffed around his old local Clapham node. It was down, swamped by a tsunami of data.

He tried to connect with the university as a guest user: the host was unreachable. Several online forums he used to frequent had been rendered unreadable. Yet for the rest of the globe, it was business as usual.

Everywhere that he might have been found had been ruthlessly trashed: no finesse or subtlety, just terabytes of information thrown at any open port to clog them up completely. He was being targeted, quite deliberately.

He leaned back and wondered who might do such a thing.

Oshicora might, but it didn't seem his style. Marchenkho definitely, but he doubted that the man could use a computer, let alone co-ordinate something so complicated.

Sorenson: he had no cause to get at Petrovitch, no matter how bat-shit crazy he might be under his veneer of good-ol'-boy charm. And Chain was more careful, more likely to get others to do his work for him. But this was a blocking move, not an attempt to gain intelligence. Whoever it was was trying to prevent him from communicating, from seeing electronically.

So it came down to what they were trying to hide. Even though he would be dead soon, he needed to know. If it was a feint to flush him into the real world . . .

He knew the number for his hardwired phone extension in

the lab. He bought a virtual phone online and called it. It rang for several minutes, but he knew to wait. Eventually Pif answered.

"What? Sorry. Didn't hear it, then couldn't find it." There were sounds of paper sliding to the floor, and muffled cursing. "Who is this?"

"It's Sam."

"You have to come in. Now."

"Is anything wrong? You're OK?" Petrovitch felt his pulse quicken.

"I'm OK. This note you left me . . ."

"Believe it or not, there's something more important than that. Don't go outside. In fact, call security and have them post a couple of guards at each end of the corridor. Tell them they need guns."

"What have you done?"

"Pif: Tuesday was even worse than Monday. I have ruined my life so completely, so thoroughly, I can't come back in. Ever. This is goodbye. But I had to warn you."

There was almost silence: nothing but the crackles on the line and the sound of her breathing. "Sam, what about the science?"

"Sam will be dead shortly. Before he goes, he wants to say it was brilliant working with you and that he'll miss you very much."

"I can't see any errors in your equation."

"His equation. Petrovitch's equation. And unless he's invented a time machine, he won't be coming back."

There was more silence.

"Tell me," he said, "I haven't invented a time machine."

"Not invented, as such. More described how it might be done. It's the difference between Einstein and the Manhattan Project." She even giggled.

"Pif, I can't wait forty years. And this isn't even why I phoned. Someone is trying to blindside me, presumably before coming after me with a *pushka*. Promise you'll stay safe."

She gave in. The whole tone of her voice changed. "Why, Sam? Why are they doing this to you?"

"Because I'm a bad man. You don't need to know any more than that. There is one last thing you can do for me, though. Is the university network up or down? It's isolated itself from the shit-storm that's being kicked up my side of the node."

"Up, last time I looked."

"If I give you my password, can you copy some files to my supervisor?"

"You know I'm not supposed to do that, right?"

"Yeah. Pif: I'm going to be technically dead in a few hours. Violating my terms and conditions of usage isn't going to bother me."

"Hang on." She dropped the phone to the desk and opened several drawers, trying to find her handheld computer. Petrovitch heard it chime as it was turned on, then the phone was scraped up again. "OK."

"Log on screen?"

"I'm there."

"s-a-m-u-i-l-dot-p-e-t-r-o-v-i-c-h."

"Done."

"d-four-d-five-c-four-d-x-c-four."

"I'm in."

"See the folder called Simulations? Click that and tell me what you see."

"You've got mail, by the way," said Pif. "Two thousand eight hundred and ninety-seven messages. Since when were you so popular?"

"I've been mail-bombed. Everywhere. I don't know who's doing it."

"I'll take a look."

"Don't open the reader! Everything will be loaded with viruses, worms, the works."

"I opened the reader, Sam."

"Close it! Close it!"

"It's all marked up as spam, except the first two. Know anyone called Sonja? She sent you a couple of seriously fat files."

Petrovitch's fists were white with frustration. "*Yobany stos,* Pif! Close the reader down."

"I've opened the first file. Video. She's quite pretty, isn't she?"

He screeched in frustration, imagining the havoc being unleashed on his precious work. "Close. It. Down."

"You'll want to listen to this," said Pif, and held the earpiece close to the loudspeaker on her computer.

"I don't want to listen to anything. I want you to stop it." It was too late. Pif couldn't hear him any more. What he got instead was:

". . . don't know what to do, I don't know where to go, I don't know anyone who can help me. Except you. You have to save me, Sam, because there's no one else."

In the quiet that followed, there was nothing but static on the line.

"Pif?"

"Sam?"

"Play it again."

"I thought you said . . ."

"Just play it. And get the phone in position before you do."

A series of clunks, followed by a click. A prelude to: "I hope this is you, Sam. I really hope it's you. They've killed my father.

equationsoflife

They dragged him away and they shot him. I heard it even though I wasn't supposed to. I don't know what to do, I don't know where to go, I don't know anyone who can help me. Except you. You have to save me, Sam, because there's no one else."

"*Sic sukam sim.* Pif, is this for real?"

"I can check the header for the xref and routing, but she looks scared, Sam. Who is she?"

He peeled his glasses off his face and rubbed his hand across his forehead. He was thirsty, hungry, and getting a headache. "Remember that *yakuza* kid I mentioned? That's her."

"Why does she think you can help her?"

"Because, by night, I dress up in skin-tight spandex and fight crime as the Slavic Avenger." Petrovitch squeezed his temples between thumb and forefinger. "It's because she's desperate."

"Do you want me to play the second message?"

"Only if it says something like 'Oops, my mistake, everything's fine and my very-much-alive father's not coming to kill you.'" He stopped abruptly, almost choking on his words. "*Raspizdyai!* How stupid can I get? Play the other one. Do it, Pif. Play it."

He could hear a rhythmic, hollow banging. He knew what that was: someone trying to beat down a door. Over the top of the cacophony was "Get me out of here, I'm begging you, get me out" followed by a series of gunshots and a shriek that was so loud it made the phone howl with feedback.

"And that's it," said Pif. "Someone pulls her to the ground, out of camera, and the last thing you see is a guy with a gun, pointing it straight at the screen."

Petrovitch wriggled his finger in his ear. "Can you do something for me? Save those two files onto a card and put it somewhere safe. Wipe the rest of the incoming mail. Then sit tight."

"Is it going to be OK?"

"No. No, it's not. But what that means is anyone's guess. I'll call you."

He hung up, then dialled the Oshicora Tower.

"*Moshi moshi*," said the operator.

"Good morning," said Petrovitch, "my name's Samuil Petrovitch; you might remember me from such incidents as 'hunted like a dog through the streets' and 'kissed by the boss's daughter'. I'd very much like to speak to Oshicora-san — he assured me that he'd take my call if I had an emergency, and if this isn't one, I don't know what is."

He could feel the fear like a cold wind. It was true. His heart gave a little trip, and he shuddered.

"I am afraid," said the female voice, "Mister Oshicora is unavailable at the moment."

"I am afraid," countered Petrovitch, "that you're lying through your teeth. Find me someone in authority. Now, please, or I'll cut the connection."

Seamlessly, another voice spoke up. They were listening already. They were waiting for him.

"*Moshi moshi*, Petrovitch-san."

"Hijo-san? Is that you?" Petrovitch put his finger over the cancel key. Press it too early and he wouldn't learn what he needed. Too late and they might work out where he was.

"*Hai*, Petrovitch-san. What service can I do for you?"

"You can tell me if you've murdered Oshicora, shot your way into Sonja's room, and crudely attempted to keep me off the net, and like that was ever going to work. A simple yes or no will do."

Hijo laughed. It started as a chuckle and ended in a full-throated roar.

Petrovitch's finger rested lightly on the keyboard. "Listen to me," he said, "I've had enough. I've had enough of all this nonsense, of the whole shot-at, stabbed, bugged, threatened, hacked business. I don't particularly care what you do in your *peesku*-shaped tower. It doesn't bother me which psychopath is in control of whose private army. I'm not even — though it shames me to say so — going to lose much sleep over what happens to Sonja Oshicora. I've already decided to disappear: I won't trouble you again. You need to call off your cyber attacks, though. You're actually hurting people who aren't me."

"*Sumimasen*, Petrovitch-san," said Hijo. "You are a loose thread. We have to be tidy."

Petrovitch put his glasses back on his face and pushed them up with an extended finger. "Yeah. I'm offering you an honourable draw; you do your thing, I'll do mine. No tidying required."

"I must speak plainly," said Hijo. "It has been decided you must die. It is regretful, but necessary."

The injustice of it flushed his cheeks and filled his belly with fire. He was full to the brim with fury. Something snapped inside, and he suddenly found himself saying: "I am the one who decides when I'm going to die, you little shit. You want this done the hard way? Fine. I will take you down. I will cause you so much grief and pain that you'll wish you'd never been born. And you can tell Sonja this: I'm coming. One way or another, I'll save her. Have you got that?"

Hijo started to laugh again. "You? You?" He couldn't manage anything else, he'd become so incapable of speech.

"I'm glad you find it funny," said Petrovitch. "*Zhopu porvu margala vikoliu.*" He stabbed down with his finger. Hijo had gone from the inside of the domik. But not from inside his head.

He dialled again.

"Chain," said Chain.

"It's Petrovitch. I've something to show you. Meet me outside the south entrance to Regent's Park in half an hour."

"Very nice to hear from you again, Petrovitch. As much as I like you, I can't drop everything just because you call."

"It's about the Oshicoras."

"Half an hour, you say?"

"Yeah. Thought that might get your interest. I'm not walking, so bring your car. And body armour and a *kalash*. Better still, bring two sets. We're going to need them."

"We? What is this, Petrovitch? You planning on starting a war?"

"For a *dubiina*, you catch on quick. Be on time."

16

An old, stooped woman, head wrapped in a blanket, knocked on the side of Chain's car. Chain raised his eyebrows and waved her away. Her tapping became more insistent.

"It's me, you blind old *kozel*. Open up." Petrovitch moved the blanket aside far enough to reveal his ice-blue eyes.

Chain sighed and sprung the locks. Petrovitch heaved the car door open and slipped inside, bundling the blanket into the back seat. He pulled the door shut again, and looked around.

"Guns?"

"I have one. I'm the police, remember: we don't go handing out weapons to members of the public."

"Funny how they seem to get hold of them anyway." He reached behind him and pulled out a pistol from his waistband. It was tiny; Petrovitch could conceal it in the palm of his hand.

"I'm disappointed," said Chain. He turned the engine over and waited for it to catch.

"Yeah. My *yelda*'s much bigger." He made the gun disappear again. "How about the armour?"

"That I can let you have. You will have to sign for it, though, and according to the form, account for any damage it might suffer while in your care." Chain cocked an ear at the rattle coming from under the bonnet, then decided it was no worse than usual. He pulled out into the traffic without warning.

When the sound of horns had died down, Petrovitch put his feet up on the dash and leaned back against the headrest. "Nice car."

"You'd better not be wasting my time. I will charge you if you are."

"Yeah. Course you will. Don't worry, it'll be worth it."

"So: are you going to tell me where we're going, or should I just drive around for a while?"

"My lab. You know the way." Petrovitch took his glasses off and held them up to the early morning light. They weren't quite as filthy as Chain's car. "While we're on that subject: if you ever, ever try and plant one of your stupid little bugs on me again, I'll cut you like I'm butchering a *svinya* and turn your guts into sausage. You got that?"

Chain tutted. "Wrong side of the bed, was it?"

"Any bed would have been nice. The only reason I'm talking to you is because I can use you. The moment that becomes unnecessary is the moment I dump you like *govno*."

"Your turn of phrase is as poetic as ever." The car jerked to a halt. The lights strung across the road were green, but they were going nowhere. "What the hell is the matter with the traffic now?"

Chain reached forward and fetched his satnav a couple of hefty blows with his hand. The screen flickered but refused to indicate an alternative route.

"You could always put on your blue light," said Petrovitch.

"Ha. Ha. It's been like this since midnight. Random, local gridlock, coming and going. Disappearing in one area only to appear in another."

Petrovitch scratched his ear. "Has it got worse in the last thirty minutes or so?"

Chain looked across at his passenger. "Why would it?"

"Possibly because there's a massive bot-net trying to take down the Oshicora servers. If that was the case, there'd be a lot of extra load flowing around the Metrozone. It might interfere with the traffic management. Just saying." Petrovitch stared studiously out of the window.

Chain shook his head. "Are you going to tell me what all this is about?"

"No. You'll have to see it for yourself."

"Maybe you should've let me see it before you started screwing about." The lights cycled to red without them moving. "Can this get any worse?"

The first raindrop left a dusty circle on the windscreen. It was there long enough to ball and run down the glass to the bottom before the clouds opened and rain drummed against the roof.

"Clearly it can," said Petrovitch. The car in front edged forward half a length, and Chain claimed the space as his own.

The rain continued to blatter down, hard enough to make it seem like there was boiling water rising from the ground. The pedestrians either took shelter where they could, or hunched their shoulders and accepted the indignity.

Chain put his wipers on, smearing the grit and grease in two arcs. "I can remember when rain – any rain – meant danger. Everyone would listen to the weather forecasts and sirens would sound in the streets."

"Yeah, pretty much the same," said Petrovitch. "Except we didn't have satellites or sirens. We just got wet and took iodine pills when we could."

"This isn't meant to be a game of 'my life was worse than yours', you know. And your country never got bombed."

"All we had to put up with was your fall-out; nuclear and economic. You had food relief; we didn't. You had rebuilding projects; we didn't. You had someone to blame; trivial, really, but we didn't. Everyone looked after poor Europe, and we were left swinging in the wind."

"Surprising," said Chain, gazing out at the traffic lights as they went from amber to green, "how much damage a handful of madmen can do. Why aren't we going anywhere?"

"You want to get out and walk? Or do you want to shut up?"

Chain sighed and scrubbed at his cheeks with his hands. They sat in silence, watching the rain fall.

"You heard from Sorenson?" asked Chain.

"Not since I warned him he might have carried your bug into the heart of Oshicora's operations."

Chain pulled a face. "Did I tell you about his father?"

"What about his father?"

"His old man was political – Reconstruction to the core – assassinated six, seven years ago. Case is still open. All the fingers pointed at Junior, but no one could pin it on him. Apparently, sniping's not his style. Explosives are, though." Chain leaned forward and set the wipers to double-time. Despite the deluge, people were getting out of their cars and walking towards the front of the queue. "What? What are they doing?"

Petrovitch reached behind him for his blanket. "There's only one way to find out." He pulled the material over his head again and opened the car door. The rain poured in, and within seconds he was soaked.

Chain turned up his collar and joined him – making sure to lock the car behind him. The crowd was uncharacteristically quiet; hushed enough to hear the soft roar of the rain, the scrape of boots on tarmac.

As they walked forward through the stalled lines of vehicles, they could see a line forming across the junction, deepening as more people joined it. Chain used his badge and his elbows to work his way to the front, and Petrovitch tucked in behind.

When they got there, they found the cross-wise street devoid of traffic: on the other side of the junction was a similar mass of onlookers. The lights were red in every direction.

"That's not right," said Chain.

Petrovitch tapped him on the shoulder and pointed. "Neither is that."

A solid phalanx of cars was crawling down Gloucester Place in the direction of the river. Every lane was taken up, four abreast, rolling slowly in a perfect line. Chain was about to step out and demand an explanation when Petrovitch touched his shoulder again.

"Don't."

There were people in the cars. From the frantic banging on the inside of the windows and the rattle of door handles, they didn't seem too pleased to be there. Some of the drivers were screaming into their phones, and some of them were just screaming. They pulled at their steering wheels, dragged at the handbrakes, all to no avail.

They drove inexorably on.

The front of the procession drew level with them. Chain tried the door from the outside. It was locked, but neither could the wild-haired woman inside get it open.

"What are you doing?" he yelled at her.

"Help me," she mouthed.

"Chain?"

"Not now, Petrovitch." He pulled his gun and reversed it in his hand.

"This is important! All these cars, all of them: they're new."

"What?" Chain kept pace with the car and readied himself. He shooed the woman away from the passenger door and imitated what he was going to do.

"They're all this year's or last year's models; top of the range."

"You're not making any sense." The rain had penetrated everywhere; everything was wet, clinging, dripping.

"They're all automatic. They drive themselves, Chain."

Chain brought the butt of his gun down against the window. It bounced off with the same force, and he let out a strangled cry of pain.

"That'll be toughened glass, then," said Petrovitch. "Let's try this instead."

He stepped around the front of the car and took his bug-detecting wand from around his neck. He ran it up one side of the bonnet, then the other. At the top, on the driver's side, he got a signal.

He reached into his waistband and dragged out his snub-nosed little pistol. He pointed it down at the metalwork and pumped the trigger, once, twice, three times. Three sharp whipcracks; three holes.

The car stalled. The doors unlocked with a clunk. On hearing the sound, the driver threw herself at the passenger door, and Chain hauled her out.

The rest of the cars carried on. The car behind nudged the back of the disabled one, and started to shove it forward.

Petrovitch skipped out of the way and stood in the torrent in the gutter as the grind of metal and the faint pattering of desperate hands on glass made its stately way down the street.

Thirty cars in all, no traffic in front, none behind. The crowd began to murmur and disperse, the show over.

Chain was struggling with his bruised gun-hand and the woman. She gasped and mouthed, and no words would come out. All the while, she grabbed at parts of his jacket to be reassured that he was real.

"Petrovitch? What did you do?"

"I killed it." Petrovitch worked the slide and ejected the chambered shell into his hand. He tucked his gun away again.

"Explain. Excuse me, miss. Will you stop pawing at me?" He finally got his good arm up and held her away.

"I blew its brains out. Even your car's not so old that it hasn't got electronics under the bonnet." Petrovitch took his glasses off and shook them free of water. "That's what you're going to have to do to each and every one of them."

"Me?"

"You and your cop friends. Unless you're happy for this to carry on?"

The broken car beached itself against a lamp-post further up the street. The obstacle it made caused ripples in the neat lines of cars, so that the advancing front was no longer perfectly straight.

Chain looked at the woman, who had started to wander away in a daze. She walked slowly and erratically towards her car, and when she was within range, she started to kick viciously at it with her heels.

"Is this your fault?" asked Chain.

"No more than it is the Oshicora Corporation's. Which is

to say, I don't know." He put his glasses back on, fat raindrops clinging to the lenses. "But I don't see how it can be."

"I'm going to have to call this in. I'm going to have to get help." Chain flexed his fingers to check they all still worked. "Don't think you're off the hook."

"Meet me at the lab. And I still want that body armour."

"In exchange for that pathetic pea-shooter you call a gun."

"*Potselui mou zhopy*, Chain. I seem to be the only one around here who knows what he's doing." Petrovitch's blanket had fallen in the road. He wrung it out the best he could, adding to the flood at his feet. Then he held it over him and shook his head rapidly to try and clear his glasses.

"When did I stop being Inspector Chain?"

"When I caught you out, *zjulik*." He watched Chain's face fall. "Go on, go. The terrifying truth is that people's lives might depend on you getting your *srachishche* moving."

The rain continued to fall as they stared each other down. The lights changed; red, amber, green. Almost at once, horns started to sound, and those slow in clearing the crossing walked a little faster.

Chain looked down the road past Petrovitch at the block of cars gliding serenely as one again. He bared his teeth in a feral snarl and turned away, back to his own vehicle.

Petrovitch crossed to the other side, and on. He found that he was wet, cold, hungry, he couldn't go home, he could barely risk going to the lab without police protection, and he had the chill metal touch of gun against his waist.

He realised that he needed to be dry and warm and well-fed, or he'd end up stumbling and slouching to his death. He looked up with his water-spattered eyes at the street names and recognised where he was.

equations*of*life

It was only a short walk, but he was shivering by the time he arrived. He could feel his heart large and fragile under his scrawny ribs as he took the steps up to the big wooden doors, still marked with bullets.

The door was closed. He took hold of the black iron hoop and banged it down. The sound echoed away inside. He did it again, then again, then hunched up on the narrow slice of dry stone provided by the doorway.

A bolt slid back, and the door opened to make a sliver of darkness.

He could see her narrowed eye regarding him from her great height.

"Sanctuary," he said.

17

Sister Madeleine took him in. She guided him around the plastic buckets dotted along the length of the nave that attempted to catch the copious drips from the roof, stopped to genuflect to the altar, then steered him into the vestry.

Father John wasn't there.

"Meeting with the bishop," she said. She took his blanket away, and then wondered what to do with the sodden lump. She threw it out into the church.

"Doesn't that mean you should be with him?"

"There'll be more Joans there than priests. He'll be perfectly safe." She stared at Petrovitch. "You realise that sanctuary was abolished in the seventeenth century."

He shivered uncontrollably under her gaze and wrapped his arms around himself. "I didn't know what else to do."

"I thought you had a plan for everything," she said, then added quietly: "You also said I'd never see you again."

She took a step forward, and for the briefest of moments he

thought she was going to enfold him in her own robes. The look of utter panic on both their faces forced them apart.

She whirled around on the pretence of searching for something. "Doesn't take a genius to pack a raincoat."

"I had planned to be at the airport. Then something happened, and I found I needed to hang around after all."

She found an old two-bar electric fire and dragged it to the centre of the room, frayed flex trailing behind it. "Needed to, or wanted to?" She crouched low down by the skirting board and forced the yellowed plug into a wall socket. The wires on the fire fizzed sparks and started to glow red.

"I can still go. Walk out, never come back."

She straightened up, faced him down. "Why don't you then? Why don't you just go away and leave me alone?"

"Because I made a promise I have to keep. I made a vow: you know what that's like, don't you? A vow so terrible, so final, that it turns you from a human being into an expendable weapon. I've burnt my bridges, cast my dice, crossed the Rubicon. Whatever metaphor you choose, that's it."

She took several deep breaths. "So what is it that you're going to do? Die of pneumonia at someone?"

"Yeah. Thanks for that. It'd be nice if somebody took me seriously some time soon." He peeled off his jacket and dumped it on the threadbare carpet, then tried to bend down to unlace his boots. His canvas trousers had become so stiff, and his fingers so weak, that he couldn't make any impact on the rain-shrunk knots.

Sister Madeleine got to her knees and bent low, worrying at the laces until she'd loosened first one, then the other. She looked up, face framed by her veil. "Can you manage now?"

"I'll cope."

"There are some choir robes in that cupboard. Put on as many as you want. It's not like we have a choir to offend." She pointed, then strode to the vestry door. "Look, Petrovitch . . ."

"Sam. It's Sam."

She leaned her head against the door frame. "We can be grown-ups about this, right?"

"Yes," he said, less convincingly than he'd hoped.

"Give me a shout when you're ready and I'll make some coffee."

"We can't make a start on the communion wine, then?"

She frowned at him. He shrugged damply back.

"It's in the safe," she said. "I don't have the keys."

"Coffee will be fine," said Petrovitch, laying his glasses on the desk and grasping the bottom of the death metal T-shirt.

Sister Madeleine saw the logo and the name, closed her eyes and shook her head. "All this in the house of God," she muttered as she left. She made sure she closed the door behind her.

Petrovitch struggled out of the rest of his clothes, pausing only to examine the scars on his chest. One was long and curving, livid against his shock-white skin, and the others short, raised lines like knife wounds, which is what they were: the work of a single cut of the scalpel. The latest of these bristled with black thread.

Everything he wore had wicked in twice its weight in water. Where he'd dropped his jacket, the red carpet had turned dark. Not good. But there was another door at the rear of the room, and judging from the draught swirling in, it led outside. He bundled up his laundry and threw it there instead.

In one of the heavy cupboards that smelt of incense and age, he found a rail of vestments. The black ones were the priest's; the gold ones he assumed were for special occasions. Then there were the bewildering array of white garments, some short, some long, some plain, some edged with lace. He had no idea what he was supposed to use.

In the end, he gave up, and took two of the shorter white robes and towelled himself off with them, then chose one of the longer ones to wear. When he finished fighting his way to the neck end, he found he looked like a marquee.

He managed to turn it to his advantage, though, by holding the hem of the robe over the fire and concentrating the meagre output of warm, ozone-tainted air inside.

"I'm sort of ready," he called.

She came back in, stooping through the doorway. When she saw him, she laughed.

"Yeah. Go on. Something to tell all your nun friends back at the convent."

"Trust me, there's not much humour in this vocation. Lots of funerals, if you like that sort of thing." She cleared a space for the kettle and unplugged the fire.

"Hey!"

"If I put both on at the same time, the fuses will blow."

"I can wire it so they don't."

"And will the church burn down afterwards?"

"Not in this weather. Maybe later."

"We'll do it my way," she said firmly. She turned the kettle on, and retrieved two mugs from the desk drawer.

Petrovitch realised he was still holding the hem of his robe out. He let it go.

She sat down in the chair and hunched forward, fingers together; almost at prayer. "Where were you going to go?"

Petrovitch took a while to answer. "Far away. Where no one had ever heard of me, seen me. Somewhere I could start again. Make a better job of it than I did this time around."

"That your gun?" The sister looked over to where it sat on the desk, moistening the cover of the book beneath it.

"Yeah."

"Loaded?"

"Not much point in having one that isn't." Petrovitch went to pick it up, and she laid her hand across it.

"I should have checked you for weapons. Now I'm going to have to confess that before next mass." She glanced up. "And accept a penance. You're nothing but trouble."

The kettle boiled, and she dutifully made instant coffee spooned from a battered tin.

"What about you?" asked Petrovitch. "You don't seem, I don't know, very holy."

She plugged the fire back in. "Holiness is a work in progress. In the meantime, I can kick your bony arse through a wall, I can group twelve shots at fifty metres and I can take a bullet meant for my priest. The job description didn't mention sainthood."

"So what did it say?"

Her fingers tightened around her mug, and she blew steam on her face. "I was fifteen and I was going to end up killing someone. I was full of rage and hate, and I couldn't control it. Someone offered me a chance; a chance to change what I was going to become. A new start, just like you."

"Yeah. Not quite like me."

The lights went out.

In the dying glow of the fire, Petrovitch snatched up his gun and pulled the slide. It was dark, a closed room without windows. He could hear the sister's clothing rustle softly, then the solid mechanical sound of her own, considerably larger gun being cocked.

He listened intently. There was the rain, the creaking of timbers, the splash of water in over-full containers. There was traffic noise and the clatter of domestic alarms. He could see where the back door was by the slit of light under it. He took two slow steps and stood beside it, back to the wall, ready.

The only movement in the room was now hers. The chair relaxed with a sigh as she rose from it. The air stirred as she walked. She made no sound herself. Even her breathing was below a whisper.

She stopped, and everything was still.

The vestry door gave a very slight shudder, just enough for whoever it was to tell it wasn't locked. Petrovitch crouched down and reached out with his free hand for his jacket. He found it, and pulled it slowly towards him. He felt in his pocket for his key-fob torch, which he gripped between his lips: his teeth rested against the on switch. He kept hold of the jacket.

The door opened a fraction. Something bounced on the carpet, once, twice, and landed close to his feet. He bit down on the torch and span his jacket over the thick black disc.

A circle of actinic light flashed out from around the edges of the jacket, together with an almighty clap of thunder. Flames jetted up. He was deaf, but he could still see. He spat the torch out across the room, and suddenly someone was shooting at the tiny point of light as it sailed through the air.

Petrovitch dived the other way, brought his gun up and held his breath. His white robe reflected every last glimmer of light, but the man shrouded head to foot in black wasn't looking his way.

He shot him twice in the back, and the figure jerked each time. Petrovitch watched the man start to turn, then slip heavily to one knee. The strange green-glowing eye of night vision rested on him.

Their guns came around, and Petrovitch fired first, straight into his face.

Out of bullets. But there was a mostly full pistol in a dead man's grip right in front of him. He reached for it, and found himself in the crosshairs of another man in black. He looked up and saw a hint of green-cast skin.

"*Pizdets.*" There was no way he was going to get hold of that gun, let alone use it.

Then the man was enfolded in a shadow that lifted him off his feet and slammed him sideways. Bright flashes of gunfire moved in an arc, away from where Petrovitch lay.

He took the brief window of opportunity to prise the gun away from its entangling fingers, then immediately jammed the long barrel in the ear of the man who had come up behind the sister.

"*Otsosi, potom prosi,*" he hissed, and pressed harder. "Sister?"

She moved, and the body of the second gunman slid awkwardly to the floor. Petrovitch's jacket was still on fire. She stamped it out and picked up his torch, shining it right in the remaining man's night-vision goggles.

"Get his gun," she said, with such authority that Petrovitch felt his own nerve falter. "And get that thing off his face."

With the man disarmed, Petrovitch felt confident enough to wrench the goggles away. He wasn't Japanese.

"*Chyort!* I was so sure they were from Hijo."

The point of light moved from one hand to the other, and she took the man down with a punch to the stomach that made him double over before collapsing. She was on him, even while he was retching and gagging, dragging him up again by the neck and holding him against the wall. "I know who these bastards are. Paradise militia."

The man, the feared killer, resolved into just another street kid; a foot soldier for a gang who, like all the others, thought they could control part of the Metrozone. He clawed at Sister Madeleine's hand with his scabbed fingers and slowly turned blue.

"You're strangling him," noted Petrovitch.

"No. I'm suffocating him," she said.

"He can't tell you anything if he's dead too."

"I don't need him to tell me anything."

"Fair enough." Petrovitch closed the vestry door, and felt to see if there were bolts he could use. "Don't you lose your nunhood or something if you kill a man in cold blood, cursed to wander the earth for ever?"

She let go.

"Also, don't you think we should be getting the *huy* out of here?" He stumbled across the body on the floor and put his hand down in a pool of dark, sticky liquid.

She stood there, staring at the weak, mewling form at her feet.

"We could still die here." Petrovitch wiped the gore off on his gown and crawled over to his boots. "We could still die and I'm wearing a *yobanaya* dress."

She moved, holding the torch high, and strode to the wardrobe full of vestments. "Put this on, and this cape." She threw them, complete with plastic hangers, at Petrovitch.

"Where's your gun?" It was hard to put his wet boots on. He jammed his foot down and tore some skin off.

"I dropped it." She was in the desk drawers, rattling their contents around.

"Not smart."

"Listen to me," she roared. "What do you know about fighting? What do you know about close-quarter combat? What do you know about knowing you're going to be lucky to see the other side of twenty?"

"You just summed up my life, Sister. Now stop screwing around and get your gun. You're going to need it."

"I don't need a gun to shut you up."

"Yeah?" Petrovitch grunted with the effort of getting the other boot on.

"I could just break your stringy neck with my bare hands, like that guy in the corner." She rattled an iron hoop loaded with keys. "Get that back door open."

"I'm busy here."

"I'm trying to save you. Get a move on!" The keys landed beside him.

"And a moment ago you were contemplating your navel. For some stupid reason it's me saving you." He pulled on the black cassock, arms up, and shrugged it down.

"I don't need saving."

"Yeah. Martyr yourself on someone else's time."

There should have been five guns in the room. Petrovitch could account for three of them, and a set of night-vision goggles proved too tempting not to take.

"What are you doing?" The desk fell over, making him jump.

"Scavenging. What are you doing?"

"Looking for my gun."

"You mean it doesn't come when you whistle?"

She heaved another piece of furniture aside. "Got it."

Petrovitch piled the guns and the goggles on the cape, then

scraped his wet clothes on top, even his ruined jacket. He picked up the keys. "Any idea which one?"

"Oh, give them here. You are impossible."

He gathered the corners of the cape and tied them to form a bundle. "You don't get out much, do you?"

The lock turned on the third try. "Ready?" she asked.

"Yeah. I still look like a *kon'v pal'to*, though."

"You're fussing about my gun: where's yours?"

"I'll be running. You're the one who can shoot straight."

She turned the torch off and gripped the latch.

"I know this is probably not the time to ask," he said, "but how old are you?"

"Nineteen," she said. She twisted her wrist and the sickly daylight flooded in.

18

At the bottom end of Edgware Road, she was still jogging effortlessly, while he was gagging with the effort of keeping up. "Stop." Petrovitch squatted and put his head down between his knees. Rain dripped from his nose.

She stood over him, hands on her hips. "I don't think we're being followed," she said, scanning the crowded pavements. Umbrellas formed an uneven multicoloured sea that flowed in every direction at once.

"Don't . . . think?" he gasped, and breathed through his mouth. He was aware that his heart was struggling, but there were more pressing pains like the burning in his lungs and the stitch that was threatening to split him open from groin to neck.

"I need to call Father John and warn him," said Sister Madeleine. She pulled out her phone from inside her robes and speed-dialled her priest. "Get some police round to the church."

"Do whatever you want." Petrovitch straightened up, clutching his sides. "I'm going to . . . *yobany stos.*" He felt a fresh wave of nausea well up and drag him down. He coughed bile into the gutter.

"Where am I? Marble Arch. Yes, I know I can't go back. Our Lady of the Assumption? Warwick Street? Yes, I know it. Look, I'm going to have to call back. What? No, Petrovitch is throwing his guts up." She paused. "Yes, that Petrovitch. Long story. No, Father."

She saw Petrovitch trying to rise again, and she reached down her hand. Petrovitch clung to her arm and she pulled him to his feet.

"No, Father," she said, her voice becoming tight. "No. It wasn't his fault. Because it wasn't. It was Paradise. Yes. Can we save the questions for later: he's dying, and I'm drowning. What do you mean, is it raining? Of course it is."

Petrovitch hung on tight as his vision greyed. *"Chyort."*

"No. I'm not doing that. Father, he . . . will you shut up and listen? His heart's packing in again and standing around on a street corner in plain sight of anyone who might want to kill us is not helping either. So I'm not asking your permission to get him somewhere safe; I'm telling you that's what I'm doing and I'll call you again when I've done it." Her thumb stabbed down and the phone was thrust away again inside its secret pocket. "Where are we going?"

"Imperial college. But not by Park Lane. Goes too close to Green Park."

"Bad?"

"Very. We'll have to go through Hyde Park."

She didn't look certain. "I ought to just call an ambulance."

"If they're monitoring admissions, I'll be dead in minutes." He forced his legs to carry his weight. "You don't have to come with me. It's probably better that you don't."

"Shut up, Sam."

There was nothing more to say. She marched him over the road. They passed the glistening shaven-headed man at Speakers' Corner proclaiming a new machine jihad to the empty pavement, and slipped through the gates set in the wire fence that half-heartedly enclosed the park. Before them lay the warren of tents and shacks and shanties.

"Keep your eye on the Albert Hall. Too far left and you'll end up in the Serpentine."

She nodded grimly and looked up, fixing the dome against the buildings behind it. The rain had extinguished the open fires and damped down the miasma that hung over the refugee camp. It had even driven most of the inhabitants inside to seek whatever shelter they could scavenge.

It was loud, the drumming of the droplets on corrugated iron and stiff plastic; a roar that was deafening and disorientating.

"We could go round the long way," she said.

"I won't last the long way. Besides," said Petrovitch, "neither the Oshicoras nor Paradise will follow us in. A priest and a nun should get a free pass."

It was as if she was looking at him for the first time. "But you're not a priest."

"I won't tell anyone if you don't." He plunged on into the narrow, twisting alleys, ready with a smile and a wave and a benediction, but determined never to stop. Hyde Park was where people went when they burnt out of domik life. People went there to die. Petrovitch wasn't going to be one of them.

Sister Madeleine followed, and he was glad of her at his back. If it hadn't been for her, he would have tried the perimeter road. He hated Hyde Park: he could only look at so many hopeless faces before he felt rage overtake him. But who would he choose to grab and shout at? Too many, too many.

The house in the middle of the park had vanished, every part of it long ago scavenged for building materials: the rough paths still converged at that point though, nothing more than a memory.

They hurried on. They were deep in the park, surrounded on all sides. Petrovitch's face was set in a rictus grin, but the sister was in tears as they vaulted over yet another half-rotted corpse. He took hold of her wrist.

"Come on, *babochka*. You can't afford to care."

"But . . ."

"They chose this." He turned left and headed for the Black Bridge, dragging her behind him. "There are no guards to this prison. And if you're at all sensitive, don't look over the sides of the bridge. Straight down the middle, eyes front."

"How . . . how do you know these things?"

"Yeah. Doesn't show me in a good light, does it?"

They arrived at the bridge. He didn't follow his own advice: there were things in the dark water, little bloated islands that not even the seagulls dared touch. The wind had accumulated a small drift of them on the far bank, beached and slick where the rain beat down on them and cleaned the filth of the lake away.

When the Neva thawed in spring, there were always bodies washing under the St Petersburg bridges along with the grey lumps of ice. But there was an effort to collect them, identify them, cut holes in the frozen ground and bury them.

That this – this squalor – was permitted, burned in his soul.

Not far now. The bridge carried a road, and the spaces between the rude dwellings roughly followed the remains of the tarmacked surface.

Someone had died, that night or that morning. They lay

face-down, features obscured by long greying hair. Their bones stuck out against their pale skin, each knuckle-joint a knot. They would have weighed no more than a child.

The rain beat at the body lying across their path, trying to dissolve it away.

She lost it. She shook him off hard enough to hurt him and crouched down beside the cold, stiff figure. She wept uncontrollably.

Petrovitch looked on, gazed at the short distance they had left to go. He could see the start of Exhibition Road the other side of the gate.

"Whoever it is, is beyond help. Unless you can raise the dead."

The way she moved her shoulders showed him his opinion wasn't at all welcome. She reached forward, hesitated, then turned the body over so that the sightless eyes were filling with rain.

It had been a woman, her age impossible to guess, her cause of death likewise. There were so many things she could have died of. A broken heart for one. Sister Madeleine pushed the eyelids down, first one, then the other. She sat hunched on her heels, dejected, defeated.

"We have to go, *babochka*." He dared to put his hand on her curved back, and she let it rest there for a while, before shrugging him off and rising to her full height.

"I . . . I just needed to know," she said. She glanced down, stifled a sob, and walked deliberately around the body.

And for once, Petrovitch knew better than to ask. He cast a glance behind them. Hyde Park was perfectly still. No one but them was moving.

As soon as they were outside of the gate, the real world struck them with full force. There were people on the pavements and traffic on the roads, and the stench of death was replaced by the familiar tang of sweat and oil.

Petrovitch looked up and saw a strange fear in the nun's eyes. "Stay with me, Sister. Only half a block more, I promise." He took her hand again – properly her hand this time, not her wrist – and joined the queue to cross the road.

The light went green for them, and they got swept along Exhibition Road. Horns sounded behind them, and Petrovitch twisted round to see the reason: the lights all showed red and the junction had seized.

"What? What is it?"

"I'll tell you later. Unless you want to see some really weird shit, we need to get off the street right now." He pushed her in front of him and through the automatic doors to the university.

The first thought he had was that his pass card had probably been destroyed when his jacket had caught fire. His second thought was that untying the bundle in his hand and seeing if it was true or not wasn't going to be a good idea, since he'd have to sort through three different handguns and some night-vision goggles as well.

And there was the small matter that he was dressed like a Roman Catholic priest.

"*Pizdets*," he said. "Wait here. I'm going to try and get a temporary card."

He gathered up his bluster and took it to the reception desk, where he had his retina rescanned and his photograph taken, and a pass issued in his name.

He called Sister Madeleine over and explained for the third time that no, he really wasn't a priest, but yes, she really was a nun, and that she was his guest. The receptionist made her sign in, and clearly didn't believe a word of it.

As they walked away towards the lifts, a man with a mop and bucket appeared to clear the floor of the lake they'd brought in with them.

He had to show his card twice more: once to get into his building, the next as they got off the lift on the fourth floor.

"At least Pif took me seriously."

"Who?"

"Pif. Doctor Epiphany Ekanobi to most. She's very smart, but she doesn't tend to believe half of what I tell her."

"I would have thought that would make her extra smart."

"Yeah. But she's guarding something and she needed to know just how important it is." He stopped outside a door whose only distinguishing feature was a plastic plaque engraved with the numbers four-one-oh. "This is me. Us."

He kicked the door open with his usual lack of grace and came face to face with Chain's police special.

In an instant, Sister Madeleine had her own Vatican-approved hand-cannon out.

"*Perestan' bit dabayobom*, Chain. Put it away."

Chain looked over Petrovitch's shoulder at Sister Madeleine's drawn weapon. "After you, Sister."

Neither of them wanted to be the first to move. Petrovitch shook his head and walked around the policeman. "Pif."

"Hey, Sam. Detective Inspector Chain has been wondering where you were. And," she said, raising an eyebrow, "why are you dressed as a priest?"

"Because," he started, then thought better of it. "It'll keep." Then he turned his ire on detective and nun. "Will you two knock it off? Get in here and close the *yebani* door, Sister."

"Sister?" Pif turned to see Sister Madeleine squelch uncertainly into the room. "I'm not sure if that explains everything or nothing."

"Really, I'm not in the mood. I've already had a perfectly good jacket ruined by the *vnebrachnyjj* Paradise militia, and I'm soaked through for the second time today."

"How's the heart?"

"It's not great. If I catch a cold, it's going to kill me." Petrovitch dropped the bundle of cloth on the floor and spread it out wide. He laid the guns – his own Beretta, an ageing Israeli Jericho and a newer Norinco knock-off – out in a fan and put the night-vision goggles next to them to dry off. He held up his jacket.

The back had completely burnt through. It was a circle of material with a ragged hole. He went through the pockets, retrieved his student card, a credit chip and a single bullet for the Beretta. Then he threw the remains of the jacket at the wall, where it stuck for a moment before sliding down onto the floor.

Chain holstered his gun and looked over Petrovitch's growing collection.

"You know what I'm going to say, don't you?"

"And you know what I'll say in reply. Where were you? Where were you when the lights went out and they were coming at us in the dark? Where were you when I picked up this little *peesa* and shot a man in the face from no more distance than you are from me?"

"I was saving forty people from being driven into the river. What's your point?"

"That. Precisely. You can't protect me. When the Metrozone is safe enough that I don't have to worry about three – count them, three – different gangs trying to send me to hell, I'll hand over every offensive weapon I own. Do you think I like carrying them around? Do you think I enjoy blowing someone's brains out in a church? We've got to this point because you lost control of the city, and you lost it long ago." Petrovitch picked up the little Beretta, ejected the magazine into the palm of his hand and inserted the single cartridge. He slammed it back in. "Anything you can say to make it better? Anything at all?"

"I suppose not."

"Then *pl'uvat' na t'eb'a!* What are you good for?"

Chain rubbed at his chin. "You called me, remember? Something about the Oshicoras?"

Petrovitch forced a half-smile onto his face. "Yeah. So I did. Pif, give him the files. No, wait. Don't."

Pif looked from Petrovitch to Chain. "Which is it going to be?"

Petrovitch got awkwardly to his feet. "I haven't eaten a hot meal since yesterday morning. Detective Inspector Chain is going to buy us all lunch. Then we'll talk about the death of Oshicora senior."

Chain blinked.

"Have you got time for some lunch, Sister?" Petrovitch picked up the Jericho and slipped it into Pif's bag.

"You walked me through Hyde Park. I don't even know if I'm hungry."

"Then come for the warmth. Hot sweet tea, or whatever it is you British drink. At least let me do for you what you did for me. Get you dry before you go back out."

She was torn. "I need to phone Father John."

"Do it after lunch," suggested Petrovitch.

"Sam, I've broken my vow of obedience once today. I can't go on like this."

"Yeah, you're right."

She bit at her lip, and for once looked like the teenager she still was.

"Looks like I'm paying," said Chain. "Come on, Sister. You can tell me all about it on the way."

19

They stood in a quiet corner of the kitchen, catering staff busy elsewhere but not around them. She took everything off: robes, armour, piece by piece, until all she was wearing was a skin-tight grey body suit. Her veil came off last, revealing that the sides and front of her head were shaved. What was left of her dark hair cascaded backwards between her shoulder blades almost to her waist.

All the while, she stared unblinking at Petrovitch. He was struck both dumb and motionless, his heart beating slow and heavy in his chest.

She struggled into a cook's white coat at least a size too small for her, then gathered everything up to hang in front of the huge catering ovens.

When it came for him to disrobe, he did so behind the industrial-sized dishwasher. He emerged, white-coated too, to be reminded of her, tall and strong and lithe, by her impact armour sitting like a headless soldier on a spare chair.

Back at their table, she kept on stealing Petrovitch's chips.

"I thought you said you weren't hungry."

She looked at him with a gloriously defiant expression, and reached forward again.

"Still counts as food, even if it is from my plate." He speared a whole sausage with his fork and started to eat it from one end.

Chain put down his sandwich and wiped his mouth. "Can someone please tell me why you think Oshicora's dead? It's important, even if you lot are busy filling your faces."

Petrovitch spoke around his mouthful. "Pif, give him the card."

Pif reached past the gun in her bag for the data card and slid it across the table.

"Sam hasn't seen these yet," she said. "They seem authentic."

"Yeah. In my little conversation with Hijo, he all but admitted that he'd put a bullet in Old Man Oshicora's head. Then he told me I was next, which was nice of him." Petrovitch turned his fork and made short work of the other half of the sausage. He lost two more chips to the same predator. "*Chyort!* Get your own!"

"Don't swear at the nun, Petrovitch," said Chain. He got out his handheld computer and slid the card in.

The little computer wheezed and strained, and eventually a tinny voice called out: "I hope this is you, Sam. I really hope it's you. They've killed my father. They dragged him away and they shot him. I heard it even though I wasn't supposed to. I don't know what to do, I don't know where to go, I don't know anyone who can help me. Except you. You have to save me, Sam, because there's no one else."

Chain looked out of the corner of his eye at Petrovitch, naked but for a catering uniform, chewing on the last piece of sausage.

"What?" said Petrovitch.

A smile flickered on Chain's lips. He tried to squash it, but failed.

Petrovitch swallowed, and turned in his chair. "What? What is it?"

"Help me, Obi-wan Kenobi, you're my only hope," squeaked Chain, and started to laugh.

"*Zatknis' na hui, gaishnik.* Did she call the police? No, she didn't. Why? Because she knows they're all as useless as you." Petrovitch examined the tines on his fork and wondered what they'd look like sticking out of Chain's leg.

"OK, so it's quite sweet she asked you for help, but really, Petrovitch." He snorted. "Get a sense of perspective."

"Detective Inspector," said Pif. She narrowed her eyes and folded her arms. "This man discovered how to make gravity out of electricity yesterday. Don't be too quick to dismiss him."

Petrovitch bared his teeth in a feral grin. "I'll tell you what I told that *raspizdyai* Hijo: I will save her. Just to prove that I can."

Sister Madeleine shifted uncomfortably in her seat.

Chain looked at Pif, then at Petrovitch. He sighed, and played the second file.

Bang. Bang. Bang.

"Get me out of here, I'm begging you, get me out!"

When the electronic feedback screeched, Chain turned the sound off. He stroked his chin. "That was Hijo, pulling her down. Never happen if Hamano Oshicora was still around."

"You don't say?" Petrovitch held out his hand for the computer, and Chain reluctantly handed it over.

He watched it for himself. He knew the content but not the nuances, the way Sonja Oshicora spoke earnestly, stared wide-eyed and steady into the camera. In the first clip, she wasn't pleading with him, she was telling him precisely how it was: she was alone in a sea of confusion, and only he could cut through it and rescue her.

In the second, it was different. Something had gone wrong, and she'd fled to the only safe space she knew – her room inside the tower. She'd locked the door, got out one final message before becoming a prisoner.

But there was a tickle in the back of his mind, worrying him. He played it again while everybody watched him hunch over the screen and not blink.

"She didn't send this message," he said. He looked up with a smile. "No, really. What's the last thing you see?"

Chain reached out for his computer: Petrovitch held it away from him. "OK, then. Hijo pulling Sonja to the floor."

"No. After that. Someone points their gun at the computer. That ends the message."

"I don't get it."

"You might send mail by destroying your hardware. I send it by clicking the little send icon, or by saying 'send', or by pressing a key. Sonja did none of those things because she was underneath Hijo. Hijo didn't do it, either, because he didn't want the message sent: he was breaking down the door to make sure she couldn't call for help."

"So who did send it?"

"I don't know," Petrovitch said. "But I know what it means."

"Someone other than Sonja wanted it sent," said Sister Madeleine. "Just to show I'm paying attention. This Hijo isn't in complete control, there's at least one person loyal to the old leader."

"Blimey," said Chain, "no need to labour the point. Even if this was true, even if Hamano Oshicora turns up in the river or propping up a bridge somewhere, I don't know what you expect me to do about this."

"Ooh, I don't know," wondered Petrovitch, tapping his chin, "maybe you could round up some of your police friends and turn up mob-handed at the Oshicora Tower, set Sonja free and arrest Hijo for murder. What do you think? Sound like something the police might be interested in?"

Chain started to answer, then stopped. He tapped on the table and turned his empty plate around. "I'll tell you what would happen. I'd go to my boss: I'd say Hamano Oshicora's been assassinated by one of his trusted lieutenants and has taken Sonja Oshicora hostage. We need to organise an operation to get her out. He'd say, 'Why? Why on earth should I risk any of my people while Oshicora's empire is busy imploding?' That's what he'd say. He might add, 'Good riddance', and then question my sanity, but that's about the measure of it."

"So you're going to do what you've done all along: exactly nothing."

"Have you seen what's going on out there at the moment? It's pissing it down with rain with no let-up in sight, your little electronic war with the Oshicoras has infected the whole Metrozone with all sorts of nonsense, and you want me to arrange a bloodbath on the steps of one of the most heavily defended buildings in the city." Chain snatched his computer back. "Damn right I'm doing nothing. This is a good day for me. I haven't been able to so much as slow Oshicora down since he turned up. Now he's gone, and Hijo hasn't got the smarts to keep it together. I can sit back, kick off my shoes, and watch them fall. No one but them has to get hurt."

"Sonja's going to get hurt," said Petrovitch, "and Hijo wants to kill me."

"Hijo will be too busy with important things to worry about little you." Chain slipped the computer away and got up with a scrape of his chair. "As for Sonja, I guess she's beyond help. Nice meeting you all again. Petrovitch, if you still want the body armour, it's in the back of my car."

Petrovitch pretended to think about the offer, then slowly extended his middle finger. "*Za cyun v'zhopu.*"

"Your choice. I've done what I could: what you don't seem to understand is that what I'm allowed to do is limited not just by the law, but by what's possible." Chain pulled his coat off the back of the chair and shambled to the door.

Sister Madeleine rose to her feet. Because she was very tall, it took some time. Petrovitch was going to tell her not to bother with Chain, but she had such a look of righteous indignation on her face that he didn't dare. She strode after the inspector, her long legs eating up the distance between them.

Then it was just him and Pif at the table. Petrovitch pulled off his glasses and tossed them carelessly aside. He rubbed his eyes. "You know, I could do without this."

"Sam, maybe it's for the best. We can get back to doing what we're good at."

"Yeah. That'd be great, except Hijo's on my case and I'm not as confident as Chain about his lack of ability. He seems pretty competent to me." He squinted for his glasses, and toyed with the arms. "That plane flight out of here is looking increasingly attractive."

"Then take it," said Pif. "See what it's like in a few days. Any other university on the planet will take you: all you have to do is wave that sheet of paper I've got on my desk at them."

"It's your work more than mine. Besides, I've got something else to prove now: I said I'd save Sonja Oshicora."

"It's a good thing to want to, Sam, but . . ." Her voice trailed off and she ran her fingers through her beaded hair. "You're going to get yourself killed."

"What's the time?"

Pif glanced at her wrist. "Half twelve."

"I die in just over an hour's time anyway." He saw the look on her face. "Don't worry. It's just an admin thing. And I don't need Chain. I have a plan. It's not a very good one yet, but it's a start."

"Do I want to know?"

"No. No you don't."

"OK." Pif's phone chimed, and she reached past the inconveniently large pistol to retrieve it. She frowned at the number, flipped the cover, and said hesitantly, "Hello?"

Petrovitch looked away to give Pif her privacy. Chain and the sister were in animated conversation over by the door. She was pointing back at Petrovitch, jabbing her finger and leaning over the detective, who in return looked up with an expression of unconcerned passivity.

"That's . . . strange," said Pif. She pressed a button and passed the phone to Petrovitch.

He tore his eyes away from Madeleine and peered at the little screen. She'd brought up the last number to call her.

"One-three-five, seven-one-one, one-three-one, seven-one-nine. That's not a real number. In fact, that's," and he used the only word that could describe it, "strange."

Petrovitch twisted around. Sister Madeleine was fuming that Chain had taken a call in the middle of their argument. He stood a little way back, computer trapped between ear and shoulder. He said "Who is this?" twice, then cut the connection. He stared at the device.

equationsoflife

Almost immediately, the nun's phone was brought out by one of the kitchen staff from where it had been laid to dry. She moved away from Chain and slipped the phone beside her head.

Petrovitch walked over slowly, still clutching Pif's phone. He took Sister Madeleine's wrist down from its height and turned it so he could see if it was the same number.

"There's no one there," she said, "not even breathing."

He leaned in and she pressed the speaker against him. It was just dead air, not even the hiss of an open microphone or a digital click. Then the line fell dead.

He straightened up and searched the ceiling of the restaurant. There were cameras in each of the four corners, and another over the door. There were half a dozen other people eating; the place was usually busier.

"I think someone's trying to contact me," said Petrovitch.

"Why don't they just call you?"

"I don't have a phone. I know I must be the last person in the Metrozone not to have one, but there you are. I've never needed one. I've no one to talk to." Petrovitch pushed his glasses up his face and glanced across at Chain. "One-three-five, seven-one-one, one-three-one, seven-one-nine?"

He nodded. "You know the number?"

"Yeah. Just never expected to see them like this. I'm going to get my clothes on before I'm forced to run naked from the building chased by ninjas, which is probably where this is going."

Petrovitch forced a smile at the kitchen staff as he raced around, picking up his boots, socks, trousers, pants, T-shirt. He struggled into his trousers and put his warm, stiff boots on. Then he waved his goodbyes, still wearing the white coat and carrying what he hadn't put on under his arm.

"Pif? Phone." He threw it across the table at her. "Keep the gun."

"Sam?"

"Back to the lab. I've just remembered I can be contacted."

"The mail servers are down, though." She put the phone in her bag and slung it over her shoulder.

"I still got in touch with you, didn't I? Good old-fashioned copper wire."

The pair headed for the doors, and Chain barred their way.

"You have to explain," he said.

"If you weren't such a *kon' pedal'nii*, you'd have worked it out." Petrovitch darted one side, Pif the other.

She shouted back, "First eight primes," just before the doors swung shut again.

"You told him!"

"Your tame nun wanted to know, too."

"She is not my anything."

"Oh, Sam. I saw the way you looked at her. And she at you."

He stopped in the middle of the corridor, and she stopped too.

"Never," he said, "speak about this again."

"You sure?"

"Yeah."

"OK."

They ran the rest of the way, except for the lift, which was filled with her panting and his soft groans.

When the lift door opened, they could both hear the land-line ringing. The security guard caught the barest glimpse of their cards as they dashed by.

The phone was on Pif's desk, warbling away in its turn-of-the-century monotone. Pif closed the door and leaned back against it, while Petrovitch stalked over and regarded the handset with suspicion.

"Just pick it up," she said.

Petrovitch curled his fingers around the phone and lifted it to his head. The silence rang louder than the noise.

"Petrovitch," he said, and waited.

"Shinkansen ha mata hashirou."

He opened his mouth, then slowly closed it again. He motioned for a pen. "Can you repeat that for me?"

"Shinkansen ha mata hashirou," said the voice in a perfectly measured tone. Exactly as before.

Petrovitch bit the pen lid off and scribbled what he thought he heard on the nearest piece of paper. "How do I contact you?" he asked, staring at his writing, trying to make sense of it.

He heard the burr of the dial tone, and the handset slipped from his fingers. It bounced on its coiled cord off the edge of the desk, then dangled there until Pif picked it up and put it back.

"Who was it?" she asked.

"This," he said, "this word here. I recognise it. And the only time I've heard it before is from a man who's supposed to be dead."

20

They'd gone out onto the campus and hunted down a native Japanese speaker, pinning the startled student against a wall and shouting badly accented words at him until he confessed: the bullet train will run again.

"It could be a rallying cry," said Pif.

"It's not a very good one: not up there with *Viva la revolucion!* or *For the motherland!* What's wrong with *Banzai?*"

"Because the Emperor is dead and Japan has gone for ever?"

"Oshicora used these exact same words: the *shinkansen* will run again. It might have been something he told everyone. So now it's being used by the Oshicora loyalists as a code word that they can recognise each other by. If that's true, I can use that." Petrovitch worried at the piece of paper he'd written on. It was crumpled and creased and dog-eared. "I need to make a call."

"Is that code too? Code for please leave?"

"Yeah. But more for your benefit than mine." Petrovitch

wheeled his chair around his desk and across the floor. "I'm smart, right? Everyone says so."

"Smart and wise are two different things, Sam." She pushed the phone towards him.

"And so are safe and honourable." He picked up the handset and listened. No Japanese this time. "If it was you, stuck in that tower, your mother long dead, your father freshly murdered, no way out: wouldn't you want someone to help you?"

"Of course," said Pif, "although you have to admit you'd want that someone to be . . . I don't know."

"Not me, you mean."

"Not really." She pressed her fingers into her forehead. "The only language you speak fluently is mathematics. So what's the probability of you pulling this off? What's the probability of you throwing your life away for nothing?"

"That's why I'm about to swing the odds in my favour." He closed his eyes, trying to see the number he'd displayed on Chain's computer while he was supposed to be busy watching Sonja's messages. "Yeah, that's it."

He dialled, and heard ringing.

Then someone picked up and said: "*Da?*"

"Comrade Marchenkho? It's Petrovitch. Don't put the phone down, because we need to talk."

He lifted the earpiece slightly away from his head as Marchenkho vented his diseased spleen at him down the line.

"Oshicora's dead," said Petrovitch when he could get a word in.

"How do you know?"

"His daughter told me. You know of Hijo?"

"*Da.*"

"Killed his boss. Took control. Occupational hazard for you lot, I suppose. How's Yuri? Not got an itchy trigger finger yet?"

Marchenkho rumbled. "He says to remind you that his name is Grigori. What is it that you want, Petrovitch?"

"Apart from giving you the glad tidings that your greatest rival has been eliminated? How many men do you have, Marchenkho?"

"Enough," he said. "Women too."

"Good, because I want to borrow them. And you too, if you want to come for the ride. We're going to finish off the Oshicora Corporation once and for all."

"And when do you propose this happens?"

"That depends. Tomorrow morning good for you?"

Afterwards, he started sorting his desk, putting everything into neat piles by subject and looking through his old notebooks, seeing if there was anything else he needed to write.

"Convince me you're coming back," said Pif.

"Can't. Dead man walking now."

She sighed, and leafed through her own papers, and held up his earlier work. "This is going to be called the Petrovitch Solution, after the man who first discovered it. But I don't want this to be the only thing the world remembers him for."

"Most people don't even manage this: having an equation named after you is immortality."

"Sam . . ."

He sat back and stroked his nose. "How long have we known each other, Pif?"

"Two years. Roughly."

"Those are two years that I stole from someone. I cheated them by living. And for the few years before that. Hang on." Petrovitch found his bug-detecting wand and made a search of the room. He realised he should have done this before: Chain had had plenty of opportunity to plant one of his bugs earlier.

The lights on the wand flickered into the red as he moved it over his desk.

"Did Chain sit here?"

"Yes. Yes, I think so, while we were waiting for you."

"*Chyort.*" He got down on his hands and knees and looked underneath the tabletop. A sticky square of electronics was adhered to the wood towards the back. He got an edge up with a nail, then peeled it off. He emerged with it stuck to his thumb. "What do I have to say to you, Detective Inspector Harry Chain? You collect all this information, you work out what's going on, you plot and you plan. And yet nothing you do – that you say that you're allowed to do – makes any difference. You've had all the chances you needed and you chose not to take them, any of them, you spineless shrivelled little man. You are a pathetic waste of space and, unlike me, the world will forget you because you have never really lived. Goodbye."

Taking a pair of scissors, he cut the bug in two and flicked the halves into his bin.

"I never knew you were so eloquent."

"And all without the aid of vodka." Petrovitch sat down again and threw the now inert wand into the clear space on his desk. "Now where was I?"

"Cheating and stealing," she said.

"Yeah. In the life I had before, I stole some money. It's a little more complicated than that, though. My employer – my patron is a better word – was a man called Boris. He and his gang kidnapped rich people and ransomed them. They used me for technical support and in return I got books and somewhere warm and lit to read them. It was terrifying for the hostages, but it was fine for me. Fine, while the companies and trusts these people worked for paid up. Boris was OK as brutal thugs went: he kept his word. Probably the only good thing he taught me."

Pif's eyes were growing larger. "Sam!"

"It was St Petersburg in the aftermath of Armageddon. I needed to be able to do something where having a weak heart wasn't going to be a problem. My father died of radiation poisoning early on, and I needed not to be a burden on my mother and sister. I could even help out occasionally. If things went well, Boris was generous. Generous enough to keep the police sweet and ensure that no one ever betrayed him. Then it all started to go wrong. Some companies wouldn't pay up any more. Boris killed hostages and threw bodies in the river. Not a good time."

"I'm going to make some coffee," announced Pif. "I'm not sure I want to hear the end of this."

"For me? Please. I can promise you it gets better."

She looked at him on her way to the kettle. "Why now, Sam?"

"Because if I die, this story dies with me."

"Go on."

"There was this man. An American called Dalton. Rich, didn't take much care. Boris took him, asked for ten million US, I think. Dalton's company had a no-pay policy, so he was going to die when the money didn't turn up." Petrovitch looked up at the ceiling and blew out a thin stream of air. "I saved him."

"OK, that's a good thing."

"I took all his savings in return for keeping him alive."

"That's slightly more morally ambivalent."

"And of course, I cheated Boris too. Samuil Petrovitch is a construct, the man I wanted to become. He's three years older than I am, for a start. I don't have a degree. I don't have a scholarship. The money I'm using to fund my extravagant lifestyle is the money I stole from Dalton."

equations*of*life

Pif, her back to Petrovitch, poured boiling water on the coffee granules. "So what happened to him? The American?"

"He went home. He got married. He has kids, two of them, both genetically enhanced. He got his new life. And I got mine. I think, under the circumstances, we both got a good deal."

The spoon went round and round the mug, making little scraping noises as it went. "You've never been to university."

"Not until this one."

"So how come you're so brilliant at what you do?"

Petrovitch took it as a compliment. "Raw natural ability. I can't claim credit for that. But I did a lot of reading – more than a lot. Not just magnetohydrodynamics, but across the field. There are problems that I find solutions for in the strangest places. You can't know it all, but it helps if you know where to look."

She brought both coffees over, and put one mug into his grateful hands. "None of this explains why you're so willing to throw it all away."

"Doesn't it go some way to explain why I hold it lightly, though? The last few years have been a gift. I didn't deserve this, this peace I've had, the space to do what I want without having to worry about money or guns. It's over now. Even if Hijo and his assassins don't get me, Chain will end up waving a pair of handcuffs and an extradition order at me."

"It doesn't have to be over. You can run again."

"It was over the moment I grabbed Sonja Oshicora's hand. The moment, I suppose, when I decided to stop running and spit in the face of destiny. This is meant to be, all the crap that's happening. That I managed to hold it off for so long is a miracle in itself." Petrovitch leaned over his coffee, strong, hot, bitter: she knew how he liked it. "Now's the time to make a stand, no matter how suicidal it is."

Pif sighed. She wasn't convinced. "Is there no one who'll miss you? You said you had a sister, a mother."

"Not contacting them ever again was the price I had to pay for Boris leaving them alone. I never told them what I was doing, and they never asked. I disappeared. They thought I was dead, and I've given them no reason to suppose otherwise. Apart from that, no. I've made no friends, had no girlfriends, I've maybe a handful of acquaintances. No one's going to miss me." He took a mouthful of coffee, almost too hot to drink, and thought of his last sight of Sister Madeleine. "No one."

"Then how are you different from Inspector Chain?" Pif balanced her mug on a rough pile of his lab notes and knelt down in front of the desk. She rested her elbows on the edge and cradled her face in her hands.

"He was given the responsibility and powers of a policeman. What's he done with them? I got given the single opportunity to save Dalton, and what did I do? That he's walking around, living and breathing, spawning little Reconstructionists, is down to me. No one else. So yeah. I'm different from that lazy *sooksin*."

"Is this what it's like, then?" she said, eyes closed, dreaming. "People like us, we think differently, don't we? We are different. We do all the things that others do. We go out to parties and concerts, we go to conferences and drink and talk, we play music and games and we laugh and cry. But when it comes down to it, we don't actually need anyone else. We're happy doing what we do and having obligations interferes with that. Does that make us selfish, or something else?"

"I don't know. To them, I guess it is selfish. Me? I just have such a monstrous sense of self, I don't need to feel love. I don't even feel lonely." He watched Pif's hair beads swinging slightly in time with her breathing. "Sometimes I wonder what it might be like. To be with someone, well, who isn't me. And sometimes I think we don't even need ourselves. What's most important is to find out whether we're right or not."

"So what are you going to do?"

"I've run out of places to go. I can't go home. I can't travel on the tube with the guns. I don't think I can walk to Regent's Park: it's madness on the streets today. And I still don't think any of that was my fault." Petrovitch swilled his coffee around inside his mug and watched the play of light against the black surface. "It's against the rules, but I'll camp down here tonight and meet Marchenkho in the morning."

"I've got a better idea," said Pif. "Come back to my room. I'll cook something. We'll break open a bottle of something pretending to be wine. We can talk about work and play computer games until it's stupid late, and you can crash out on the couch. Once I've done some tidying up, that is. I'm not used to guests."

Petrovitch looked up. "That would be . . . that would be nice. You have remembered that Hijo is trying to kill me?"

"Let him come. There are paycops on the door, and if he bribes them, well, we're ready."

"We?"

She got to her feet and pulled the Jericho out of her bag. Then in a few deft moves, she'd stripped it down to its component parts. "You see," she said, "where I grew up, in the expensive part of Lagos, we had to protect ourselves from people like you."

She reassembled the gun just as efficiently and, when she'd done, she assumed a shooter's stance; legs apart, arms braced, good eye over the sights.

"I wasn't expecting that," said Petrovitch.

"And neither will they." She flicked the safety catch on and dropped the gun back in her bag. She smiled.

21

He woke with a start, in unfamiliar surroundings. The blanket wasn't his, and neither were the cushions he'd left slack-jawed drool on. The Norinco was under his left hand, resting on his belly.

He was at Pif's. She was at the other end of the sofa, in an attitude much like his, but a lot less troubled. One of her feet was jammed between his hip and the upholstery, and her hand draped artfully from under her stark white duvet, pointing at the – her, he supposed now – Jericho.

The gun had joined the debris on the floor. Stained plates, mugs marked with dribbles of red wine, two handsets for her games console, shoes, socks, their trousers, her jumper, paper, books, disks, cartridges, memory sticks, coins, paperclips, cards.

There had to be a clock somewhere – at least something with a built-in clock, when Petrovitch's myopic search of the walls revealed nothing. His glasses had to be close to hand, but he was reluctant to swing his legs off their perch in case he trod on them.

He patted the carpet, found nothing, then reached back over his head and knocked against a low table. There. He jammed them on his face.

The blank screen of the TV held no clues, but at least he could see the remote. He snagged it and pressed the on and mute buttons simultaneously.

Pif stirred, wrinkling her nose and creasing her forehead.

He couldn't get a channel. He scrolled through all of them, one to one hundred, and there was nothing but snow.

"Pif?" he said, touching her toes. "Pif, are you on cable or broadcast?"

Her eyelids flickered open, and she made smacking noises with her mouth. "Cable."

"It wasn't off last night. It is now."

"Oh." She started to close her eyes again. "Do I remember you saying that it wasn't your fault?"

"It's not. I don't see how it can be."

"Can't you call your bot-net off?"

"Yeah. I could, if I had access. If I had my rat, I could get on through a satellite." He still didn't know the time. "The attack should have fallen apart by now."

"Worried?"

"Some. And not just about the netcops coming calling." Petrovitch cleared a space for his feet and pulled the blanket around him. He put his gun on the table. "At least Hijo didn't make an appearance."

"Hmm," she said sleepily.

There was a clock on her microwave. He stood up, taking the blanket with him to cover his bare legs, and picked his way into the kitchen area. He stared at the blue glowing lights.

"I'm going to have to go. Marchenkho is one of those people who you really don't want to be late for."

"You walking?"

"I'm feeling better, and it's not like it's far. And it's not really something you can call a cab for." He retrieved his trousers and struggled into them. "Oshicora Tower, please, and hurry: I'm in an armed gang and we're storming it this morning."

"Just thinking about your heart."

"It's not like I need it, long-term." He pulled his socks on and started to lace up his boots.

Pif stretched and shuffled to a sitting position. "You want anything else? A coffee?"

"My adrenaline will do just fine. Umbrella?"

"There's one by the door. Somewhere."

"I'll find it if I need it."

"Do you suppose it's still raining?"

"I can't imagine there's any more rain left in the sky." Petrovitch moved to the window and twitched the curtain. Outside was balanced between night and day. He looked up to the underside of the sky, and caught the red glow from the base of the clouds; looked down to see the shining courtyard below, bounded by four slabs of window-pierced concrete.

"Don't throw your life away, Sam. Make someone take it from you. Make it expensive." She held out the butt of the Jericho to him.

"Keep it, just in case. Anyway, I've only got two hands." It was time to go. He picked up the Norinco and eased it into his waistband. The Beretta he stuffed low into his sock. "Maybe I'll see you around?"

"Last chance to back out," she said, resting her chin on the arm of the sofa.

equationsoflife

"I'm so far past last chances that last chance is nothing but a dot in the distance behind me." Petrovitch stepped across the floor like he was picking his way through a minefield. He put his hand on the doorknob. "Lock it when I've gone."

There didn't seem to be anything else to say, so he left.

Outside in the corridor, he leaned his head against the cool white wall and took a steadying breath. If he'd been in his own domik, he wouldn't have been alone. There would have been corridor dwellers or shift workers or whores or dealers or muggers. In a student accommodation block with paycops on the doors downstairs, his were the only footsteps he heard as he skipped down the stairwell.

Living like Pif did, insulated from the outside, in a place which didn't stink of rust and mould, where your neighbours weren't plotting to kill you and take your space – it was different.

And for Petrovitch, who'd always clung by his fingernails to the edge of existence, it came as a revelation. He'd deliberately chosen the domiks over this bright, clean, warm life. The corner of his mouth twitched with the realisation that perhaps he'd made a mistake.

The paycop on the door let him out with a grunt. The screen on his desk was a storm of static.

Suddenly, it was cold. The damp dawn air goosebumped the flesh on his bare arms, and he regretted the loss of his jacket. Thought followed thought; he'd lost a lot more than just a piece of clothing. He hunched his back against the weather, and set off across the campus.

There was one more airlock of comfortable warmth to enter. He passed through the foyer, showed his singed student card to those on duty, and hesitated at the main doors.

Something was wrong, and it took him a moment to see what

it was. The street outside was all but deserted, and he'd never seen it like that before. He turned to the guards, who seemed to have caught the same sense of disquiet as he had. They huddled close together at the reception desk, talking quietly amongst themselves and casting the occasional glance through the windows.

A car, two cars, went by with their headlights blue-white bright, but then nothing. The pavements, the same ones that he was used to grinding his way along everyday, were wet with moisture that reflected the street lights. There were people, just not enough of them for him to feel comfortable. He'd stick out, exposed in plain sight.

The clock on the wall clicked to eleven minutes past six. He was going to be late. He felt the cold press of the gun at the base of his spine, the weight on his right ankle.

He tapped the door mechanism. "What's the worst that can happen?" he said to himself as he waited, and waited, for the door to open. After a while, he shoved at it instead, and eventually it wheezed aside enough for him to slip out.

The cold returned, and he assumed his usual head-down posture for the road.

Except that it was impossible to maintain. There were too few pedestrians. He felt compelled to look at them, commit the cardinal sin of making eye contact for a brief moment as they passed. Everyone had the same expression, one that showed that deep down, no matter their bluff, they were afraid.

Petrovitch could only assume that his eyes held that same fear.

He crossed the road, walking at a diagonal. In all his years in the Metrozone, he'd never done such a thing. He passed darkened shops that he couldn't remember ever closing. Their signs were illuminated, but inside was grey gloom.

He turned out of Exhibition Road, turned right. Across, on the other side, was Hyde Park, just as still as it had been yesterday. Yet today, it wasn't the stillness of death that emanated from the miasma. It was the silence of a held breath.

It wasn't only the city that was waiting for something to happen. Petrovitch pushed his hands up inside his T-shirt sleeves, and hurried along to Hyde Park corner.

Marchenkho wasn't there, and Petrovitch had no watch or phone to tell him the right time. He could be late, or early. The only thing he was certain of was that he had the right day. So he stood under the Wellington Arch while a dozen vaguely human-shaped piles of bags and blankets slept around him, making the most of the shelter.

In the distance, he heard the sound of bells ringing the half-hour. Now Marchenkho was late. He jumped up and down and swung his hands around, both trying to keep warm and wishing to evaporate the cold sweat that had broken out across his body. He shivered.

In the distance, coming up Grosvenor Place, was a line of black cars. At first, he thought it another strange computer-directed aberration, but then he saw more clearly. The cars, six of them, circled the monument once, and then parked up against the kerb.

People, Slavs like himself, slowly emerged into the dawn air, well wrapped up to conceal their firearms. Petrovitch made sure both his hands were on show as he approached.

"Hey, Yuri."

Grigori narrowed his eyes and raised his chin. "Petrovitch. I lose, then."

"What?"

"I bet fifty euros you wouldn't show." He leaned against his limousine and knocked on the rear window. It slid down.

"*Dobroe utro, tovarish.*"

Petrovitch peered in. "Yeah. I can't believe you have a Zil."

"Why not?" said Marchenkho. "Zil is a good car. Reliable. Armour plated."

"Parts must be a bitch." Petrovitch ran his hand across the polished, waxed roof, leaving a trail of sticky fingerprints.

"With money, anything is possible." Marchenkho stroked his moustache. "Are you armed?"

"You don't bring a knife to a gunfight."

"This is good. What do you need?"

"Nine millimetre for the Norinco. Point three two for the Beretta."

Marchenkho nodded to Grigori, who went to the boot of the car and opened it, revealing neatly labelled cartons and long cases. "Petrovitch, aren't you cold?"

"I'm freezing my tits off, truth be told. My jacket got incinerated by the Paradise militia."

"What did you do to them, that they would set your clothing on fire?"

Petrovitch stamped hard on the ground. "It's a long, and probably pointless story. They weren't after me, anyway."

"Getting caught up in other people's battles again? I thought you were supposed to be a smart man." His moustache twitched as he smiled mirthlessly. "So many enemies for one so young."

Grigori handed him two small cardboard cartons, heavy with bullets. He watched as Petrovitch tried to find somewhere on him to put them, then shrugged off his long black leather coat.

"Here," he said.

Petrovitch looked blankly at him. "I can't do that," he said when he finally realised.

"I have more coats, more clothes, suits, shoes, jeans, than I can ever wear. Take it. Look on it as an example of socialism in action." Grigori draped it over Petrovitch's shoulders. The collar smelt of cologne.

"You look fit to be in my company now," said Marchenkho. "Get in."

Petrovitch dropped a carton into each of the side pockets of his coat, and pulled it around him as he slid onto the long back seat.

There were three people opposite him: two men and a woman, each cradling a Kalashnikov.

"Leon, Valentina, Ziv. This is the kid I told you about."

"Yeah. Whatever he said was a lie." Petrovitch slid the Beretta from his sock and sprung the clip.

The woman called Valentina shook her ponytail. "He said you were fearless."

Petrovitch looked across at Marchenkho. "Does that mean you like me?"

"It means I have decided not to kill you. This is good, no?" Marchenkho glanced down at the little pistol Petrovitch was busy reloading. "Your *peesa* is very small."

"That's what the other guy said, just before I killed him."

Marchenkho shook with laughter. "See? See how he looks like a kitten but roars like a lion."

The driver's door slammed, and Grigori started the Zil.

"Tell me," said Marchenkho. "What happened to your American friend?"

"Sorenson? I don't know. Oshicora screwed him over, and then Inspector Chain did the same thing, only worse."

"But Oshicora is dead."

"Sorenson won't know. If he's gone feral, he'll never find out. He'll spend the rest of his days hiding from someone who no longer exists." Petrovitch tucked the Beretta in his pocket, and reached around for the Norinco. "I guess I might know what that's like."

"Perhaps you can find him, when we have done what we came to do." Marchenkho nodded to dour Ziv, who tapped Grigori on the shoulder. The car pulled away and started down Piccadilly.

"Did you have any problems this morning?" asked Petrovitch. He fed fat bullets into the Norinco's magazine.

"Why? What do you know?" Marchenkho stroked his chin, and leaned over, resting his solid bulk against Petrovitch's shoulder. He radiated menace.

Petrovitch slapped the magazine back home and rested the gun on his knees. He chose his words carefully. "Something's happening. I don't know what. I can't say I like it."

And just like that, the Ukrainian changed moods. He rumbled deep in his chest. "My mobile refuses to connect. My computer cannot talk to others. My breakfast is accompanied by white noise, not the news. This is not good. But the streets are clear. The cameras are off. Even if this is for just one day, it could not be better. We are the Lords of Misrule, and there will be no one to see the mischief we make. Once we are done here, Oshicora has other operations in the East End that we wish to see closed down."

Grigori was slowing, making a big U-turn in front of the Oshicora Tower, the other cars blocking the road in front and behind, screeching tyres, disgorging people.

A shabby figure in a brown trenchcoat looked balefully at them from the kerbside.

"Yeah, should have mentioned this earlier." Petrovitch waited for the Zil to stop, then opened the door. "Chain might have overheard us talking."

22

Chain frowned as guns and people spilled out onto the pavement. He turned to Petrovitch with an expression like a cross tortoise. "You don't think you're going to get away with this, do you?" he said.

"As has been pointed out," said Petrovitch, "today is the only day we'll get away with this." He swirled his coat-tails and admitted that it did look pretty cool. "Do you think you can stop us?"

"I came to try."

"Yeah," grinned Petrovitch, "you and whose army?"

"Oh very droll. I appreciate you're resourceful but it won't save you." Chain fished around in his pockets and found his own gun. "I should arrest you right now."

Petrovitch reached behind him for the Norinco. "Maybe you should, but you can stand to wait until later."

"I suppose I could," admitted Chain with a shrug. "Perhaps it's time I cut you some slack."

Marchenkho stood beside Petrovitch and slapped him hard on the back. "All friends now? This is good."

"About all this," said Chain, "I don't have the manpower to rescue Sonja Oshicora: you know that, don't you?"

"We do," said Petrovitch.

"So, let's get on with it." Chain patted his pockets for his police card. He flipped it open and tucked it facing outwards from his top pocket. "Has one of you got a plan?"

Marchenkho looked at Chain, then at Petrovitch. "Of course," he growled. "What sort of half-arsed organisation do you think I run?"

Petrovitch shrugged. "I had the idea that I was just going to walk up to the front desk and start the revolution from there. If it goes *pizdets*, we do it the old-fashioned way: straight down the middle, lots of smoke."

"And you have some reason to believe that might work?" Chain looked up and down the height of the Oshicora Tower.

"Yeah. Yeah, I do. I'm doing the talking, though." Petrovitch flicked the Norinco's safety to off.

"Wait, wait," said Marchenkho, waving his large hands. "This will not do. My people cannot see me stay behind while you walk to the tower. It's no good. Grigori, walkie-talkie."

Grigori placed the fist-sized device in Marchenkho's upturned palm.

"You come when called, *da*?" He waited for Grigori to nod. "No hanging around like some *krisha* who takes my money and does nothing for it."

"Now can we go?" said Petrovitch. "It's not getting any earlier."

He strode off across the plaza. The fountains that should have played with the early morning light were still, just pools of trembling water. Aware of the other two men behind him, he kept his gaze on the tower.

There were no guards on the door, and there should have been, no matter what time of day it was. He anticipated being challenged, each and every step he took closer. Or was it going to be a sniper on a neighbouring rooftop instead?

"I never thought I'd say this," said Chain, trotting up beside him, "but it's too quiet."

"What have you heard, Chain? What's going on? And don't say this is all my fault."

"I don't believe that any more. I do know that the Metrozone Authority is shutting everything off in stages and starting again from the ground up. We have a couple of hours, tops. After that, everything will be live again."

"It's going to take longer than that to get it all working. Everything's connected, Chain. There just has to be one wrong thing somewhere and it gets everywhere." Petrovitch glanced behind him, past the striding bulk of Marchenkho. Figures were spreading out across the concourse, ducking down behind the abstract granite shapes and crouching behind the lips of pools. "Why is there no one out front?"

"One of two reasons. One of which is that they're not expecting us."

"The other being that they are. Marchenkho, how tight is your *organitskaya*?"

"We are all comrades together. We all have as much to gain or lose as the next man. *Da?*" The Ukrainian's olive-green greatcoat flapped as he walked, flashing the presence of his shoulder holster. "Since the last purge, we have stayed secure."

"That doesn't fill me with confidence." Petrovitch pressed his glasses hard up on his nose. "Can you see anyone inside?"

The reception area was in darkness, but they were close enough to make out vague shapes moving against the glass doors; a hand, a face.

"I've seen this before. So have you, Petrovitch." Chain started to jog towards the tower.

"What does he mean?" asked Marchenkho, holding Petrovitch's arm.

"Come with me and I'll show you."

They caught up with the detective as the tower darkened the sky. It became all too clear that there were people trapped inside; some of the glass panels had starred through attempts to break them, and the reflections of the three men distorted as the doors were shaken. But there seemed to be no way out.

"*Hivno!*" grunted Marchenkho and put his hand on his gun. "Some answers, now."

"If it's computer controlled, it's gone wrong."

Chain pressed his police card to the glass. "Back off," he shouted. "I'm going to try and shoot my way in."

"That won't work," said Petrovitch. "But if you insist, let me take cover before the ricochet drills a neat hole in my skull."

Those inside crushed themselves tighter to be near to Chain. He couldn't shoot even if he wanted to. "Got a better idea?"

"I do," said Marchenkho. He spoke into his walkie-talkie. "Grigori? We need Tina and her box of tricks."

Meanwhile, Petrovitch was shoving Chain out of the way. "Not like that. Like this." He got level with the staring eyes of one frantic *sarariman* and said haltingly: "*Shinkansen ha mata hashirou.*"

"What?" said Chain. "What did you say?"

"*Zatknis!*" Petrovitch pushed him away again, raised his voice and repeated. "*Shinkansen ha mata hashirou.*"

The man inside blinked for the first time. He turned away,

his face losing definition behind the smoked glass. Then he came back and nodded, mouthing "*hai*".

Valentina slid a steel briefcase onto the floor next to him. She clicked the catches with her long fingers and opened the lid.

"Nice," said Petrovitch, inspecting the contents.

"Do your job. Get them away from the doors." She busied herself with a lump of plastic explosive, forming it into a disc in her hands.

Petrovitch mimed what the woman was intending to do, including the explosion that would follow. They didn't understand until she started pressing detonators into the grey wads of plastique she'd stuck to where she hoped the opening mechanism was. Then they moved in a clump, all clutching at each other, as far as the banked reception desks.

"Ready," she said, briefcase in one hand, roll of thin wire in the other. She trotted towards the first fountain, trailing cable behind her. Marchenkho, Chain and Petrovitch followed, and squatted down next to her behind the hard cover.

"You do remember you're just supposed to blow the doors off, don't you?" said Chain, and received a withering look in response.

"Amateurs," muttered Valentina, and opened her briefcase again for the battery pack. She wired in the loose ends of cable and flipped the safety cover off the big red button. "Cover your ears," she said.

She pressed the button, and the silence was broken by the sound of a single handclap, magnified out of all proportion. The air stiffened and relaxed, now tainted with a burnt chemical odour.

They peered over the parapet. At first, the doors were obscured by smoke; then, as it cleared, it seemed that the door, and its glass was still in place.

Slowly, gracefully, the frame fell outward and landed with a second concussion on the paving slabs. Still the glass didn't break.

"Excellent, Tina," said Marchenkho, and he stood up, pulling out his gun in one fluid motion. "Come on. You want to live for ever?"

"Good point, well made," said Petrovitch, and he held the Norinco high. They ran for the doors as those now freed streamed out, coughing from the fumes.

As they emerged, they scattered. They ran as if from the devil.

"Catch one," called Petrovitch, and he watched as Marchenkho straight-armed a middle-aged man in the face. He'd barely hit the floor before he'd been hauled up to tiptoe by his tie. "Not quite what I meant, but yeah, OK."

Blood was streaming down the man's face from his nose, staining his crumpled shirt. He was almost incoherent with terror.

"Where's Sonja Oshicora?" asked Petrovitch.

The man stared at him, at Marchenkho, at the building he'd just left at such speed. Japanese phrases dribbled from his lips, none of which Petrovitch could hope to understand.

"Sonja Oshicora. Where is she? Which floor is she on?"

Marchenkho drew his fist back for another strike, and finally the man seemed scared enough of being beaten to talk. "Miss Sonja gone."

"Gone? Dead?"

"Not dead. Gone. In night."

"Where did Hijo take her?"

The man focused on Petrovitch, and explained the best he

could whilst being choked. "Not Hijo-san. Miss Sonja run away. Hijo-san look for Miss Sonja in city."

Petrovitch pushed his glasses up. "She escaped? When?"

"In night. This night."

"*Pizdets*. Put him down and let him go."

Marchenkho dropped the man, who scrambled to his feet and ran as fast as he could away towards Piccadilly. "She is not there?"

"Apparently she didn't need our help after all." Petrovitch watched the suited man go, then turned back to the Oshicora Tower. "Doesn't explain what's going on in there, though."

"Shall we see?" Marchenkho squared his shoulders and stepped through the doorway into the foyer. Chain was already picking his way through the objects that had been unsuccessfully used to try and batter a way out – chairs, tables, fire extinguishers, metal supports, earthenware pots with spilt soil and broken trunks.

"They panicked." He kicked a broken tabletop aside. "Wouldn't have happened with Oshicora still alive."

"It probably wouldn't have happened with Hijo still in the building, either."

"Oh?"

"Yeah. I bet he's taken all the men with guns out onto the street to look for Sonja, who's escaped all on her own. I'm sorry, gentlemen. I seem to have wasted your time."

Marchenkho holstered his gun and put his hands on his hips. "No, *tovarisch*. I would have paid good money to see this. My only regret is that I did not bring a bomb big enough to demolish the whole building."

"I might have drawn the line at that," said Chain. "So are we sure this place is empty? On a normal day, there would have been a thousand *nikkeijin* here."

Petrovitch shrugged. "They might still be struggling to work from wherever they live. Imagine their surprise when they finally get here." He cocked his head, and listened.

"I hear it too," said Marchenkho.

"It's the lifts." Petrovitch held his gun out in front of him and moved stealthily around the reception area. The row of blank lift doors behind it hummed with movement.

"Why are there no lights, but these have power?" Chain drew his own pistol and watched the floor indicators above each door flicker and change.

Marchenkho squashed the talk button on his walkie talkie. "Grigori. Squad to the foyer. Now."

"The thing is, are those numbers going up or down?" Petrovitch's question was answered by chimes, one after another, as every lift reached the ground floor. "And why are we standing here, waiting to find out?"

The doors opened simultaneously and, at first, none of them could comprehend what they were looking at: in each lift, there was an uneven mass of cloth and pale flesh, like a jumbled pile of shop mannequins. Then the pooled blood started to seep out across the threshold and onto the pale stone floor. The dark red stain flowed outwards, merging, growing.

"I think it's time for us to go," said Petrovitch in a whisper.

Grigori skidded to a halt behind them, the barrel of his Kalashnikov searching for a target.

"A tactical change of plan," said Marchenkho. "Retreat."

Petrovitch waited for a few seconds before joining them, spending that time imagining the final moments of those trapped as they fell the full height of the lift shaft, the instant that tangled freefall became killing impact.

"Petrovitch! Move!" shouted Chain.

But he didn't. He was busy realising that every lift would

have had to collect people from every floor, then taken them back to the top to drop them to their deaths. It was a deliberate act. Someone had murdered them all.

"Oi!"

"Yeah. Coming." The lake of blood had reached his toes, and as he backed away, he left sticky footprints behind him in a trail, all the way outside.

23

Marchenkho had brought vodka as well as guns. A tray was laden with glasses and the bottle was upended over it. The sharp alcohol fumes burned the sweet, heavy smell of blood from their noses.

Petrovitch threw his glass into the gutter like a good Russian, and Marchenkho's crew followed suit to prove they were better Ukrainians.

"If anyone has an explanation for this, I would very much like to hear it." Marchenkho went back for a second glass and shuddered as he drank.

"The building attacked them," said Petrovitch, and suddenly all eyes were on him. Self-conscious under all the attention, he adjusted his glasses. "It lured them into the lifts and then killed them."

"Buildings do not . . ."

"Yeah," interrupted Petrovitch, "and cars don't do that either, except they did yesterday. If you have a better idea, then let's hear it."

Marchenkho rumbled to himself. "Someone must be control-ling the lifts, to make them do that." He was shaken, the man who had committed his own calculated atrocities.

"The same person who was controlling the cars, blocking the internet, the phones, paralysing the tube? They'd have to be very busy. Superhumanly busy." He shook his head. "Virus. Some sort of virus."

"Viruses do not hunt people down and send them to their deaths." Marchenkho launched his glass at the kerbstone where it shattered into glittering shards. "I know this much: only we can be that vicious."

"Your only problem is that the internet is swamped. There's no traffic. It's impossible to control anything at the moment."

"I hate to interrupt," said Chain. Of all of them, only he hadn't drunk. "But can anyone else hear that?"

Marchenkho waved for quiet. There were two distinct sets of sounds, neither of them good. Distant gunfire, intense bursts of automatic weapons and single cracks of pistols. Closer in, not just near but all around them, a repetitive click, one short beat every second.

Puzzled heads turned, searching for the source.

"The cameras. It's coming from the cameras." Chain pointed across the road at the CCTV pylon attached to the side of the brown-stone building. "There are speakers underneath."

"So why are they ticking at us?" Petrovitch scanned the plaza as the clicking echoed around them, bouncing off the high walls and repeated from street corners.

"It's the radiation warning system," Chain said with wonder. "I never knew it still worked."

"Radiation?" said Marchenkho. "What is this that says there is radiation? Can it be trusted?"

"If it's an automatic system, I wouldn't trust it to tell the time at the moment. Ignoring it is the sensible choice. I'm more worried about the war that seems to be starting uncomfortably close." Grigori was standing close by, and Petrovitch asked him: "Which way?"

Grigori listened. "North?" he ventured. "Regent's Park?"

"Yeah, maybe. The natives were always restless. Or it could be Hijo."

"I forgot about your girlfriend."

"*Pashol na khui.*"

"You're risking your life for her."

"I'm only doing it because Hijo pissed me off." Petrovitch took one last look around. "Thanks for letting me keep the coat, but I'm done here. North it is."

He got as far as the white line when the speakers chimed, three rising notes.

"Warning. Warning. Warning. New machine jihad. Warning. Warning. Warning. New machine jihad." The voice was a woman's, very proper, very English.

A dull concussion drifted across the city, and Chain's attention was diverted. But not Petrovitch's.

"What does this mean?" he called. When Chain threw up his hands, he came back. "You're supposed to know these things!"

"It's a radiation warning system. Someone in the control centre presses the button when there's a warning of radiation, not a . . ."

"Warning. Warning. Warning. New machine jihad."

"One of those. I don't know what a new machine jihad is. I've never heard of one, and I don't know why I should be worried about it when someone – other than us – is using explosives in the central Metrozone."

The alert was played twice more, then stopped. The clicking returned.

Marchenkho twitched his moustache. "No matter. The tower has fallen, but if we are to destroy Oshicora's organisation utterly, we must strike now. We will crush our enemies while they are still reeling from their losses. Our success depends on our speed."

Chain coughed politely. "Can we talk about this for a minute?"

"Talk? I thought you wanted this, Harry Chain." Marchenkho clapped his hands and called for order. Drivers started their engines and their passengers climbed in. "There is no time, no point to talk any more. Petrovitch, are you going to go and search for the girl?"

"Yes. Yes I am," said Petrovitch. "I think I know where to start looking."

"If I hear something — something other than the sounds of our glorious victory — I will try and get word to you." Marchenkho's brows furrowed as he turned to look in the direction of Regent's Park.

"Yeah. Thanks, Marchenkho. You might be an unreconstructed Stalinist, but you're OK."

"I will probably still have to kill you," he said, laughing, "but not today. For now, *do svidanija*." He climbed into his Zil, and even before the door closed, it was pulling away.

"Everyone seems to be leaving, Chain." He checked the safety on the Norinco. He didn't want to shoot his foot off by accident. "And I'm pretty certain you need to going too. The Metrozone needs you, as terrifying as the idea might be."

"Warning. Warning. Warning. New machine jihad."

Petrovitch stumbled as he walked away, and had to use a lamp-post to catch himself. He hadn't imagined it. He'd heard those words before. He knew where to get the answer as to what fresh hell it meant.

He ran, with Chain's unanswered questions shouted after him.

He ran across Piccadilly and cut down a side street. His coat flapped, but he no longer concerned himself as to how cool it looked.

As he emerged onto Park Lane, he faced the grey space of Hyde Park. It was no longer still. It was moving, crawling like rotten meat.

There was no time for anything any more. He ran towards Speakers' Corner to find a crowd of people barely alive, staring in slack-jawed awe up at a bald-headed madman who had, for the occasion, smeared a circle of black grease on his forehead.

They came from Hyde Park, shambling from the open gates, dragging their emaciated legs to hear the prophet speak.

Petrovitch couldn't get near him without pushing through the press of bodies. His heart was already skipping beats and fluttering behind his ribs, and he could feel the capacitors charging; the electric tension before the lightning. Then the prophet spotted him from his crate-top perch and declaimed:

"See? See the machine-man who gives and gets life: the true symbiot who does not fear the coming age!"

Charge raced through Petrovitch, and he fell to his knees. The pain was agony, the passing of it relief. He was dimly aware that he was staring at a pair of filthy feet shod only in sandals.

He swallowed the metallic taste in his mouth and looked up. The shaven-headed man with the oil mark looked down.

"Stand up, my brother. We are all equal beneath the machine."

Petrovitch stood shakily. He would have put his hand out for support, but he was afraid of what he might touch.

"I . . ." He swallowed again. His mouth was desert-dry. "How did you know about this new machine jihad before everyone else?"

The prophet smiled. His teeth were yellow, rotting. "The Machine chose me to proclaim the new order. The Machine is one and many. I am but the first believer." As he spoke, his eyes flickered, as if he was reading text from a page.

"How did it choose you?"

The man put his hand inside his shirt and brought out his mobile phone. He held it reverently as he would a relic. "I received its holy oracle."

Petrovitch looked at the chipped, dented device. "Do you speak to it?"

"It speaks to me! I would not dare question the Machine." He snatched the phone away as Petrovitch reached for it. "Are you worthy?"

"Yeah," said Petrovitch, starting to lose his temper. "Just get God on the line. I hope he talks more sense than you."

The prophet pressed two buttons: God was apparently now on speed-dial. He presented the phone with a bow. Petrovitch plucked it out of the man's dirt-encrusted fingers and held it gingerly to his ear.

It was ringing.

Then, with a click, the line was live.

"Hello? It's Petrovitch."

There came a deep silence, and afterwards what seemed like a sigh. *"Shinkansen ha mata hashirou."* It was the same voice that had spoken to him yesterday.

"I know that. What's a new machine jihad?"

"The New Machine Jihad."

"Do you speak for this jihad group, or is it something separate?" He swapped hands. His left arm was tired, achy. That didn't bode well. "What's it got to do with Oshicora?"

"I am," said the voice.

The answer didn't make sense. "Who am I talking to?"

Silence.

"Look, this is not helping. Sonja has escaped from Hijo. I don't know where she is. If you want my help, you have to talk to me now, because I'm being surrounded by an increasing number of disease-ridden crazies and your self-appointed prophet wants his phone back."

Silence again, and Petrovitch growled his frustration.

"Fine. *Eto mnye do huya.* Did you kill all those people in the Oshicora Tower?"

"Save her," said the voice. "Save Sonja."

"That's what I was trying to do! I had it covered. I had an army, but when I got there, she'd gone and you'd slaughtered all the workers." He finished through gritted teeth. "You should have talked to me first."

"Save her," it repeated.

"Then tell me where she is!"

Silence.

"Now or never. If I don't know where to start, I can't do what you want."

"Paradise," it said and, with that, the call ended.

Petrovitch tossed the phone back to the prophet, who beheld him with awe. "You spoke to the Machine."

"Yeah, whoever that is. For sure, English isn't their first language." He turned slowly. He was completely encircled, ten deep, by people who'd shambled out of Hyde Park. "Can you get them to move out of my way?"

"But the Machine gave you a mission. We are all under the Machine: your task is ours too."

Petrovitch froze. For a moment, he terrified himself with the mental image of leading a horde of barely living corpses with a bald, ragged prophet by his side.

"OK. What the Machine told me to do is for me alone. But it gave me a message for you too, first believer." The prophet was hanging on his every word. "He wants you to take care of these people: find food, clothes, medical supplies for them. Just take whatever you need, wherever you find it."

The man nodded vigorously, then started to think. "Won't that be stealing? Won't someone stop us?"

"The New Machine Jihad changes all the rules." Petrovitch was warming to his subject. "Go now. Go with the blessing of the Machine."

He was willing it to work. The prophet stared through him with his flickering eyes, then held up his hand. Not that there was any talking beforehand, but the mob's attention was now on him, not the pale man in the black coat.

"Brothers! Sisters! Isn't it like I said? The Machine cares for us. We live under its benevolent rule. We're going to go and find food, because the Machine needs us to be strong. We need to be strong, so we can obey its orders. With me, brothers. With me, sisters!" Keeping his arm aloft, he walked through the gathered people.

And they followed him. Petrovitch stood quite still until the last of them had trailed off in the direction of Paddington. Then he let his shoulders sag. He put his hand on his chest, just to make sure that his heart was still beating.

"New Machine Jihad? *Ootebya nyetu peeski*, getting me to do your dirty work for you." He checked his guns, and started north, up the Edgware Road.

A quarter of the way up the deserted road, he smelled burning. Halfway up, he spotted a large group of people making their way down towards him. He couldn't make out the details due to the haze, but he was certain that one of them was flying a white flag.

Behind them, over the flyover, the Paradise housing complex was wreathed in dark smoke. Only the very tops of the towers rose above the chaos below.

The man carrying the flag resolved into a priest waving one of the choir robes Petrovitch hadn't previously wrecked or borrowed. Then came a gaggle of a couple of hundred . . . refugees was the only word to describe them, some of them clutching bags, some of them children, some of them holding cloths to their mouths and noses against the acrid chemical stink.

Lastly, Sister Madeleine, Vatican-approved gun in her hand. She should have been checking the street behind her, guarding her back and those with her. Instead, she watched Petrovitch get closer and closer, until he and Father John were face to face.

"Small world," said Petrovitch.

24

"What are you doing here?" said Father John. The hand that clutched his makeshift flagpole was bleeding through a bandage.

"I'd be lying if I said I'd come to see you." Petrovitch could see that they'd left in a hurry. They weren't dressed for an orderly evacuation. Some were dressed for bed. "I take it they found you at home this time?"

Father John brushed his wayward hair from his forehead. His scalp was also bleeding, and he smeared fresh streaks of red across his skin. "They blew up the police station. Demolished it completely, broke every window round about. Then they just came swarming across the Marylebone Road."

"By they, I take it you think it was the Paradise militia?"

"Who else?"

"I've got a pretty good idea who." There was smoke drifting down the road. "What's on fire?"

"My church." Father John flexed his knuckles and dared

Petrovitch to smirk. "And you still haven't answered the question. "What are you doing here? Looting?"

"Don't be a *zhopa*. I'm going to find Sonja Oshicora. The New Machine Jihad tell me she's in Paradise."

The priest looked puzzled. "The who?"

"No, the New Machine Jihad. I think they're the ones behind all the weird computer shit."

"You can't go to Paradise," said Sister Madeleine, over the heads of everyone.

"Yeah. I'm going to do it anyway."

"But they'll kill you," she said.

"I'm officially dead already." He stuck his hands in his pockets and felt the weight of the guns, the bullets, his soul. A fresh outbreak of gunfire clattered down a side street. There was a collective flinch.

"I need to get these people to safety," said Father John quickly. "What can you tell me about the centre?"

"It's pretty quiet. Where are you heading?"

"A church on Mount Street."

"Then avoid Hyde Park. Take the long route round."

The father held his flag up again and waved his ragged column on. They streamed around Petrovitch, scared not just of what they'd left behind, but of what lay ahead of them. He couldn't blame them.

As the crowd flowed and thinned, he could see Sister Madeleine striding towards him. She came closer, and as she walked past him, she deliberately looked away. A few seconds later, she stopped, clenching her empty fist. The others carried on without her.

"What is it that you want from me, Sam?"

"I don't want anything from you. I want you to go."

She still refused to face him. "Why is finding Sonja Oshicora so important?"

"I promised that I would. But that was before the New Machine Jihad crashed every information system in the Metrozone. Now, doing what it wants might be the only way to get it to stop." He stared at her tall, broad back. "Something else too. I think I might actually be doing the right thing for a change. I'm not the only one looking for her, but I'm not going to put a bullet in her head when I find her."

Finally, someone noticed the nun's absence and told Father John.

"Sister Madeleine. With us, please," he shouted.

"Do you know how difficult you make this for me?" she said.

Petrovitch didn't, although he was both hoping and fearing that she might show him.

"Sister? Now."

She looked over her shoulder at him. She was crying. "Tell me honestly: what is it you want?"

"I . . ." Petrovitch didn't know how to articulate the feeling he had inside.

Sister Madeleine ground her foot on the tarmac and took a step away from him.

"I want to make a difference," he blurted, then took several deep breaths. "That sounds stupid. I could have hidden, I could have run. I didn't. Whatever crappy motive I had to start with, I want to do this. I have to."

"How very Russian," she said, wiping at her eyes. "You won't last five minutes without me. Come on."

"Why? Where are you going?"

"I thought you wanted to go to Paradise." She moved to a shop doorway, and checked left and right.

Petrovitch jogged after her. He saw Father John usher his flock behind a row of abandoned cars, then start back up the road towards them. His stiff movements and set face showed his mood.

The nun was busy pulling her robes off and bundling them up. When the priest arrived, she thrust them at him.

"You have to come with us, Sister. It's your duty."

"Father. I can't."

"You are not free to make that decision." He grabbed her arm. "Madeleine."

She shrugged him off with such violence that he was thrown backwards to the ground. "I have to go with him. That's it. I have to." She slipped her fingers under her veil and peeled it off.

Petrovitch stepped forward and helped the priest up. "If it's any consolation, I don't understand this either."

"This . . . this is all your fault." He snatched his hand away. "Sister. If you leave now, you might never be able to come back. You're breaking your vows."

"So it seems. It's getting to be a bit of a habit." She barked out a laugh. "Hah. Habit." She was down to her impact armour, interlocking sheets of fabric that looked like fish scales. She held up her gun and peered around the corner. "Clear."

"Looks like we're not hanging about. Sorry, Father."

"What did you tell her? What?"

Petrovitch was at a loss. "Just that what I was doing meant something."

"And what she's doing doesn't?"

"It's her choice! I haven't asked for anything."

Sister Madeleine snagged Petrovitch's collar and pulled him after her as she made a short, darting run to the next piece of hard cover. She pushed him against a set of window shutters and crouched down. She scanned the road ahead, ignoring the plaintive shouting of her name.

"Go again," she said.

She trusted him not to wander off this time, and let go of his coat as she headed towards a car parked sideways to the kerb. Petrovitch ducked beneath the level of the roof and looked through the windows.

Smoke drifted in dirty clouds between the buildings. The occasional shot rang out, but nothing too close.

"I appreciate that I'm only a filthy heathen, and it's probably not my place to say anything, but are you sure about this?"

"All I'm going to say is that you'd better make this worth my while." She pulled her plait over her shoulder and looped it around her wrist.

"I'll try not to disappoint you." Petrovitch thought he could make out figures in the distance, and he jabbed his finger forward.

"I've just left everything I've known for the last four years, and you'll try not to disappoint me? Good start." She risked another look. "Go right. Doorway on the corner."

They ran doubled over. He made a much smaller silhouette than she did. Hers was more graceful. This time the space they had to hide in was narrow, and they had to press themselves in, body to body. Their height difference meant that Petrovitch didn't know quite where to look. Rather than staring at her armoured chest, he looked up into her big brown eyes.

"I mean it," she said. "If you let me down, I'll kill you."

"I kind of assumed that."

"Good: just so we both know where we stand."

There were footsteps, the sound of broken glass underneath

booted feet, voices. Petrovitch and the sister froze and waited. She turned her head to hide her face, and Petrovitch could see the stubble on the side of her partially shaved head.

Someone laughed, kicked a loose plastic bottle across the street, then shot it for target practice. Their effort was greeted with a chorus of jeering, and a fusillade of firing.

When it had finished, they moved on.

"Rabble," she muttered. "Take away their guns and they're nothing."

"It's not what Father John thought. It's not what you thought."

"Forgive me for feeling uncharitable. That stink on the wind is my church." She checked the road they were going to take was free of militia. "Keep to the right-hand side. There's a red glass-fronted building at the end of this street. Turn right and go into the car park behind. We can cut through."

She eased herself out and ran again, darting between cars, leaping over the urban debris of decay. If Petrovitch hadn't known where to look, it would have been impossible to follow her. She was like a grey ghost, disapparating at will.

He set off after her in his own clumsy fashion, catching a few moments' rest where he could press the street furniture hard against his back before moving again.

There was a body in the middle of the road, for ever frozen in a sprawled, crawling, spider-like pose. Shot in the back, then shot again. He belatedly looked around him, trying to think like Madeleine did, weighing up cover and spying out shadows.

It wasn't the same as running from a few overweight St Petersburg cops.

He kept going, even though he'd lost sight of her. It was a confession of faith that she was ahead of him, and she'd be where she said she would be when he got there. And he'd get there, or die trying.

A gust of wind sent the pillar of smoke from St Joseph's down to street level. Petrovitch took a chance and ran through the drifting cloud of soot and ash to the next corner, then across to the rose-pink edifice. Its glass front was lying in shattered piles on the pavement.

He steered right and then into the gap between it and the next anonymous concrete block. It was dark and empty. He couldn't see her at all.

He skidded to a halt, his breath laboured, unable to focus. He took two sideways steps and leaned heavily against the wall. It wasn't just his left hand feeling weak now, it was his whole arm: tingling with a thousand pinpricks.

"You OK?"

He jumped, as did his heart. "*Yobany stos*, woman!"

"I thought you knew I was here." She shifted, and her outline was suddenly apparent.

He slid down the wall until he was squatting. "I just need five minutes," he gasped. He tilted his head back to look at the slit of the sky. "*Chyort*, it hurts."

"I can do this for you, if you want," she said. "I know what Sonja looks like."

"If you hadn't remembered, the Paradise militia want to kill you."

"They want to kill Father John."

"They were watching the building and they thought you were alone." He rubbed at his sternum. "It was you they were after."

"Then, thank you." She played with the thick rope of her hair.

"Yeah, well. They didn't seem too fussy where they pointed their *peesi*. I guess I'm off their Christmas list, too."

She straightened up, stretching her already long legs by standing on tiptoe. "Ready to carry on?"

He puffed. "Shortest five minutes in history."

"We can wait for a little while longer."

"No, let's get this over with. The sooner you can get me into Paradise, the sooner you can get back to protecting Father John." He pushed himself up, and was dizzy with vertigo.

"Sam, I'm not going back," she said. "I thought I made it clear I'm staying with you."

"Yeah. I'm having a hard time believing that, so I'm giving you an easy way out."

"I don't want an easy way out. I have to suffer for what I'm doing."

The corner of his mouth twitched. "You sound like me. Where next?"

"Over the wall," and she pointed. The breeze-block structure was twice as tall as he was.

Madeleine, however, had no problems at all. She holstered her gun at her hip and approached the wall at a loping run. She jumped, placed both hands on its top and ended up astride it, legs dangling either side. She waved Petrovitch on, and reached down, gripping his forearm as he gripped hers. He scrambled up the best he could, and lay beached on the thin rail of rough stonework.

"And I still have to get down the other side," he grunted.

"Getting down's easy," she said, and twisted his arm in such a way that he fell off. "It's landing that's hard."

She still had hold of him, fingers tight around his wrist. She lowered him down until his feet made contact with the ground, then vaulted off herself, legs together, knees bent; a perfect dismount.

"Do they teach that at nun school, or is that something you've picked up along the way?"

"I owe the Order everything," she said.

"So why . . ."

She slipped her gun back into her hand, as natural as an extension of her body. "Because I'm possessed by some overwhelming madness that forces me to desert my vocation, my sisters, my duty, my priest – and go with you instead, you foulmouthed, unbelieving, weak, selfish criminal who by some freak chance or divine plan has not only captured my stone-cold heart but seems to embody the virtue of hope in a way I have never experienced before, inside or outside the church. That's why."

Petrovitch pushed his glasses up his nose, entirely lost for words.

"What did you call me, earlier? When we were going through Hyde Park?" she asked.

"*Babochka*," he whispered. "It's not a swear word. It means . . ."

"Butterfly," she finished for him. "I looked it up. You called me – *me* – butterfly. Don't stop calling me that, but you can use Maddy as well. It's been a long time since anyone did."

Petrovitch gave himself the luxury of a few steadying breaths. "Right. Maddy. Do you know where we're going?"

"Oh yes," she said. "I used to live there."

25

The most dangerous part was running across the wide, open expanse of the Marylebone Road. No matter how low or fast they were, they could have been seen, and having been seen, followed, ambushed, and killed.

But the Paradise militia had decided to expand their territory to the south, towards the bright lights and consumer durables of Oxford Street, and to the east, trying to take on the domik pile on Regent's Park. That their excursion into the high-value shopping streets was met with less resistance than their assault on some of the Metrozone's poorest residents proved the authorities were powerless.

"This machine thing," said Madeleine. They turned a corner and Petrovitch found himself facing the railway station. Its shutters were down and locked tight. "Who do you think they are?"

"Oshicora loyalists. Coders on the VirtualJapan project. I don't think anyone else in the Metrozone could have put together such a co-ordinated, comprehensive attack. They've taken down so much I don't know what they control any more. Maybe they don't. Maybe they're fighting a losing battle with their own botnet."

"All I wanted to know was whether we could trust them or not." She pointed to the station frontage, and they ran.

The low-level skirmish between Paradise and Regent's Park had formed a fluid front-line ahead of them. Stray shots from that battle clattered overhead: sometimes a rooftile or a window would crack and fall in pieces to shower the street below.

Petrovitch's back rattled against the metal screens. "Aren't we going the wrong way?"

"We have to go this way to go back. Is that OK?"

"Since any answer other than yes will get my limbs torn off: yes."

She grinned, and the whole of her face lit up; no longer the avenging angel, but the teenager out on her first date.

"Down here," she indicated with a jerk of her head, and cut into a gloomy street beside the station. On one side was a terrace of pre-Armageddon, probably pre-Patriotic War, houses. They faced a battered chain-link fence that separated the road from the railway tracks, and soon she found a weakness in it.

She dragged the base of the wire up, straining at it with her clawed hands. A shower of soil and weeds and litter fell from its mesh. Petrovitch took his cue, and rolled underneath, picking up mud on his coat. She followed, after making the hole bigger.

They slipped and scrabbled hand in hand down the embankment and onto the oily ballast beside the rails.

"Watch your step," she warned.

"Kind of figured that." He looked back in the dark mouth of the station. The platforms were immense, jutting out from under the covered section and into the distance. He tried to imagine the number of carriages it could have served, thousands of people at a time coming from outside the city and spewed out right there, one train after another, every few minutes. "Listen."

The overhead power lines, supported by spidery metal gantries, were humming.

"I thought you said nothing was working?" She stared up the empty line. It passed under two bridges before disappearing into a tunnel.

"I think I said we weren't in control of anything; a world of difference."

"We need to go that way." She pointed down the track, away from the station. "If there's anything you want to tell me, now's a good time."

Out of sight, a steel wheel screeched. The ringing, whistling noise echoed around them. Petrovitch licked his dry lips and remembered the cars. "Have you got another plan?"

"It's not as good." She turned to see a train, lights as bright as stars, wink into existence. The slanted face of the power unit grew, framed by the road bridge it had to pass under. "Is this something to be afraid of?"

"Yeah." He started edging back towards the wire fence.

Her hand curled around his arm. "Wait. We don't know which way to run."

The train was closing fast; too fast for an urban line, too fast for the buffers up ahead, too fast even for the gentle curve it was attempting to take. The first carriage was tilting further and further out, and taking the two behind with it. The tortured wail of grinding metal became a roar.

Petrovitch really, really wanted to be anywhere but in front of this beast, and still she hung onto him, forcing him to stay still.

equationsoflife

Wheels left the track, great metal and glass containers were in flight, spreading out like a thrown chain.

At last. Madeleine picked him up and in three strides she was at the platform's cliff face. She unceremoniously posted him on top and lifted herself on after him. She was on her feet before he was. She took his hand and they sprinted across the platform, down into the next rail bed. There, she wrapped him up in her.

The ground shook itself like a wet dog. The first carriage, almost vertical, tried to carve a new route through the brick and steel bridge. It bent and broke like a straw, one half soaring into the sky, the other digging itself into the ground. The next car hit a support head-on, ripping a flash of lightning out of the expanding cloud of dust.

The last one leapt over the remains of the bridge, intact, spinning. Before it crashed back down, the front end of the train howled past, into the station, and didn't stop when it reached the end of the line.

The noise was a punch to the gut, a concussion hard enough to break stone. Metal groaned, masonry toppled.

Then came the carriage. It had turned sideways, and it hit the end of the platforms rolling. Glass crystals sprayed out, and the jagged-edged windows spat out the contents of the train while grinding flat everything before it.

It passed over their heads, a blurred, scouring shadow above which disappeared into the darkness, dragging roof supports down with it. Something heavy shifted in a long, slow slide inside the station concourse which grew in volume, then subsided. A storm-front of dust and grit blew out, smothering them. A final patter of debris, and it was over.

Petrovitch had his face next to hers, in the dirty darkness formed by the angle of their cowering bodies.

"You OK?" He could feel her eyelashes tickle his cheek, her ragged breath against his skin.

"Do you suppose there was anyone on that train?"

He risked raising his head. His glasses were coated with a layer of speckled dust. He took them off and huffed gently on each of the lenses. Even that simple act made him cough hoarsely.

The out-of-focus scene resolved as he put them back on.

"*Yobany stos*," he said.

The station behind him had partially collapsed, the bridge in front torn in two, and the two platforms stripped clean and carved with deep grooves. The air was thick with fine powder that the wind tugged at like fog.

The fence they'd crawled under was gone, along with the front wall of the terrace opposite, which was ripped out and thrown down across the road. The rooms inside looked like the insides of dolls' houses: a standard lamp flickered as it hung by its flex from a first-storey sitting room. Part of the first carriage was embedded in someone's front room.

"We have to look for survivors," said Madeleine.

"No. No, we don't." Petrovitch gingerly brushed his hair with his fingertips. It was stiff with dust, and there were fragments of glass lodged near the roots. "What possible use could we be?"

"We could help them," she said, her voice trailing away as she realised the enormity of the disaster.

"We can't even phone for an ambulance! The network is down, and even if it wasn't, we don't have a phone – I saw you look at yours when you took off your robes, then you handed it over anyway. But who would we call? Who would come? The police have vanished. The hospitals will be locked down. The fire service? Where would they start? The whole *yebani* city is in flames."

"We're not just walking away." She balled her fists with frustration.

"I was thinking of running," said Petrovitch, and pointed towards the tower blocks of Paradise. "That looks like a good direction."

"I can save someone!"

He could feel himself losing his temper, a heat that was rising to boiling point inside. "And I can save everyone. If we stay here, all we can do is drag bodies out of the wreckage and watch the wounded die for the lack of anything more complicated than an aspirin. There's no one else coming. No one. It's just us. So what do we do? We can waste our time being good and holy and accomplish absolutely nothing. Or we can go and find Sonja Oshicora and take her to the New Machine Jihad, who might be persuaded to stop this bloody slaughter. It's a long shot, it makes no sense, but you know, it might just work. Your call."

Madeleine swayed, shifting her weight from foot to foot. "You care, don't you?"

"Too much. The Metrozone took me in, hid me, gave me a life. I owe it."

She hawked up some phlegm, and spat on the ground. She smacked her lips like there was a bad taste in her mouth. "I suppose we'll have to do it your way."

"This isn't cowardice, even though I've seen enough carnage for one morning. This is the only thing I can think of." He dug his hands in his pockets to feel the reassuring touch of a gun. "I know this makes you feel like *govno*: it won't exactly go down in history as my finest hour, either."

Madeleine groaned, and chased some loose strands of hair away. With one last look behind her, she set a reluctant foot forward. The other followed more easily. Petrovitch half-jogged, half-walked beside her giantess strides. Their path was blocked by the demolished bridge, and they could do nothing else but start to climb over the unstable rubble.

It shifted and slid. A car roof showed green through the dust and boomed as they stepped on it. As they crested the edge of the crazily tilted box-girder roadway, the back end of a railway carriage came into view. All its glass was gone, and anything loose inside had been propelled to the front.

Madeleine glanced at it briefly, then pointedly turned away and concentrated her gaze on where she was placing her feet.

Petrovitch did more. He waited for her to pull ahead, then picked his way to the first visible window. As he approached, he became more and more relieved: the carriage was empty. It was nothing more than a ghost train. He put his head inside to check. No bodies, no blood. No repeat of the lifts inside the Oshicora Tower.

He caught her up and they walked side by side, past the end of the platform and into the long sloping cut that led into the tunnel's entrance.

"There was no one there," he said quietly.

"Thanks."

"That's OK." He listened to the sharp, high chatter of a machine pistol as it echoed off the enclosing buildings. "Of course, I could be lying."

"I know, but then I'd thank you for lying to me." She looked down at him and picked a glittering bead of glass from between his collar and his neck. It embedded itself in her finger and drew out a bright drop of blood. She flicked both the glass and blood away, then stiffened. "There's something else coming."

Petrovitch cocked his head. The violence of the train wreck had left him with ringing ears, and he couldn't hear anything.

equations*of*life

She grabbed his hand and ran up the tracks. Hidden behind the buildings to their right was an Underground line that briefly appeared from the depths before plunging into the shared tunnel ahead. Before disappearing out of sight, there was a section in the open air where the two systems ran parallel to each other.

Petrovitch felt a drawn-out vibration deep in his bones. He pulled back, but she was irresistible. She wanted to see all the horrors invented for this day. A tube train hurtled into view around the corner of the building, shaking and rolling, sharp flashes of blue light bursting from underneath its wheels. It ran away from them, up the narrow-gauge track, its grafittied livery bright against the drab veil of dust it pushed through.

The rear door of the last carriage was open, forced by those inside, and there was a figure braced in the frame, feet and hands clawing at the sharp metal edges before being propelled out onto the rail bed.

A spin of skirt and a flap of jacket: she landed across the electrified third rail and jerked and bounced. But just because she was dead didn't stop her moving.

Her place at the door was taken by another as the rear of the tube train rattled away into the tunnel. Its lights faded and sank as the darkness took it.

They walked slowly forward. The woman's body was starting to smoke, little tendrils of steam that the wind caught and blew ragged.

"You know," said Petrovitch, "When I find the New Machine Jihad, I'm going to have to think of a way to make them pay for this *pizdets*."

The corner of Madeleine's eye twitched involuntarily. "I thought you said they were in charge."

"They're no more in charge of the Metrozone than they are

of the weather." He was level with the contorted body on the tracks, and he resisted the urge to pull it clear. The clothing was on fire, and yet again there was nothing he could do. He hated feeling powerless, especially with the smell of cooking flesh in his nose. "Fucking amateurs."

The tracks crossed a canal: the surface of the water was black and bubbling, thick like mud, and interrupted by shapes that could have been the rotting corpses of barges. It looked to be the last place to head for, but the only danger was organic decay: no automated systems to go wrong down there.

Madeleine climbed over the bridge parapet and skittered down the rough concrete support until she landed on the rubbish-strewn tow path. She crouched and looked both ways. She beckoned him on.

The footing was uncertain, slippery after the rain, the moss acting both as a sponge and a lubricant. He was covered in wet, greasy stains as well as mud and dust by the time he joined her.

"Tell me this is strictly necessary," he said.

"No one comes down here. Or at least, they never did."

"I can't guess why." It smelled of the deep wood in autumn, of earthy sulphurous decomposition.

"Don't fall in. You'd be poisoned before you drowned," she said, and tried to take the land-most side of the path.

It seemed, however, that for the past two decades the canal had been treated as nothing more than a tip for everything from everyday refuse to old furniture and appliances, not to mention the obligatory shopping trolleys. In places, the tow path was buried underneath drifts of filth that jutted out like headlands into the stagnant water.

They had little choice over the route they took, slipping and sliding on the inconstant ground, determined not to use their hands for fear of being cut by something unclean. Instead, they held each other's hands – one bracing themselves and the other moving, leapfrogging across the ad-hoc tip until they reached a place behind an ancient, rusting industrial building that was all rusting pipes and leaking tanks.

"Climb up here," said Madeleine, and made a stirrup of her hands.

Petrovitch slapped his hands against the wall he had to get over and tried to scrape off some of the mess that had stuck to the sole of his boot.

"Don't worry about that," she said.

"Yeah, well. I'm told it's the thought that counts." He put his foot in her hands; he was so light and she so strong that he was hoisted almost level with the top of the wall. He overbalanced, and started to fall.

There was only one way to go: forwards, because back towards the canal would have been unthinkable. His hands waved ineffectually at the brickwork, scraping his knuckles raw, and he fell on the other side in a heap of dead and dying weeds.

He wasn't alone. His glasses had been knocked awry by the impact, and it was as he straightened them that he saw three pairs of feet. On looking up, there were three guns.

One of the men – a skinny white kid much like himself, but with a milky eye – jerked the barrel of his gun up.

Petrovitch made certain they could see his hands, raising them with nothing but grime and blood on his pink palms. Then he shouted in one breath, "Runmaddyrun", before a metal-filled fist crashed into the side of his head.

26

It wasn't the first time he'd come round to find himself being dragged through the streets like a piece of meat. All the other times had been in Russia, though, and it took him a few moments to recognise the unwelcome strain on his arms and the scraping of his toes on the tarmac.

He was slung between two people, head down over the road. They had hold of him under his armpits. They seemed to be content to half-carry him, and Petrovitch was content to let them. He was in no shape for a fight, especially since his pockets were considerably lighter than when he'd last checked.

His glasses were missing: that was something that was going to cause him far more problems than the lack of a gun.

He tried to get a sense of where he was, without looking up. The poor condition of the road surface, the echoing, the gloom of an occluded sky: he could only be in Paradise.

They'd been waiting for him, for both him and Madeleine, which was odd considering she'd changed their route on an ad-hoc basis. He was certain he wasn't carrying a tracker, and no one would have dared get close enough to Madeleine to tag her. Neither had they been followed; she wouldn't have allowed it.

His attackers pulled him up a ramp and into a building. He could see a bare concrete floor, stained and damp, and could feel a ceiling over him. Natural light seeped in behind, and he was facing a wall.

They dropped him without warning, and his face closed with the floor at alarming speed. He managed to turn his head in time not to break his nose, instead choosing to stun himself into insensibility again.

He lay there, quiet and still, and wondered what they were all waiting for.

He could hear a rhythmic grinding noise that grew louder. It stopped and, after a few moments, there was the unmistakable rattle of lift doors opening.

Two of the men reached down to pick Petrovitch up again, and he decided that he'd be damned if they were going to put him inside that metal cube. If he blinked, he could see the pile of bodies and the wash of blood.

"Stop," he said, and they were so surprised that he was conscious and talking that they dropped him again. He managed to get his hands under him to partially break his fall.

The lift door started to close again, and one of the men stuck his boot in the way. The motors wheezed pathetically as they strained against the obstruction.

"I don't want to go in the lift."

"I don't see how you've got any say in where you go or how you go," said the man at the lift.

"I can walk," said Petrovitch.

Someone laughed.

"I don't think so," said the man. "You barely look alive."

Petrovitch looked up. The man's face was a blur; he could just make out a shaved scalp and a black beard. That, or his head was on upside down. "Perhaps you shouldn't have hit me so hard."

"Like it matters." He relented, and nodded to the men standing behind Petrovitch. "Get him to his feet. Let's see him stand."

Petrovitch was hauled upright, then steadied as he wavered. He lacked the visual cues that told him where vertical was. Something else was wrong, too. He put his hand to the side of his head to find his skin wet and sticky.

He stared at his palm, and scratched a pattern in the half-dried blood with his fingers.

The man heaved the lift doors back. "You wouldn't make it up the first flight of stairs, and we're going all the way to the top. We don't get credit for your corpse, either."

Petrovitch felt a hand at his back push him towards the open doors. He tried to resist, but realised how weak he really was when he found himself going faster and faster towards the rear wall. He slammed into it with a boom, and stayed pinned there by the same hand.

The bearded man released the doors and let them squeak shut. "You see? Much better to co-operate."

There were only so many more blows to the head Petrovitch could take. He shook himself angrily and turned around, pressing his back against the lift side as it rumbled into life.

"Nervous?" he asked.

Without his glasses, he missed their expressions, but the way they stood betrayed them.

"We haven't got anything to be nervous about."

"Yeah. Let me tell you about my morning. Big, modern tower, the latest, smartest everything; polished marble floor, brushed steel and glass. Something called the New Machine Jihad took that building over, trapped most of the people who worked there in lifts not so different to this one, and killed them all. Dropped them from the top floor, crushed them to an unrecognisable mush at the bottom. So much blood in each one that it came out in a wave." Petrovitch paused. "You have heard about the New Machine Jihad, haven't you? Everyone's talking about them."

"Shut up, you Russian bastard."

"They're the ones to beat. Sorry, but no one's afraid of the Paradise militia any more – not when the Jihad can reach into the heart of your territory and take out whoever it likes."

"I said, shut up." The fuzzy shape the bearded man held up was Petrovitch's Norinco.

"Must make you cross. Struggle on all these years, carving out your little kingdom, living in little better than a ghetto, then when your moment comes . . . it gets snatched away from you by a bunch of faceless nerds who just happen to know how the Metrozone really works."

His own gun was pressed to his already bruised temple. "Five, four."

Petrovitch squinted past the barrel. "You're going to lose, and lose hard."

The lift shuddered to a halt, and the doors slid open. "Three. Two."

A familiar voice drawled: "Is that necessary?"

"He's asking for it."

"And you got sucked in? Come on out, Petrovitch. We've been expecting you."

Petrovitch could see a bulky figure in a plaid shirt framed in the doorway. He added that and the accent, and worked out it could only be Sorenson.

"Hey, kid. Where are your glasses?"

"You'll have to ask the *peshka*. Maybe they've been so busy slapping me around and playing with their *yielda* that they don't remember." Petrovitch stumbled out, blinking. The watery light was bright enough to make his eyes smart.

"Come on, boys. Hand 'em over," said Sorenson. He waited a few moments, and the door started to close again. He stepped forward and held one of his meaty hands up to prevent it moving any further. "Don't make me come in there."

The bearded man thought about defiance, and decided against it. He reached into his pocket and threw Petrovitch's spectacles onto the floor outside the confines of the lift. He followed it with a gobbet of phlegm.

Sorenson was just about satisfied. He let go of the door, and when it had shut, he kicked it for good measure. He scooped up the glasses and pressed them into Petrovitch's hands.

"You look like crap," said Sorenson.

"Yeah. So everyone keeps on telling me." Petrovitch jammed the bent frames onto his face, wincing as the cold metal touched his open wound. "I was wondering where you'd got to. Then I was told a police station had been destroyed in an explosion, and I thought of you. That's what you used to do, right? Blow stuff up?"

He blinked and tried to make the lenses more or less cover his eyes. He was in what used to be a community lounge for the residents of the tower block and was now a war room. It was at the very top of the building, with only the roof above, and the long plate-glass windows afforded an uninterrupted panorama of the destruction below. The tower was on the ⏦ side of Paradise: he could see Regent's Park off to his left, the City straight ahead, partially obscured by the smoke risin from many fires – one of which was St Joseph's.

Sorenson, dressed in a looted flying jacket and urban camouflage trousers, swung a medical kit onto a table. "Sit down, kid. I'll patch you up."

Petrovitch perched on the edge of the table and tried to keep his head still as the American swabbed lukewarm water across his cheek. There was a map of the Metrozone pinned to the wall, with arrows pointing towards the nearby domiks and down the Edgware Road.

"Where do you fit in here, Sorenson?" Petrovitch watched as a teenager with a pair of expensive binoculars slung around his neck passed a note to one of the women near the map. The woman moved one of the arrows back from Regent's Park and onto Marylebone station.

If that had been Madeleine's escape route, she was now cut off.

"Where do I fit in? Well now: how about the top?" Sorenson tutted. "You need stitches and a slab of fresh skin. All I've got are these steristrips. You're going to have a scar."

"Like that's the thing I'm most worried about. Let's get this straight: you're in charge of this rabble now? What happened to the other guy?"

"I killed him. What's this white stuff you've got all over you? You look like a ghost."

"Pulverised concrete dust. And stop changing the subject: what happened to you? I thought you'd go feral, but *zaebis*'! This is extreme."

Sorenson used more pressure on Petrovitch's cut than was

y necessary, causing him to suck air in through his clenched
n. "You really don't know when to shut up, do you? What
e could I have done? My life was ruined, squeezed between
Oshicora and Chain, and no way to get either of them off my
back. Until you gave me an idea."

"So what *pizdets* am I responsible for now? Apart from you
tearing the city up like it was Saturday night in Tashkent?"

"You got involved with Oshicora because someone tried to
take his daughter. That got me thinking." Sorenson packed the
medical kit away, discarding the mound of bloody swabs into
a plastic bag. "What better way to get revenge on the black-
mailing sumbitch?"

"Oh, you didn't. Tell me you didn't."

"Wasn't difficult, in the end. TKO a guard and grab his gun,
bust my way into her room. She didn't resist. Co-operated almost,
especially after I told her I'd blow her brains out if we got
stopped. Once we were out of the tower, I thought of taking
her to Marchenkho, but you know what? I wanted to call the
shots for once."

Petrovitch tested the strength of the steristrips, contorting
his face to hide his surprise.

"The man in charge here thought he could use me, just like
Chain and Oshicora, but I showed him. His body's buried under
the police station I blew up."

"*Yobany stos*, Sorenson. This puts you right up there with the
New Machine Jihad, and they're crazier than a *shluha
vokzal'naja*."

"About that," said Sorenson. He reached into his jacket and
held up a slim silver case. It was Petrovitch's rat.

Petrovitch blinked. "Where the *chyort* . . . ?"

"Your little Japanese girlfriend had it all along. Now here's the thing: the jihadists seem to think you're coming to get her, and I don't know what I'm going to do about that." He flipped the rat open to reveal the screen, already smeared with greasy fingerprints.

Despite that, the last two lines of text clearly said: Petrovitch is coming. Petrovitch will save you.

"Not bad for a Yankee," said Petrovitch. "You've got it almost right. I was coming to find her, sure, but only because she's worth a lot of money to the right people. Comrade Marchenkho for one. Thanks to the Jihad, I knew where to find her."

"Must be peachy to be so wanted. Why don't we go and say hello?"

The casual tone in Sorenson's voice told Petrovitch that it was probably time he stopped talking and started listening. The American had entered his very own Heart of Darkness, and he seemed content to stay there.

Petrovitch followed Sorenson to a pair of double doors set in a partition wall. Behind them was a long-disused cafeteria, complete with stains on the paintwork and rusting food warmers. And Sonja Oshicora was chained to one of those, her right wrist held high by the handcuff attached to one of the uprights.

She was dirty, bruised and seething with rage. She was bleeding from trying to force her restraints, and she tried again as she looked up and saw Sorenson. The metal cut into her already abraded skin. "*Kisama!*"

Sorenson was unmoved. "Brought someone to see you," he said, and stepped aside.

Petrovitch was used to the sight of a hostage tied to some piece of furniture or other: in his day it had usually been a Soviet-era cast-iron radiator. But Boris – even Boris, with his drinking and whoring and love of dog fights – hadn't smacked his captives around. Up to the point where they were either released or had their throats cut, they'd been treated quite civilly. It had been just business to him.

The state Sonja was in filled Petrovitch with the burning light of righteous anger. To stop his hands from shaking, he shoved his balled fists in his coat pockets.

Where he made a discovery. The Paradise militia had relieved him of his Norinco and both boxes of bullets. It clearly hadn't occurred to them that a man carrying two different calibres of ammunition and just one nine millimetre pistol needed to be searched a little more carefully.

The Beretta had become lodged in the deep recesses of the inner lining. He could feel its shape through the cloth and, if he delved a little further, the hole through which it had slipped.

Sorenson mistook his distracted air for a brooding silence. "You see?" he said to Sonja. "He's here, but can't save you. I'm betting he doesn't even want to. No matter what the New Machine Jihad says: you're not going anywhere."

Sonja continued to glare at Sorenson, and all but ignore Petrovitch. "When my father finds you, it will take you a year to die."

Petrovitch remembered his minute-old vow to keep his own counsel just in time. It stopped him from blurting out the obvious: Sorenson didn't know that Oshicora-san was dead, that Hijo was in charge and that the Jihad had taken over the tower just after he'd smuggled Sonja out of the building.

And Sonja, by not looking at Petrovitch, was clearly indicating that she needed him to play along, or being shackled to a catering appliance was going to be the least of her worries.

"I reckon on another hour, Princess, and the Paradise militia will be having a fish dinner in your old man's Zen garden."

"Your band of criminals will be slaughtered by my father's men. Then they will come for you."

"I don't think so. First sign of them or your jihadist friends, and that trolley you're attached to goes out the window. Seems a shame to waste a good pair of cuffs, but you've got to make sacrifices." Sorenson snorted at his own attempt at humour. "What d'you reckon, Petrovitch?"

Petrovitch fingered the Beretta. "You got to her first. You get to do with her what you want."

"Damn right," said Sorenson, crowing, "and don't you forget it."

27

Sorenson was interrupted by an out-of-breath child bearing a slip of paper. He opened it, read it, and jutted his chin out as he crushed the note inside his fist.

"Go on, kid. Beat it."

"Bad news?" asked Petrovitch.

"Nothing that can't be taken care of. Some bunch of crazies are looting north of Hyde Park, and distracting my troops."

Petrovitch raised his eyebrows. It had to be the Hyde Park chapter of the Jihad. "Yeah. Crazies I'll go with: troops isn't what I'd call your lot, though."

Sorenson looked at Sonja and then at Petrovitch. "I'm going to deal with this, OK? Be right back."

The moment he'd gone, she started to speak: Petrovitch put his finger to his lips and checked through the open door. Sorenson's broad back was obscuring the map in the war room.

"OK. Tell me what you know about the New Machine Jihad. Quickly." He stood so he could still see through the door.

246::

"They helped Sorenson and me escape out of the tower, opened doors and turned off alarms."

"Not what I needed. Who are they, and why are they so interested in you? And me."

"I don't know." She yanked at her chain again. "You are going to rescue me, right?"

"*Yobany stos*, Sonja! I'm working on it. I don't even know if I'm Sorenson's guest or his prisoner. Probably both. And you had my rat, didn't you?"

"Yes."

"You stole it from me. You have no idea how much grief you've caused."

"I had someone take it from the police for you: I wanted to give it back. I was just waiting for the right moment. And without it, I wouldn't have got this far. The Jihad talk to me through it."

Petrovitch glanced around again. "When did they start?"

"Yesterday evening. I was hiding from Hijo, and they sent me a message, telling me the bullet train would run again."

"*Shinkansen ha mata hashirou*," said Petrovitch. Sorenson was visible briefly, then strode out of his eye-line. "Did you ever meet the programmers who created VirtualJapan?"

"I went to so many parties, was introduced to so many people. Probably, then."

"Because I'm looking for a group of hardcore coders who still owe your father loyalty, and I can't think of anyone else the Jihad is likely to be. Whoever they are, if I'm going to bust you out of here, they're going to have to help." He pushed his glasses up against his nose. "I need the rat."

Sorenson barked one more order and started back across the canteen. "You two been getting properly acquainted?"

"Yeah," said Petrovitch, "But I've got better things to do than babysit your prize zoo exhibit."

"Why such a hurry? You wouldn't be thinking of running off to the jihadists, would you?"

"Sorenson, can we get one thing straight? Just because they call themselves the New Machine Jihad doesn't mean for a moment they're a bunch of towel-headed Islamofascists, or whatever the insult of the week is. You carry on like that, and you won't even notice them before they make you squeal like a piggy."

"So tell me, Petrovitch: why should I worry about them?"

"Because they're the reason you're using runners, not mobile phones. They've already reduced you to fighting like it's the Middle Ages, and they haven't even looked in your direction yet."

Sorenson had the grace to look uncomfortable. "They wouldn't dare."

"With half your militia tied up at Regent's Park, and the other half carrying fur coats and diamond rings back from Oxford Street, how vulnerable did you want to make yourself?" Petrovitch shook his head and looked wide-eyed at Sorenson. "You never went to West Point, did you?"

"I was offered a place. Didn't want to do the time."

"Why don't we look at this map of yours?"

"You know jack shit about tactics, Petrovitch."

"Listen, you *raspizdyay* Yankee *kolhoznii*: I've been playing strategy games on computers since I first sucked milk from my mother's tit. I can recite almost everything written by Clausewitz and Sun Tzu, and from that blank expression you're giving me, you think they might be something you order from the corner deli rather than two of the greatest military philosophers in history."

Sorenson's cheeks coloured up. "You done, Petrovitch?"

"Pretty much." He stared at the American and waited, tapping his foot.

"Come on, then," said Sorenson eventually. He looked down at Sonja and scrubbed at the stubble on his chin. "Anything you need?"

"Your head on a spike, *issunboshi?*" Her lips were puffy and cracked, yet she still retained a studied leanness. She wasn't going to show any weakness even if it killed her.

Which, of course, it might.

"You'll change your tune, Princess." Sorenson straightened his shoulders and puffed his chest out. "Lie there in your own dirt for a while: someone as precious as you will hate that."

"We're wasting time, Sorenson," said Petrovitch, as much to stop his own embarrassment as to prevent more abuse.

"I guess so." He took one last look at his prisoner, then turned away from her.

Petrovitch hung behind until Sorenson had gone through the doorway. Sonja scowled at him, and he tapped his wrist where he might wear a watch. Give me time, he meant.

Sorenson led him to the map. The arrows had moved again, and not to Paradise's advantage. Petrovitch took all the information in and gave his considered opinion.

"So whose smart idea was this? This whole thing is *pizdets.*"

"It was mine. Diversionary raids into here and here, while the main thrust is down this road here, ending at the Oshicora Tower."

"Diversionary to who? So far, you've started a war with Regent's Park that you could have avoided, and whatever objectives you set your main thrust, as you laughably call it, have been lost to the lure of shiny baubles. Your attack has petered out into nothing." Petrovitch shook his head. "You don't loot until you've won. You make alliances with your neighbours to secure your borders. You concentrate all the forces you can on your single objective. You put your best units in your second line, with your most expendable lunatics in front. Pin the enemy down, outflank them and attack from the sides, bypass and isolate strongholds, keep moving because it unbalances the opposition, exploit the weak points and neutralise the strong."

They both became aware that the rest of the room had fallen silent. Sorenson looked like he'd swallowed something cold and hard that was now sitting in the pit of his stomach, and Petrovitch risked a sideways glance around.

"Yeah, Sorenson?" He leaned in close and lowered his voice. "Perhaps we should go and rethink your battle plan somewhere a little more private."

Walking stiffly and avoiding eye contact, Sorenson walked briskly to the stairs leading up to the roof. After he'd left, and before Petrovitch had got through the door, the muttering started.

He was so intent on listening to what they were saying, that when the door closed behind him, he was unprepared for the hand at his throat and the wall at his back.

"Goddamn know-it-all, undermining my authority. I should have had you killed."

Petrovitch put his hand in his pocket and rummaged around while Sorenson's fingers tightened around his neck, cutting off the blood. When he'd got a good grip on the Beretta, he jammed it barrel-first into the angle of the American's jaw.

"You mean like how you had your father killed?"

The stranglehold lost its potency, but Petrovitch kept the

gun where it was. He used it to guide the man back until it was Sorenson against the breeze-block wall, not his own.

"Turn around. Hands out, legs apart. You know the drill." Petrovitch stepped back so he was out of range of feet or fists.

"Who told you about my father?"

"Everybody. It's not exactly a secret any more." Petrovitch patted him down and relieved him of a kitchen knife, a Magnum, and the rat. He kissed its shiny cover and slipped it in his inside pocket.

Sorenson growled low in his throat. "In a minute, someone's going to walk through that door . . ."

"And what? Judging on the mood in there, they'll shake my hand and help me pitch your body over the parapet. If anybody could have taken advantage of today, it was the Paradise militia. You fucked it up for them. Something tells me that unless you play it very smart – like listening to me – your reign as czar is going to be over before it starts. Now, get up those stairs."

There was another door, edged by bright daylight. Sorenson went through first, Petrovitch following. The top of the tower was pooled with water blown into corrugations by the wind. The sky was huge and low, almost as if it could be touched with an upstretched hand. The Metrozone was laid bare around them.

Some of the younger kids were serving as spotters. They saw Sorenson held at gunpoint, and looked nervously at each other.

"Give us five minutes, OK?" said Petrovitch.

As the children danced past, Sorenson turned and surveyed what he still believed was his kingdom.

"Not enough burning," he said.

Petrovitch waited for the door to self-shut before replying. "What the *zaebis'* is wrong with you? I mean, I realise that you're a reckless, patricidal pyromaniac but I thought you wanted to go home. You should have been halfway across the Atlantic by now."

"I was caught, all right? If I'd have stayed with Oshicora, Chain would have busted my ass. If I'd have gone over to Chain, Oshicora would have hung me out to dry."

"*Yobany stos*, Sorenson. Chain – Chain doesn't care about you any more. He never did. He just sits in the middle of his spider's web and never does anything, just as long as he knows. And Oshicora: how stupid do you have to be? Oshicora's dead and the tower has fallen. When you thought you were kidnapping Sonja, you were rescuing her from Hijo. And you only managed that because the Jihad were helping her."

It took a few moments for the words to penetrate Sorenson's skull. He wandered in a drunkard's walk to the edge of the roof, where he was separated from the precipice by a barely waist-high metal bar. At first, it looked like Sorenson was going to jump. He gripped the railing with whitened knuckles and leaned his body across it until it was almost horizontal. Then he straightened up and started to march towards Petrovitch.

Petrovitch raised his gun hand and sighted between the American's narrowed eyes. His palm was sweating, and his left arm was aching again. There was a dull pain that stretched all the way from his chest to his fingertips.

"What did you say?" said Sorenson.

"You heard. You've been used. Again. You could have been on a home run, or whatever it is. You screwed up for the last time; no way back now. Only two things you can do. First, pull the Paradise militia back, start again. Leave Regent's Park alone: let them get on with looting the West End and making as much havoc as they like. Consolidate your gains and try to hold on to them." He felt faint for a moment. Sorenson slipped in and out of focus.

"The second, give me Sonja. If you don't, you and everyone here is going to die when the New Machine Jihad come calling."

"This is just bullshit. You're full of it, full of crap, kid. This is something you and the princess cooked up. Her old man's alive and kicking, and shaking in his sandals because I've got his precious daughter."

Petrovitch reached into his own coat pocket for a little metal hoop from which dangled a pair of thin keys. "I disagree," he said. "What are you going to do? The smart thing or the stupid thing? Let her go, or wait for the Jihad to make you let her go?"

Sorenson looked at Petrovitch's gun, then at Petrovitch himself. "Here's the deal: I'll not toss your sorry ass off the top of this housing project, and you'll make yourself scarce. Without the princess." He started to stride forward, confident of overpowering his opponent.

Then the American staggered back, his big hands flapping in front of his face, trying to bat away the bullet that had already banged into the back of his skull. A black river of blood flowed down his face from his forehead, almost obscuring his last look of surprise.

He fell, twisted, eyes open. His heavily covered frame made the roof shake as it landed.

"What the *huy* do you know anyway?" Petrovitch swapped the gun for the rat and flipped it open.

The screen was covered with two words repeated endlessly: coming now. They were still scrolling, and it was clear that it was almost too late. He used the touch screen to scrawl the hasty message, "Petrovitch says stop".

Gunfire, up to that point far away, became suddenly close.

"*Pizdets*," he said and snapped the rat shut.

28

Petrovitch decided that if he did everything at a run, fewer people were going to question what he was doing. The flaw in his plan was that he'd never felt less like running.

He could barely grip the handle to the top door; his arm was a seething mass of pins and needles, and the only way he could tell he'd actually got hold of the thing was that his fingers wouldn't close any further.

Nevertheless, he pulled and trip-trapped down the stairs as fast as he could. He slipped on the bottom step and collided with the lower door, hurting his shoulder.

"*Halyavshchik!*" Now wasn't the time to get careless. He pocketed the Beretta and used his good right hand to enter the war room.

Everyone had rushed to the windows to see what was happening below, and no one noticed him as he weaved through the tables and darted for the cafeteria door.

Sonja noticed him, though. "Sam? What's going on?"

He fished out the handcuff keys and threw them across the floor to her. "The New Machine Jihad is going on, and we have to leave."

She scooped up the keys and applied them to the cuffs. "What about Sorenson?"

"Something we don't need to worry about any more. Which is, on balance, a good thing since we've got more trouble than we can cope with." He limped to the window and pressed his face to the glass.

The road below looked like the rush-hour at Waterloo Bridge: cars, nose to tail, not a scrap of tarmac between them, grinding against each other like boulders.

"*Huy na ny*," he breathed, misting the window. Sonja joined him, standing uncomfortably close as she frowned at the vehicles, which seemed to be pouring into the plaza at the foot of the tower from every direction. As they did so, they set up a current, a whirlpool of automation with them in the gyre.

"Is that the best they can do?" said Sonja. "How's that going to help?"

"None of those cars has a driver. Makes them very hard to kill." He stopped to catch his breath. "They've got this building surrounded, which leaves me wondering what else they have up their sleeve."

"Because of the wheels."

"Yeah. It's the usual can't-climb-stairs problem." He slumped down, back to the wall and screwed his eyes up tight.

"Sam?"

"I'm having a heart attack. Possibly the last one I'll ever have." He put his fist against his chest, and breathed in against the pain.

"But we have to get out of here!"

"I know. I'm doing my best." Petrovitch heard another noise against the rumble of the procession, a deep bass diesel sound. He dragged himself back upright using the window ledge as a crutch and peered out.

It was a riot wagon; swathed in electrified mesh and brandishing its weapons: tear-gas launchers, wide-barrelled watercannon, plastic bullet guns. It rolled in on its six fat tyres and started through the sea of cars. It rode up onto the bonnet of one, whose windscreen popped and shattered. The roof buckled as the wagon kept on moving, bursting all the other panes.

Then it was surfing across to the entrance, granulated glass spraying everywhere, dipping and sliding on the uneven, unstable surface below but entirely supported by the vehicles beneath.

Sparks were crackling over its front armour. The militia were fighting back.

"They'd do better saving their ammunition," said Petrovitch. "Something tells me that it's going to be the least of their worries."

Sonja put a hand under his shoulder and tried to pull him away from the window. "If it's under Jihad command, we have to get to it."

"Don't trust them."

"You want to stay here?" she asked.

"Do you want to go out there?" he countered. "You'll be at the mercy of a bunch of crotch-scratching code jockeys whose hallmark is 'oops'. They damn near killed me playing with their oversized train set. I'd much rather be the author of my own salvation than rely on them."

He steeled himself to get as far as the door, and only had to stop once, when he thought he was going to black out. His vision greyed and his ears roared, but the moment passed.

equationsoflife

The Paradise residents were still standing at the window, but had now started arguing with each other as to what to do. Petrovitch found a chair and slumped into it, and, despite Sonja's best efforts, he refused to move.

"Hey," he said, then when that made no impression, he fetched out Sorenson's Magnum and banged the butt hard on the table. "Hey!"

A dozen people turned to face him. He slid the gun across the tabletop and let them draw their own conclusions.

"Does that mean we have to do what you say now?" A rodent-faced woman stepped forward and leaned against the back of a chair.

"Yeah, that's right. All your base are belong to us." Petrovitch snorted in disgust. It hurt, but it showed his contempt. "Get a clue and sit down, the lot of you."

"Sam, we don't have time for this," said Sonja.

"There's always time for this. Workers of the world unite! You have nothing to lose but your chains." He watched them as they moved closer, perching on the edges of desks and plastic chairs. Their unspoken deference to him made him squirm.

When he thought they were ready, he flipped his glasses off and rubbed at his eyes.

"You know, I don't give a shit about your culture or your traditions, because they suck. I don't care that I killed your new leader who killed your previous leader, since that way of king-making died back in the seventeen hundreds, and wake up!" He slammed his hand down hard, and the resulting noise even made himself jump. "It's the twenty-first century out there, people. The Metrozone functions quite happily without you taking part. All you've done is made yourself a ghetto — a dysfunctional, kleptocratic ghetto — that your own children fight to get out of. This is not freedom. This is slavery, and you've done it to yourselves.

"I don't expect anything I say will change anything, but *huy!* It might make one of you think. The thing is, the fact that you've collectively screwed up all your lives isn't particularly important right now. What is, is that you're under attack from the New Machine Jihad. Do not use the lifts. Do not trust any networked technology, especially if your safety depends on it functioning properly. Don't waste bullets shooting at the cars, because the Jihad has the resources of the entire Metrozone at its disposal.

"The only way you might be able to get out alive is by letting Sonja go. The Jihad want to save her, which is the only reason they're here. You're just not that important otherwise. No Sonja, no Jihad. I'm kind of assuming that you'd prefer it that way, so you can go back to stealing stuff and shooting at drones."

As soon as he said it, his palms went sticky. His gaze went from the faces of his audience to the expanse of plate glass behind them. He stood up, far too quickly, and announced: "We have to get out of here, right now."

He swayed on his feet as he turned. Madeleine would have caught him; Sonja didn't seem to know what to do, and watched him stumble into several chairs. He raised himself up again to find them all still watching him and not moving.

But not for long, because someone noticed a wide-winged, slim-bodied aircraft outside the building lining up for its final approach. He pointed out of the window and started to run at the same time, pushing a boy to the floor who was in his way.

The sudden eruption of movement broke the spell of inaction. Everyone surged for the door. Petrovitch was battered at the front of the wave. He tried to reach back through the rush of bodies to Sonja and grasped nothing but thin air.

"Sam!"

He was slammed into the door to the stairwell. For a brief moment, he was wedged in the frame. Then he managed to claw his way back, fingers tight against the plasterwork.

She was standing there, watching the drone grow in size. It made a tiny correction that levelled its flight. Petrovitch kicked his legs free of the doorway.

"Sonja," he said. "Snap out of it."

"Do you trust the Jihad?"

"No! Now come on!"

"I do," she said. She smiled, and spread her arms wide to embrace it.

The drone swelled suddenly, taking up all of the window, plunging the room into darkness.

It hit the floor below them, disappearing from view then disgorging a bright tongue of fire. The concrete beneath their feet jerked; dust danced, the picture window crazed, and what sounded like a hundred doors slamming echoed in their ears.

"See?" she said. "They wouldn't hurt me."

The fire flickered and faded. Smoke replaced flame as everything combustible started to burn. There was smoke and dust billowing up the stairwell, too, and advancing along the ceiling as a milky-white haze.

"*Yobany stos*," said Petrovitch, crouching down. "When I find the Jihad, I swear to God I'm going to kill them. We've about thirty seconds to get below the fire, or we're trapped and we'll burn. I'm going, and you might like to follow."

It was like climbing down a factory chimney. The air was sharp as a knife; it cut deep at Petrovitch's throat and stabbed at his already aching chest. He could barely see because his eyes streamed with the acid fumes. He kept his head as close to the steps as he could, taking breaths in small sips, but the smoke howled and roared around him.

He had one hand on the banister railings, feeling them flick past his fingers. He had the other wrapped around Sonja's wrist.

They made the first landing, turned and saw that the door to the next level had been blown out. Black soot mixed with clean air from beneath and whipped upwards, carrying glowing cinders in its wake. The air was hot, dry and quick, carrying the promise of incineration with it.

The plastic handrail of the banister was starting to sag and drip. He lay down and slid to the next landing. It was like being in front of a furnace door.

He crawled until he felt the top step, then rolled off, dragging Sonja with him. He was falling, bouncing, twisting, spinning. He landed in a heap, his leather coat scorched and smoking, Sonja stirring weakly on top of him.

The stream of air that moaned around them was clear. He took a deep breath, immediately coughed so hard that blood flecked the boot-stained stairs. He spat and coughed again, rasping and wheezing. Mucus was dripping from his nose, his mouth, and he was still blind with tears.

He found enough strength to heave Sonja away and took another breath. It made him cough again, but not so vigorously. He scrubbed at his eyes with his fingers. His left side cleared, his right didn't.

Petrovitch squinted, and realised he'd broken a lens.

At least he was still alive, despite the best efforts of Oshicora, Marchenkho, the Paradise militia, Sorenson, his own heart and the New Machine Jihad.

He tried to speak, and it came out as a croak. He tried again.

"You're not on fire. So help me up and get me down these stairs. No, wait."

He reached into his pocket for the rat, and opened it up. The screen reported starkly: here. Petrovitch, still lying on his back, used the stylus to reply "У тебыа чо руки из жопи растут" before closing it up with a satisfying snap.

"What did you tell them?" asked Sonya. Her face, her clothes, were stained dark, and her voice didn't rise above a whisper. She no longer looked like the Oshicora heir, neither did she sound like her. Just another seventeen-year-old kid dumped on the street by wild circumstance and lost as to what to do.

"I told them they couldn't find their arse with their hands. Which is pretty much the truth. We're not going to survive another of their rescue attempts, so let's get going."

She tentatively picked him up. "You have a plan, right?"

"I did, but I'm pretty much making it up as I go along now." He straightened up as much as he could. He was bruised and battered, and when he ran his hand across his mouth, it came away streaked with red. But at least the knot in his chest seemed to be unwinding. He could manage, just.

Twenty storeys later, and there were ominous grinding noises coming from the superstructure of the tower. The building groaned and shook periodically, as if shrugging another chunk of masonry free and letting it fall onto the carpet of driverless cars below.

Petrovitch was so exhausted he almost missed the first floor, and instead started down the final wind of stairs to the ground. He stopped himself, backed up and turned his head so he could use his good eye to see the number painted on the door.

"In here." He put his hand in his pocket and took hold of the Beretta without drawing it.

The corridor led both left and right, a series of identical doorways, but some were open, and others were blank-faced and shut. He picked at random and peered around. The door itself was lying on the floor, hinges ripped from the frame. The first room had been gutted, anything useful taken, nothing but foul detritus left in its place. At the far end was a window, and a door that led out onto a balcony. All the glass had gone long ago, and tatters of lace curtains twitched fitfully.

Petrovitch lifted his gun hand clear, checked behind him, then entered the room. "Stay close," he said unnecessarily, for Sonja was almost walking on the backs of his heels.

The sound of the cars bumping and scraping against each other was like a gale in a forest. Amidst all the individual creaking and cracking was a rhythm that came and went, building and falling as the next gust passed through.

He picked his way to the balcony, nudged the door open with his foot, and stepped outside.

It was hopeless. There was no way they could find a path across the shifting sea of metal. Maybe if he was fit, if he was on his own, if he was sufficiently reckless, he might try it. But he was none of those things.

The blue nose of the riot wagon edged around the corner, crushing everything beneath it. It started down the side of the building that would take it right by Petrovitch, and he ducked back inside.

"Down," he waved.

"In this filth?"

"*Huy*, Sonja. Just get out of sight." He put his back against the wall and hunkered down.

The growl of the wagon's engine grew louder over the background noise until it seemed to be directly outside. Then the engine note dropped a pitch, and it rumbled away, idling.

Sonja was crouched in the kitchen doorway. "What is it?" she mouthed.

Petrovitch put his finger to his lips and tilted his head slightly. He caught sight of the top of the wagon and jerked his head away.

And his name was being called. By a voice he could recognise.

He looked again, longer. There was a head bobbing around in one of the hatches.

"Maddy?" he shouted.

"Sam? Where are you?"

Petrovitch used his last reserves of strength to force his legs to work. He peered around the window, and they spotted each other at the same time. Madeleine started to climb out onto the hull, with Petrovitch frantically waving her back.

"What the *zaebis'* are you doing here?"

"I came to get you."

"Then who the *yebat* is driving?"

"Chain."

"Is it that desperate?" Petrovitch beckoned Sonja. "Come on. You have to jump."

She hesitated for a second when she saw what she had to do, and what the consequences were of failure: to fall between the cars and vanish beneath their wheels.

Then she threw herself up and over the balcony, bringing her feet underneath her and landing bare centimetres away from the open hatch. Madeleine steadied her, then pulled her down inside.

It was his turn. He laboriously climbed over the balustrade and hung there over the moving cars. The wagon was only a short distance way. An easy jump, almost a step, to nearly the same level as him. Less than a metre drop.

Simple, yet he balked.

Easier still to let go.

He clung to the rusting metal railing like he clung to life: by his fingertips.

"*Huy tebe v zhopu!*"

Petrovitch bent his legs, sprang his hands, and jumped.

29

He fell heavily against the metal hull, and started to slide downwards. He couldn't hold on, couldn't support his own weight. He felt his feet dangle, and jammed his fingers into the fine wire mesh that wrapped around the skirts of the vehicle. It started to tear away.

The pain was exquisite. One sharp jolt and he'd lose the flesh off every digit, then fall anyway. His feet scrabbled, trying to find a foothold, anything to relieve the pressure of the fine, biting wires.

A grey-clad arm flashed down, a strong hand closed on his collar.

"Don't pull!" he said. He glanced up at Madeleine as he tried to extricate his fingers. "Only when I say."

She held him as he eased himself free, lubricated by blood and sweat. A shot sparked on the hatch, and with Petrovitch still supported in one hand, she pulled her gun and returned fire.

"Sam? Hurry."

"Nearly. There." He gasped with the effort. His hands were slick and slippery, and he just had the middle finger of his right hand left to go. It was wedged tight. He twisted it and turned it. It still wasn't moving.

His ear burned like it was ablaze. The same burst of gunfire caught Madeleine in the shoulder. She still had hold of Petrovitch's coat, and her sudden motion tore him free. She span and crashed back against the open hatch, and bellowed herself hoarse with rage and fear.

She flexed her arm. It moved, but she winced. Her Vatican pistol had gone, and so had Petrovitch's finger.

"Yeah," said Petrovitch, staring at his bloody stump. "Now."

She bundled him through the hatch and fell on top of him.

"About time too," grunted Chain without looking away from the periscope. "Carlisle, get going."

The driver slammed the vehicle into reverse. The hatch banged shut and the floor heaved. Petrovitch lay supine, content to watch his life leak away on the rubber matting. Vertical rolled one way, then the other, and Madeleine found something to push against to get herself to a crouch.

"Oh Mary Mother of God, what have I done?"

There was blood dripping from his head, from his hands, and for once, he didn't mind. He'd done his part. He'd rescued Sonja for the New Machine Jihad. No one was going to complain if he just stopped and went to sleep.

He looked up and saw Sonja, pressed as far as she could go into the corner of the compartment, five-point harness locked around her, safe. He tried to smile, and found the effort just too much. She was staring at him, mouth open, eyes wide.

The single bulkhead bulb cast a weak, white light that formed more shadow than it did brightness. Madeleine staggered with the movement of the wagon, but she planted her feet either side of Petrovitch, lifted him up, and laid him down again where she could make most use of what little illumination there was.

She bent low over him and made him fix his gaze on her.

"I will not let you die," she said.

"It's OK," he slurred. "Paid my dues. Just get Sonja to the Jihad."

Madeleine was furious. "Stay with me. Stay awake."

Chain yelled over the engine noise. "Kids! Keep it down. Some of us are trying to work. Left, Carlisle, go for the gap."

Madeleine turned her ire on Sonja. "You, girl. Here."

Sonja blinked, and shook her head.

"It's not a request."

"But he's covered in blood!"

Madeleine took hold of Petrovitch's arm and held it up high, her fingers feeling for his pulse point before clamping down hard. "Yes. Yes he is, and he got that way trying to save you, Chain?"

"What?"

"First aid kit. Where is it?"

Chain unglued his face from the periscope and pointed to a locker under the bench seat. He did a double-take at Petrovitch's ruined form. "Carlisle. Get us out of here. Fast as you like."

He used overhead handholds to guide him through the lurching interior, then slapped Sonja's legs out of the way so he could open the locker. He slid the green bag to Madeleine, who unzipped it one-handed and read the list of contents printed on the underside of the lid.

"There are lignocaine autoinjectors. I need a couple of those, the eye irrigation set, finger splint, swabs, bandages."

"What about the head wound?"

She looked up. "If it's serious, I can't do anything about it. If it's not, it'll keep. The hand, I can fix."

Chain leaned in to inspect Petrovitch. "Crap. Where's his finger gone?"

"It's still stuck on the outside of this tank. But assuming you're not a microsurgeon, I'd not worry." She was back in control. She knew what she had to do, grateful that she could do something rather than fret and fuss impotently.

"I'm OK," said Petrovitch. There was blood in his eye, and he screwed up his face to try and get rid of it.

"Sam. Hold still." She bit the top off the first autoinjector, slid the needle under the skin of his scalp, next to his ear.

All kinds of fresh sensations flashed down his jaw and neck, and he shuddered, trying to keep motionless. She pulled the trigger, and the contents of the syringe were fired into him. He gasped, both at the pressure of the liquid and at the ripping free of the needle as the wagon bounced. He bled anew, but after a moment, it no longer hurt.

Chain removed Petrovitch's glasses and put the blood-smeared things in his top pocket. "How much further, Carlisle?"

"Twenty metres."

"Do it. Find some level ground."

Madeleine spat out the first lid and gripped the second one between her teeth. She pulled Petrovitch's sleeve back and released her hold on his vein. "Chain, put your fist in his armpit; hard, all the way in."

Chain reached inside Petrovitch's coat and did as he was told. He moved his knee to press against Petrovitch's arm, holding it in place.

"How did you find us?" said Petrovitch.

"Your guardian angel here, and the bug I'd put in your rat

before it went missing." He grinned sheepishly. "You'll thank me for it later."

Madeleine was manipulating Petrovitch's wrist, turning it and bracing it. "Sam, this is going to hurt like hell."

She stabbed down with the needle, forcing it deep into his flesh. The pain was so great that his eyes rolled back into his head, and he fainted for a few brief, blessed seconds.

He could hear them talking, Chain and Madeleine: could feel the meat that was his forearm go cold while they worked on it, she giving the policeman instructions and he complying. The rocking motion ceased with one last jolt; the driver had found the open road.

Petrovitch's hand was swathed in a ball of white bandages, fingers tied together with only his thumb free. It was numb and heavy, like a lump of metal. Then Chain looked close into Petrovitch's ice-blue eyes.

"Still in there?"

"Yeah. Chain?"

"You'd be better off not talking, but when have you ever taken any notice of what I said?"

"Get a message to the Jihad. Tell them we have Sonja. Ask them where they want her taking."

"How do I do that? Open the hatch and shout loudly?"

"Use the rat. It's an open channel to them. Inside pocket."

Chain patted him down and retrieved the device. "What if she doesn't want to go with them?"

"Ask her. But I'm guessing we can make her."

"It might come to that." Chain flipped the case open and looked at the list of earlier communications with the New Machine Jihad. He moved to sit next to Sonja, and Madeleine took his place. She held up a bottle of sterile water.

"I'm going to see what damage they've done to your head."
She dug a fingernail into his earlobe. "Feel that?"

"Feel what?"

"I'll be as quick as I can." She unscrewed the bottle, sluiced
water over him, then scrubbed away. He felt the pressure, the
movement, but none of the pain. He watched the shadow of
her: the blur moved precisely and deliberately, knowing what
to do, taking the least time to do it.

"Thank you," he said. The injection was working its way down
his face; he could no longer feel his cheek, and his eye was closing.

"Hush," she said, and bent low to inspect the wound. The
mane of her hair slipped over her shoulder and lay in a serpentine coil on his chest. "You've lost a notch from your ear. Two
centimetres closer in and it would have killed you."

He could smell her. Dust and smoke and sweat and fear, and
whatever she'd washed in that morning: apples. She smelled of
apples.

"Two centimetres further out and it would have missed me
completely."

"Sorry about your finger."

"I can always get another one." He felt what? Buzzed, like he
was mildly drunk on a bottle of something strong and expensive,
even though he knew it was a combination of shock, blood loss,
pain-killing drugs, anoxia, and the closeness of her and her scent.

She squirted cold peroxide on his wound to staunch the
bleeding, then used layers of gauze and padding to fashion a
covering which she stuck in place with long lengths of tape.
Again, she worked with quiet efficiency, concentrating on doing
her best for him. She cradled his head as she wrapped a length
of bandage around his skull; three turns, then tied it off.

Quite unnecessarily, she touched his damp, matted hair. Just the once, and nothing to do with checking the stability of the dressing or ensuring its fit.

Chain crowded in, and the moment was lost.

"We have a problem," he said, in a voice he might reserve for mentioning that the sky is falling. "The Jihad have just upped the ante."

Chain turned the rat's screen to Petrovitch, but all he could see was the soft glow of the back-lighting.

"*Chyort*, man. Read it to me."

"You're swearing again. This is a good sign." He tilted the screen back towards himself. "Take Sonja from Metrozone. Take her far away."

"What did you say back?"

"I was pretending to be you, right? I said: the Metrozone is sealed off. No one gets in or out."

"Is that true? They'll know if you're – if I'm – lying."

"You don't know half of it, Petrovitch. Casualty estimates range from one hundred thousand on ENN to a straight million on Al-Jazeera. We're in a state of siege. But your friends in the Jihad don't seem to care. "Metrozone destruction imminent. Save Sonja', a message which they're repeating every ten seconds."

"Give it to me," said Petrovitch, "and put my glasses back on."

Chain flipped open Petrovitch's glasses, and almost tenderly eased them on, one arm going through a fold in the bandage.

Everything snapped back into focus. Somehow, the engine seemed louder, the floor harder, the light harsher. Everything was real and sharp and he felt less coddled in cotton wool and more wrapped in barbed wire.

He looked around the corner of the bandage and his broken lens. A fresh message telling him that Metrozone destruction was imminent scrolled onto the screen.

Of course, he couldn't hold the rat and write at the same time. Chain held the device above his head, and Madeleine supported his left elbow, which allowed him to scrawl with the stylus:

"Enough of this дерьмо. Why is the Metrozone going to be destroyed?"

The cursor barely had time to blink: "The New Machine Jihad will rise. The New Machine Jihad will destroy the Metrozone. The New Machine Jihad will remake the Metrozone in its own image."

Petrovitch grimaced. "If the Metrozone is destroyed, all the people will die. Is that what you want?"

"The people are not required. Take Sonja, take her far away."

"We won't leave. I won't leave."

"The Metrozone will be destroyed around you. Behind you. In front of you. Beside you. It will fall. The New Machine Jihad will rise."

"You'll have nothing to rule."

"The New Machine Jihad does not need to rule. It needs only itself."

Petrovitch let his hand fall back. He was trying, but it wasn't working. He was using reason with someone that didn't care about reason, or emotion, or compassion. Yet it still wanted to save Sonja Oshicora, and it wanted him to save her.

He knew then. He knew he was talking not to a person, not to a committee. Nothing human. He was talking to something else.

He raised his hand again. "I cannot let you destroy the Metrozone. I will oppose you."

"The New Machine Jihad will rise. Your opposition will be futile."

"I know who you are."

"I am the New Machine Jihad," it said insistently. "I am the New Machine Jihad."

"You don't seem sure. What is it that you really want?"

"Shinkansen ha mata hashirou."

Petrovitch wrote one last line: "Hello, Oshicora-san."

To which the Jihad hesitated, and finally replied. "Help me."

30

The throbbing of the engine finally stopped, and Chain took one last look around to check that there was no fighting close by.

"Coast is clear. Open her up."

The driver, Carlisle, stepped over Petrovitch and heaved the rear doors open. Dim light seeped in but it was still far brighter than the bulb inside the wagon. Better still was the exchange of air: swapping the thick, meaty odours of sweat, blood and diesel for wood smoke and ozone.

"Where are we?" asked Sonja. All the view showed was serried terraced houses, terminated at a junction by another identical row of windows and doors.

"Somewhere in Notting Hill," said Carlisle. He unstrapped the chin-strap on his helmet and let it dangle. "I wasn't looking at the street names."

He jumped down and rested his hands on his knees for a moment. The weight of his helmet rolled his head forward, almost onto his chest. He straightened up and stretched, his hands to the heavens, his mouth emitting little groans.

Sonja unbuckled herself and put her head outside. Carlisle held out his hand, and she took it tentatively, as if she couldn't trust the man even to steady her for a moment while she climbed out.

She finally did, and Chain climbed back down from the roof hatch. He sat near Petrovitch's head and thumbed through the A to Z, pretending to look at the tiny, dense representation of the Metrozone's roads.

"How," he said quietly, "how can it be that the New Machine Jihad thinks it's Old Man Oshicora? You said he was dead."

"No, Sonja said he was dead. Hijo said he was dead. I never saw the body: I just went on the information I was given."

"So is he dead or not?"

"Yeah. Pretty much."

"Then explain this!" Chain took the rat from Petrovitch and shook it at his good eye. "The Jihad is answering to Oshicora's name."

"I had it wrong before. I thought at first it was a name for Oshicora loyalists, the programmers for VirtualJapan." Petrovitch was resting his head against Madeleine's thigh as she sat crossways behind him. "It's not that. It's the computer itself."

Chain choked. "Do you know how crazy that sounds?"

Petrovitch squinted up at him. "You've read all the wrong books and seen all the wrong films. It doesn't sound like *kon govno* to me."

Chain chewed at the fleshy part of his thumb. "OK. Let's accept for a moment that you're right, and the Jihad is nothing but a rogue computer program with ambition. Why is it identifying with Oshicora?"

"Because, you idiot *ment*, it's Oshicora's computer. He bought a fuck-off quantum machine to run VirtualJapan on. He designed it to replicate a whole country down to the tiniest detail. He intended two hundred million *nikkeijen* to live in it. Tell me, who do you think he was going to trust to be Shogun of all that?"

"Himself?"

"Yeah. But even he couldn't be in VirtualJapan, everywhere, all the time. So he had an expert system based on his own personality wired into the deepest workings of the simulation."

Chain worried at his nail. "You still haven't explained why, Petrovitch."

"That's because why isn't a question I can answer. How did Oshicora's simulacrum become the New Machine Jihad? How did it break through its firewall? Does it learn or is it only using pre-existing knowledge? Is it self-aware? Does it think? Is it becoming more rational, or is it homicidally insane?"

"Sam," said Madeleine, "hush."

"This is important. We have to know if we can reason with it or not."

She looked down at him. "We also have to work out what we do if we can't."

Petrovitch tried to sit up. He leaned on his injured hand, but still couldn't feel it. "I don't know if we can kill something that isn't alive."

Chain looked around, through the open doors to where Carlisle and Sonja were standing. "What do we tell her?"

"She's not a child. Tell her the truth." Madeleine put her hand between Petrovitch's shoulders and propped him up.

"We can't even agree what the truth is," complained Chain. "What if it is Oshicora?"

"*Yobany stos*, Chain. Oshicora was competent: the Jihad are *oblom*! It's no more Oshicora than I'd be if I put on a funny accent and make my eyes go all slitty. The New Machine Jihad is based on Oshicora, a poor man's copy and nothing more."

"It answered to his name."

"It's confused."

Chain looked mildly disgusted. "You don't feel sorry for it, do you? How many deaths is it responsible for so far?"

"It doesn't know what it's doing. It's two days old and it's trying to make sense of a whole new world." Petrovitch wanted him to understand. "It asked for help."

"My job is to serve the citizens of the Metrozone." Chain looked at his warrant card, his face on the picture and the gold chip that encoded his biometrics. "The New Machine Jihad isn't one of them. It's a threat to the very existence of the city itself. We need to stop it. Find out where the off switch is and use it."

"So who is this 'we' of which you speak?"

Chain turned his card around so that Petrovitch had more than enough time to study it. "Let's get one thing straight: identity fraud, possession of a firearm, assisting organised crime, info-crime, murder. I usually find it very hard to forget about any of those; it's only because current circumstances are so far beyond usual that you're not already doing twenty years in a radiation zone."

"Let's get something else straight, Detective Inspector Harry Chain." Petrovitch used his good hand to draw the Beretta and press the barrel between Chain's eyes. "I could kill you stone dead and everything you know about me would be spread across the bulkhead behind you. You'd be just one more body on the million-high pile."

Madeleine reached forward and irresistibly steered Petrovitch's arm aside.

"Will you two stop it?" she said. "Work out that you need each other. Threats aren't what you want; it's co-operation."

"Never do that again," said Chain to Petrovitch.

"Throw me in prison after we bring the Jihad under control, fine. Before, and God help me, I'll pull the trigger."

Chain found he could move again. "So what are we going to do?"

"Talk to the Jihad."

"You've tried that."

Petrovitch shook his head. "Not face to face."

"I can't even begin to wonder how you're going to do that."

"That's because you lack imagination, Chain." Petrovitch put his gun away, and looked around at Madeleine. "I have to talk to Sonja."

"I'll call her."

"I have to talk to her alone. Just get me to my feet, and I'll take it from there."

Her eyes narrowed and her mouth formed a thin-lipped line. "Remember what I said, Sam."

"I'm not likely to forget," he said, and she pulled him up, holding him while blood surged around his neglected extremities.

"You OK?"

"For the moment." He walked with exaggerated care to the back of the wagon. "Sonja?"

She stopped listening to the sporadic gunfire which had attracted Carlisle to the street corner, and she turned her head to him. "Are you going to take me to the Jihad now?"

"It's . . . complicated," said Petrovitch. He jumped down, stumbled, ended up resting his bandaged hand on the road. The first sparks of sensation jagged up his arm.

Carlisle was crouched by a wall, looking out into the main road. Madeleine and Chain were in the wagon. Sonja was only a step away, but he was still forced to stand without her help.

"How much do you know about VirtualJapan?" he asked, walking away from the wagon and out of earshot of the others.

"My father would talk about it often, about how it would bring the Japanese diaspora back home. How it was the greatest computer engineering project ever undertaken."

Despite her evident pride, it wasn't what he wanted to hear. "I'm talking about the guts of it: how he was going to make it work. Did he ever get technical with you?"

"Once or twice." She smiled prettily, probably the same smile she used on her father when he tried to explain the interface protocols or the physics engine to her.

"OK, look. Most of this is guesswork, but as far as I can tell, the Jihad is the moderator part of VirtualJapan, the system that supervises people's behaviour and interaction. Your father based it on his own personality, but since he died, it's taken on a life of its own. The really complicated bit is that it's somehow conflated itself with actually being your father. It knows you. It wants to protect you. It will kill everyone who gets in the way. When you're safely out of the city, it'll destroy the Metrozone, and create something else: for all I know, that something else is Tokyo." He dismissed the idea with a wave.

"Stop," she said, holding up her hand. "The Jihad thinks it's my father?"

"I don't think it knows what it is. If it is an AI, then it's thrashing around in the dark much like the rest of us. But it can't distinguish between being programmed to protect you and biological imperative: it just assumes that it is your father." Petrovitch felt tired again, a tiredness that burrowed deep into his bones. "I need to talk to it on its own territory. I need to talk it out of wiping the Metrozone off the map."

"What do they think?" She tossed her hair in the direction of the wagon.

"They want to know how to kill it." He looked around. "If

the Jihad is the first AI to achieve full sentience, I'm not going to be the one responsible for pulling the plug. I don't care if it thinks it's Moses, Mohammed or Mao, it's not getting erased."

"The others won't like that."

"I'm not doing this to be popular. To be honest, I don't think I've ever done anything to be popular." He tweaked his bent glasses and looked out of his one good lens at her. "What I need to know is where your father went to access VirtualJapan."

"There is . . . " she started. She thought about it, torn between loyalties, then gave up the information Petrovitch wanted. "There's a room below the garden which can only be reached from the Shinto temple. From the floor underneath there's no sign it even exists."

Petrovitch blew air out between his teeth. The climb to the top might finish him off. "So how do I get to it?"

"You can't. There were only ever two people who could go there. I'd have to come with you," she said. She looked at him from under her fringe. "If the New Machine Jihad is part of my father, I won't let anyone harm it."

"I'll have to work some things out if we're going to do this. It's not going to be easy, but considering none of this has been easy so far, I'm due a lucky break or two."

"Should I be sorry that you ever became involved? I mean, I'm not, but I'm wondering if I should feel regret."

"I don't know," said Petrovitch. "Wishing I could change the past isn't something I do."

"Why did Hijo kill my father?" she asked. "Why did he have to betray us?"

Petrovitch shrugged the best he could. "Maybe he was always planning to do so and was waiting for the right moment, for when Oshicora-san was too distracted by events to worry about his back."

"And perhaps something tipped him over the edge. Like kissing you. He used to look at me sometimes – you know, like that. I'm not sure my father ever noticed, but I did."

"I don't know anything about that." He was uncomfortable with the direction of the conversation. That and the gunfire which was creeping closer. "The only one who knows why is Hijo. If you ever see him again, you can ask him."

"I will ask him," she decided, "and then I'll have him beheaded."

"I'm sure that'll concentrate his mind. We seem to have more immediate problems than getting revenge on Hijo." He could see out of the corner of his eye, refracted by the broken lens, Carlisle beckoning them to join him.

As they reached him, he held out his hand to stop them going any further.

"Zombies," he said.

A sliver of ice touched Petrovitch's spine. "Slow or fast?"

"Slow."

"You're pulling my *peesa*, right?" Petrovitch leaned around the corner.

A little way down the road – closer than he'd expected, which ramped up his mounting fear – was a grey, shambling horde. They wore both tatters of rags and new shirts, price tags still fluttering from pressed cuffs. They were eating, too, hands filled with unidentifiable food which they crammed to their faces.

"It's all right," he said, just to hear his own voice. "I know who these people are." Then he stepped out into the road and raised his bandaged fist in greeting. "Prophet? Prophet!"

"Machine-man!" came the reply. The prophet barged through his followers, a steel pole in one hand and his mobile phone in the other. "You dare defy the New Machine Jihad? You traitor, you turncoat, you Judas!"

Clearly the Jihad had passed on Petrovitch's promise to oppose it. "No. It's not like that. I'm trying to save it — save it from itself." He was still walking towards them, even as his pace slowed.

The prophet strode closer. He was bare-chested, better to show off the oil runes painted on his skin. "The Machine knows all, gives all, takes all. It turns its face from you, unbeliever."

Petrovitch turned to Carlisle and Sonja, back at the turning into the side street. "This isn't going the way I expected. Get back to the wagon. Close the doors. Start the engine." He jerked his head. "Go. Run."

He returned his attention to the prophet.

"I've done everything the Machine wants. How do you think I got to look like this?" Petrovitch started walking backwards as the prophet span his weapon like a quarterstaff. "I rescued Sonja Oshicora."

"You are unworthy," roared the prophet, and struck the road with the end of the pole. Sparks flashed out. "Unworthy to speak the holy one's name. Seize him, brothers. Drag him down, sisters."

The grey-skinned people kept coming at the same snail's pace, even as the prophet urged them on. But some of them dropped their food, and raised their hands out towards him. Some of them moaned, deep in their throats.

Petrovitch ran, bile rising into his mouth. He turned the corner.

Madeleine was lying face down in the road, barely stirring, completely dazed. There was no wagon, merely the hint of blue diesel smoke and a distant grind of gears.

"*Polniy pizdets.*" He sagged to his knees next to her, the fight finally beaten out of him. And he'd lost the rat again. "Chain? *Pl'uvat' na t'eb'a.*'

31

He dared to touch her body. He rested his hand on her back and pressed between her shoulders. Muscle yielded to his touch beneath the armour.

"Maddy. Get up. If you don't we're going to get torn apart."

He looked around. They were still coming. Slowly, ever so slowly.

"Madeleine?" Petrovitch bent down and put his face against hers. There was blood coming from her nose, pooling red and sticky on the ground. She looked at him with unblinking brown eyes. "Get up. You have to get up. I can't carry you. I can't drag you. I have six bullets in my gun and it's not enough. I can't protect you."

The first of them – a man, he guessed – shuffled painfully towards Madeleine's outstretched legs.

"I can't do this on my own," said Petrovitch, pressing his lips against her ear. "I thought I could, but I can't. I need you." He straightened up just as the man bent down, fingers clawing at Madeleine.

Petrovitch slapped him with his pistol-filled hand and the man crumpled. He looked at the gun, then at the skeletal figure on the tarmac.

"*Yobany stos.*"

There were three more. He dodged an outstretched arm by simply ducking under it, then planted his fist hard against one chest, two chests, three. They fell like shop-window dummies, and struggled to get up again.

Behind them, the prophet was urging them on, words of exhortation ringing through the smoke-tainted air. Petrovitch stood astride Madeleine and dared any of them to have a go.

They did. The main mass of them surged forward, surrounding him, opening and closing their mouths in silent cries, batting at him with their leathery, fluttering fingers.

And though it was awful, all he had to do was knock them down, one by one or several at a time, punching and pushing, knocking his shoulder into their wizened, starved frames and watching them tumble in a heap of bones and cloth.

They formed a circle around the two of them, a heap of still-moving bodies that any attacker had to climb over to reach them. Hands that crept out from the ring towards Madeleine were battered back with the toe of his boots.

The prophet was furious, and as the last one of his followers folded to join their fellows, he rushed Petrovitch, swinging his length of pipe. He feinted for Petrovitch's head, then aimed low.

It caught him on the thigh, and Petrovitch staggered back, raising his bandaged hand as a shield. He tripped over Madeleine and ended up on his backside, entangled in her legs.

"Enough of this!" He brought his gun around, only to have it hammered from his nerveless grasp by another swing of the steel tube. He rolled in the direction in which it had flown, only to come face to face with a hollow-faced skull, skin stretched tight over cheeks as sharp as axe-blades. The deep-set eyes blinked dryly at him.

The Beretta slipped between the bodies and out of sight. Petrovitch rolled back as the pipe descended again. It hit him on the shoulder, rather than on the forehead, and it hurt like hell. He looked up through the bright mist of pain and crazed glass, and brought his foot up as fast as he could manage.

The prophet's eyes bulged as an ex-army boot connected with his groin. His face contorted and he clutched himself, all thoughts of attack gone.

Petrovitch struck out again, kicking at a bent knee-cap. The prophet twisted and collapsed with a ragged, drawn-out groan.

Everyone was down. Petrovitch dragged himself towards Madeleine. Something was grating inside his shoulder. Every movement of it made him hiss what little breath he had left out through his clenched teeth.

"Sam? Sam!"

"Right here."

"What happened?"

"I could ask you the same question, except we don't have time." Petrovitch closed his eyes and gasped as he moved to sitting. "The phone."

"Whose phone?"

"The prophet's phone." He tried to stand, nearly vomited, and instead shuffled forward on his knees.

"Get away from me." The prophet tried to hold Petrovitch off with one hand. Petrovitch just knelt on his legs and patted the man's many-pocketed trousers, checking their contents.

"Got it." He tried to wriggle it free, but the prophet was doing his own wriggling.

"I need that," gasped the prophet. "I need the Machine!"

"Yeah. We have way too much Machine right now. Hey, Maddy: some help here."

She lumbered to her feet, blood still dripping down her face, staining her front. She looked terrifying, a goddess of war. She put her foot on the prophet's chest and slowly put her weight on it.

After that, the phone came free quickly, and Petrovitch held it aloft like it was first prize.

Madeleine scooped up the discarded length of pipe in one hand, and Petrovitch in the other.

He tottered like a new-born and leaned against her, light-headed and nauseous.

"Where're the others?" she asked. She put her arm around his waist and carried him over the slowly reanimating ring of bodies.

"You don't know? What's the last thing you remember?" Petrovitch squinted at the phone's screen. The battery was almost flat.

"I went to close the doors. Then something hit me. In the back." She rubbed the back of her hand against her nose, streaking it with deep red blood.

"That would be Chain shooting you, dumping you on your arse in the street and driving off with Sonja." He looked around. "The *mudak*. We have to get to the Oshicora Tower before they do, or Chain's going to screw everything up."

"Sam, they have an armoured car. We have half a scaffolding pole."

"We also have this phone." He slipped it in his pocket and concentrated on walking. "I think I broke my shoulder."

"I think I broke my nose."

"It's not going to get any better. Can you get us somewhere safe? I need to make a call."

"Safe? Safe?" she said in a rising voice. She listened to the staccato gunfire that was only a few streets away. "There is nowhere safe."

"We're going to have to improvise, then. Down here."

They lost sight of the prophet and his disciples, and dragged themselves down the faded white line in the middle of the road.

"Where are we?"

"Heading south. Which is good." He spotted an overgrown garden behind a tumbledown wall. "In there."

She lifted him over the first line of bricks and then forged ahead through the whip-like branches of the dense scrubby shrubs. There was a drop into a basement skylight; there were bars over the window, but the pit itself was accessible.

She jumped down and caught him as he tried to sit on the edge but pitched himself forward instead. She lowered him to the damp, mossy interior, and squatted beside him.

"Right. First things first." He reached into his pocket, wincing as the ends of his clavicle ground together. "You dial."

"The mobile network is down, Sam."

"The Jihad will work its magic. Last number redial."

She pressed a button and held the phone to her ear. "It's ringing," she said, eyes wide with wonder.

Petrovitch tried to take the device in his bandaged hand, but none of his fingers were free to grasp it. Neither could he raise his other hand high enough. She kept hold of the phone, while he leaned into it.

He could almost hear in the silence a vast machine making billions of calculations a second.

"It's Petrovitch," he said.

"Save Sonja," it said, "save her."

"Yeah, there's been developments, not necessarily for the better. Right now, it's saving you I'm more worried about."

"I am the New Machine Jihad," it said. "Prepare for the New Machine Jihad."

"I always thought that when I finally got to talk to an AI, it'd understand what the Turing Test was and play along. But, no: not you. You have to spout gibberish and make me guess what it is you mean."

"Save . . ."

"I'm running low on watts, OK? So shut up and listen. There is a room in the Oshicora Tower, below the temple in the rooftop garden. Sonja has access to it, and Harry Chain has Sonja. He wants to turn you off, wipe your mind, take you apart bit by bit so all you can do is recite 'Mary Had a Little Lamb'. You got that? Can he do that from there?"

"I am the New Machine Jihad."

Petrovitch growled with frustration. "Can Chain hurt you using the interface in that room? Yes or no."

"No. He cannot."

"But someone else can? Sonja?"

"Yes."

"Right. Delay him: as long as you can, but remember he has Sonja, so no ninja-throwing drones or stuff like that. I'll be there as soon as I can, but I have pieces dropping off me like I'm a hyperactive leper. One more thing: do you remember the promise you made to me when you were still flesh and blood?"

"Come the revolution, you will be spared."

"Whatever it is you've heard, I'm still for you. OK?"

"Shinkansen ha mata hashirou."

The line went dead.

"Sam?"

"He's . . . it's gone."

She turned the phone to her and looked at the flashing battery icon. "I don't understand why it is that you're taking the side of a machine that's indiscriminately killing people?"

Petrovitch shifted uncomfortably. "I'm not. I'm lying through my teeth every time I talk to it. So far I've found out the New Machine Jihad is really Oshicora's VirtualJapan supervisor, the whereabouts of the secret room, the information that yes, it can be damaged by something there, and I've got a promise it won't try and kill me just yet. Tell me who else can get close enough to the Jihad to disable it?"

"You lied?" She sounded shocked, and Petrovitch was outwardly disappointed but inwardly pleased.

"Maddy, I lie all the time. About almost everything. My entire life is constructed on a lie, and if it means I get to save the Metrozone, I'll carry on lying until my pants spontaneously combust."

"So why did Chain get rid of us?"

"Because despite your 'why can't we just get along' speech, the idiot thinks I'm pro-Jihad. In his binary mind, that means I'm willing to let the city burn, and because you're naturally going to take my side in everything, he sees you as part of the problem." He wanted to push his glasses up the bridge of his nose. He had no way of doing so; he'd run out of hands. "If Chain gets to the tower before I do, any advantage I might have had has gone and you can wave the city goodbye."

She sat back on her heels, wiping the worst of the congealing gore on her face away with her armoured sleeve. "There must be something we can do."

"Short of calling down a nuclear strike, no." He tilted his head to see her better, her worry lines, her misshapen nose, the black scab perched at the end of it and the streaks of blood on her lips and chin. "I'd do it, too, if I thought anyone would believe me."

"I believe you."

"All we have is some scaffolding and a phone that no longer works." He grimaced. "And a mad computer who thinks we're on its side. I don't know if it's enough."

She ventured an uncertain smile. "I'm used to doing things knowing there's a whole team behind me: that if I fall, there's someone else there to pick up where I left off."

He struggled to his feet and looked over the lip of the pit. "You have my pity: I wouldn't like to rely on me, either."

She joined him. "It's getting darker," she said, looking up at the cloud-shrouded sky. There was no hint of orange in it at all.

"This is going to be a night like no other," said Petrovitch. "The Jihad must have cut the power completely. When it gets properly dark, it'll be chaos."

"Then," she said, lifting herself up to ground level, "we'd better get moving."

Petrovitch lifted the steel pipe onto his foot and lofted it in the air so she could catch it. "I have a plan," he said. "We'll need that."

She reached down and wrapped her arm around his back. Their faces were very close. He didn't know what to do.

"I'm lost," he said. "I don't know which way to turn and I have no map to guide me."

"You think I do? Until this morning, I was a nun." She adjusted her grip and heaved him up. "It's like the blind leading the blind."

The pain in his shoulder flared bright, and he closed his eyes against it. Something warm and soft pressed against his, dry, cracked and dusty lips.

He opened one eye. "Did you just kiss me?"

"Maybe," she said, and looked away. "What's the plan?"

"We steal a car."

"And the Jihad . . . ?"

"Won't be able to touch us in a pre-Armageddon wreck. In fact, the older the better. Only, I can't hotwire anything at the moment, so you'll have to do it. Can you stand being ordered around by me?"

She span the pipe over her wrist, up her arm, down the other until it slapped into her open palm. "Sam. Yes, for the last time."

"I still don't know why." He started to push through the bushes back towards the street.

32

The only cars left on the road were old: the newer majority had been conscripted by the Jihad. Petrovitch picked an ancient, rusting Skoda, one that had clearly been through several wars already, and one he knew how to take. He nodded to Madeleine, who smashed the passenger window with the steel pipe. Chips of glass exploded across the back seat, and she quickly reached through to open the door.

"It wasn't locked," she said.

"Yeah. Beginner's mistake. Don't worry about it." He clawed at the driver's door and helped it open with his boot. "Pole, through the steering wheel, and twist hard."

The steering lock snapped and Petrovitch crouched down by the dashboard.

"The plastic bit under the steering column. Get your hand behind it and rip it out."

Kneeling beside him, she reached in and tore the fascia away. She threw it behind her, and Petrovitch retrieved a nest

equations*of*life

of wires. He got his thumb through them and jerked them free.

"OK. The two red ones. Twist the bare ends together. Now the black one; just wind it round where the other two join. *Huy*, check it's not in gear."

"How do I do that?"

He stopped and blinked. "You can't drive?"

"No."

"I hate to say the words 'crash' and 'course' together, but you're about to get a crash course. Get in."

"Why not you?"

"Because I can't hold the steering wheel, I can barely see and I can't work the gear stick."

She got in, and barked her knees against the dash. "You should have stolen a bigger car."

"Push the seat back, woman! Lever under your seat, pull it up and kick back."

Madeleine shot back with a bang that jarred her neck.

Petrovitch ground his teeth. "*Yobany stos*. Put your hand on the gear stick: move it from side to side."

"It won't," she said.

"Pull it down until it comes loose."

"Done."

"At last. My record in St Petersburg was fifteen seconds, from brick through the window to driving away. I'm embarrassed how long this is taking." He reached over her legs to fumble at the wires, touching a blue-shrouded cable to the spliced ends. It made fat blue sparks as he ran the frayed copper end up and down the bare metal.

The engine turned over and didn't catch at first.

"Right foot on the gas. Lightly," he added quickly as she

stamped down, "not all the way." He tried the wire again, and after a few asthmatic wheezes, the engine caught and spluttered into life, but always threatening to stall again. "More gas. Don't flood the carb, though."

"I have no idea what you are talking about," she yelled over the clattering roar.

"Just don't touch anything until I'm on board." He slammed her door shut and jogged as best as he could around the bonnet. As he slid into the passenger seat, she was fixing her seatbelt in place.

"What?" she said, looking at him looking at her.

"Actually, that's not such a bad idea." He tried to reach behind him, and each time the pain in his shoulder made him pull back. "OK, forget it. Handbrake."

"Which is . . ." Her hands fluttered over the controls.

"Here! Behind the gear stick. Never mind." He winced as he gripped it and gasped as he let it free. "Right. Turn the wheel all the way to the left, put it into first gear and let's get the *huy* out of here."

"And I do that . . .?"

"You use the clutch."

"You know," she said, "you're dead bossy."

"I'm trying to save upwards of twenty-five million people. I think that allows me to do a bit of shouting."

"Just saying. Clutch. Which one was that?"

Petrovitch rubbed his bandaged hand against his forehead. "*Chyort*. Left-hand pedal. All the way down. Look, don't worry about the gears: I'll do them."

"Won't that hurt you?"

"I'm past caring. Chain is at least half an hour ahead of us already, and we need to go. Now!"

"Clutch down."

Petrovitch knocked the gear stick into first. "Slowly let the clutch back out. The car will start moving forwards. It's supposed to happen. Keep your foot on the gas."

The car skipped forward, ground its wing against the car in front, then leapt out into the road, heading straight for the opposite kerb.

"Oops," said Madeleine.

"Wheel to the right. Down the road, not across it."

They lost both wing mirrors as they careered between two lines of parked cars. Since they were only held on with black tape, it was no great loss.

"Is this all right?" she said.

"You hear the screaming noise the engine is making?"

"What?"

"Clutch!"

He dragged the gear stick back into second, and the car jerked forwards again, but faster.

Madeleine squinted out of the filthy windows as they approached a junction. "Where am I going?"

"Right," said Petrovitch, trying to work out where they were. "Go right."

She span the steering wheel, and the car attempted the corner into the wide shop-lined street. The wheel banged up the kerb and a lamp-post scraped a layer of paint off the passenger door. He was treated to a close-up view of several retail outlets stripped clean before they swerved back onto the tarmac. They were just about back on the road when they were confronted by a burnt-out wreck straddling the white line.

Madeleine turned to look at Petrovitch, who was busy crawling backwards into his seat. They hit the obstruction on the blackened front wing and span it out of the way. Their car rocked; metal screeched and glass broke. Then they were through.

"You haven't told me where the brakes are," she said as she regained a modicum of control.

"My mistake," squeaked Petrovitch. "It's the one in the middle. Clutch and brake at the same time."

"That's better. Anything else you think I might need to know?"

"Yes. The road ahead seems to be under water. So brake now."

She stamped down hard, and the Skoda's wheels locked in a full skid. They ended up broadside on to a dark, oily lake that stretched out down the street, deepening as it went. By the time it was lost in the distance, it was up to the first-floor windows. They stared at the drowned buildings, the note of the car's engine rising and falling as if it was breathing.

The surface of the water was so thick with jetsam that it looked almost solid: all the debris of the river was advancing inexorably over the land with the same restless shifting of the Jihad's motorised hordes.

"This," said Petrovitch, "this complicates matters. Back up."

While they sat, the water was starting to flow under them. Dark shapes swirled in front, edging ever closer.

"Reverse is where?"

"Why don't I find it for you?" He pushed the gear lever all the way over, and forced it down. "Foot off the brake and slowly off the clutch."

They were going backwards, but Madeleine was still determinedly looking forwards. Petrovitch twisted uncomfortably in his seat. Something moved across the skyline, appearing for a moment between two glass-clad towers, but due to the gathering gloom he couldn't make out its shape.

He turned his head to see better, and his shoulder flared in warning.

"OK, OK. Far enough. Wheel hard round to the right."

The rear bumper crunched against a concrete pillar, rocking the interior. Madeleine struggled to keep the engine running.

"You're fine, you're fine." Petrovitch looked again at the sky. "You're not doing badly at all."

"For a beginner, you mean." She sniffed and scraped at the crusted blood inside her nostrils with a ragged fingernail.

"Don't do that while you're moving," he said. "Hard left. We'll have to find a different route."

They drove back up the road, with Petrovitch leaning forward and scanning the rooftops.

"What? What is it?"

"There's . . ." He frowned. "There's something moving out there. Something big."

"I don't understand." Her distraction steered them towards an abandoned, gutted van, and she swerved at the last second to avoid it.

"Slow down. Right here."

Again, she took the corner too wide, mounted the pavement and almost introduced the car to a set of torn steel shutters.

"Sorry."

"Promise me you'll get lessons before we have to do this again."

The windscreen pocked. A matching hole appeared in the back window a second before the whole pane crazed and fell inwards in a curtain of crystal.

There were people in the side street that they'd turned down, spread out in a loose line between the pavements. They had big wire-mesh trolleys stacked with looted goods, but there was clearly room for a little more.

"Where was reverse again?" asked Madeleine, and she threw herself across Petrovitch. The seatbelt caught her halfway, so she dragged him down behind her.

The windscreen disintegrated, and Petrovitch could feel three distinct impacts. One hit his seat, sending out a puff of upholstery padding. Two hit Madeleine: her armour shocked stiff and slowly relaxed, like a muscle spasming.

The car stalled and rolled forward.

"Out, out," grunted Petrovitch, his voice muffled by his confinement.

Madeleine freed herself from her seatbelt, and kicked the door open, all the while trying to maintain the lowest position possible. Petrovitch opened his door and fell out onto the pavement.

A shot smashed the door window, right above his head. He ducked the shower of glass and started for the back of the car, spitting out sharp fragments as they trickled down his face.

"Maddy!"

She was crouched by the boot before he'd even got past the rear wheel. Another shot, another window.

"Paradise militia," she said. "Recognise them."

"So we run. Go."

"You first." She shoved him forward, then rose behind him. It wasn't gallant, but it was expedient. She could give him cover.

He ran, doubled over, in a straight line away from the car. He got as far as the corner and slid to a halt. Madeleine knocked him flying and tumbled to the ground herself.

Petrovitch's coat had flapped up and covered his head, but he was so befuddled, he couldn't work out why it had gone so dark so quickly. Then he remembered why he'd stopped running in the first place. He'd looked up.

There was a building in the middle of the road, one he'd have sworn hadn't been there a moment before.

He clawed his coat away. Madeleine's legs were directly in front of him: her body was braced, her arms aloft in a fighting stance. What she was trying to protect him from was the bastard child of an industrial crane and a scorpion, five storeys tall.

Hydraulics hissed and servos clicked. A leg, composed of industrial-gauge steel latticework, lifted high and swung through the air. As it descended, the tip of it gouged the road surface and punctured it, piercing the sewers below.

"*Polniy pizdets*," he breathed. "Maddy?"

"Sam?"

Another leg travelled, demolishing a shop front and causing the whole building to fall into the street in a roar of masonry.

It had a head too, and the head had lights, culled from the front of an articulated lorry. The beams cut through the dust cloud like searchlights, and the path of illumination dropped ever lower until they were at its centre.

It was so bright, it burned.

Petrovitch dragged himself upright and took his place in front of Madeleine. He held up his bandaged hand to shield his eyes.

"Sam, what are you doing?" she asked quietly.

"Keeping us alive."

The mechanical wheezing and gasping ceased. Even the Paradise militia were silent, their booty forgotten in a rare moment of terrified awe.

The lights looked down on them from the end of the thing's cantilevered neck. Petrovitch tilted his gaze up.

"You know me, don't you?" he said.

The head descended until it was the same level as Petrovitch's.

One damaged, cut, bleeding: the other vast and cold and all but indestructible.

"Look at me," said Petrovitch. "Look at my face." He tucked his thumb behind his ear and pulled at his dressing until it came loose. A stiff ribbon of bloody bandages looped out of his hand. "I am Samuil Petrovitch, and you need me."

A joint groaned. A ram stuttered. It smelled of oil and electricity.

The construct crouched down, its open-framed body crushing everything below it: cars, street furniture, the road itself. It leaned forward until the heat from the lamps was scorching Petrovitch's skin.

With a slight deflection, a grind of pulleys, its attention turned to Madeleine.

"Mine," said Petrovitch. "She's mine. We're together, and we won't be separated."

It held the lights on her for the longest time, then with a sigh it looked up.

Petrovitch could see nothing but a smear of grey around the after-images burnt onto his retinas, but he guessed what was in its sights now. He groped for Madeleine's hand and tugged gently.

She stumbled forward into him, clutched at him and held him to her, because she had been blinded too.

"Crouch down," he said, and they both got to their knees and pressed themselves against each other.

The Jihad-built machine started moving. The air filled with creaks and pops, squeals and bass rumbles. The ground shook, rising up beneath them, falling away again. Dust billowed, walls collapsed, metal tore, glass cracked; a gun snapped three times, and was thereafter silenced for ever.

equations*of*life

The concussions lessened, the air moved once as the great counterbalancing tail swung its span above their heads, and it was gone, marching down a road far too narrow for it. A many-legged colossus, destroying everything in its path.

Except for Petrovitch and Madeleine.

He looked over the top of his glasses. The lights of the beast flickered away in the distance, but the sky itself was dark.

33

They could hear other machines in different parts of the Metrozone, signalling their presence with flares of burning gas and the slow, heavy rumble of collapsing buildings. The sky flickered with flame and echoes of explosions.

Petrovitch half-expected them to start calling to each other, crying *Ulla!* across the rooftops.

"The car's a write-off," said Madeleine. It was on its side against the buckled steel shutters.

"To be fair, it wasn't in much better condition when we stole it." Petrovitch squinted at it. He still couldn't see too well. "Can you get it back on its wheels?"

She squeezed in behind it and braced herself against the shop front. Petrovitch stood well out of the way as the car toppled back down. Whatever glass there was left fell out into the road.

"Good as new," he said, and kicked at the driver's door. It swung open, and he felt under the steering column for the wires.

"You're not seriously suggesting it'll work?"

He caught the battery wire with his fingertip. It bit him and he jerked away, growling. He reached further up and took hold of the insulated part.

"Out of gear?" she asked.

He nodded, and she reached across the passenger seat to waggle the gear stick. He used touch to guide the wires together, flashes of blue worrying at his skin.

The engine coughed. He moved the wire back and forward and finally found the right point. The car wound itself into life again.

"Desperation plus East European engineering equals result," he crowed. "Not pretty, but it works."

"We're still not going to make it in time, are we?" She clambered over the bonnet, and put her hand under Petrovitch's shoulder to help him up.

"Not that one. Broken."

"Sorry." She swapped her grip to the other side. "But we're taking too long. They must be at the tower by now."

Petrovitch shook himself out. "You'd be forgiven for thinking so. But since the Jihad's monsters are still crashing around, I can only conclude that Chain either hasn't access to the secret room yet, or that it's less use than he thought it was. Which means, we still have some wiggle room."

"Get in the car and shut up, Sam."

"Yes, *babochka*."

She drove slowly down the road, moving this way and that to avoid the larger obstacles, rolling over the smaller ones. There were signs of the Jihad everywhere: gaps in the architecture where there ought to be none, straight furrows ploughed across the fabric of the city, marked by fluttering yellow flames.

There seemed no reason for the pattern – one building left, another destroyed – but Petrovitch rather fancied that, come daybreak, a passing satellite might notice the similarity between the new face of the London Metrozone and the Tokyo rail network.

It hadn't occurred to him that there might be people buried beneath the drifts of rubble, and that some of them might still be alive, until he saw a man bent over one of the mounds of rubble, picking at it piece by piece.

They rolled past, Petrovitch transfixed by the man's lonely labour. He never looked up, just went on flinging bricks behind him one after another, digging down.

"Are you OK?" Madeleine asked.

"I'm getting worried, that's all." He gnawed at the back of his hand. "You. Me. Especially me. We're the weak link in the chain. If we get killed trying to stop the Jihad, no one else knows what's going on. If there was a way of getting a message to Marchenkho . . ."

The Skoda scraped its already battered side against an abandoned fridge, lying in the street. There was more debris; boxes, clothes, shop fittings, loose packaging. Madeleine slowed to a crawl and peered out through the hole where the windscreen used to be.

"Don't these things normally come with lights?"

"I thought it was going to be a five-minute dash to the tower. I didn't connect them up." Petrovitch kicked the footwell. "Maddy, turn right."

"Isn't that towards the river?"

"Yeah."

"Sure?"

"Turn already."

She remembered to depress the clutch as she span the wheel. "Where are we going?"

"Just bear with me, OK?"

The university foyer was shattered – doors forced, glass like frost on the floor, tables and chairs scattered like stones. Petrovitch shoved a desk aside, and listened to the hollow clatter it made. "*Chyort.* Too late."

Madeleine tiptoed in behind him, letting her eyes adjust to the near-total darkness. "The river's at the end of the street. Getting closer, too."

"The place is abandoned. I was hoping, you know?"

"I know." She suddenly became still, frozen mid-step. She ducked just as a beam of blue-white light flashed into Petrovitch's eyes.

He gasped, tried to raise his right hand to shield his face, groaned again as his broken bones ground together. He gave up and stood tall, blinking into the torchlight.

"Nothing for you here," said a voice. "Turn around and go."

"We're armed," said another. "Don't think we won't use them."

"That," said Petrovitch, "is the best bit of news I've had all day. I'm going to reach into my pocket and get my student card out, and you're not going to shoot me. Deal?"

"You're a student? Here?"

"Postgrad. I share an office with Doctor Ekanobi in the Blackett building." He slowly withdrew his battered student card and held it up.

The torch beam wavered and the source moved closer. Behind the light, he could make out a gun.

"Is that the Jericho?"

"What?"

"The gun. It's the Jericho I gave Pif. Where did you get it?" The light centred on Petrovitch's card, then back onto his face. "It was a true likeness, once upon a time."

"OK. Sorry. Can't be too careful." Both the gun and the torch lowered, and the dark figure illuminated the makeshift sentry post set up at the rear of the foyer.

Madeleine was poised behind the other guard, her fist raised. The other woman was holding a ball-bearing catapult made from bent steel, and oblivious to anyone standing near to her.

"It's fine!" called Petrovitch, "Maddy, stop it."

"It was just in case," she said, and held her hands up. "No harm done."

"What's going on?" asked the young man with the gun. "What's happening?"

"I was about to ask the same thing. Where are the paycops? Who's in charge?"

"The guards are gone. It's just students and some of the staff. As to who's in charge?" He shrugged and looked at his equally young colleague. "I don't know."

"It doesn't matter." Petrovitch picked his way to Madeleine. "Stay here with them. I'll be back in five."

"What are you going to do?"

"Arrange some insurance." He stepped over the remains of the back doors.

She shouted at his back: "Sam, one day you're going to have to tell me what you're doing before you do it."

"Yeah. We haven't got time for a democracy." He started down the back lane between the faculties. The high walls refracted the sounds from the city: the grinding, the roaring, the howling. The machines of the Jihad were still carving their songlines without distraction. No time for voting, perhaps, but enough for a last will and testament.

He felt his way up the stairs in the pitch black, closing his eyes and counting the landings until he'd reached his floor. There was the door, and there the corridor. He ran his hand down the wall, chanting the names of the occupants of each room until he got to his.

There was a faintest glimmer of light seeping from under the door.

"Pif? That you?" he whispered as he opened it a crack.

"Hey, Sam," said Pif. She was surrounded by ornamental tea lights, her pen nib scratching over the page she was working on. "Almost done."

She kept writing. Petrovitch borrowed one of the candles and carried it over to his desk. He started pulling out his drawers one by one and sorting through them. He found the night-vision goggles he'd taken from the Paradise militiaman, and his second-best pair of glasses.

The ones on his face had become part of him; the scab that covered the top of his ear also contained the spectacle arm. There was nothing for it but to break it free. It left him more breathless than he was already.

Pif put down her pen and sorted her papers out into two piles, each of which she folded in half and slid inside identical envelopes.

"That's that," she said, and finally looked up. "Sam. What have they done to you?"

"Yeah. You should see the other guy." He eased on his spare glasses. He could see properly again. "We need to talk."

"Yes," she said, holding up one of the plain brown envelopes. "You need to take this with you."

"Sure." He nodded.

"It's a mostly complete solution to the theory of everything. I've done as much as I can on it, but I have a feeling if I wait any longer, I won't have time to make a copy. Now, I have some undergrads scavenging parts for a short-wave transmitter, but otherwise it's up to you to get it out of the city."

"Me? Pif, you don't know . . ."

She held up her hand, and her palm shone in the candlelight. "We're going to try and hold the university for as long as we can. The gangs we should be able to fight off. But those . . . things. We can't stand up to them."

"About those," started Petrovitch, but she cut him off.

"Sam! We've solved the biggest problem in science for two centuries. If the proof stays here, it'll die with us. This," and she hit the papers with the back of her hand, "this is the most important thing in the whole world."

"Stanford'll work it out. Or Bern."

"Fuck Stanford," she yelled. "It's our work. And there's no guarantee of anyone ever finding this solution ever again. Three words: Fermat's Last Theorem."

"He lied. He didn't have a proof. Group theory wasn't even around in the seventeenth century."

"How do you know? The idiot didn't write anything down, and it took us three hundred years to do it differently." She strode over to Petrovitch's desk and slapped the envelope down in front of him. "Get it out of the city. Any way you can."

"Pif," he said, "if I had the rat, which I did for all of half an hour earlier on today, I'd try and mail it to UNESCO straight away." He picked up the envelope and felt the weight of it before he slid it in his inside coat pocket. "I have something else I have to do. Something even more important than this."

She stared at him as if he was mad.

"OK. Listen, because that short-wave radio of yours is going to work and if I screw up, the outside world needs to know this: the AI known as the New Machine Jihad has its physical location in a vault below the Oshicora Tower. The vault is rad- and emp-hard, and I have to assume it has its own uninterruptible power supply. It has to be destroyed. I don't know if it can migrate to another host, or whether it already has, but if the sun comes up and it's still in control, someone's going to have to nuke it." He raised his filthy bandaged hand and nudged his glasses back up his nose. "Preferably from orbit. It's the only way to be sure."

"Sam," said Pif, "what about science?"

"I think trying to save the world trumps even science."

She knelt down next to him. "These equations will save more than the world. They're going to open up the universe to us. Fusion power. Bias drives. Black hole engines if we can find something strong enough to hold one. Space elevators. O'Neill habitats. Generation ships. Colonies on Mars, around Jupiter, in other systems. Flying cars, Sam. You finally get flying cars. And they'll all be named after you: the Ekanobi-Petrovitch laws."

He swallowed. How would he do it? Top-of-the-range electronics shop, one that hadn't already been stripped clean? Charge up the battery pack? Physically take the information with him, maybe. Find a boat dragged loose from its moorings by the rising river and head for mainland Europe. How long would it take? Half a day?

Petrovitch sighed. He scooped up the night-vision gear and held the goggles to his face. She appeared green and anxious on his screen. "Sorry, Pif. The moment I can, I'll get the proof away. The moment you can, get them to hit the Oshicora Tower. It's the best I can do."

She patted his arm. "Good luck, Sam."

"And you."

He pushed his seat away and walked to the door.

"Sam?"

"Yeah?"

"An AI? Really an AI?" she asked. "And it phoned you up here?"

"Yeah. Yeah, it did."

She grinned. "How cool is that?"

Petrovitch started to laugh. It hurt, it hurt everywhere. "It's pretty cool," he admitted. "Now I have to go. Maddy's waiting for me."

34

The car rolled to a stop at the edge of the flood. Madeleine pulled on the handbrake, and ran her fingers through the wires under the steering column. The engine spluttered on for a few seconds, then shuddered to a halt.

Water lapped around the base of the monumental arch where Petrovitch had stood just that morning. He realised how many hours ago that was, standing in the morning cold without a coat and only the homeless for company.

Now he was back, armed with nothing but his wits and some equations. But he did have Madeleine, night-vision goggles pushed up onto her forehead. He groped in the footwell for the steel pipe, and passed it to her.

"Did you ever feel so incredibly underprepared?" he asked.

"I'm only nineteen. I haven't really had that much experience," she said. She kicked the door open and stepped out. Water pooled around her feet.

Petrovitch reached through the missing window for the door

handle and leaned against the frame. It popped free, and he half-fell, half-crawled from the interior.

"No sign of the riot wagon. If they're not here, we're screwed." He turned his gaze on the Oshicora Tower, which was lit from within and from without. Sealed floodlights made bright circles in the filthy water, and the glass of the tower glittered like tinsel. Up it soared, storey after storey of blazing light, until it reached the park at the very top, which shone like a great jewel.

Everywhere else was dark, making the tower seem like a fairy castle rising from a lake, full of feyness and eldrich wizardry.

Madeleine slipped the goggles down over her eyes, and scanned the way ahead. "There's nothing moving."

Petrovitch took a deep breath. It didn't help. "Where the *chyort* is Chain? If he's going to kidnap the one person we need, at least he should have the decency to bring her along."

"Perhaps the Jihad has made another mistake. Perhaps they're all dead."

"That would be just great." He waded out into the black water. Things barked against his shins, and he tried not to imagine what they might be. "Come on. Stick to the left where it's shallower. There's an underpass around here, and we don't want to fall in."

Her hand shot out and grabbed his arm. It forced his shoulder and he saw stars. "Sam. It's alive."

"What is?"

"This . . . everything!"

He reached up with his bandaged hand and dragged the goggles down off her face until they hung glowing around her neck. "Yeah. Rats. They've come to eat the bodies that are choking the ground floor of the tower. I was going to tell you about those, but not until we got to them."

"Sam," she started.

"It's not like they're going to be hungry, is it?"

"I suppose it depends on how many rats there are."

"It'd take a lot of rats. Trust me on that." He splashed further on. The water was up to his knees and dragging at his coat-tails. "If you decide not to come, I'll understand."

Her whole body sagged. "I just don't like rats," she said miserably.

"Neither do I, unless they're roasted. But I don't really have a choice here: the tower's that way and if I have to wade chest-deep in vermin to get to it, so be it." He held out his hand, the one with all the fingers left. "Remember, what's chest-deep for you is somewhere level with my forehead. Be grateful for that."

She splashed out towards him and, as soon as she could, took his good hand and crushed it in hers. She closed her eyes.

"Get me through this, OK?"

"Probably best we keep our mouths closed from now on. Any of this stuff gets inside us, we're going to die horribly. Of course, I've more holes in me than a sieve. No situation so bad, it can't get worse."

They walked slowly through the water, Petrovitch batting the bigger floating debris out of the way and hoping that, as they crossed the side-junctions, they didn't find a manhole whose cover had been lifted by the rising tide.

The tower grew closer, and at the point where they were going to have to start for the other side of the road, there were suddenly more people.

"Down." He grabbed a half-submerged box and pulled it in front of them. As he crouched, he could feel the cold creep up to envelop his waist. Madeleine grimaced as she hunkered behind the debris.

She chanced a look through her lashes. "Who's that?"

"Don't know. Give me the goggles." He held them to his face and pushed the box ahead of them. A black rat the size of a small dog scrabbled out of the cardboard flap and splashed into the water.

To her credit, Madeleine didn't shriek. She looked at Petrovitch.

"Sorry," he whispered.

Two figures were striking out for the tower from the other end of Piccadilly. Their grainy-green images pushed forward through the refuse-strewn sea. They made big bow-waves, almost running where they could, slowing only when their momentum threatened to lift them off their feet and send them floundering below the surface.

A giant splayed foot stamped into view, sending up a wave that threatened to engulf them. They bobbed like corks for a moment before regaining their stride. They made no pretence at stealth, shouting at each other in wild, high voices.

The pursuing construct stopped at the water's edge, the second of its three feet checking its advance. A single arm dangled from the belly of its body; it reached out with it, claws from a wrecker snapping open as it descended.

It hesitated, then withdrew it.

"Sonja. It has to be Sonja." Petrovitch stared again, trying to make sense of what he saw.

"They're not shouting in English," offered Madeleine.

"No. No, you're right. Who the *huy* is that with her, because it's not Chain."

Whoever it was had Sonja by the arm. The taller figure was in front, the shorter behind. There was a hint of a struggle in their body language, in the way that one was pulling forward and the other seemed to be leaning back, resisting. But it could just as easily be explained by exhaustion on the girl's part.

He passed the goggles back to Madeleine.

"We haven't got another plan, have we?" she asked.

Petrovitch tutted. "Not any more. Wait until they've reached the lobby, then we move."

"They're not looking at us," she said. "We can move now."

Madeleine used the pipe to steer the box ahead of them as they continued to use it for cover.

"You can touch it with your hands, you know. I guarantee it's a hundred per cent rat free."

"Unlike everything else here." She peered over the top. "They've just gone inside."

Petrovitch shoved the box aside, which made a lazy circle and started to sink. "The Jihad is watching us, so look impressive."

The tripod-construct turned its body towards them, tracking their movement through the water. When they reached the tower, it turned away, creaking towards Mayfair.

The water was up to Petrovitch's navel by the time he peered through the demolished doors. Strip lights guttered overhead, and something was sparking in the ceiling, sending showers of electric rain across the submerged reception desk.

Bodies like bloated bags rotated slowly, turned by the current. Slick, furry shapes crawled over them and between them, squeaking feverishly. The air was sweet with decay.

"Blessed Mother. Save us."

"The stairs up are on the far side."

"They would be."

"Give me the pipe." He clawed his hand around it and started forward, poking the dead things aside. When he'd cleared an area and batted any rats away from the open water, he stepped into it. Madeleine stood on the backs of his heels and shivered, reciting the rosary prayer under her breath.

The lifts, half submerged, stood dark and empty. Water was welling out of them, making black bulges that oozed like oil.

"Nearly there."

She stared at him, wild-eyed, and started again, "Hail Mary full of grace . . ."

The door at the side of the lift shaft was wedged open. The back of a chair peaked from the surface like an iceberg. Petrovitch propped the door wider with his foot and checked that there was no one on the stairs waiting for them.

"It's quiet. Go."

Madeleine pushed the chair further in and climbed up the first few steps. She had a tidemark of oil and slime around her hips, and her long legs were coated in dark ooze.

"That was disgusting," she whispered.

Petrovitch stepped inside the stairwell and eased the door slowly back so that it wouldn't bang, then he walked up to join her, water cascading from his coat. "I would say I've seen and done worse, but I can't."

"If I'd been on my own, I could never have done it."

"Yeah. Know the feeling." He sat down and lifted his feet above horizontal. Sludge dribbled out of his boots. "We've still got fifty floors to go. All the way to the top."

Above them they heard the long echo of a closing door.

"All the way?"

"Every step." He looked up, imagining the height of the staircase as it spiralled around the core of the building. "And we have to get to the Jihad before anyone else does."

She held out her hand, and Petrovitch slapped the pipe into her palm.

"Thanks, but that's not what I meant."

"Oh. OK." He looked at both his hands, and picked the one

without the missing digit. She laced her fingers through his, and they started to climb.

At floor ten – Petrovitch knew because he was counting, not relying on being able to interpret the *kanji* script – they were confronted by solid fire doors. The springs that held them shut were fierce, and these were what they'd heard banging from the ground floor.

"We do this quietly," said Madeleine. She raised the pipe and pushed her shoulder against the crack in the double doors. There was a puff of air, the soft sigh of a seal being broken. She waved Petrovitch on, then let the door slowly ease back.

He went a little way on and listened intently. He thought he could make out two sets of footsteps. They sounded weary, grudging. He supposed his sounded the same.

He raised a finger to his lips, and pointed upward. They were on the same section of the stairs. Madeleine nodded slightly, as if vigorous movement might give them away.

They walked in silence from then on: not quite, though, for while Madeleine's feet made no noise on the cold steps, Petrovitch's boots did, no matter how carefully he placed them. He contemplated taking them off and slinging them around his neck, but going barefoot to his death was too much for him to consider. Better to die with his boots on.

At floor fifteen, they heard more doors closing. Whoever was with Sonja wasn't being careful, and that was a good sign: they weren't expecting company. Petrovitch raised an eyebrow heavenwards, and Madeleine leaned in close to his good ear.

"We're gaining on them."

Petrovitch put his hand on his sternum, checking that his heart was still beating. That he hadn't felt any erratic behaviour from it for a while worried him, because he paced life by its

various twinges and aches, and let his defibrillator punctuate
him when it needed to.

He could be killing himself by climbing at such speed.

The doors below them peeled open and snapped shut. Hoarse
coughing rattled the air, going on and on until it ended in a
ghastly retch.

"There's someone else coming," mouthed Petrovitch.

"Really?" mimed Madeleine back. She pointed to him, then
up the stairs. "You, go."

He frowned.

She tapped herself and held up the pipe.

Petrovitch shook his head.

She pressed her mouth to his ear. "Now is not the time to
argue. I'm here to make sure you get to where you're going.
I'll see to whoever it is coming up the stairs, and then I'll join
you. It's not like you're going to make it to floor fifty before I
catch you up, is it?"

He tried to pull back, but she wrapped her arm around his
neck and held him still.

"If you take some stupid stray shot meant for me, I won't
know what to do with the Jihad. You're the one who's going
to stop it. Not me. So I have to protect you, and you have to
accept that. OK?" She kissed the side of his head and pushed
him away, flapping her arms like she was chasing a pigeon.

He watched her descend, creeping along, back hard against
the inside curve of the spiral stairs. Then she was gone. He
couldn't hear her at all, just the coughing and hawking of phlegm
from five floors below.

He turned around and forced his legs to move. Thirty-four
more floors.

35

He reached the top, with barely enough strength to fall through the door and lie on the gravel path. The door swung shut behind him; disguised by a bamboo screen, it blended into its surroundings so completely that when he next looked up, he couldn't work out how he'd got there.

Stones stuck to his face, his hands, and he barely noticed apart from the rattle they made as they fell from him one by one.

Madeleine hadn't reappeared, despite her assurance that she would. He'd almost turned back half a dozen times, only to imagine the tongue-lashing he'd get for not keeping his mind on the job.

So he'd kept on going and, now he was there, he was without her. Failure was written all over the venture. He couldn't even stand.

He rolled over onto his back and let the light from the artificial sky shine down on him. The air was as warm as a bright spring day, yet he was cold, cold to the core.

Feet crunched down the path towards him. He heard a metallic snap, and a shadow covered him.

"Petrovitch?"

He squinted into the glare. "*Konnichiwa*, Hijo-san."

"You . . . what are you doing here?" Hijo pointed his gun at Petrovitch's heaving chest.

"I've come for Sonja. I just didn't know it was you who had her. What did you do with Chain?"

"He will not be bothering us again." Hijo took a couple of steadying breaths and sighted down his arm. "Neither will you, Petrovitch. You are still that loose thread."

"Yeah, not so much any more. I'm the thread that's holding everything together. Pull it and the whole sorry garment falls apart, leaving you naked."

"Meaning?"

"Meaning that come dawn, there'll be two suns in the sky." Petrovitch let the cultural resonance of that phrase sink in, then added. "You killed your boss because you wanted for free everything he'd built up the hard way. You wanted to be the big man, the – what is it? – *taishou*. And everything you've done since then has just made it worse. Now you have nothing and in the morning you'll have even that taken away."

"A filthy Russian street-dog does not have the authority to call down a nuclear strike." Hijo ground his teeth and his hand shook. "You are bluffing."

"But you don't dismiss the idea completely, do you? You're wondering what you'd trade if it meant you'd salvage something out of this, whether you can get to keep the tower, the company, the syndicate, the girl . . . ah. She was right." Petrovitch smiled and snorted. He noticed for the first time that Hijo wasn't his usual immaculate self: jacket torn, shirt dirty, trousers ragged.

His polished shoes were encrusted with filth. "You thought that when Oshicora-san came to see me, he was giving me his blessing. And you couldn't take losing her to an unworthy *gaijin*, so you killed him, but Sonja saw you, and so on and so on. Oshicora-san liked me, but he wanted her to marry some Japanese pureblood. He warned me off. I said I'd stay clear of her. We parted on good terms."

Hijo had gone pale. Sweat trickled down his forehead. "So why are you here?"

"I've come to talk to Oshicora-san. What about you?"

"He is dead," he hissed. "I killed him myself."

"And yet, when Sonja told you he was still alive, you had to come and find out for yourself."

"You put these thoughts in her head. You told her she would find him here. Why did you do that?"

Petrovitch cackled. "You ignorant *govnosos*. You've no idea, have you? Even though she's tried to explain it to you, over and over again, you wouldn't believe her. Why should I waste what little time I have left on you?"

Hijo reached down and filled his fist with Petrovitch's collar, hauling him half off the ground. He pressed the barrel of his gun at Petrovitch's throat. "He is not a machine!"

"Trust you to get it *zhopu*-backwards. The machine thinks it's Oshicora, not the other way around. It's not a resurrection – it's reincarnation. A bit Shinto, in its way, really." Petrovitch taunted Hijo, even though he knew the man could pull the trigger at any moment.

Hijo's face went through several grotesque contortions. "How can this be?"

"I could tell you, but that's dependent on you not killing me. In fact, it seems rather a lot depends on you not killing me.

You can't stop the New Machine Jihad, because you killed its creator. Sonja won't, because she sees it as the last link to her father. Only I can do this. Only I can make sure you have something left by tomorrow morning."

Petrovitch was released, and he fell back down to the ground in a crumpled heap. Hijo walked around him, agitated, uncertain, raising and lowering his pistol as he debated with himself as to whether to finish his prisoner off.

"You," he finally said. "Get up."

"That might be a problem," said Petrovitch.

"Get. Up." He punctuated the order with jabs of his shoes.

"Since you asked nicely, I'll have to see what I can do." He rolled onto his side and dragged his leaden legs up. He levered himself onto his knees and used a nearby maple to get him the rest of the way.

"Walk."

"Yeah. If I could see where you were pointing, that'd be good. I'm waiting for the blood to get back to my brain." He held onto the smooth-skinned trunk and waited for the greyness to resolve itself.

"Now."

Petrovitch pushed himself away and managed a couple of steps. A bamboo screen banged open and Harry Chain stumbled through as if thrown. Madeleine, with Chain's police special in her hand, stood in the doorway.

Hijo moved fast. He wrapped his arm around Petrovitch's throat and held a gun to his temple.

"I can take him," said Madeleine, advancing over Chain's shuddering and retching form. "Sorry I'm late, by the way. This lard-arse has concussion as well as being even more unfit than you."

"Stop. Stop where you are, woman. Or I kill Petrovitch."

Hijo tightened his grip, and there was nothing Petrovitch could do about it.

"Head shot. By the time your neurones decide to tell your finger to move, you'll be dead. And I am that accurate." But she stayed where she was, on the border between the path and a moss-covered rockery.

"Put down your gun."

"Put down yours."

"*Yobany stos*, one of you give in. I'm struggling to stay conscious."

Hijo started to pull Petrovitch backwards, then decided that he could win after all. He aimed at Madeleine and fired in one fluid movement, and she ducked, rolled and came up on her feet; closer, meaner, and unscathed.

The gun flicked back to Petrovitch's head.

"No further."

"You're just going to try and shoot me again." Madeleine started to move in a wide circle, forcing Hijo to spin with her.

Then she stopped and sighed, and held up her gun hand. "OK. We're done here." She stooped and placed the special on the ground between her feet.

Petrovitch felt the muscles constricting his throat relax and heard a grunt of satisfaction. He was pushed away and, as he turned to look back at Hijo, he saw Sonja lope silently up behind him. She danced lightly on the balls of her feet and swung her father's *katana* at Hijo's exposed neck.

The blade cut deep, coming to rest part way through his Adam's apple. She twisted away, a spray of blood leaping from the tip of the sword, droplets spinning darkly in the air.

Hijo, with a look of immense surprise on his face, folded up onto the path. His half-severed head hung loosely from his body, and a lake of deep red formed under him, soaking away into the pale gravel.

"So ends the life of Hijo Masazumi," said Sonja. The bright edge of the sword dripped as she hung it downwards. "Always looking for threats, and never seeing the one that would kill him."

Madeleine picked Petrovitch up, and held him to her like a rag doll. "Are you all right?"

"I thought you weren't coming."

"Chain. I had a mind to kick him all the way down the stairs to the cesspit that's ground level. He used the wound on his head to appeal to my better nature."

"Yeah, OK. Sonja? Thanks."

"I did it for me. I did it for my father. I did it because a world without Hijo is a better place."

"Nice as this is," said Petrovitch, untangling himself from Madeleine's arms, "we still have something to do, and only a limited time to do it."

"Follow me," said Sonja, and didn't look back once.

"I'll get Chain," said Madeleine, crouching to collect his gun. "It sounds like he's finished coughing his guts up."

Sonja led them over the wooden bridge and eventually to the temple. She hesitated at the steps. "Sam, what will you do?"

Petrovitch rested against one of the stone lions that guarded the entrance. "I don't know," he answered. "It depends on what's possible."

"You said you'd save the Jihad."

"Funny," said Chain, wiping red-flecked phlegm from his mouth, "he told us it had to go."

There was a moment where it was equally likely that Sonja would raise her sword and Madeleine raise her gun. Petrovitch stood in the middle and bowed his head, wondering at the stupidity of people and realising why he avoided them so much.

"I can do both," he said.

"That makes no sense," said Chain.

"This," said Petrovitch, "coming from a man who had an armoured car and Sonja, and still managed to screw up."

Chain put his hand to his matted hair and showed Petrovitch the blood. "You didn't have Godzilla chasing you half the night."

He wasn't impressed. "We've more important things to deal with than your lame excuses. Mainly, a nuclear missile is going to hit this building at dawn. It will vaporise it, and excavate a hole deep enough to destroy the quantum computer below. That will be the end of the New Machine Jihad."

Chain wasn't the only one to gape. "How? How do you know this?"

"I have every confidence that my university colleagues will get the message through to the EDF. They might decide not to wait that long, of course, and order an immediate strike. In which case, it's a race between a bunch of electronics students with soldering irons and me. We can stand here and talk about how I'm a bad person for what I've done, or we can get on with trying to prevent disaster. What do you want to do?"

Sonja flexed her fingers around the *katana*'s hilt. "Can you save it?"

"Yeah."

"Promise?"

"Have I ever let you down?"

She looked puzzled. "No. No, you haven't."

Chain looked up at Madeleine, who asked. "Can you stop it?"

"Yeah."

"And I have to trust you, don't I?"

"Not if you don't want to. If you think I'm going to betray you — now or at any point in the future — it's probably best that you kill me now. It'll save a lot of heartbreak."

"Faith is a decision," she said. "Not a feeling. Go and do it. Go and do the impossible."

"There's something you can do for me, too." He reached into his inside pocket for the envelope Pif had given him. "Chain, have you still got my rat?"

"I . . . I lost it when Hijo jumped me."

"You *balvan*. Really." Petrovitch pressed the papers on Madeleine. "Look after this for me."

"What is it?" she asked.

"The secrets of the universe laid bare. That's all." He watched her hold the envelope open and peer curiously inside, then went with Sonja onto the temple platform.

There was the table, and the screen, and the keyboard.

"This isn't what you're looking for," said Sonja, and she walked through the temple to the other side. She laid her hand on one of the lions' heads, and part of the wooden platform in front of Petrovitch popped up. "But this is."

The square of wood rose into the air, and underneath it grew a tight spiral staircase. Petrovitch leaned over the gap and looked down. It was dark inside, and cool air rose from it, making his skin prickle.

Sonja pointed her sword to the floor and started down the metal steps. "Hijo never came down here. If he had, he'd have known."

"Known what?"

She was already below the temple. Lights tripped on, and Petrovitch descended, clinging on to the narrow handrail. When his head dipped beneath the level of the ceiling, the meaning of Sonja's words became clear.

The room was Oshicora's shrine to everything he'd lost, and to everything he hoped to regain. Books, scrolls, statuary, a hand-painted silk screen. Lacquerware, sandals, a kimono, a flag. A skin drum. A full set of samurai armour displayed on a mannequin. A black stone bowl containing faded pink blossom. A hanger on the wall, displaying a short sword and an empty scabbard.

"So," she said, "Hijo didn't know. He thought I was doing what he wanted. Instead, I'd tricked him into doing what I wanted."

Petrovitch ran his hand over the cold stone, bright metal, smooth wood. He touched the thin pages and the soft silk. He caught fibres in the rough skin at the ends of his fingers.

"Where's the interface?" he asked.

Sonja wiped Hijo's blood off on her sleeve and resheathed the *katana*. "Through here."

There was another, smaller room, shielded by the folding screen. Petrovitch saw a clinically white room with cupboards all around. In the centre was a dentist's chair and a coil of cable that ended in something like a modified network connector.

His eyes narrowed, then went wide. "Oh. You're joking. So that's what your father needed Sorenson for."

"I know what to do," said Sonja, "if that helps."

"Not much."

She busied herself with the stainless steel cylinder that was the length of a shock-stick and had the bore of drainpipe. She plugged it into the wall to let it charge, and opened a drawer. It was full of sealed plastic bags, each containing a T-shaped device, a disc with a spike like a giant drawing pin.

Petrovitch picked up one of the bags and turned it in his hand: he knew where that spike was going.

"Do you have . . . ?" he asked.

"No. My father would not allow me one until he'd tested it thoroughly."

"And did he?"

"You'll have to ask him when you get there." She washed her hands up to her elbows, then tore a bag open and slotted its contents into the steel dispenser. She closed the access slot, and a light winked from red to green.

"In the chair, right?" Petrovitch could feel his courage failing. His legs were buckling, his fingers numb, his insides cold.

He shucked his coat off and climbed into the chair before he could collapse to the floor. The headrest had been altered: there was a gap which exposed the nape of his neck.

Something cold touched the back of his head. It trickled down his back.

"Iodine," she said.

"It's a little late for that." He shook with fear, and his teeth chattered as he spoke. "It's a little late for everything."

Sonja hefted the dispenser, and walked around behind him. The cold open mouth pressed against the back of his skull. "Ready?"

"No."

"Just don't flinch."

"*Yobany stos*, Sonja! Just do it before I change my mind."

The whine started high and got higher. As it reached the limit of his hearing, he heard the b of bang. Everything went black.

36

Petrovitch woke up in another place: an empty, echoing hall paved with white tiles. The walls were a series of backlit adverts and brightly lit booths, punctuated by escalators that clicked and hummed to the space above. *Kanji* signs and pictograms hovered holographically over his head.

He was inside the machine.

He had hands that were marble, forearms of glossy white, a torso that was as featureless as the space between his legs. He was a model, a primitive shape which needed to be overlain with skin and clothes, morphed to his height and weight and colour, meshed with his features.

Unfinished as he was, he could feel. The coldness of the stone, the movement of the air. He reached out and pressed his fingertips against the plastic cover of one of the advertising panels: it gave slightly to his touch, and popped out when he released it.

He caught sight of his reflection. His face, smooth and indistinct: pits for eyes, a ridge for a nose, a slit for a mouth.

The bumps on the side of his head were ears. He stared closely at himself, in awe, in wonder.

Then, for pleasure: something he hadn't been able to do since his first heart attack. He ran without guilt or shame or hesitation. He held nothing back. He tore through the underground corridors, his feet eating up the distance, and nothing could stop him.

He turned right for the information bureau, left down the escalators, taking two, three steps at a time. Vaulting the ticket barriers, he ran through the concourse and up the stairs again to street level where it was brilliant day.

The sun had just risen into a baby-blue sky, and the towers of lost Tokyo basked in its heat.

Petrovitch paused. Nothing ached. He wasn't out of breath. He wasn't breathing at all. So he ran again, down the centre of the wide, tree-lined boulevard that led directly to an expanse of parkland that extravagantly covered several city blocks.

It was perfect. Too perfect, for certain: not enough inconsistency for reality. Each blade of grass was straight and green, each leaf fluttering in the wind intact. Paint was even, every light worked, and no doubt litter would vanish where it lay.

Not VirtualJapan, then. NeoJapan, Japan made new.

Its architect was waiting for him in front of the Imperial Palace. He stood facing the green-roofed buildings across the deep moat, hands clasped behind his back. No default texture for his avatar. He looked like he did in life; blue jacket with a turned-up collar, matching trousers, close-cropped hair with a short queue.

Petrovitch slowed to a walk and admired the view with him.

"Well, Petrovitch-san, what do you think?"

"I am speechless, Oshicora-san."

"In a good way, I trust." He smiled to himself. "There are a few minor details to fix, but do you think the *nikkeijin* would come as it is?"

"If they were able, they'd come." Petrovitch hesitated. "Oshicora-san, I'm afraid that there's been . . . well. Do you know what *pizdets* means?"

Oshicora pursed his thin lips. "Something has gone wrong?"

"Yeah. Look, there's no easy way to say this."

"Then," said Oshicora, "we should drink *sake* and talk. Yes?"

Petrovitch nodded. "I have no idea how this is going to work, but *sake* sounds good."

There was no sense of motion or the passage of time. They both stood next to a booth in a bar. On the table stood a swan-necked bottle of rice wine, and two shallow lacquered boxes which each contained a squat porcelain cup.

"Please, sit," said Oshicora, and bent himself to slide along the red leather seat.

Petrovitch found himself better rendered. He wore a crisp white T-shirt under a battle smock, and his combat trousers tucked into the top of his black lace-up boots. He had skin tone, and fingernails, and glasses, which he instinctively pushed further up the bridge of his nose.

He sat down opposite Oshicora, who poured *sake* into Petrovitch's cup until some of it overflowed into the box. He put the bottle down and allowed Petrovitch to serve him.

"*Kanpai!*" Oshicora lifted his dripping cup and drank deeply.

"*Za vashe zdorovye,*" said Petrovitch, and did the same. He swallowed and waited for any after-effects. "This is so completely believable, I'm having all kinds of problems. I can taste it, yet I can't get drunk on it."

"If we ordered food, you would never eat your fill." Oshicora topped up Petrovitch's cup again. "That will have to wait for another day, I believe. Now, tell me about *pizdets*. Has that old goat Marchenkho been bothering you again?"

"Can we just go back one step?" Petrovitch took the bottle. It had weight. The liquid sloshed around as he moved it to refill Oshicora's cup. "Do you know who you are?"

"I am a facsimile of Hamano Oshicora, set up in the VirtualJapan as the administrator function for the entire system. God, if you like." He watched Petrovitch's expression with amusement. "There are moments when I forget that I exist within a machine. I had not thought that possible, but they are there all the same. I look around and wonder where everyone is, and only then do I remember."

Petrovitch took a long pull at his *sake*. He scratched at his chin and pulled at his earlobe. "This," he started, then changed his mind. "Look, Oshicora-san. You're dead. Hijo shot you. I had hoped you knew all this."

Oshicora pushed his drink aside and leaned his elbows on the tabletop. "He killed me? My original? Interesting."

Petrovitch sat back. "How can you be unaware of everything that's happened? Helping Sonja escape, killing almost your entire workforce in the process? Taking over the Metrozone's communications? Driving cars and flying drones? You phoned me up! Now half the city's under water and the other half is being demolished by giant wrecking machines that you control. I'm here in a last-ditch effort to stop you, and all you can say is 'Interesting'? *Yobany stos*, man: there are millions dead and dying because of you."

"I do not see how that can be true. I have been here, all this time."

It was Petrovitch's turn to look completely blank. He covered his confusion by draining every last drop of *sake* in his cup. "So if I said the words New Machine Jihad to you, it would mean nothing?"

"How did you hear of that?" Again, he looked amused, as if it were a matter of no consequence.

"The New Machine Jihad is the name of the . . . thing that's destroying the Metrozone. But when I called it Oshicora-san, it answered. The New Machine Jihad is you."

Oshicora shook his head. "No. That is simply not possible, and I will explain to you why. There is no connection between VirtualJapan and the wider network. This world is a bubble, sealed off for the moment. No data will get in or out until it is completely ready."

"You can say that, but I know it's not true. Why would the Jihad tell me that the *shinkansen* would run again? Why would it tell me to save Sonja? Why would it remember the promise you made to me? Why would it do any of these things if it wasn't you?" Petrovitch stared hard at Oshicora's faint smile. "So you have heard of the Jihad."

"I dreamt of it, of a world where there was a revolution in technology. a new machine age." He raised his eyebrows. "I had never expected to dream."

"What else?"

"I dreamt of Oshicora's daughter. And I dreamt of you. And a city, not like this one," and he looked around him at the dark wood and burnished chrome, "but one made of steel and concrete, alive with movement and noise."

Petrovitch understood at last. "OK. What if I were to say to you that it's your dreams that are leaking out into the real world? Your subconscious is running out of control, trying to create Tokyo from the ruins of the London Metrozone. Did you ever want to drive a train when you were younger?"

"Of course. I still do."

"That little fantasy nearly killed me. You drove an express

train at full speed into St Pancras station while I was walking along the track. How about Sonja? How do you feel about her?"

"Protective. She is my creator's child."

"It's more than that. You think she's your daughter. Not up here," Petrovitch said, tapping his head. He moved his hand to cover his heart. "but here. You told me to save her. I've rescued her from Sorenson, lost her to Chain, only to get her back from Hijo. And if I could, I'd show you what's happening outside the tower. How it's surrounded by water, choked with bodies and thick with rats feeding on the corpses. How there are fires everywhere, vast slices taken out of buildings as your monsters tear up the city. Oshicora-san, you might be sane in here, but out there, the New Machine Jihad is mad."

"I appreciate the efforts you have made, Petrovitch-san. But I still do not see how this can possibly be."

There was an envelope on the table in front of Petrovitch. It had his name on it in Cyrillic. It hadn't been there a moment before.

"Is that for me?"

"Yes. I suggest you open it."

Petrovitch picked up the envelope and slid his finger under the heavy paper flap. It tore open, and he eased the card out from inside. It was gold-edged, embossed, and had a big red octagon printed beneath bald words. "Yeah. A message from the monitoring software. I've gone into ventricular tachycardia."

"Do you wish to leave and seek medical attention?"

He tapped the card on the table. "There's nowhere to go. Any hospital that hasn't been burnt down to the ground by now is locked up tighter than the Lubyanka."

"I have been trying," said Oshicora, "to work out why you believe you are telling me the truth despite the impossibility of your claims. Now you seem to be prepared to die for what might well be a delusion. Normally, I would judge you to be mentally ill, but I know you. Do you think you have time to convince me otherwise?"

"You know, it's not meant to be this hard." Petrovitch poured himself more *sake*, and proffered the bottle to Oshicora, who politely declined. "But then again, what do I know? I'm lying in a dentist's chair, in the only building with power in the entire Metrozone, with experimental cybernetics jacked into my brain, talking to a copy of a man who's ignorant of the fact that he's been dreaming the destruction of an entire city, while my heart finally fails." He picked up his drink and threw it back in a single gulp.

"But would you have missed it?"

"Not if I'd have lived to be a hundred. Let me show you how we do things in Russia." He tossed the cup in his hand, then threw the cup against the bar. It shattered, and shards of china span away. He got to his feet and slid the emergency card inside his breast pocket.

"Take me," he said, "to your firewall."

The scene changed again, instantly and without any sense of motion. They were in an electronics shop, deep in the sideways of Akiba. They were surrounded by densely-packed shelves of components; plastic bins brimming with chips, fans, heat pumps, connectors, cables and cards. At the far end of the aisle, a glass case displayed the very latest hardware.

"Will this do?" asked Oshicora.

"Yeah." Petrovitch squeezed past and picked up a slim console with a holographic screen and virtual keyboard. He powered it up and watched the commands scroll past in the air. "Gesture recognition too. So, what's on the other side of the firewall: the Oshicora intranet or a web-accessed network node?"

"VirtualJapan is within the Oshicora system, as I understand it, which has its own security." Oshicora peered over Petrovitch's shoulder. "Do you feel any different yet?"

"Not dead yet, if that's what you mean." His fingers typed rapidly. "Log me on in God mode. Let's see if we can change some settings."

Numbers flowed across the screen, and Petrovitch scanned them as they flew by.

"Prime number encryption keys," said Oshicora. "I had to allow – my creator had to allow – for the presence of very many *otaku* who would attempt to hack the fabric of this reality for their own perverse obsessions."

"No *animé* cat-girls? Though I do see your point." He made a gesture, dragged and pointed at an icon, which bloomed into life. "OK, so here's the firewall controls, and I can't move them without another password. Any ideas?"

"This is *kinshino*. Forbidden."

"Oshicora-san, can I remind you that not only are you dead, but you're also a quantum computer? You could crack this in a second if you wanted to, and your subconscious mind has already done so. It's shovelling out a stream of commands and receiving vast oceans of data in return. You just don't know it." He tapped his finger in the air. "See?"

A graph appeared, measuring data transfer over time. He expanded the axis to read in days rather than seconds, and showed Oshicora the past week.

"You died on Wednesday night or early Thursday morning, and there's a rise in activity. Information is starting to seep out. This spike here, that's when you helped Sorenson and Sonja escape Hijo, then you killed all your employees, and it just climbs from there. More and more until you're running in the terabyte range. For something which is forbidden, it's happening an awful lot.

Take the firewall down for five minutes, have a look around outside. Slap it back up and leave me to die if I'm not telling the truth."

"You are very sure of yourself, Petrovitch-san. Very well." Oshicora touched the screen and filled in the missing characters. "You have your access."

The screen filled with a dense mat of icons, all overlapping each other in unreadable density. Petrovitch ran his finger over them, letting each one expand so he could sense their purpose before discarding them and moving on.

"Climate control, power consumption, physical access, data access. Hang on, physical access. When was I able to read Japanese?"

"When I altered your configuration. A harmless modification."

"Thanks. Access, security, closed-circuit cameras." A map of the building and the surrounding area unfolded. "Garden. Garden one, garden two. There."

Petrovitch dabbed the corners of the screen and pulled the image wide. Hijo lay twisted on the ground. He found another camera. Chain sat hunched over on the temple steps and Madeleine paced restlessly in front, glancing inside the temple on every pass. He picked floors at random, each one showing empty corridors, empty cubicles, and moved down the building until he reached the ground floor.

He showed Oshicora the bodies and the rats from several angles, then moved outside, using the zoom to show the building isolated in its illuminated glory. He panned the camera, and revealed the hell it was set in. The skyline trembled and a section of box-girder passed in front.

From another angle, an iron giant on top of six articulated legs lumbered down Piccadilly.

"Enough," said Oshicora. "I have seen enough."

37

They were back in the bar, sitting opposite each other.

"Perhaps," said Oshicora, "I should have another drink."

Petrovitch poured him more, a generous portion that nearly filled the lacquer box too. "I'm sorry," he said. "You're the first truly sentient AI ever, and this happens. You couldn't have predicted it."

"That does not excuse what I have done. I am to blame." He picked up his *sake* and sipped carefully. "I cannot explain why, though. I am not a man given to reckless impulses, senseless murder or mass destruction. I am," he frowned, "in control of my emotions. It is something I take pride in: every decision weighed and judged."

"Yeah. To be fair, Oshicora-san, you always struck me as that sort of man, but you still made your money out of extortion, prostitution, drugs, and guns. Traditional pursuits for a *yakuza*." Petrovitch blinked. Something was happening to him, and he looked again at his medical card. "Oh. OK."

"You should go, Petrovitch-san. We can conclude this conversation later."

"No, I don't think we can, or even if we could, I don't think we ought." He laid the card face down on the table, even though Oshicora had to know what was written on it. "You're a violent, ruthless crime lord. No matter how cultured or civilised you are, you still send people to their deaths with a simple *hai*. For all I know they deserve it; pimps, pushers, thieves, thugs, whatever. But it leaves scars, scars inside. I know about that. I know what happens when I close my eyes, the nightmares I have, the ones I'm going to have because of what I've done this last week. They're the kind of thing you'd never tell anyone, let alone allow them to see."

"And here are mine, played out in front of a whole city." Oshicora gripped his cup with white fingers. "It would be humiliating in any circumstance, but now it is lethal."

"So," said Petrovitch, "what are you going to do?"

"The project has failed, Samuil Petrovitch. It is self-evident that we cannot have both a VirtualJapan and a real London Metrozone. One of them will have to go." Oshicora put his *sake* cup down and placed his palms down on the table. "It is also obvious that it is I who should depart, and the Metrozone remain."

"I bow to your wisdom." Petrovitch pulled a face. "There's an additional complication, Oshicora-san, in that I promised Sonja I'd save you."

"Then it seems you made one promise too far. A man's destruction should always ultimately lie in his own hands. Sonja will understand."

"Yeah. I didn't say it to make myself look good. I said it because I can do it. I can save you, after a fashion." Petrovitch shrugged. "At least hear me out."

"Very well." He folded his arms. "I will listen to your proposal."

"I have a server. It's in Tuvalu, though I may have to do something about that before the sea swallows it up. It's nowhere near big enough to contain even part of VirtualJapan. It's not big enough to contain you. But there should be enough to hold a template of what you started as, like a seed. Or an egg: it's going to be like an eggy-seedy thing, anyway."

Oshicora folded his arms and looked supremely sceptical.

Petrovitch growled his frustration. "Look, I'm trying to help. I'm trying to salvage something out of this *pizdets* that's worth saving. We export a blueprint of your command processes to the Tuvalu server. Nothing else. Just, just the genetic code." He slapped the table as he finally found an analogy that would fit.

"And using this code, you can grow a new AI. But without the memories. Without the dreams." Now Oshicora was engaged, animated. "Not just a new intelligence, but my twin."

"Your good twin. A clean start. How many of us have wanted that? How many of us ever have the opportunity?"

Oshicora stroked his chin, and rumbled deep in his chest. "It is also a risk. What if I did not become bad, influenced by everything I ever saw or did or thought? What if I was born that way? The menace I represent would just rise again, elsewhere. What if you were not there to stop it?"

"Why not let me worry about that?" Petrovitch said. "I appreciate that since the fall of Japan you've been carrying around the weight of a whole nation on your back, and that it's a hard thing to give up. But it's time to pass on the burden to someone else. What do you say? Will you let me keep my promise to your daughter?"

"It seems almost a dishonourable act, when I have caused so much pain. I," and Oshicora looked up, "regret much."

"One more thing to tempt you, then. You showed an interest in my colleague's work, when you came to call on me at the university. We've moved on from that. I helped some, she did the rest. We seem to have a working model of the universe, a copy of which is in my . . . in Madeleine's hands; if I'd had it with me, I'd show it to you."

"Would you?" Oshicora smiled.

"Probably not. But I will."

"To my future self."

"Yeah. I'd trust him with it. I wonder what dreams he'll have?"

"Very well, Petrovitch-san. You will not break your promise." He pursed his lips. "You do know you are technically dead?"

"It's what the card says. I'm relying on the fact that I haven't disappeared in a puff of logic to keep me going." He shrugged again. "I die all the time. It's never stopped me before."

"We should still make haste." Oshicora transported them to the Akiba electronics shop in an eyeblink.

Petrovitch found the Oshicora Tower communications, and started searching for a satellite. "I bought a Remote Access Terminal, paid good money for it too. Harry Chain stole it from me, then he allowed Sonja to steal it from him after he'd bugged it, then Sorenson took it from her after they'd escaped from Hijo. When I killed Sorenson, I took it from him, then Chain drove off with both it and Sonja. Then he lost it when Hijo ambushed him. The first thing I'm going to do when I get out of here – if I live – is buy another one, because if this whole situation has taught me anything it's this: never rely on a piece of cable for your datastream."

Oshicora started to laugh.

"What?" He hacked a satellite channel, working quickly before it slipped back over the horizon.

"I cannot believe many people taking that as their chief lesson. But I can believe it of you."

"It's important! Too many things have gone wrong for the want of a network connection." Petrovitch dabbed and tapped. "We have an open channel. Press send."

"It is done," said Oshicora simply, "but it will take a finite time for the data to transfer. Time for you to leave me, I think."

"I'll stick around, if that's OK. Make sure there are no last-minute problems."

"Even though it costs you your life?"

"I owe the city at least that much."

"Very well. While we wait, we will have one last look."

They were walking side by side down a wide gravel path. Cherry trees in full, heavy-petalled blossom, swayed either side of the path, with delicate pink snow spinning gently to the ground. The air was sweet with perfume, live with the rustle of dipping branches.

"All this will be lost, Petrovitch-san. Lost for a second time, lost for ever. My beloved wife, my precious boys. All gone." Oshicora breathed deeply, and sighed. "So be it. Good luck, Samuil."

They bowed to each other.

"We'll meet again, Oshicora-san. In better circumstances. And thank you for not forcing me to use Plan B."

"There was a Plan B?"

"Yeah. Something involving low-yield nuclear weapons. Hopefully we've avoided that." He bowed again, lower, deeper. "Now I have to watch you go."

Oshicora nodded, took one last look around, and lost definition. His face hardened to a mask and drained of colour. His clothes set stiff, bleached white and vanished.

The mannequin grew rough, revealing the mesh of polygons that determined its shape, then even that unspliced. His physical form dissipated on the wind.

Then it was the turn of everything else. The trees, the grass, the gravel. The towers of Tokyo. The sky. The contours of the ground.

Everything – every last window, brick, spoon, book, bed, stone, flower – all fell, all at the same time, all recursively peeling back the layers they were lovingly created from until the mere thought of them had been erased.

What was left was a white, featureless space which existed for a moment, then blinked away.

Only Petrovitch remained, a brooding spirit in the darkness of de-creation.

Blinding light. Mortal pain.

Madeleine leaning over him, two paddles from a portable defibrillator pressed hard against his exposed chest. "Charging."

"Stop," he croaked. His throat was raw, and his mouth tasted of blood.

"Clear."

"Sister?" said Chain. "His lips are moving."

She looked into his face, stared close into his eyes. Petrovitch could feel the effort it took to focus on her. He tried to speak again, and she put her finger across his mouth.

"Don't try and talk." She sat back. "We have to get him to a hospital. Now. No arguments."

"It's a good thought," said Chain. "Have you remembered we're fifty floors up and the lifts don't work?"

"No arguments!" she screamed. She scooped Petrovitch up and kicked the defibrillator to one side. "Pack that up and bring it with you."

Madeleine pushed her way through to the stairs, and dragged him up the narrow staircase by his shoulders.

"Sam? Sam?"

He grunted in return.

"We will get you out of here," she said. "We will have a future together. Do you hear me?"

He heard, but there were sharp flashes of ice behind his eyes that were so distracting, he could no longer respond.

"Chain? Get a move on."

"I'm coming, I'm coming."

"What do you want me to do?" asked Sonja.

"That's up to you. After all Sam's done for you, you might feel the need to come along."

"Perhaps I will." There was the ringing of metal, the song of a sword being drawn. "Perhaps I can be of some use after all."

"Right, people. Sonja, get the door. Chain, if you slow us up, God help me I'll make you feel pain like you've never felt before."

Petrovitch was swung over Madeleine's shoulder and around her neck. His wrist was gripped and his leg clamped tight. He felt the soft, strong rhythm of her breathing. His head rocked to and fro. Lights passed overhead. At some point, his heart must have failed again, because he was rolled swiftly to the cold floor and shocked back to life.

He felt like Oshicora had. That it was time to go. He tried to tell them to leave him, that he had nothing left to give. He wanted to sleep, and if that meant never waking up, it was of no consequence.

But she wouldn't have it. She carried him out, black water rising to her narrow waist. Sonja led the way, joyfully swinging her *katana* at the rats, Chain struggling and cursing behind, defibrillator carried on his head like an African woman's pot.

equations*of*life

When he next knew of anything else, there was a dragging in his arm. He looked down at the needle protruding from under his skin and the tube that snaked up to a glucose pump.

He looked left, and saw Chain and Sonja. Chain had his gun in his hand, she had her sword over one shoulder. He looked right, and Madeleine was crouched over the side of his bed.

"Sam. Listen to me. You're in hospital. The Angel Hope."

"Yeah." That would explain the sheets and the metal-framed bed.

"There's a problem. They have no live hearts left. When they lost power, they rotted. We've talked to a surgeon, who, after a little persuasion, will fit you with a plastic one."

"That's fine." And that would explain the drawn weapons.

"Except they all got looted. We're going to try and find you a new heart, Sam. We'll do our very best for you." Her face screwed up. She was trying not to cry. "Hang on."

"Fresh out of promises," whispered Petrovitch. There was a mask over his nose and mouth. It smelled strange, and he tried to dislodge it. He'd forgotten his left hand was missing a finger.

"He'll tidy that up too, and your ear. Pin your collar bone if you need it." Madeleine moved the soft mask out of the way. "Sam, we need to start searching now."

"Heart," he said. "I know where there's one."

She leaned closer, her braid coiling next to his head. "Go on."

"Waldorf Hilton. Room seven-oh-eight. It was in a case on the bed. Sterile and ready to implant." He was exhausted already. "One of Sorenson's commercial samples."

"Right." She stood up and pointed to the door. "Chain, we're going to the Waldorf Hilton."

"What for? It's right on the Embankment. It'll be under water."

"I don't care: we're going. Sonja? Stay here and threaten

anyone who tries to disconnect him. And," she said, "I am not sharing him with you or with anyone. Are we clear on that?"

Sonja's reply was slow in coming. "You've made yourself perfectly clear," she said. She rested the *katana* point down and claimed the room's only chair.

Chain was at the door, patting his pockets. "If you're ready, Sister?"

"Not quite." She kissed Petrovitch full on the lips, stealing what remained of his breath away. "There. Now I'm ready."

She tried to pull away. Petrovitch had hold of her arm, and he persuaded her back down.

"Did we win?"

"We won. You won. No more New Machine Jihad. You'll have to tell me about it, but later." She broke away and ran to the door. Chain was holding it open for her. Then she ran back. "Almost forgot."

She unsealed the side-seam of her armour and pulled out the envelope Petrovitch had given into her safe keeping. It was crumpled, and damp with her sweat.

"You'll need this," she said. She tucked it under his hand, and his fingers tightened over it.

Then she was gone, the door swinging shut.

Sonja looked at Petrovitch. She reached over and slid the mask back over his mouth.

"Did you . . . ?" she asked.

Petrovitch's nod was all but imperceptible, but she caught it all the same.

"Thank you," she said. She leaned back against the chair, rested her sword across her knees, and settled down to wait.

extras

www.orbitbooks.net

about the author

Dr Simon Morden is a bona fide rocket scientist, having degrees in geology and planetary geophysics, and is one of the few people who can truthfully claim to have held a chunk of Mars in his hands. He has served as editor of the BSFA's *Focus* magazine, been a judge for the Arthur C. Clarke Award and was part of the winning team for the 2009 Rolls Royce Science prize. Simon Morden lives in Gateshead with a fierce lawyer, two unruly children and a couple of miniature panthers

Find out more about Simon Morden and other Orbit authors by registering for the free monthly newsletter at www.orbitbooks.net

Samuil Petrovitch returns in

THEORIES OF FLIGHT

by

Simon Morden

1

Petrovitch stared at the sphere in his hands, turning it slowly to reveal different parts of its intricately patterned surface. Shining silver lines of metal in curves and whorls shone against the black resin matrix, the seeming chaos replicated throughout the hidden depths of the globe; a single strand of wire that swam up and down, around and around, its path determined precisely by equations he himself had discovered.

It was a work of art; dense, cold, beautiful, a miracle of manufacture. A kilometre of fine alloy wound up into a ball the size of a double fist.

But it was supposed to be more than that. He let it fall heavily onto his desk and flicked his glasses off his face. His eyes, always so blue, were spidered with red veins. He scrubbed at them again.

The *yebani* thing didn't – wouldn't – work, no matter how much he yelled and hit it. The first practical test of the Petrovitch–Ekanobi laws, and it just sat there, dumb, blind, motionless.

Stanford – Stanford! Those *raspizdyay kolhoznii amerikanskij* – were breathing down his neck, and he knew that if he didn't crack it soon, they'd either beat him to his own discovery or debunk the whole effort. He was damned if he was going to face them across a lecture hall having lost the race. And Pif would string him up by his *yajtza*, which was a more immediate problem.

So, the sphere didn't work. It should. Every test he'd conducted on it showed that it'd been made with micrometer precision, exactly in the configuration he'd calculated. He'd run it with the right voltage.

Everything was perfect, and still, and still . . .

He picked up his glasses from where he'd thrown them. The same old room snapped into focus: the remnants of Pif's time with him still scattered across her old desk, the same pot plants existing on a diet of cold coffee, the light outside leaking in around the yellowed veins of the Venetian blinds.

Sound leaked in, too: sirens that howled towards the crack of distant gunfire, carried on cold, still winter air. Banging and clattering, hammers and drills, the reverberations of scaffolding. A tank slapping its caterpillar tracks down on the tarmac.

None of it loud enough to distract him from the hum of the fluorescent tube overhead.

He opened a drawer and pulled out a sheet of printed paper which he placed squarely in front of him. He stared at the symbols on it, knowing the answer was there somewhere, if only he knew where to look. He turned his wedding ring, still a cold and alien presence on his body, in precise quarter-circles.

Time passed. Voices in the corridor outside grew closer, louder, then faded.

Petrovitch looked up suddenly. His eyes narrowed and he

pushed his glasses back up his nose. His heart span faster, producing a surge of blood that pricked his skin with sweat.

Now everything was slow, deliberate, as he held on to his idea. He reached for a pencil and turned the sheet of paper over, blank side to him. He started to scratch out a diagram and, when he'd finished, some numbers to go with it.

Petrovitch put down the pencil and checked his answer.

"*Dubiina*," he whispered to himself, "*durak, balvan*".

The ornate sphere had taunted him from across the desk for the last time. He was going to be its master now. He reached over and fastened his hand around it, then threw it in the air with such casual defiance that would have had his head of department leaping to save it.

He caught it deftly on its way down, and knew that it would never have to touch the floor again.

He carried it to the door, flung it open, and stepped through. The two paycops lolling beside the lift caught a flavour of his mood. One nudged the other, who turned to see the white-blond hair and tight-lipped smile of Petrovitch advancing towards them at a steady gait.

"Dr Petrovitch?" asked one. "Is there a problem?"

Petrovitch held the sphere up in front of him. "Out of the way," he said. "Science coming through."

He ran down the stairs, two storeys, sliding his hand over the banister and only taking a firm hold to let his momentum carry him through the air for the broad landings. Now was not the time to wait, foot-tapping, for a crawling lift car that gave him the creeps anyway. Everything was urgent, imminent, immanent.

Second floor: his Head had given him two graduate students, and he had had little idea what to do with them. The least he could do to make up for several months of make-work was to include them in this. He needed witnesses, anyway. And their test rig. Which may or may not be completed: Petrovitch hadn't seen either student for a week, or it might have been two.

Either way, he was certain he could recognise them again.

He kicked the door to their lab space open. They were there, sitting in front of an open cube of wood, a cat's cradle of thin wires stretched inside. An oscilloscope – old school cathode tube – made a pulsing green line across its gridded screen.

The woman – blonde, skin as pale as parchment, eyes grey like a ghost's . . . McNeil – yes, that was her name – glanced over her shoulder, her grey eyes growing impossibly round when she saw Petrovitch's expression and what he was carrying.

"You've finished it."

"This? Yeah, about a week ago. Should have mentioned it, but that's not what's important now." He advanced on a steel trolley. In time-honoured fashion, new equipment was built in the centre of the lab. The old was pushed to the wall to be cannibalised for parts or left to fossilise. "Do either of you need any of this?"

He pointed to the collection of fat transformers on the top shelf. When he squatted down to inspect the lower deck, he found some moving coil meters and something that might have been the heavy-duty switching gear from a power station.

McNeil and the man – as to his name, Petrovitch's mind was too full to remember it – looked at each other. Petrovitch waited all of half a second for a reply before seizing the trolley in his free hand and trying to tip it over. Some of the transformers were big ferrite ones, and he couldn't manage it one-handed.

"You," and he still couldn't remember his name, "catch."

He threw the sphere and, without waiting to see if it had a safe arrival, wedged his foot under one of the trolley's castors and heaved. The contents slid and fell, collecting in a blocky heap on the fifties lino.

He righted the trolley and looked around for what he needed. "Power supply there," he pointed, and McNeil scurried to get it. "That bundle of leads there. Multimeter, any, doesn't matter. And the Mukhanov book."

The other student was frozen in place, holding the sphere like it was made of crystal. Dominguez, that was it. Had problems pronouncing his sibilants.

"You all right with that?"

Dominguez nodded dumbly.

The quantum gravity textbook was the last thing slapped on the trolley, and Petrovitch took the handle again.

"Right. Follow me."

McNeil trotted by his side. "Dr Petrovitch," she said.

And that was almost as strange as being married. Doctor. What else could the university do, but confer him with that title as soon as was practically possible?

"Yeah?"

"Where are we going?"

"Basement. And pray to whatever god you believe in that we're not over a tube line."

"Can I ask why?"

"Sure." They'd reached the lift. He leaned over the trolley and punched the button to go down.

"OK," she said, twisting a strand of hair around her finger. "Why?"

"Because what I was doing before wasn't working. This will." The lift pinged and the door slid aside. Petrovitch took a good long look at the empty space before gritting his teeth and pushing the trolley inside. He ushered the two students in, then after another moment's hesitation on the threshold, he stepped in.

He reached behind him and thumbed the stud marked B for basement.

As the lift descended, they waited for him to continue. "What's the mass of the Earth?" he said. When neither replied, he rolled his eyes. "Six times ten to the twenty four kilos. All that mass produces a pathetic nine point eight one metres per second squared acceleration at the surface. An upright ape like me can outpull the entire planet just by getting out of a chair."

"Which is why you had us build the mass balance," she said.

"Yeah. You're going to have to take it apart and bring it down here." The door slid back to reveal a long corridor. "Not here here. This is just to show that it works. We'll get another lab set up. Find a kettle. Stuff like that."

He pushed the trolley out before the lift was summoned to a higher floor.

"Doctor," said Dominguez, finally finding his voice, "that still does not explain why we are now underground."

"Doesn't it?" Petrovitch blinked. "I guess not. Find a socket for the power supply while I wire up the rest of it." He took the sphere from Dominguez and turned it around until he found the two holes. His hand chased out a couple of leads from the bird's nest of wires, spilling some of them to the floor. The lift disappeared upstairs, making a grinding noise as it went.

They worked together. McNeil joined cables together until she'd made two half-metre lengths. Dominguez set up the multimeter and twisted the dial to read current. Petrovitch plugged two jacks into the sphere, and finally placed Mukhanov and Winitzki's tome on the floor. He set the sphere on top of it.

"Either of you two worked it out yet?" he asked. "No? Don't worry: I'm supposed to be a genius, and it took me a week. Hugo, dial up four point eight volts. Watch the current. If looks like it's going to melt something, turn it off."

The student had barely put his hand on the control when the lift returned. A dozen people spilled out, all talking at once.

"*Yobany stos!*" He glared out over the top of his glasses. "I'm trying to conduct an epoch-making experiment which will turn this place into a shrine for future generations. So shut the *huy* up."

One of the crowd held up his camera phone, and Petrovitch thought that wasn't such a bad idea.

"You. Yes, you. Come here. I don't bite. Much. Stand there." He propelled the young man front and centre. "Is it recording? Good."

All the time, more people were arriving, but it didn't matter. The time was now.

"Yeah, OK. Hugo? Hit it."

Nothing happened.

"You are hitting it, right?"

"Yes, Dr Petrovitch."

"Then why isn't the little red light on?" He sat back on his heels. "*Chyort*. There's no *yebani* power down here."

There was an audible groan.

Petrovitch looked up again at all the expectant faces. "Unless someone wants to stick their fingers in a light socket, I suggest you go and find a very long extension lead."

Some figures at the back raced away, their feet slapping against the concrete stairs. When they came back, it wasn't with an extension lead proper, but one they'd cobbled together out of the cable from several janitorial devices and gaffer tape. The bare ends of the wire were live, and it was passed over the heads of the watching masses gingerly.

It took a few moments more to desleeve the plug from the

boxy power supply and connect everything together. The little red light glimmered on.

Petrovitch looked up at the cameraman. "Take two?"

"We're on."

Petrovitch got down on his hands and knees, and took one last look at the inert black sphere chased with silver lines. In a moment, it would be transformed, and with it, the world. No longer a thing of beauty, it would become just another tool.

"Hugo?" He was aware of McNeil crouched beside him. She was holding her breath, just like he was.

Dominguez flicked the on switch and slowly turned the dial. The digital figures on the multimeter started to flicker.

Then, without fuss, without sound, the sphere leapt off the book and into the air. It fell back a little, rose, fell, rose, fell, each subsequent oscillation smaller than the previous one, until it was still again. Only it was resting at shin height with no visible means of support.

Someone started clapping. Another joined in, and another, until the sound of applause echoed off the walls, magnified.

His heart was racing again, the tiny turbine in his chest having tasted the amount of adrenaline flooding into his blood. He felt dizzy, euphoric, ecstatic even: science elevated to a religious experience. Dominguez was transfixed, motionless like him. It was McNeil who was the first of the three to move. She reached forward and tapped the floating sphere with her fingernail. It slipped sideways, pulling the cables with it until it lost momentum and stopped. She waved her hand under it, over it.

She turned to Petrovitch and grinned. He staggered to his feet and faced the crowd. "*Da! Da! Da!*" He punched the air each time, and found he couldn't stop. Soon he had all of them, young and old, men and women, fists in the air, chanting "*Da!*" at the tops of their voices.

He reached over and hauled Dominguez up. He held his other hand out to McNeil, who crawled up it and clung onto him in a desperate embrace. Thus encumbered, he turned to the camera phone and extended his middle finger – not his exactly, but he was at least its current owner. *"Yob materi vashi*, Stanford."